D0960581

WRECKED

ALSO BY JOE IDE

IQ
Righteous

WRECKED

An IQ Novel

Joe Ide

**MULHOLLAND
BOOKS**

New York Boston London

Mulholland Books / Little, Brown and Company
Hachette Book Group
1290 Avenue of the Americas, New York, NY 10104
mulhollandbooks.com

First Edition: October 2018

Mulholland Books is an imprint of Little, Brown and Company, a division of Hachette Book Group, Inc. The Mulholland Books name and logo are trademarks of Hachette Book Group, Inc.

The publisher is not responsible for websites (or their content) that are not owned by the publisher.

The Hachette Speakers Bureau provides a wide range of authors for speaking events. To find out more, go to hachettespeakersbureau.com or call (866) 376-6591.

ISBN 978-0-316-50951-0
LCCN 2018933154

10 9 8 7 6 5 4 3 2 1

LSC-C

Printed in the United States of America

To Josh Kendall
I can write some. Josh taught me to write books.

We are not trapped or locked up in these bones. No, no. We are free to change. And love changes us. And if we can love one another, we can break open the sky.
—Walter Mosley, *Blue Light*

WRECKED

Prologue

"D o you know what Abraham Lincoln said after a six-day drunk?" Jimenez said.

"What?" Hawkins said.

"I freed *who?*"

They laughed in wheezing coughs. Hawkins took another hit off the joint, leaned back in the chair, and put his size ninety-five combat boots up on the table. Jimenez felt sorry for the table and even sorrier for the chair.

"Want some?" Hawkins said, offering up the joint.

"No," Richter said, "that shit makes me sleepy." He was eating a massive burrito, napkin tucked into his collar, carnitas smeared all over his mouth. He was smoking between bites. *What a pig,* Jimenez thought. He took the joint, took a hit.

"Do you know why General Santa Anna only brought six hundred soldiers to the Alamo?" Hawkins said.

"No, I don't."

"Because he only had two cars."

That afternoon they'd driven out to Simi Valley. A commuter town; row upon row of tract houses surrounded by parched hills. There were a lot of baseball fields. Teams played at night because it was too damn hot in the daytime. Walczak owned an industrial park. There was a big FOR LEASE sign you could see from the freeway. Plastic bags blew across the empty parking lot like urban tumbleweed. Pigeons peered down from the roof. They parked in the delivery bay and dragged Sneaky Pete out by his elbows. Hawkins had worked him over in the van. He liked doing that kind of shit. Jimenez didn't mind but he didn't enjoy it. Hawk was the only person he'd ever met that was mad all the damn time. Richter was useless, never doing anything until he ran out of excuses.

Sneaky Pete was limp and babbling when they dragged him up the stairs into a third-floor office. Nothing there but some cardboard boxes, overflowing wastebaskets, and a few tables and chairs. Half the fluorescents were out and tiles were missing from the ceiling, wires dangling down.

They enhanced-interrogated him but he held out. Damn good for a private citizen, better than a lot of professionals. Jimenez wished Slayer was here. You want to get somebody to talk, put a big, black snarling German shepherd three inches away from his dick. Motherfucker will pay you to confess. Jimenez had neon lines and floating rectangles in his head but he took another hit anyway. His mouth watering for one of those crazy munchies Hawkins liked to make; hot Cheetos, Nutella popsicles, chocolate chip waffles with peanut butter and bacon. Hawkins liked to do shit like that. Put stuff together. Once, when they were home between tours, Jimenez watched him make cannabis oil to treat his mother's cancer symptoms.

"First, you gotta wash it," Hawkins said. He put a couple ounces of primo weed in a bowl, poured in some benzene, and carefully rinsed and squeezed the leaves. "Extracts all the cannabinoids," he said.

"Doesn't benzene mess you up?" Jimenez said.

"Cooks off. Leaves no residue. You just gotta remember to have a fan on and not to smoke." Hawkins put the liquid into a coffee filter and strained out the stems and debris. Then he poured what was left into a rice cooker and reduced it down to something that looked like axle grease with a reddish tint. He put the stuff in a double boiler and added some coconut oil.

"Is that for flavor?"

"No. It homogenizes and activates the cannabinoids," Hawkins said, Jimenez wondering if Hawk knew what he was talking about.

"It's a lotta damn trouble. Why don't you just give her a joint?"

"You can't control the dose. A gram of this stuff a day helps her out and doesn't make her high."

"Still, it's a lotta damn trouble."

Hawk gave him a look that used to scare the shit out of the Iraqi prisoners and everybody else on the tier too. *"It's my mother."*

Eveline Owens came in, an unfiltered Camel behind her ear. She was carrying a cardboard tray from Starbucks, her turn to make the coffee run. Owens was raised on a cattle ranch in Montana or North Dakota, somewhere. She was tall and knobby-looking, like she had too many elbows and knees, with a long Jersey Maid face and the biggest hands Jimenez had ever seen on a girl. She probably won a lot of blue ribbons for roping cows or churning butter or whatever the fuck they did out there. Jimenez had tapped that ass a few times, but there weren't a lot of options over there. She was what they called a 4-10-4. A 4 in her hometown, a 10 over there, and a 4 when she got back home.

"This drink is for faggots," she said. She handed Hawkins a cup of something that had the word *caramel* in it twice.

"What'd you get?" Hawkins said. "A bale of hay?"

Owens was a little glassy-eyed. She'd been drinking since they'd arrived, a six-pack all herself. She drank a lot at Abu Ghraib but now she was a full-on alcoholic. Jimenez reminded himself not to rely on her. She gave Richter his coffee.

"Thanks," he said, not looking up from the paper. You could hardly read for the blotches of burrito grease.

"How are the wife and kiddies, Jimenez?" she said.

"I don't know. Carla won't let me come home."

"She find out you had shit for brains?"

"No. I boned her too good and wore her ass out."

Jimenez, Hawkins, and Owens were all on tier 1, where they kept the security detainees, the poor bastards who were suspected of attacking US troops or knowing something about it. Jimenez was a military intelligence reservist, called up for duty because there weren't enough officers to abuse the detainees. Hawkins and Owens were both MPs. The lieutenant colonel and chief warrant officers were supposed to be in charge but you pretty much did whatever you wanted. A couple of the other guys had served at Guantánamo, but other than that nobody from the CO on down had any experience in running a prison, collecting intelligence, conducting interrogations, or any other relevant subject. At the time, the insurgency was everywhere, the entire area in chaos. Whole families were scooped up. Maybe two or three out of a hundred had anything to say that you could call intelligence and the longer they were detained, the older and more meaningless their information became.

Nobody really knew who was doing what. There was the CIA, military intelligence, the outside contractors, CACI and Titan and OGAs or "Other Government Agencies." Everyone called them ghosts because you didn't know who they reported to; MI, Task Force 121, the FBI, the Defense Intelligence Agency, or some other secret organization full of mysterious motherfuckers with a budget hidden in the farm bill. The CIA guys and outside contractors did most of the interviews, if you could call screaming, threatening, breaking furniture, slapping, punching, or throwing the detainee down a stairwell an interview. The MPs were instructed to *soften them up,* which really meant they were turned loose to do whatever the hell they wanted. No instructions, regulations, limits, guidelines, or supervision.

When Jimenez looked back on it, he still had to shake his head in wonder. Take a bunch of grunts who were hard sons of bitches to begin with and who'd watched the 9/11 tape a thousand times or maybe had a friend shot in the head by a sniper or blown up by an IED and put them in one of Saddam's filthy, overcrowded, medieval dungeons with no water, power, or ventilation and shitty food, and then shell them night and day and kill some of them so they were afraid all the time, and then leave them alone in concrete bunkers with their fear and their testosterone and their angry, pent-up frustration, and then tell them to *soften up* the inmates who might have a cousin out there lobbing mortar rounds at you and surprise-surprise, bad shit was bound to happen. Even when you got time off, how were you supposed to relax? Your recreational choices were video games, video games, and fucking anything with a pulse. The only available liquor didn't even have a name. They called it *raw drink.* A fifth for ten bucks. It was so strong even Owens had to mix it with grape soda.

The whole world had seen the photos. Detainees wearing hoods and standing on boxes with their arms straight out or hung from railings in stress positions or piled on top of each other naked or bleeding and beat to shit. Poor Lynndie England. She was the poster child for that clusterfuck. She was the short girl with the boy's haircut who got her picture taken leading a prisoner on a dog leash and standing next to a line of hooded detainees grinning and pointing at their dicks. Fortunately, she wasn't in the photo of a prisoner kneeling with his mouth open and another prisoner masturbating in front of him, but she did quip, "Look, he's getting a hard-on!" A remark that didn't help her at the trial.

Charlie Graner took the pictures. He was a specialist, a rank somewhere between a private and a corporal. He unofficially ran the tier along with some other untrained, unqualified assholes. Graner was all over Lynndie as soon as she arrived. He was twice her age and *smelled* her vulnerability. Once he had his grappling hooks in her she did anything he said, and he was a mean bastard too.

Lynndie got three years, Graner received ten. Hawkins, Jimenez, and Owens were dishonorably discharged because there wasn't enough evidence to indict them. Walczak knew he'd never get a promotion unless he singlehandedly killed everybody in Al Qaeda, so he resigned.

And get this: Nobody in the top brass got busted. Not a single one. Not the brigade commander, prison commander, operational supervisor, or anybody else above the rank of sergeant. All they got was a reprimand. *A reprimand?* What the hell was that anyway? They called you into the principal's office and smacked your hand with a ruler? And do you know what the head of the CIA, that chickenshit Panetta, said? That the officers were paid to do a job, they did it, and he was giving them the benefit of the doubt. *The benefit of the doubt?* Those motherfuckers get the benefit of the doubt? The ones who gave the orders, encouraged them, egged them on, told them they were doing a good job? *They* get off without a scratch? Meanwhile, you were a pariah. Tell somebody you were at Abu Ghraib and you might as well say you went to the Congo and had sex with a howler monkey.

Jimenez felt bad about what he'd done. He told himself he was a different person back then, that it was circumstances, that anybody would have gone crazy if they were put in that position. But the shit still haunted him. He wondered if Walczak and the others were haunted too. Did they wake up at 2 a.m. hearing the prisoners scream and seeing the agony on their faces as they cowered in a corner bloodied and pleading for their lives?

He wondered if Panetta ever felt bad about letting everybody off the hook except the people who were responsible. Unlikely, Jimenez thought. You know what he'd say? *What was I supposed to do? Turn the CIA, MI, and CACI upside down? Take depositions from the hundreds of people connected with Abu Ghraib? Interview every prisoner and stack up so much evidence they'd have to keep it in an airplane hangar? Reassign every attorney in JAG and Department of Justice to handle the cases? Spend years and millions of dollars sorting out who was to blame for each individual act of abuse and who was responsible for supervising them all the way up to that moron Rumsfeld? No. Better to bust a few ordinary soldiers and heap the blame on them. I mean, let's move on, shall we? We've got two wars to fight.*

Jimenez finished off the joint and dropped it on the floor. His cell buzzed. "Shit. It's Fuckhead. You want to talk to him?"

"Hell no," Hawkins said.

"I'm eating," Richter said.

"Well, I ain't talkin' to him," Owens said, popping the cap off another Coors. "I'm drunk."

Jimenez put the call on speaker. "What's up, Balzac?"

"It's Walczak," Walczak said, like his name was a rank. "Status report." Jimenez looked at Hawkins and Owens. *Do you believe this asshole?*

"I'm Mexican, sir. We don't have no status." Owens grinned. Hawkins laughed out loud. Richter kept eating.

"Not funny, Jimenez. I want a status report."

Jimenez suddenly sounded panicky and desperate. "Sir, we're taking fire from hostiles, battalion strength!" he shouted. "We're black on ammo, sir, and the Stryker's down." Hawkins started whistling like incoming rounds and making that explosion sound kids make, Owens ack-acked like a machine gun. "They've got eighties, MBTs,

9

RMGs, forty mike-mikes, SAMs, and ICBMs!" Jimenez screamed into the phone. "Get us out of here, sir! We need air support! We need evac! Oh no! It's Owens, sir! She took one in the ass crack!" Owens and Hawkins were doubled over with their mouths wide open.

"Stop screwing around!" Walczak shouted. "What's going on, Jimenez? I want to know *now*."

"Nothing so far but we're working on it. Say, Balzac, you're Polish, aren't you?"

"It's Walcz—yeah, what about it?"

"Do you know what they call a Polack with a hundred and fifty girlfriends?"

"No, I don't."

"A shepherd."

More hysterics. Richter blew out a mouthful of carnitas. Hawkins fell over backward and crashed to the floor.

"Are you finished?" Walczak said.

"Yeah, yeah, I'm finished," Jimenez said, tears in his eyes.

"Has the detainee said anything?"

"No, he hasn't said anything."

"Could somebody check on him, please?"

"I'm eating," Richter said.

"Don't look at me," Owens said. "I made the coffee run."

"Hold on," Jimenez said.

Jimenez and Hawkins went over to the supply closet and opened the door. It was empty, bare walls, the carpet ripped out. It was cold, the air conditioning was turned up high. A demonic voice spewed hate rock from a boom box so loud you'd think it would shatter Owens's beer bottles. Sneaky Pete was curled up on the bare cement. His hands were zip-tied behind his back. He was naked and shivering and groaning. He was wearing a hood they'd dipped in hot sauce before they'd put it on him but the effects had worn off, or at least he'd stopped screaming.

Jimenez turned the music off. "How long's he been without water?"

"Since we picked him up," Hawkins said. "Let's see if he's ready." Hawk used the toe of his boot and gave Sneaky Pete a stiff nudge in the ribs. He groaned in pain. Hawkins had punched him there a bunch of times, you could see the bruises. Jimenez knelt down and ripped off the hood. Sneaky gulped fresh air.

"What's up, Sneaky?" Jimenez said.

"Water ... please, water," he croaked.

Owens came in with her beer. "You tell us what we want to know and you can have all the water you can drink." She emptied the bottle on the floor. "Don't that look good?" Sneaky opened his mouth and tried to catch some of the drops splashing on his face.

Walczak was yelling from the phone. "Okay, that's it! You've had him all day and you're supposed to be professionals! I want results by nineteen hundred hours, no excuses!" He ended the call.

"He's right," Jimenez said. "We should get this done. It's our asses too."

"Then enough of this bullshit," Hawkins said.

He hauled Sneaky to his feet and slammed him against the wall. He leaned in close, nose-to-nose. "You think this is bad, asshole? This is nothing. This is a day at the beach. This is Disneyland. I'll put you in so much pain you'll be beggin' for me to slit your throat." Hawk put his hand around Sneaky Pete's jaw, his fingers like the claws of a crane, squeezing so hard Sneaky's cheeks were almost touching. Hawk screamed into his face, spit flying out of his mouth. "NOW START TALKING MOTHERFUCKER OR I SWEAR TO GOD I'LL CUT YOUR GODDAMN DICK OFF AND HANG IT AROUND YOUR NECK!" Hawk banged Sneaky Pete's head against the wall. "DO YOU HEAR ME? DO YOU FUCKING HEAR ME?" Hawkins kept banging and screaming. "TELL ME WHAT I WANT TO KNOW AND TELL ME RIGHT FUCKING NOW! OPEN YOUR GODDAMN MOUTH AND TELL ME!"

"Hold it, hold it, Hawk," Jimenez said. "You're gonna kill the guy." Richter was standing in the doorway, an unfeeling mother-fucker if there ever was one, and even he was incredulous. Hawk was breathing hard, glaring into Sneaky's eyes. Sneaky looked back at him, in pain but unafraid. More blank, like. Stoic. A tough motherfucker.

"Fuck it, " Jimenez said. "Owens, find a table where we can lay him down. Did somebody bring a bucket?"

"It's in the van," Hawkins said.

"Get it. Fill it with water. And see if you can find a towel too." Hawk let go of Sneaky and let him slump to the floor.

"You gotta admit," Jimenez said. "The guy's pretty tough."

"What's this asshole's name again?"

"Isaiah. They call him IQ."

CHAPTER ONE

Motherlove

Isaiah hadn't seen Grace since he'd met her in TK's wrecking yard. He'd helped her remove a wiring harness from an old car. He was intrigued by her, but she'd given no indication that she had the slightest interest in him. It was a month later when he saw her again, standing in front of an art supply store talking to her friend. He'd watched them awhile, and when the friend left, he wanted to say hello but was too intimidated. Instead, he sent Ruffin to smooth the way, the slate-gray pit bull with fierce amber eyes that scared the hell out of most people. The dog ran over to Grace and sat at her feet and she responded the same way she had at the wrecking yard. She smiled, big and warm and glad, kneeling down to scratch him behind his ears. Ruff was usually standoffish with people, but you could feel the connection between them, like sister and brother reuniting after years apart.

"Hello, beautiful," she said. "How are you, huh?" Ruffin could hardly sit still, waggling with his butt still on the ground and mewling with happiness. She stroked his head and beamed at him. "How are you, huh? You doing all right?"

"Hi," Isaiah said as he approached. She gave him a quick glance and went back to stroking the dog.

"Hi."

"How's it going?"

"It's going fine." Her voice was flat, not a hint of friendliness or anything else, the pale green eyes giving nothing away.

"Did the wiring harness work okay?"

"Yeah, it worked okay."

"Good. That's great."

He had reached the limits of his conversational skills and a couple of awkward, endless moments went by, the girl holding the dog's big head in her hands. He felt her sadness again. He recognized it from before. Like his, far away but imminent, anguish buried in a shallow grave.

"It's Ruffin, right?" she said.

"You have a good memory." At the wrecking yard, she'd chided him because the dog was unruly and hadn't been neutered. "I did some training with him," Isaiah said. "Got him fixed too." If she was impressed there was no sign of it. "I'm Isaiah," he said, getting desperate. "Isaiah Quintabe." He knew her name but didn't want to say it because it would sound creepy. She thought a moment, like she was gathering her memories of him, deciding if he was okay.

"Grace," she said simply. She was wearing worn jeans and a chambray shirt over a gray T-shirt. She smelled faintly of turpentine. He remembered the pocket watch tattoo on her forearm. It was an antique, the numbers in an ornate font and nicely done too. Crisp lines, subtle shadowing, the sheen on the bezel just right, the time frozen at five after eleven.

Isaiah said the only thing he could think of. "So you're an artist." She looked at him sharply, a little alarmed.

"How do you know?"

He rushed to explain. "In the wrecking yard you had paint on your shoes and a Royal & Langnickel T-shirt. They make paintbrushes. I just happened to notice, that's all. Sorry, I didn't mean to pry."

"Don't worry about it." She looked like he'd taken her wallet and given it back. "Gotta go." She scratched the dog one more time, turned, and walked away, the dog trotting happily beside her.

Isaiah wanted to say goodbye or ask if he could walk with her or invite her for coffee but those things were beyond him. "Ruffin? Here, boy."

The dog stopped, looked wistfully at Grace, and reluctantly came back. Isaiah snapped on his leash and watched her. She was walking fast, like she was escaping. Had he done something threatening? Was he giving off some kind of weird vibe? Was he so bumbling she had to flee so she wouldn't laugh in his face? Probably. She was an artist. Cool. White. Creative. She probably hung out with other cool, white, creative people. Actors or documentary filmmakers or somebody who raised seven different kinds of heirloom cucumbers or had a line of yoga pants or made crazy sculptures out of old dental chairs, and if there *were* some black guys in her circle they were probably named Zado or Ska and they had dreadlocks and walked around barefoot and wore white peasant shirts and sacred beads from a monastery in Machu Picchu and had tats that meant fight the oppressor and performed at poetry slams or played the timbales in a reggae band.

Grace was almost a block away, just turning into an apartment building. Isaiah got in the car and drove past it. It was an old stucco low-rise called the Edgemont; scarred with gang graffiti, front steps scuffed down to bare wood, the burglar bars weeping rust. He parked the car and went furtively to the intercom. He checked the list of names. *G Monarova* resided on the top floor. #406. Monarova? What kind of name was that?

He drove away wondering what had gotten into him. Twice now, he'd been clearly rejected, and here he was almost stalking her. It was ridiculous. Why was he so intrigued? Okay, she did remind him of himself; removed, wary, her eyes searching for a crack in your armor, trying to see inside you, see what was really going on. Those weren't exactly attractive qualities. Dodson had told him about meeting Cherise and how he'd been hit by the thunderbolt like Michael Corleone when he saw the shepherd girl in *Godfather II*. It bordered on the mystical, being so drawn to someone you didn't know; longing to be with her after two minutes of conversation. No, Isaiah thought, this is crazy. What was he going to do, knock on her door with a bouquet of flowers? This was some kind of errant brain wave or a whim of imagination. Drive on, he told himself. By this time tomorrow you'll have forgotten all about her.

Isaiah was meeting Dodson at the Coffee Cup, a neighborhood institution stuck between a dry cleaners and a Mexican market. He was nervous about it. They were going to talk about partnering up, the conversation long overdue. Dodson had been busy with his new baby. He'd sold his half of the food truck to Deronda and was presumably living on the proceeds. He'd promised to bring in high-profile cases with serious paychecks and Isaiah could sorely use one. As usual, his client fees were dribbling in, along with the usual assortment of casseroles, cookies, needlepoint homilies, left-over Christmas presents, home repairs, and knitted woolen scarves so perfect for the California weather. The whole Erwin family had painted the house. Javier had installed a new water heater. Mr. Yamasaki had reroofed the garage. Things that needed doing but didn't pay the bills.

"There's my hero," Verna said. She said that every time he came in, which was almost every day. Awhile back, he'd saved her from a robbery, and she wouldn't let him forget it. Verna was a wizened sprig of a woman who must have been in her eighties. She wore a waitress's uniform even though she owned the place and arrived before dawn to bake her fresh goodies. Danish, muffins, cinnamon rolls, and sourdough bread from a starter that was forty years old.

Her croissants were what Isaiah craved. Verna said her recipe only had two ingredients. Warm snowflakes and a tub of butter.

Isaiah was still embarrassed about the conversation with Grace. He was apparently less appealing than a four-legged creature that ate dog food, shed like a dying Christmas tree, couldn't speak English, and crapped all over the yard. He was twenty-six years old and couldn't carry on a conversation. Pitiful. Just pitiful. On the other hand, the nut he'd chosen to crack was as hard as the sidewalk and cold as a bag of frozen peas. Maybe pick someone easier next time, someone who already liked him. Maybe Winetta Simpson, a neighbor who was always inviting him over for coffee and a chat. He'd felt bad about turning her down all the time, so he'd gone over there once. She greeted him at the door with a bottle of Crown Royal, glittery purple eye shadow, and a negligee that looked like a lace tablecloth thrown over a buffalo.

Since the 14K Triad case, Isaiah had handled the usual assortment of neighborhood woes. Store thefts, break-ins, lost children, wife-beaters, bullies, and con men. The only halfway-interesting case involved a girl who'd been accused of hanging her boyfriend and making it look like a suicide. There wasn't enough evidence for an arrest but the boyfriend's family was sure she'd done it. Isaiah made some initial inquiries and discovered the boyfriend was a meth dealer who stalked his estranged wife, beat his twin girls, and had kiddie porn on his laptop. Isaiah decided the world was better off without him and turned down the case.

"What's flamin', son?" Dodson said. He strolled in like the landlord; an icy breeze with an attitude, condensed of stature but walking large. He'd gained a few pounds but was still thin and roped up; immaculate in a white T-shirt, jeans, and a modest gold chain. "So what's up with you?"

"Nothing special. How's Micah?"

Dodson made a face like he was remembering a car accident.

".Man, that baby is *work*. You know he can't do *nothin'* for hisself? Can't even hold his oversize head up. You got to watch him all the damn time."

"You didn't know that going in?"

"Knowing and doing is two different things. You know Cherise makes me wash my hands *every time* I pick him up? I don't keep my toothbrush that clean, and the kid is always spittin' up and he farts like he's full of propane. I couldn't believe it the first time I changed his diaper. He don't eat nothing but mother's milk and his shit's the same color as hot dog mustard and got birdseed in it."

"Birdseed?" Isaiah said.

"It *looks* like birdseed," Dodson replied, "and for some reason, we're always hurrying and rushing around, why I couldn't tell you. Damn baby ain't no bigger than a pot roast and he ain't goin' nowhere. And *everything's* a damn crisis. The boy gets a rash on his ass, and Cherise and her mama carry on like he had a tumor on his neck. I said, what are y'all worried about? *Everybody* gets a rash on they ass at one time or another. I got a rash on my ass right now."

"How'd that go over?" Isaiah said.

"Like I farted at a funeral, and Cherise done lost her sense of humor altogether. Other night, I was changin' the boy's diaper, trying to keep it light, you know how I do. I said, 'Cherise, check this out. The baby's got a hard-on, and he takes after his daddy too!' Girl didn't crack a smile and her mama looked at me like I was Crip Walkin' on her grave—and check dis. I got to use my *inside* voice. The fuck does that mean? I *am* inside. And pictures! Lord have mercy. It's like we got to record every minute of that li'l nigga's life. Might as well get a movie camera and set it on *forever.*"

"So you're not enjoying this at all?"

"Sometimes," Dodson said, thoughtful now. "But mostly when it's just me and him. Like when he's asleep and I'm carrying him on my shoulder. All that other stuff goes away." Dodson went quiet a moment, like he was feeling the love and wonderment of having a child.

The moment was too heartfelt for Isaiah. He fiddled with his spoon. "So we're partners."

"I'm ready," Dodson said, coming out of his reverie. "But we need to talk about some other things first. Are you on social media?"

"No," Isaiah said, perishing at the thought.

"Do you advertise?"

"No."

"Have you got a list of former clients?"

"No."

"Do you keep books?"

"No."

"Do people owe you money?"

"Yes."

"How much?"

"I don't know."

"You don't know?" Dodson said. "How can you not know?"

"I don't keep track. I figure people will pay me sooner or later."

Dodson looked at him like he'd flunked his GED. "If this is business, we got to run it like a business."

Over the next couple of weeks, Dodson got a Facebook page up and running and had his nephew design a simple web page. Isaiah was shocked when he found out Dodson had named the partnership.

"IQ Investigations?" Isaiah said. "Where did that come from?"

"The company needs a name. What are people supposed to tell each other? You need help, go to Isaiah's house?"

It's a company now? Isaiah thought. The word smacked of cubicles and secretaries and employee handbooks. At least Dodson hadn't inserted his own name. That would have been too much.

"After we get going, get some size to us?" Dodson said. "I want my name on the door." He made Isaiah write out a couple of lists. The first was his former clients, Dodson saying the best contacts were the ones you already knew. The second list was all the people who owed Isaiah money and how much.

"It's a lot of people," Isaiah protested.

"You got a memory like a tape recorder. Just write the shit down and quit whinin' like a bitch."

Isaiah almost snapped back but managed to restrain himself. He wished they'd talked about the partnership in more detail. How long would it last? A year? Five years? Was it 'til death do us part? There should have been a trial period, and what happened if you wanted out? Could you just cut the cord, no hard feelings? That didn't seem likely.

Dodson got serious about collections. He called, wrote emails, badgered and harassed and made house calls on the recalcitrant. Tudor was a mortgage broker and a wealthy man. Isaiah had tracked down a young couple that had wrecked one of Tudor's rentals, and Tudor had never paid a nickel for his services. Dodson went to his office.

"Pay him?" Tudor said, dusting imaginary lint off his shiny gray suit. "Why should I pay him? I hold the mortgage on his house. And that other one too, for that kid, Flaco."

"And you think that entitles you to what? Not paying your bills? I'm not leaving this office 'til I have a check for the full amount."

"Is that so? Well, you might need a sleeping bag and some groceries because you'll be here a long time."

"And you might need a security guard to guard your house at 674 Piru Drive," Dodson replied. "Be a shame if somebody broke all those fancy windows, kicked down your door, and made off with your bling collection and that raccoon coat your wife wears in the summertime."

"It happens to be mink," Tudor said. "Are you threatening me, young man?"

Dodson went into his gangsta stance, chest to chest, his head tipped to one side, weight on his back foot, hands down but curled. "You're goddamn right I'm threatening you. That's our livelihood right there and if you take food out of my baby's mouth I'll flush your whole life down the toilet." Dodson left with the check.

He started contacting former clients, introducing himself and explaining the new situation. "We're here," he'd tell them. "No need to stress yourself out. When life throws some bullshit curve ball at you, me and Isaiah will catch it for you and throw it right back." Make it an opportunity like they did on the shopping networks. *If you don't have that dress that goes from work to date night with hubby? Ladies, do we have the answer for you.*

Dodson presented Isaiah with an Excel spreadsheet. There was a list of client names, dates, payments, accounts receivable. This was exactly what Isaiah feared. Being controlled by the bottom line. But his fear took a backseat when he saw how much money Dodson had collected and how much was still owed.

"That's incredible," Isaiah said.

"It's a damn shame is what it is. And these people over here said they already had deals with you." Some handwritten notations were on the bottom of the page.

Orlando Suarez Clean carpet. Three rooms only
Billy Phan Build doghouse.
Adam Papadakis Reupholster sofa.
Louella Barnes Reindeer Christmas sweater

"Reindeer Christmas sweater?" Dodson said.

"Maybe it'll be nice," Isaiah answered feebly.

"I saw it. Louella's eyes are bad. The sweater will come down to your belly button and only got the antlers on it. I told her she should go buy you one at the store if she can get there without getting hit by a bus." Dodson sipped his coffee, more sugar in it than a Snickers bar. "And from now on, no more sweaters, cupcakes, gardening, plumbing, or any other damn thing. Everybody pays real money. Are we agreed?"

Isaiah felt rushed. "Okay. But only what they can afford."

He thought his decision would be final but Dodson said, "But most of 'em can't afford diddly. How about this? We set a minimum. A hundred bucks."

"Too much. If you're making minimum wage that's almost a whole day's pay. That could be rent money or food money."

"Or lottery ticket money or Miller High Life money. People are taking advantage of you, Isaiah. They don't think before they call you, they just call you. What the hell were you doing looking for Winkie's cat? It was under the house and she could have looked under there herself—and what about Cheesy Williams? You helped him with that insurance thing. Took you two whole days."

"What's wrong with that?" Isaiah said.

"Nothing's wrong with it, but he's a garbage man. He makes union wages, seventeen dollars an hour, and what did he pay you with? His girlfriend came over to your house and washed the windows. He didn't do nothin' but watch." Dodson had a point, Isaiah thought. "Look at it this way," Dodson went on. "Your windows might be clean, but can you spend 'em? Let me be in charge of the finances. I know about money and you don't." Dodson was right, Isaiah thought, which was aggravating in itself.

"Okay," he said. "You're in charge of the money."

"You promise?" Dodson said skeptically. " I know you don't like people fuckin' with your business."

"I promise," Isaiah said, immediately wanting to take it back.

"Okay, how about this? A fifty-dollar minimum and they can make payments. Spread it over a year and that's four dollars and sixteen cents a month. Anybody can afford that."

"I don't know," Isaiah said, trying to draw this out until he could think of an argument.

"Do you want to live by the skin of your teeth for the rest of your life? You got to get ahead, Isaiah, put some away. What if something comes up and you really need cash? You can't get a second on a dog house. You need to be sensible."

Isaiah could feel his scalp tingling, a sign of fear, oncoming disaster, loss of control, or all of the above. So what did he expect? Partners meant being reasonable, compromising, *sharing* control. This was starting to seem like a bad idea already. "Okay," he said in a voice that was nearly a whisper.

"All right," Dodson said. "We rollin' for real."

"What about those big cases you talked about?"

Dodson smiled, ever confident. "Don't worry about it. I got some irons in the fire."

Dodson *was* worried about it. Rich people had all kinds of resources at their disposal. Needing Isaiah's services would be a rare thing. The Facebook page had received a grand total of a hundred and seventeen views, and all of them were people Isaiah already knew. Dodson posted articles touting Isaiah's accomplishments, an announcement of their partnership, a mission statement, headshots of himself posing like Kat Williams, and the only personal photo Isaiah would let him use: standing twenty feet away in the shade of a lemon tree. He looked like he was hiding. But the thing that kept Dodson up nights and made him sweat was that he hadn't told Cherise he'd sold his half of the food truck.

He could just hear her: *Let me see if I understand,* she'd say in her are-you-stupid voice. *You used all of our savings and took out loans to buy the truck and then went ahead and sold it so you can play detective with Isaiah? Do you know Louella Barnes paid him with a reindeer sweater?*

They got married at the United in God Baptist Church. Reverend

Arnall performed the ceremony. Cherise's family and friends were seated on one side of the chapel. A normal collection of black folks. Dodson's people were on the other side: his mother and sister, his father not sober or interested enough to attend. Isaiah, Deronda, and Nona were there, as well as Dodson's old friends; the kind of people you'd see on wanted posters in the post office; thugs, hoochies, gangstas, hustlers, and bruthas on parole for a variety of felonies. Their idea of dressing up was to wear whatever they wore yesterday, except for Cheesy's girlfriend, Libertine. She was heavy and round and had on a silver halter top and matching shorts. Cherise said she looked like a ball of Jiffy Pop coming off the stove. At Cherise's insistence, none of them were invited to the reception, but a few did bring gifts. A box of 9mm ammo, a cock ring, an old version of *Grand Theft Auto,* and a bong made out of a clarinet.

If Cherise found out about the truck he wouldn't see her naked again until his nuts were like dried apricots. He was paying the bills with the checks he got from Deronda, which weren't much, and Cherise was on maternity leave and getting half pay. He could feel his checkbook scraping the bottom of his bank account.

Dodson drove home from Isaiah's, pissed he hadn't stood firmer on the minimum. He was either in charge of the money or he wasn't. He stopped at Beaumont's to grab an overpriced grapefruit juice, a habit he'd developed in his drug-dealing days to get the crack taste out of his mouth. He was glad all that was behind him. The violence, the hustling, prison.

"How are you, Juanell?" Beaumont said as Dodson stepped up to the counter. "You still selling counterfeit Gucci bags out the trunk of your car?"

"I quit that a long time ago," Dodson said.

"What are you doing these days?"

"I partnered up with Isaiah."

"Isaiah?" Beaumont said in disbelief. "You mean *our* Isaiah?"

"Yes, our Isaiah."

"What are you, some kind of secretary?"

Dodson paid for the juice and left. As he came out of the store Deronda pulled up at the curb in a brand-new, bright red Miata. She was bobbing her head to Mos Def's "The Edge." She was dripping bling, her hair straightened, unflattering bangs on her forehead, her nails too long to be functional and so sparkly you could see them from Jupiter.

"Whassup, Dodson?" she said, sounding suspiciously cheerful. "How's everything in your fucked-up world?"

"Fine. How's everything in yours?" He wondered where she got the car but didn't ask, assuming she'd smothered yet another baby daddy with that world-class badonk.

"Heard you and Isaiah might be getting together."

"We've formed a partnership. We have compatible personalities and other attributes that complement each other. He appreciates my business acumen and instinct for opportunity and I'm happy to say we've far exceeded our financial goals and look forward to a successful future. Is that broke-down food truck doing any business?"

"It's not *truck* anymore. It's truck*ssss*. I got three of 'em now."

"What three?" he said.

"Do you know Tudor, the mortgage broker?" Deronda said. "That's a smart man, right there. He saw my potential, my charisma, my star quality. He got the bank to give me a fat-ass loan." Deronda looked at her nails and blew on them. "Yeah, I'm an LLC now and a CEO on top of that. Oh and by the way? It ain't D&D's Fried Chicken no more. It's just plain *D*, and I'm makin' *money*, son." She looked in the mirror and patted her hair. "I really do appreciate you sellin' me your half of the food truck for a mutha-fuckin' song. Definitely shows your business acumen and instinct for opportunity."

Dodson was silent a moment. He hadn't been this tongue-tied since his early days with Cherise.

"What was that?" Deronda said, cupping her hand around her ear. "I can't hear you? Are you okay? Because you look like you choking to death on your jealousy."

"Nobody's choking," Dodson said, struggling to maintain his cool. "And I'm happy for you. An uneducated stripper from your poverty-stricken background deserves a second chance."

"Y'all still gettin' paid with blueberry muffins?"

"No, we have new regulations about fees."

"I hope they keep you out the poorhouse." She revved the engine. "Y'all take it easy now. I wish you success exceedin' your financial goals." She gave him a wide-eyed laugh, did a few fuck-you head bobs, and sped off to the beat. Dodson felt humiliation ooze over him, hot and slimy. He'd never live this down. Never.

When he got home, Cherise was in her sweatpants and a long T-shirt that said MAMA BEAR. There was another one that said PAPA BEAR but he'd accidentally thrown it in a dumpster. Cherise was walking in little circles with the baby in her arms, cooing and patting him on the back. She was still on the heavy side but at least you could see where her waist used to be. She hadn't put on lingerie since Before Christ. All she wore now were big, white, senior citizen panties and the same bra the Russian women wore at the Olympics.

"We're out of Pampers, Juanell," she said, not even looking at him.

"How we can we be out of Pampers again?" Dodson said, wondering what happened to *Hello, sweetheart* and a kiss. "That baby shits like a grown man."

"Didn't I tell you about that kind of language? I don't want to hear it around the baby."

"Since when does he speak English? If that's the case, we don't need that baby monitor. He can just holla at us." Dodson kissed her and kissed the baby. "Whassup, Micah? How's my big-head boy? Damn, are you giving him hormone shots? He's bigger than when I saw him this morning."

"He's perfect," Cherise said with that dreamy-eyed smile she'd had since she left the hospital.

"Say, Cherise. You got an ETA on when we gonna be hittin' it again? It's been a whole month."

"And it might be another month," she snapped. "I just had a baby, okay? An *eight-pound* baby."

"That's why I thought you'd be all loose and juicy." Dodson wished the words were a boomerang that would turn around and come back. Cherise gave him a look that sliced off the top of his head.

Cherise's mother, Gloria, came out of the kitchen. "Did you see Micah's diaper rash? I don't think that ointment's doing anything. You should switch to that organic brand, Motherlove, I've heard good things about it." She looked at Dodson, scowled and said, *"Oh, it's you."*

"Yes, it's me. Who'd you expect? Your ex-husband who went all the way back to North Carolina just to get away from you?"

"Josiah was a bum just like you. I'm surprised you two aren't related."

Gloria was an ossified, dead-certain old woman who wore dark print dresses, glasses with rhinestones embedded in the frames, and nurse's shoes. She was one of those people who was right about everything and knew the proper way, the *only* way, to do everything from making a pie crust and removing stains to child-rearing and dealing with the white man. She brushed past Dodson like he was a dead branch on an azalea bush and slipped a towel between Cherise's shoulder and the baby. Gloria tossed her head. "How something as beautiful as this child could have a father like you, God only knows. If I've said it once, I've said it a hundred times,

Cherise should have married Earl Cleveland. That man is a plastic surgeon now."

"He needs to be," Dodson said. "His whole damn family is ugly."

"Juanell," Cherise said, glaring at him. *"Go get the Pampers."* Dodson turned and headed for the door.

"And some Motherlove too," Gloria said. "I think they have it at Whole Foods."

Dodson stopped. Whole Foods was way over near the harbor. It would take him forty-five minutes to get there in the traffic and forty-five minutes to get home again. He started to protest but he could feel the women's eyes daring him to turn around, and he knew if he did those eyes would become sledgehammers and beat him into the ground like a fence post. "See you in a while," he said.

He was walking around Whole Foods looking for Motherlove. He couldn't believe all the shit they sold in here. Amazing Green Grass Superfood, Deer Velvet Extract, Neptune Krill Oil, Organic Certified Noni Juice, Cranberry Proanthocyanidins, and more Omegas than there were cars on the 710 freeway. Did white folks really need all this shit to stay alive? No wonder people of color were taking over. All they needed was a bowl of kimchee and a fried baloney sandwich and they were good to go. He bought the Motherlove and went out to his car. There was a note on the windshield. He read it and dropped the Motherlove, an icy daddy long legs skittering up and down his spine. "Lord have mercy."

Hello there, Mr. Dodson! You and I have yet to meet so I will, without further ado, get to the point. I have recently come across some information that I'm quite sure might be of great interest to you. I have been informed by a source (unimpeachable) that you and your friends, Isaiah Quintabe and Deronda Simmons, are the individuals who, some years ago, relieved Junior (a drug dealer) of a large amount of money, and in doing so, caused him and a

companion serious bodily harm. It would be in your best interest
(and health) to meet me tomorrow at exactly 9 am Pacific Stan-
dard Time at 775 Atlantic Blvd, Long Beach, California 90803.
Don't be late. Warmest Regards. C Babbitt, Esq.

When Dodson was seventeen, he lived in an apartment with Isaiah. Deronda was his girlfriend, and at the time, they were broke. They either had to come up with some cash or move out and be on the street. At Deronda's urging, Dodson robbed a drug dealer named Junior, and in the process, things went very wrong. Junior and his bodyguard, Booze Lewis, were about to execute him when Isaiah came to the rescue. He shot and severely wounded both men. Michael Stokely was in charge of Junior's security and the scariest muthafucka in the hood. He was humiliated. Junior, Booze, and Stokely were back on the street now, dangerous as ever. Dodson thought about showing the note to Isaiah but changed his mind. It would put that whole painful mess in the spotlight again and he'd endured enough humiliation with Deronda. He picked the Mother-love off the ground. No, he decided. He'd dig his way out of this all by himself.

CHAPTER TWO
Everybody Pays Real Money

The partners worked their first case together. The client was Carter Samuels, a police officer who was sleeping with Dodson's Auntie May. She was twenty years his senior but they seemed to really care about each other. They went on dates to Huntington Beach, where they wouldn't be recognized, they held hands, sent each other love texts, and bought each other presents. Auntie May wasn't concerned about her religious convictions or that Carter was married and had three kids. When Dodson asked her about it she said, "The Bible says, 'The Lord is my shepherd, I shall not want.' Well, I wanted and the Lord came up big-time."

When Carter was a young man, he had appeared in an adult movie titled *Wanda's Hole in One,* starring Wanda Wonder Lips. On the box cover, the grinning porn star, naked except for golf shoes, was bent over setting a golf ball on a tee. Carter played Caddy #1 and was featured in most of the scenes because of his extraordinary nine iron.

Wanda was heard to remark, "Damn. Put a steering wheel on that thing and you could drive yourself home." Unfortunately for Carter, Caddy #4, whose real name was Spencer Witherspoon, street name Spoon, had kept a copy of the movie on DVD.

Carter met Isaiah and Dodson in the parking lot at Shop 'n Save. He was wearing his uniform and looked like somebody had driven a bus over his spirit. "Spoon's blackmailing me," he said. "He wants ten thousand dollars or he'll spread that video all over town."

Isaiah had met Spoon some years ago. Isaiah was at the Coffee Cup, sitting at the counter, having breakfast. Suddenly, this drug-crazed wild man burst in, waving a gun. He pointed it at Verna.

"Gimme the money and don't fuck around," he said. "Or I'll shoot you right through your belly button."

Verna, whose strength of will was comparable to earthquakes and the Great Wall of China, refused. "I worked my fingers to the bone for this money, and I'm not giving you one red penny!" she said. Verna picked up a pan of cinnamon buns and threw it at him. Startled, Spoon fired into the air. As he raised his gun again, Isaiah barreled into him. They grappled briefly, but Spoon threw him off and escaped. Isaiah didn't know him then, but eventually he identified him and put him in jail.

"I know him," Isaiah said. "He's dangerous, an armed robber. I don't know what he's doing now."

Carter seemed preoccupied, giving Dodson a dubious look. "What are you doing here, Juanell?"

"I'm Isaiah's partner," Dodson said.

"You are? Last I heard, you were selling counterfeit Gucci bags out the trunk of your car."

"Go on, Carter," Isaiah said.

"I can't afford ten thousand dollars," Carter said in that strangled voice of the desperate. "We barely make it as it is. What's my wife gonna say? What am I gonna tell my kids?"

"What are you gonna tell my Auntie May?" Dodson said.

Carter ignored that. "I'll lose my job over this."

"Where does Spoon live?"

Carter looked at Isaiah and lowered his voice, which didn't really matter since Dodson was sitting across from him. "He's really your *partner?*" Carter said.

"Yes, he's my partner," Isaiah replied before Dodson went off on him.

"I don't know where Spoon lives. I'll run him through the system. You've gotta get me out of this, Isaiah. You've *got* to."

Ordinarily, Isaiah would have said something like Don't worry, everything will be okay, but Dodson cut him off. "Let's talk about fees, Carter."

"Fees?" Carter reacted like he'd never heard of such a thing. "Well, okay, how about this? I know a fella who installs burglar alarms. I can get you a big discount."

"That's not gonna cut it, Carter. This is a complicated case and let me see…" Dodson did some imaginary calculations on his phone while he muttered to himself, "Two of us working on it…per diem…expenses…hazard surcharge."

"What are you talking about, *hazard surcharge?*" Carter said.

"Spoon is a dangerous muthafucka who robs people with a gun. If that ain't damn hazard I don't know what is."

"Well, quit messing around and tell me what the damage is."

Dodson smiled like he was doing Carter a solid. "With the ten percent discount for first responders it comes to seven hundred and sixty-two dollars plus tax."

Carter was shocked. "Seven hundred and sixty-two dollars? Isaiah, are you listening to this?"

Before Isaiah could reply, Dodson said, "I am in charge of the company's billing department, so going forward, please direct your questions to me. If you'd like, we can put you on our financing plan, no interest for sixty days on your good credit."

"Wait, Dodson," Isaiah said. "There's no charge, Carter. We'll take care of it."

"That's more like it," Carter said, with a triumphant look at Dodson. "I'll get back to you on that address."

After Carter left, Dodson was incensed. "The fuck was that, Isaiah? You made me look like a fool!"

"We'll get paid with something that's worth more than money."

"Oh, I need to hear this. What's worth more than money?"

"A police officer who will owe us a favor."

Spoon's last known address turned out to be fake, but Isaiah remembered that Deronda's friend Nona was Spoon's cousin. It turned out she hated him and was happy to give him up. Spoon was living in the Crest Motel on Long Beach Boulevard. Nona said, "If you see a cockroach runnin' across the floor backwards, it's him."

The Crest was a Motel 3 with two floors and a soda machine with no soda and an anchor chain securing it to an iron railing. Dodson gave the clerk twenty dollars and got Spoon's room number. "Number 204," Dodson said when he came back to the car. "He's in there. I heard him yelling at somebody." Dodson was proving useful, Isaiah thought grudgingly. "You got a plan?" Dodson said.

"Not yet. Let's hang around for a while, see what's what."

They sat in the car and waited. The silence was uncomfortable. Isaiah had overruled Dodson with an airtight argument. They both knew a favor from a police officer could save your life or keep you out of jail. But that hadn't settled the pecking order. It had only increased the sense of competitiveness. For the moment, Dodson was distracted, playing a game on his phone and sending texts to Cherise. Isaiah had a book his brother Marcus had been reading just before he was killed. *The Known World* by Edward P. Jones. Isaiah was reading the part about Satan pledging to find evil out of good when Spoon emerged from the hotel room in a do-rag and boxer shorts. He stood at the railing, smoking a j and talking on his phone. He was insistent, selling something.

"That's him," Isaiah said.

A girl came out. She was white, miniskirt, high heels and a crackhead's resignation, not enough room on her face for all the makeup. One more dreamer from Ohio or Iowa who'd watched too much E! channel, her fantasies overwhelming her common sense. Spoon muttered something threatening and the girl lowered her head and hurried down the steps.

"How old do you think she is?" Dodson said. "Fifteen? Sixteen?" She walked past the car. There were welts on her legs, a bruise on her cheekbone. "Sometimes you need a word that's stronger than *muthafucka*. I'm gonna enjoy taking Spoon down."

Isaiah could understand a teenage girl running away from home. What he couldn't wrap his head around was why she wouldn't *return* home in the face of shit like this. Was there abuse there too? Or were her parents so uncaring and belittling it was just another kind of hell? Such a waste. She'd probably get herself pregnant just to have someone who loved her and who she could love in return.

"Go on and catch her," Dodson said. "I want to talk to her."

"Why?"

"Just catch her, okay?"

When they pulled up next to her, Dodson leaned out of the window. "Excuse me. Could we talk for a minute?"

She stopped and looked them over. "I'm not getting into the car with two of you."

"Leave this to me," Dodson said, and he got out of the car. There was a taco stand right there. He gave the girl some money for her time and the two of them sat at the counter eating tacos while IQ waited in the car. Dodson's street persona gave him cred, telling the girl in a very un-social-worker-like way how fucked over she was and what a piece of shit Spoon was for treating her like this.

"He didn't mean it," she said, barely audible.

"What'd he hit you with?" Dodson asked.

"His belt."

"He took off his belt but he didn't mean to hit you with it? It's a good thing he didn't mean to hit you with a hammer."

"You're another pimp, right?" she said. "He'd kill me if he saw us talking."

"No, I'm not another pimp and nobody's gonna kill you."

"Then what do you want?"

"My beef is with Spoon. I need something in that room and if I can break you out at the same time, that's gravy." Dodson explained the situation with Carter and the consequences for his family. He told her what he wanted her to do, promised she wouldn't be hurt and that she wouldn't have to go home. "I'll take you to a shelter right after it's done. I know the people there." Which was true. The director was Auntie May's daughter. The girl was listening or she'd have left, Isaiah thought.

"He'll find me," she said, hugging herself.

"Aww, come on, girl, use your head," Dodson replied. "There's twenty million people around here. Could you find *him* if he wanted to get lost?"

Dodson was wearing her down but Isaiah could tell she wasn't completely convinced. Then Dodson leaned in close and said something. She perked up but she still wasn't sold. Then he said something else, like a sweetener, a closer. He brought her back to the car. "Bridgette," Dodson said. "This is my partner, Isaiah Quintabe."

She looked in the window. "Are you really IQ?"

He nodded. "Yes, I am." And then she smiled like everything would be all right.

Spoon was on the sofa drinking a tall can of Monster and reading a tabloid. One of many he said he bought for Bridgette but were really for him. He liked those articles about somebody getting bungholed by an alien or a senator getting his dick sucked in

35

the bathroom at Mickey D's. There was a knock on the door. He grabbed the Sig Sauer off the coffee table.

"Who is it?"

"Me. Bridgette."

"The fuck you doing back so early?"

He set the gun down, got up, and undid the chain, ready to slap the shit out of this bitch if she didn't have her daily quota. He yanked the door open and a short motherfucker came leaping at him with a goddamn Superman punch that knocked him backward over the coffee table, scattering the gun, the Monster can, the sixteen hundred dollars that Bridgette had made, and the belt he'd used to beat her with. Before he could get up, Shorty had a foot on his throat.

"Stay still," Shorty said, "or you'll never holla at a woman again."

Spoon recognized the guy who'd come in behind him. "Isaiah?" he said. "I ain't forgot what you did. I served thirty-six months because of you."

"You got off light."

"You are one sorry muthafucka, Spoon," Shorty said. "Pimpin' is a fucked-up thing to do."

"First of all, I ain't no pimp," Spoon replied indignantly, "I'm a personal manager, and second of all, y'all should be talkin' to the johns, not me. If they can't get some decent pussy on they own that ain't my fault." Spoon noticed Bridgette standing behind Shorty, her face blank but doing something with her eyes he didn't like. "You in on this?" he said. "I'm gonna kill you, bitch."

"Where's the DVD?" Isaiah said.

"What DVD?" Spoon replied.

"You know what I'm talking about."

"I'm gonna call the police on you," Spoon said for the first time in his life. "This is assault with intent to hurt somebody."

"I don't think you want to do that. How old are you, Bridgette?"

36

"Fourteen."

"You still want to call the police? Where's the DVD?"

For no apparent reason, Spoon closed his eyes. "I don't know 'bout no DVD."

They duct-taped his hands behind his back and his ankles together and ransacked the room. The whole time he talked at Bridgette. "You know what I'm gonna do to you? I'm gonna knock you into next week, you hear me? You think you got beat bad before? It's gonna be ten times worse. *A hundred times* worse." He kept going, the bitch not saying anything, standing there staring like he was a math problem she was trying to figure out.

"Here it is," Isaiah said, waving the DVD.

"This is bullshit," Spoon said. "And tell Carter he's really fucked now."

"I don't see how. He's an officer of the law and you're a low-down pimp."

"I'm not a pimp, I'm a personal mana—and how do you know I ain't copied that thing all over the place?"

"Because you're too stupid to think of it," Isaiah said, "and too lazy to get it done."

He's got you there, Spoon thought. "You ain't gonna leave me like this, are you? I might starve to death."

"I can only hope," Bridgette said.

Spoon was enraged. "You can only hope? You need to hope I don't kill you to death." Bridgette looked at Shorty like she was asking permission.

"A deal's a deal. Go on and take it," Shorty said. She scooped up the money and stuck it in her bag.

"Hey, bitch! That's my money!" Spoon shouted.

"It's mine now," she said flatly. She looked at Shorty again.

"We'll wait for you in the car," he said. The two guys left, closing the door behind them.

Spoon was alone with Bridgette and was just starting to realize he was forehead-deep in shit. "Look here, baby," he said, droppin' his suave game on her. "Let's put this behind us, aight? You know I love you. Get this tape off me and we'll start all over again." He expected her to forgive him and fuck him like she always did but she casually picked up the belt, doubled it, and snapped it just like Spoon had done. He smiled like it was a joke. "Hey, baby, whatchoo doin' with that?"

"Stop calling me baby." She swung the belt viciously, whomping the bed a few times, dust rising, Dorito crumbs jumping. She stopped and looked like something was wrong. Like she wasn't satisfied.

"The hell's goin' on, ba—Bridgette?" Spoon said. "Look, tell you what. I'll cut you in on it. Keep twenty percent all for yourself. That's cool, ain't it? Nobody's gonna give you a deal like that." She was looking around the room. "What?" he said. "What are you looking for?" Her eyes found the aluminum baseball bat leaning in the corner.

She looked at it like she'd never seen it before. "Well, what do you know," she said. She picked up the bat.

"Hey, hey, don't fuck around, girl," Spoon said. "Now come on and get me out of this. I'll take you to Roscoe's, get you some chicken and waffles. You like that place, don't you?"

"No. I hate it. Haven't you ever noticed I don't order anything?"

"Oh yeah, yeah," Spoon said, like he was just now remembering. "How 'bout Norms? I know you like they salads." She stood over him and took a couple of practice swings. They made a whooshing sound and he could feel the air move over his face. Before she was officially his ho, he'd seen her play softball at McClarin Park. She hit one so hard she knocked down the third-base coach and put another one over the fence and broke a windshield in the parking lot. Spoon smiled queasily, sweat running into his eyes. "Let's talk about this, get everything out in the open, air this nonsense out."

She had the bat on her shoulder and was looking at him like dog shit on her brand-new Pumas. She gripped the bat and positioned her hands, choking up a little.

"Okay, okay," he said, his throat as dry as a sandbox. "Make it thirty percent. *Forty* percent, and that's my last offer."

She reared back with the bat. "Shut up, Spoon. Just shut up."

Manzo called. He was Khan of the Sureños Locos 13 and a neighborhood entrepreneur. He invested the gang's money in equities, real estate, and small businesses. Most of the membership wasn't enthusiastic about his vision of ending gangbanging and becoming legit businessmen, but they respected him and enthusiastically cashed their quarterly dividend checks.

"What can I do for you, Manzo?" Isaiah said. The phone was on speaker. He was playing Frisbee with Ruffin, the dog chasing it, catching it, and immediately sitting down. In his mind, returning it wasn't part of the game.

"You owe me, right?" Manzo said.

"Yeah, I do."

"I want to collect."

When Isaiah was searching for his brother Marcus's killer, he had mistakenly thought Manzo was responsible. He'd beaten him severely with a collapsible baton and owed him more than a favor. They met at the Coffee Cup. The last time they were here, Manzo had been nervous, not used to the concept of people going someplace to hang and work on their laptops while they sipped four-five-six-dollar cups of coffee.

Manzo looked around, thoughtful. "You know, I'm thinking about opening one of these."

"A coffee place?" Isaiah said.

"Yeah. It'd be like a Starbucks for Mexicans. And not just coffee. Horchata, Mexican soda, all that stuff. The profit margins are like fifty-sixty percent." He took a sip of his French roast and nodded appreciatively. "The place would have cool decorations too, not just sombreros and Corona posters. People think Mexicans don't care about nice places, you know? They think we *like* hangin' out on street corners and somebody's backyard. What do you think?"

"I think it's a great idea."

"Yeah. I just might do that."

Isaiah waited.

"It's about Vicente," Manzo said. Isaiah heaved an inward groan. Vicente was a hothead with a trip-wire temper, and he had no love for Isaiah. Manzo continued. "Vicente kidnapped his own daughter and he keeps calling his ol' lady threatening to take her to Mexico because she threw him out. I want you to find him."

"Why don't you call the police?"

"Because they'll arrest him and he's got priors. He'll go away for a long time. Plus, his ol' lady still loves him, or that's what she says. You ask me, homies don't deserve the women that love them." Isaiah nodded. That was his opinion too. Manzo went on. "The other thing is, Vicente's brothers are Locos and he's got other family too. His mother knows my mother."

"What happens if I find him?" Isaiah said.

"Up to you."

"What do you mean, up to me?"

"Up to you how you get the girl away from him."

Isaiah was home again on another Saturday night. He was usually all right with it but tonight was different. He was restless. He tried reading *The Known World* again but the words were a smear on the page. He thought about Dodson, how he'd deftly handled things with Bridgette and earned himself a place at the table. It made him anxious. The future was gray and dim and complicated.

He opened his laptop. The hotshot from South Africa wanted to play online chess again but how many times can you beat a guy in twelve moves? He watched the news on his laptop and discovered nothing had changed. The same blaring headlines about mayhem, corruption, and sorrow; the same fiery commentators burning the bridges that connect us one to the other. Isaiah put on some music but it was more irritating than soothing, reminding him that no one was there listening with him. At times like these, he wished he liked to drink or smoke dope. Something to get him out of himself.

Since resolving his brother's murder, he'd undergone some changes. The albatross of guilt he'd worn around his neck had flown the coop and he'd realized what an isolated life he'd been living. He had no friends except Dodson and TK, both of whom he rarely saw. He was lonely. He wanted a girlfriend, he wanted to have fun, whatever that was. He spent most of his time with the dog.

He'd made a few halfhearted attempts to improve his social life. He went to Nona's birthday party but stayed in the kitchen helping her mother with the food. Then he sat out in the yard with her father and talked about the old guy's days as a professional boxer, music and laughter taunting him from the house. He took a class on forensic science, hoping to meet someone with similar interests, but the only female there was a cop in uniform who looked at everybody like they were bank robbers.

Cherise set him up with a dental hygienist named Leslie. He decided to take her to dinner because he couldn't think of anything else. The photos on her Facebook page showed a cute, lively young woman who looked like she could be perky during a firestorm. She liked spin training, *Gone Girl,* the book and the movie, spending time with her family, hiking, and she was a vegetarian except for bacon (*I know, right?*).

He took her to the Souplantation, a dubious name, he thought, but it had a lot of different salads.

"I work for Dr. Fujimoto, over on PCH?" she said as she picked at a pile of spinach leaves, radishes, and bacon bits that looked like dead bugs. "He's in that strip mall right next to Vons? I've *got* to get away from him. You know what he likes to do? When I'm working on a patient, he comes up behind me and bumps me with his you-know-what and says *Woopsie daisy!* Jeez, what a creep." She widened her eyes like she was announcing her engagement. "Oh my God! Today? This one patient didn't even brush his teeth before he came in! I could hardly stand it. Oh my God, it was like a garbage disposal in there. I almost said something." She crossed her eyes and wagged her head. "But you have to be a professional. Oh, did I tell you I have this friend, Jackie? She's great, you know? Really funny—and *crazy.* Anyway, she asked me if she could get a discount on bridge work and I told her it's up to the doctor and she said maybe he'd like to woopsie with her. Can you believe it? Jackie's so crazy! Are you really a detective?"

Isaiah sighed at the memory. He closed his laptop and ate some canned chili standing at the counter. It was too salty and tasted like another barren weekend. There was nothing else to do but walk. At least he wouldn't be still and stymied in the house. Ruffin sensed the plan immediately and came over panting and mewling. Isaiah slipped on his leash and was halfway out the door when his phone buzzed. An email alert. It was late and he might have ignored it but any shred of human contact was better than none.

Dear Mr. Quintabe,

I'm the person you met at the wrecking yard and again in front of the art supply store. I'm sorry I was so abrupt but I am naturally suspicious of strangers. Since then, I've found out who you are and what you do. In fact, I've heard of you before. You helped a friend of mine, Samantha Chow. She said you were a good person. I hope so. I have a problem and would be grateful if we could talk about it. Would it be possible to meet for coffee?

Grace Monarova

He was fibrillating with excitement. He'd been thinking about her a lot, trying to remember every detail and fighting the urge to show up at the Edgemont with a bouquet of flowers. He wondered what she'd found out about him and hoped she'd read the articles in *Vibe* and *The Scene* and the *Long Beach Press-Telegram*. How smart and resourceful he was. How he helped people and didn't want the lime-light. He felt a little smug too, the girl brushing him off like a pest and now asking for his help. He thought about how to answer her. Serious and businesslike, of course, and no eagerness, like her request was routine, one of dozens he got every day. He thought maybe he should wait until the weekend was over before he responded so he wouldn't seem like a lonely guy with nothing to do at ten-thirty on a Saturday night except walk his dog and read emails. He held out for a good seven minutes before he emailed her back. He wanted to meet her right now, tonight, but he didn't want to seem too needy. Tomorrow he had meetings with clients for most of the day. He wanted to cancel them but decided he couldn't. Anyway, if she had to wait, it would make him seem all the more like a Very Important Person.

Earliest time I have available is 7:30 pm tomorrow. Starbucks on Willow.

He chose Starbucks because he thought it was fancier than the Coffee Cup. When he didn't hear back immediately, he almost wrote her again to give her more options but thankfully she replied.

Thank you. See you there.

He took Ruffin for a walk. He was always alert and observant but he was so distracted he bumped into a mailbox. He wondered what it would be like talking to her. What would she say? What would she be like? He usually had a mental image of a new client, pieced together from instinct and observations, but Grace was so withholding, nothing was coming together. He was suddenly anxious, realizing the meeting wasn't so much about her as it was about him. What was *he* like? What would *he* say? Unless he was in detective mode, his self-confidence was woeful. A good thing he could slip on that persona. The other ones were embarrassing.

His client meetings seemed to go on forever. He almost told Henrietta Williams to hurry the fuck up. He worried Grace would change her mind or have something better to do. Afterward, he hurried home to change. He felt ridiculous deciding what to wear. His good clothes weren't in style when he bought them. He settled on what he always wore when he went out. Diesels, Timberlands, a light blue, short-sleeve shirt, and a Harvard cap.

He got to the Starbucks early, thinking he'd get a look at her first, see if he could catch her mood, something to give him an edge, but her white '09 GTI was already in the lot. He could see her in the driver's seat, gathering her things. Why was she here so early? Probably for the same reasons he was. She got out and came toward him, tentative, taking deep breaths like she was about to get a root canal. He got out of his car.

"Hi," he said.

"Hi," she said.

He tried not to stare. It was as if someone started with a very pretty face and then moved everything the tiniest fraction so the overall effect was more compelling than beautiful. She was wearing jeans, scuffed black ankle boots, the same chambray shirt over a different gray T-shirt. She looked neither hip nor unhip. More like she didn't care about clothes but didn't want to be a slob either.

"Thank you for meeting me." She glanced past him at the Audi. *She's looking for the dog,* he thought.

"Glad to do it." He extended his hand. She hesitated a moment and shook it with her fingertips. She was wound up tight, wary as a deer edging out of the forest. She didn't meet his gaze and moved past him toward the coffee shop. She walked fast, he had to hurry to keep up, her boot heels clicking too loudly on the asphalt. He wondered if she didn't want to be seen with him. He almost said something until he realized she didn't want to be *next* to him. She was keeping her distance.

Once inside, they made their orders, espresso for him, black coffee for her. Before he could get his wallet out, she paid. They sat down at a table. He struggled to find a starting point. *So, how are you?* seemed too stupid to say.

"I want you to find somebody," she said. "My mother. I haven't seen her in ten years." He was surprised by her directness, she'd been so reticent before. "She's somewhere in LA. I've Googled her and all that but there's no trace."

"Has she tried to contact you?"

She seemed embarrassed, looking at her hands, folded on the table. "No, she hasn't."

"Why try to find her now?"

"I saw her. She was in a car parked across the street from my apartment. She didn't see me because it was raining and I had an umbrella. I couldn't believe it. There was traffic and by the time I crossed the street she'd driven off."

"It's been a long time. Are you sure—"

"*Of course* I'm sure," she said, her voice rising. She got out her phone and showed him some photos. "Just to give you an idea. Her name is Sarah." The first picture was taken in a kitchen that might have been in the neighborhood. Linoleum countertop, mismatched canisters, an electrical plug mounted crookedly on the drywall. Like Grace, Sarah was thin and fair, same green eyes but tentative, like she was unsure of her place in the world. She was in her twenties, housewifey; a flowered apron over a dress, hair and makeup in place. She was standing at an aging stove frying something. Grace was in the picture. She was maybe seven or eight years old. She was holding a baby possum and trying to touch noses with it. Most people would have said *It was a pet* or *I was crazy about animals* but she didn't.

"Where was this?" he asked.

"We lived in Bakersfield," she said, looking like she was really glad to be out of there.

There were other shots of Sarah serving food on holidays, playing with Grace on a swing, sewing on a sewing machine. Then a family shot. Grace's father in uniform; all angles like a paper airplane, standing at attention, reporting for duty. Sarah was next to him, expressionless, her arms folded, their shoulders not touching. She wore jeans with narrow ankles and an oversize sweatshirt, less makeup, her hair was tied messily in a ponytail. She looked like a mom going back to school. Then a family photo: Sarah and her husband standing next to each other; Grace in front of them, smiling with no front teeth, happy to be with her parents. But mom and dad's shoulders weren't touching, six inches of air space between them. *Something wrong there,* Isaiah thought.

"What was your father's name?" he asked.

"Charles," she said. "Everybody called him Chuck."

Isaiah looked at the pictures. Grace seemed excessively nervous, like there were secrets in them. He didn't see anything out of the ordinary. Another shot of Sarah. She was in her mid-thirties, outdoors, shading her eyes from the sun. Her hair was lighter than Grace's and towel-dried. She wore an oversize black-and-white-checked shirt and faded black jeans. Little makeup. A small heart on a chain around her neck. There was confidence in her gaze and a wry smile like she was finally in on the joke.

"That's what she looked like when she left," Grace said.

"When was that?"

"April seventh, 2004."

"So what happened? Why did she leave?"

"Does it matter?"

"Yes, it does."

She stiffened like she wasn't going to get pushed around. "Why? I just want her found, that's all."

He was a little surprised. "Why? Well, if I know why she left, it'll give me a better idea of where she's gone."

"We already know where she's gone. She's here."

"I need context."

She looked away. "It's about something private."

She was a loner like him, he thought. Not used to being contradicted because there was no one to contradict her. She leaned back as if to say *deal with it,* but Isaiah was in his element now and he had a rule. Never let the client control the case.

"You called me because you thought I could help," he said. "So let me. Assume I know what I'm doing." They grappled with their eyes. She took a deep breath, the kind where you need a moment to make something up.

"Mom and Dad were fighting a lot. She'd had enough of him and took off." A bad liar, Isaiah thought.

"How old were you?"

"Fifteen."

The barista called her name. She immediately got up, went to the counter, and brought back their orders. "Before we go on, I want to talk about payment. How much do you charge?" Again, he was surprised by her directness. He thought about taking something off the price but thought it was condescending. He told her his per diem and she shook her head. "I can't afford that."

"We'll work something out," he said like it wasn't an issue, but she stood firm.

"No, I don't want to owe you." He sensed a struggle going on inside her. Her need versus a concession pushing and shoving each other like sumo wrestlers. The need won. "Do you mind coming over to my place?"

The Edgemont's elevator stank of piss, cigarettes, and fortified wine, creaking as it ascended. Isaiah wondered why it was always awkward riding with someone in an elevator; like whatever you said would be inappropriate and recorded by a hidden camera and you'd be a creep on YouTube for all eternity. The hallway was gloomy, the carpet runner worn and blotched with stains. It was quiet but Isaiah could hear the drunken rages, weeping women, and crying kids from behind the scarred apartment doors.

The room was surprisingly large. Somebody had removed the bedroom wall with a sledgehammer and a crowbar; chicken wire extruding from the smashed stucco. "I needed more work space," she said, not embarrassed, just explaining.

"You don't think the landlord will mind?"

"The building's been sold, they're going to tear it down."

The room looked like an artist's studio, not that he'd ever seen one. Cans of gesso, putty knives, sponges, brushes blooming from glass jars, and dozens of rolled-up paint tubes scattered on a work-bench. Strewn around the room were beveled stretcher bars, corner bars, rolls of canvas, two easels with half-finished paintings, and numerous completed ones hanging on the walls and stored in crudely made stalls, a living space carved out in a corner. Futon, dresser, nightstand, laundry, shoes on the floor. If she was self-conscious about the mess there was no sign of it.

"Have a seat," she said. There weren't a lot of options. He took a stool at the Formica peninsula, a tiny kitchen behind it. "I don't have espresso. Is instant all right?" They'd just come from Starbucks. She needed something to do, settle herself down.

"Sure. That's fine," he said.

The windows were closed and the apartment retained the day's heat. It was stifling and drowsy with the smell of turpentine. Grace was still nervous, maybe more so now that they weren't in public. She put water in an electric kettle and clanked it against the faucet. She found the instant coffee and dropped the lid. She got mismatched mugs out of the dish rack and banged them together. While they waited for the water to boil, he glanced around at her paintings. They were abstract; amorphous shapes, dark colors, overdrawn with slashes, stark lines, and thick smears of paint. Just the kind of stuff he didn't understand. She gave him a mug.

"Thanks." He took a sip. The coffee wasn't tasty or choice. It tasted brown.

She sat down on the other side of the counter. "So I guess it's obvious I'm not exactly rich." She's setting me up for something, he thought. Another deep breath, this one preparatory. Her lips were pinched together, her chin up; that look you get when you're going to say something embarrassing and want to keep your dignity. "But I have to pay my way." He didn't want to assume anything, but it was clear she wasn't talking about bitcoins or postdated checks.

"Look, don't worry about it," he said.

She was insistent. "No, I have to do this."

He was getting a little alarmed. "No, you don't, really."

"I want to pay you with my art," she said. Isaiah was relieved and a little disappointed as well. "I don't want to insult you," she went on.

"You're not insulting me."

"Don't feel like you have to. I mean, if you think it's stupid—"

"It's not stupid, I just—" He ran out of words. She shrugged, her face coloring.

"It's okay. It was just an idea, that's all." She was already moving for the door. "Thanks for coming." Isaiah heard Dodson's voice: *Everybody pays real money,* but it faded quickly in the cloud of Grace's disappointment.

"Wait," he said. "There's a lot to see." He got up, went to the center of the room, and surveyed the paintings. He had more pressing needs than starting an art collection but there was no going back now. He wanted to know her. He looked from one to the other, trying to find something recognizable; a likeness, a hidden image, a suggestive shape. His nervousness turned everything into a muddy wash. He was taking too long. He could feel her anxiety, her hope. He knew he should say something but didn't know what. New sweat was making his scalp tingle. The heat and turpentine smell were making him sick. *Why doesn't she open a window?* Seconds went by like a roller coaster chugging its way to the summit, a calamitous drop on the other side. *Say something, you idiot!*

"Take your time," she said, mistaking his inaction for focus. She drifted out of his view. Reprieved, he took a breath. *Okay, settle down. This is her work, her passion. Be respectful. Give the paintings their due.* He looked at them again one by one. To his uncultivated eye, they were artful, not paint thrown on a canvas. Composed and haphazard at the same time, balanced but not symmetrical, the colors discordant and yet they somehow blended. No amateur could have done them. The problem was, they didn't look *like* anything. *What is that? A skyline? The ocean? A screaming child?* It felt like a game show, a million bucks on the line, the clock tick tick ticking, a breathless audience waiting for the answer. *Settle down. Settle down. Think!*

Nothing.

Then it struck him. *They're abstract, dummy,* meant to communicate on some other level than concrete things. So what else was there? Feelings. Not exactly his strong suit. He tried to clear his mind and not let his brain assemble the elements into anything tangible. It was like looking at a sunset. You don't try to see some-thing in it. You let it evoke—love, sadness, wonder, hope, endings and beginnings, or something undefined and wordless at your core. He looked at the paintings again, his mind blank and absorbent, the colors and shapes affecting him osmotically. There was nothing remotely pleasant about them. Most were unsettling and brooding. There was one that stood out from the others. It was large, four feet by three, the only one with a frame. There were stormy grays, graveyard browns, and hard edges, a disastrous fracture splitting the canvas like a rip, mysterious tendrils spreading ominously from a stump of black, reaching across the fracture, darkening a patch of sky blue like an infection. It felt unbearably tense. A struggle. He'd had no idea art could affect him this way. He wondered what kind of person could create such powerful images. He turned and saw her sitting on the futon with her arms around her knees. She'd been watching him. "They're amazing," he breathed. He met her gaze and in that moment he felt it. *Contact.*

"Thank you," she said quietly, a smile in her eyes. "Is there some-thing you especially like?" He knew right away. He nodded at the one with the frame.

"That one."

"Oh God." She put her hand over her mouth, an edge of panic in her voice. "Could you pick something else? I'm kind of attached to that one."

Isaiah thought about the work he would put into the case. The time. How he'd be sacrificing real money and have to fight with Dodson. No, if he was going to do this she should sacrifice too. "I want that one or nothing," he said. Surprised, she jerked her head back as if a bee had flown by. She waited, expecting him to soften, but he kept his face neutral. He could see an argument gathering inside her, but as the moment drew longer, her face flattened into resentful acceptance.

"Okay," she said. "Can we get started?"

"Did your mom have friends?" he asked.

She shrugged. "Some but they changed. At first, they were housewives like her. They didn't work, they played tennis and did a lot of shopping. When she decided to make art, she dropped them and started hanging with other artists, writers, actors. They were way more interesting."

"Are you in touch with any of them?"

"No. They're long gone."

"Did you get along with your mom?"

She made a face like it was a stupid question. "Why does that matter?" She moved her coffee mug in front of her and held it in two hands. He waited. She shrugged. "We got along okay. We had the usual mother-daughter bullshit. Who didn't?"

"What did your dad do?" Isaiah said. Grace shifted her position, half in profile now. Again, she hesitated as if she needed time to assemble the words.

"The army," she said.

"Was he in Iraq?"

She folded her arms. "Yeah." He waited for her to elaborate but she didn't. He wondered if he would have to prompt her every time.

"Is he around?" he said.

"He died." She hesitated again. "Heart attack. And I still don't see why this stuff is important."

He ignored that and continued. "Who took care of you?"

"After my mom left, I stayed with my grandmother. She couldn't handle it so I went to a foster home. I ran away when I was sixteen." Her phone buzzed. "Sorry, I have to take this. It's about an art show." She moved away.

Isaiah believed in tells, body language that indicated deception, but they weren't always reliable. If a person scratches his nose, maybe it's because his nose itches. If he's sweating, maybe it's because he's wearing a sweater on a warm day. But the degree of reliability rose dramatically if you established a baseline or what the person was like when they were truthful. Isaiah had established a baseline by asking Grace basic questions. When did this happen. What was her father's name. How old was she at the time. Grace was forthright, looked at him directly, held the coffee mug in one hand, not all the pauses and sighs and impatience and turning into profile so she wouldn't have to make eye contact and holding the mug between them like an obstacle and folding her arms protectively. As soon as the conversation touched the past, the tells started flashing like the red and white lights on an ambulance. He wondered why she knew the exact date her mother left but hesitated before saying her father died of a heart attack. A funny thing to forget. And why the reluctance to say he was in the military? What was wrong with that, or being in Iraq? And why would Sarah abandon her daughter just because she was fighting with her husband? Why didn't she move to another neighborhood or get a divorce? Sometimes clients cherry-picked the truth because they wanted to put themselves in the best possible light or others in the worst. Sometimes they simply forgot or didn't think something was important, but more often than not, they were hiding something, and if Sarah abandoned her teenage daughter and dropped out of sight for ten years, she wasn't taking a sabbatical. She was on the run.

CHAPTER THREE

Fangs

Jimenez's father was a gardener, and on Saturdays he took his son along to rake leaves and pile cut branches in the truck. The boy learned to love the abundant jacarandas, Western oaks, and box maple trees in the rich neighborhoods, and wondered why they didn't grow that way in the barrio. Laguna Hills was lush with trees, flowers, and wide green lawns. The houses were big and there were almost no pedestrians around, the residents content to lie out by the pool or play a set with their attorney.

Jimenez pulled into Walczak's driveway, his matte-gray Jeep Rubicon bumping over the cobblestones. The hell is that about? he thought. Did Walczak want to hear his horse clip-clopping when he came home from a fox hunt? The house was a massive brick thing. Jimenez had read about it in a magazine. He wondered what it was like living in a custom-made 12,000-square-foot building with nine bedrooms and a bathroom for every ass cheek in the neighborhood.

Walczak's flunky and bodyguard Craig Richter let him in. He wasn't the usual no-neck weight lifter or chiseled Secret Service type. Richter was an ex–homicide detective from the Newton Street Division in South Central LA, the gangbangers' Promised

Land. He hadn't changed since the last time Jimenez had seen him. Burly, fifties, wide and bowlegged like a bulldog, dark bags under his eyes. He wore a cheap gray suit, a red tie that hung like a flap of cardboard, and security guard shoes. He was still a slob too. Unshaven, one shirttail out of his pants, stains on his tie, and for that cosmopolitan look, he'd added a porkpie hat like Gene Hackman in *The French Connection*. It made him look stupid.

"You're making good money, Richter," Jimenez said. "Why don't you buy some new clothes?"

"What are you talkin' about? These *are* new."

They'd met once before at a memorial service for a veteran officer who was killed in Afghanistan. Richter drove Walczak's family to the church in the Bentley. Walczak's perfect wife, Patty, elegant and vivacious, and their perfect son, Noah, twelve years old, good-looking, polite, and as shiny as the chrome on the Bentley. Together, they looked like the photo that comes with a picture frame.

Jimenez and Richter had a smoke together on the church steps while the minister droned on and on. Richter didn't seem too bright for an ex-cop, his conversation limited to the Dodgers and where you could get good carnitas.

Walczak's foyer was as big as Jimenez's apartment. The main hallway could have doubled as a driving range. The place was furnished like one of those English TV shows about lords and manors and butlers and footmen. There were crystal chandeliers, parquet floors; the furniture heavy, dark and European. Oil paintings in gilded frames hung on the walls. Boring landscapes. Crashing seascapes. Dead pheasants slung on a wooden table. If there'd been chamber music Jimenez wouldn't have been surprised.

Richter led Jimenez to Walczak's study. The man himself was sitting behind his ridiculously huge desk. Get somebody to stand on the other end and you could play Ping-Pong, assuming you could thread the ball between the gold-plated pen holder, a fifty-caliber machine gun shell, a Sharper Image gizmo that levitated a globe, a laptop in a case that could withstand an IED, a teakwood humidor that once belonged to the King of Siam or the Duke of Earl, and lots of photographs. Birthdays, anniversaries, Thanksgiving, grandparents; corny, sentimental crap you wouldn't associate with a shit like Walczak.

Walczak was already annoyed. "Glad you could make it, Jimenez."

"I'm glad too," he said. Hawkins and Owens were lounging in leather club chairs and drinking Walczak's Scotch. They looked weird holding fancy crystal tumblers, like aborigines with power drills. Hawkins grinned and they bumped fists.

"What's up, Hawk?" Jimenez said.

"Ain't nothin' to it," Hawkins replied. Owens huffed contemptuously.

"Hey, baby," Jimenez said. "Long time no see. Shouldn't you be milking something?"

"Shouldn't you be picking lettuce?"

"This is a time-sensitive matter," Walczak said. "Do you mind if we get started?"

"I don't get a drink like everybody else?" Jimenez said.

Walczak sighed and drummed his fingers on the desk. He was trim and fit, like he could run on a treadmill for weeks at a time. He had blond hair, Aryan blue eyes, and an All-American face, his smile as broad as a car salesman's, his teeth too white to be human. More like an appliance or snow. He had on his casual Friday look. Khaki chinos, a white Egyptian cotton shirt with the sleeves rolled up, a fat gold Rolex, and for that touch of hipness, six-hundred-and-eighty-nine-dollar Kanye West sneakers in fire-hydrant yellow. If he was handling your portfolio you'd give him the passcode to your brokerage accounts and not worry about a thing.

Jimenez got his drink from the bar and Walczak rose from the

Ping-Pong table. He used a remote, and a photo of a woman appeared on a large wall monitor. "Remember her?"

"Oh shit," Jimenez said.

"I hope you're gonna tell us her plane crashed in the Amazon," Hawkins said.

"Afraid not," Walczak said grimly. "She's turned up."

"It's been, what, nine, ten years?" Owens said. "Why's she poppin' up now?"

"She's blackmailing us." It went quiet except for Owens swirling the ice cubes around in her glass. "Sarah sent me these," Walczak said. "They came in an email. Untraceable, even by my guys." A slide show began. They were pictures from Abu Ghraib. They were taken clandestinely, the cameraman shooting through half-open doors and dirty windows, over partitions and around corners. They were shocking. Richter choked on his drink.

It was the four veterans torturing detainees, but there was more. Hawkins smirking as he came out of a cell zipping up his pants, a naked woman curled up in a corner, Owens threatening her with a baton. Walczak, sitting imperiously in a chair, grinning at a woman removing her burka and weeping with humiliation. The next slide made Jimenez want to blend in with the carpet. He was on top of a woman, bare-ass naked, her beseeching hand flailing in the air. Owens was there, hands cupped around her mouth, braying as if to egg him on. Walczak thrusting against a woman pinned to a wall. The group in a cell, plastic cups in their hands, leering and laughing at a naked woman. She was hysterical, pleading, her hands clenched together as if in prayer. Jimenez, sitting on a cot, Owens giving him a blow job.

"That'll be enough of that," Owens said. The slide show stopped. The silence that followed was like an unexpected ceasefire, everyone bewildered, not believing what they'd seen, not believing what they'd done.

Richter was so appalled he was laughing. "Holy shit, I thought I was bad. Jesus, you guys went nuts! Talk about a depraved bunch of assholes! Didn't you have any conscience at all?"

Everyone looked at him like he'd kicked a puppy to death.

"Shut up, you idiot!" Walczak barked. "You don't know anything about it, so until I ask for your opinion, *shut your big stupid mouth.*" Humiliated, Richter leaned back in his chair, drew in his cheeks, and looked away.

"Are these the ones you told us about?" Jimenez said. "The ones that Chuck took?"

"Yeah," Walczak said. "I don't know how he did it without us seeing him."

"Because he was a sneaky little goddamn rat," Owens said, pouring herself another drink. "Always hangin' around with that damn camera. He was worse than Graner."

"Sarah wants a million dollars or she'll go public with the pictures," Walczak said.

"She should have asked for more," Hawkins said. "You got that in your penny jar, don't you?"

Walczak ignored him and went on. "I told her I was going to split the bill with you guys and getting it together would take awhile. She gave me until Friday." He shook his head. "Stupid. It just gives us more time to come up with something."

"And it gives her time to come up with something too," Richter said.

"Didn't I tell you to shut up?"

"Wait a minute," Hawkins said. "Split the bill? That's bullshit, Walczak, you got us into this."

"Oh really? And how did I do that?"

"You were our superior, remember? You gave the orders."

"Did I order you to rape those women?" Walczak retorted. Hawkins's nostrils flared. He set his drink down hard and got out of his chair.

"Whoa, ease up, Hawk," Jimenez said. He stood in front of him with his palms out. "Walczak's gonna pay the bill because a million is nothing to him and he knows the rest of us are living paycheck to paycheck. Ain't that right, Walczak?"

Walczak heaved an exasperated sigh. "Yes, that's right. Back to business, please?"

Walczak's company had access to every law enforcement database in existence. He'd already run Sarah's name through ATF, DEA, FinCEN, IRS, INTERPOL, NCIC, Nlets, US Customs. Not a single hit. Sarah had successfully flown under the radar for a decade, not an easy thing to do.

"We have a lead," Walczak said. "Her daughter." He put another photo on the monitor. "Her name is Grace. Twenty-five years old, single, calls herself an artist. She lives in a shitty part of Long Beach."

"We paying her a visit?" Jimenez said.

"Yes, we are."

This was fucked up, Jimenez thought. Maybe Sarah was staying with her daughter, maybe not. Either way, they'd have to kidnap one or both of them and if they held out, Walczak would torture the shit out of them and kill them when he was done. Walczak was a de facto leader on the tier and like a deep-sea submersible, he explored your murky depths and discovered shit you never knew was there. Mainly, that you were capable. Capable of evil. And nobody who wasn't actually there understood what it was like to be in a world where evil was expected, where evil was the norm. Shit you never imagined you would do, shit you'd *stop* somebody from doing if you were anyplace else, was suddenly your fucking *job*. It was like you gave up the power to decide things for yourself. You were working for the devil and you did what you were told.

They had their own little cabal; Walczak, Jimenez, Hawkins, and Owens. They called themselves the Four Horsemen. If Abu Ghraib wasn't the apocalypse, nothing was. Walczak was different from the other CIA guys. He got right in there and tortured prisoners personally, which was weird if you didn't have to. He was also a clean freak, showering four or five times a day and paying somebody to do his laundry. He only went to the bathroom if he was alone and washed his hands like an eye surgeon. If he was anywhere but in his office he wore latex gloves.

With the detainees, he always went that extra mile. If they'd beaten a guy senseless and he was lying on the floor, Walczak would kick him. If a detainee had a broken leg, he'd step on it. Walczak organized contests for the dog handlers. If you were the first one to make a prisoner piss on himself, you got a bottle of booze. He ordered a detainee to be crucified. Hung him by his arms with a hood over his head. The guy died and they buried him just outside the prison walls. Why not? Who was going to dig up some asshole in a killing field?

Walczak was delighted when the detainee's family was being held too. He'd bring in the guy's wife, tell him all the different ways you were going to defile her if he didn't start talking. Then he'd grab her tits or rip off her burka. It worked better than sic'ing Slayer on him. There wasn't a lot in the news about rape but there should have been. The whole cell block was rape central. Men, women, boys, girls. Didn't matter.

Walczak's specialty was waterboarding. He'd get excited about it like he was getting the prisoner ready for a space launch. The plank had to be tilted down fifteen degrees for maximum effect, a number Jimenez suspected Walczak made up. The prisoner was strapped down completely, ankles to shoulders, even his head. Walczak didn't like wigglers. The towel had to be drawn taut over the prisoner's face so as not to impede the water flow, and Walczak's preference was to use a hose. A stream of water made the sense of drowning continuous. If no hose was available, Walczak used ten-gallon gasoline drums. None of it was necessary. A bucket and fifteen or twenty seconds and the guy would be choking and gagging and freaking out. A trained marine couldn't hack it for more than thirty. But Walczak let it go on. And on. And on. Until the guy was actually drowning and everybody in the room was alarmed.

By that time, the detainee would be screaming at the interpreter, giving up information about everything and anything, relevant or not. This way, Walczak claimed, he'd get answers to questions he hadn't asked, which made no sense at all. Anybody in that situation would make shit up just to get you to stop and the vast majority of the detainees didn't know jack in the first place. Since then, Walczak had founded his own security company, WSSI, with contracts all over the world. He was richer than his hero, Donald Trump. And what was Jimenez's reward for defending his country? A shit apartment and a job working as a dispatcher at a cab company. The payments on the Rubicon took half his income but it was the only thing in his life that made him happy.

Walczak put a diagram of Grace's building on the monitor. A dump called the Edgemont. "Here's the layout," he said. He started pointing at things and rambling on about the operation's objectives and entry points and static posts like he knew what he was talking about. At Abu Ghraib, he was a desk jockey when he wasn't torturing the detainees. Walczak went on about the "mission" and the "targets" and it reminded Jimenez of rounding up Iraqi cabdrivers, rug salesmen, janitors, store clerks, camel drivers, and any other random asshole who happened to be at home minding his own business. Jimenez glanced at Richter. He was half asleep, fiddling with the end of his tie, probably thinking about his next plate of rice and beans. Jimenez wondered why Walczak kept him around.

"Is everybody clear?" Walczak said.

"You're coming with us," Hawkins said, belligerent. "You're in the front lines with the rest of us, you hear me?"

"I never thought otherwise," Walczak said, not fooling anybody.

"Could we stop jawing and get on with this?" Owens said. "I didn't bring a piece, by the way."

"Don't worry," Richter said. "Walczak can get you a nuke if that's what you want."

They were sitting at Grace's workbench, looking at her laptop. Isaiah brought up a pay site that searched personal records.

"I can't afford this," she said.

"Part of the service."

"No, it's not. I'm taking advantage."

"If you were I'd tell you."

"I'll pay you back," she said, like Isaiah wouldn't believe her.

"You've already paid me."

"No, I haven't," she said, adamant.

"Don't you think your art is worth $129.95?"

Sarah's school, financial, property, and educational records turned up nothing relevant. "I think this is a waste of time," Grace said. "All of this happened in the past. What good does it do us now? I'm gonna make coffee."

"Could I have water, please?" Isaiah said. She got up and went to the kitchen while he brought up Sarah's criminal record. She had an unpaid traffic ticket in Reno, Nevada. And then there was this:

MONAROVA, SARAH JANE. HEIGHT: 5'3" WEIGHT: 110lb
EYES: GREEN. HAIR: BLONDE. WANTED FOR: MURDER.
WARRANT NUMBER: F7900076 USE CAUTION: MAY BE
ARMED AND DANGEROUS. IF ARRESTED, CONTACT DETEC-
TIVE SWINSON AT (661-459-0404) HOMICIDE DIVISION
BAKERSFIELD POLICE DEPARTMENT, CALIFORNIA.

A murder warrant had been issued for Sarah's arrest, dated the day after she fled Bakersfield and left her daughter behind. This was what Grace was hiding and why she didn't want him delving into her past. He wanted to tell her it was okay, that he'd help her no matter what her mother had done. Should he confront her? No. She might be humiliated and back out of the investigation altogether.

Grace put water in the kettle. "Anything else?"

"No, nothing," he said. He closed the site and was glad she hadn't made note of the password. "I've got to go," he said.

"Already? We were just getting started."

"I have to feed Ruffin, take him for a walk."

She fumed. "*Now?* We haven't done anything yet." Isaiah was annoyed. First she pays him with a painting, then she makes it hard for him, and now she's complaining because he has to go?

"What do you want me to do?" he said, a little more harshly than he intended. "Let him go hungry and crap in the house?"

She took a deep breath as if she needed a moment to find her patience. "When can we pick this up again?"

"In the morning. I'll call you."

They exchanged numbers and he left. He came out of the building and stretched. A long time to be sitting on a stool. He saw a matte-gray Jeep parked across the street. The driver was a Latino. He had short hair, his Hawaiian shirt stretched tight over an imposing shoulder, a tatted-up forearm resting on the windowsill. He had the intense stillness of a cop just before a drug raid. He glanced at Isaiah and turned to talk to a passenger. He was wearing an earbud with a coiling wire that went down under his collar. A Secret Service–style radio. Not a cop then. They used car radios or handhelds. FBI? DEA? But the car wasn't right. A new forty-thousand-dollar Jeep with BBS rims. It wasn't a fleet car. This was the Latino man's personal ride. So these people were probably private security, but what were they doing here? Why were they sitting out in the open? A staging area? Maybe. Isaiah relied on his internal sonar to alert him to possible trouble. He heard a faint *ping.*

He walked to the end of the block, turned onto a side street. His car was parked farther up. He reached the alley behind the building and saw a silver BMW M5 near the fire exit, a beast of a car, over 500 horsepower, a man in the driver's seat. His face was obscured by the reflection off the windshield. What was somebody in a seventy-thousand-dollar car doing back here at this time of night? A drug deal? *Ping ping.*

Isaiah was instinctively drawn to anything remotely criminal, and he turned into the alley and walked right past the car. The driver was white, expensive haircut, manicured nails, a polo shirt with the Versace logo, a Rolex Yacht-Master on his wrist. He was also wearing the same kind of earbud as the Latino man. They were hooked up. *Ping ping ping.*

The guy gave Isaiah a hard look and Isaiah kept walking. Why was a private security team staking out a dump like the Edgemont? Who could possibly be of interest to them? If it was a criminal matter or terrorism, they would be law enforcement. Was this about Grace's mother and the murder warrant? He restrained himself from running and reached the other end of the alley. As soon as he made the turn, he sprinted around the block, slowing as he approached the front of the building again. The Jeep was still parked across the street. He hurried inside, patting his pockets like he'd forgotten his wallet. He glanced around the lobby making mental notes and bounded up the fire stairs three at a time.

It was eleven-fifteen, the area nearly deserted. "Let's go," Jimenez said. He alerted Walczak and they got out of the Jeep. Jimenez, Hawkins, Owens, and Richter crossed the street and entered the Edgemont. Owens was semidrunk so Jimenez told her to stay in the lobby. The others took the elevator to the fourth floor and moved quickly down the hall, pulling on their ski masks. They had Tasers, Mace, duct tape, zip ties, handcuffs, and Glocks. Subduing two women, or two men for that matter, wouldn't be a problem. Then they'd be hustled down the fire stairs and thrown in Walczak's SUV.

When they reached Grace's apartment, Hawk got into position and Jimenez gave him the nod. Hawk shouldered through the flimsy door like it was cardboard. He grinned.

"Trick or treat."

It frightened her when Isaiah banged on her door. "We have to go. *Now,*" he said. She didn't know why she trusted him but here she was, chasing him down the fire stairs. For some reason, he'd picked up her umbrella as they left the apartment. They reached the lobby level and stopped.

"What's happening?" she said.

"Some people are after you—no questions, we'll talk about it later." He gave her the umbrella. "Have you ever done any acting?"

"What are you talking about?"

"They're looking for a girl in her twenties."

They went through the door and into the lobby. Isaiah held her arm like he was helping her walk. She was bent over, shoulders hunched, wearing Isaiah's hoodie, drawn tight around her face. With a trembling hand she used the umbrella like a cane and hobbled along beside him. Who were they running from? she wondered. What the hell was this about? She took a quick glance. A woman leaning back against a wall with her eyes half closed. She was tall, wearing a flannel shirt and cowboy boots. Isaiah clutched Grace's arm a little tighter. "Easy does it, Mrs. Mayfield."

They crossed the lobby, passing within ten feet of the woman. Grace could see her boots and feel her eyes crawling over her. Isaiah turned and ushered Grace into a hallway that led to a side entrance.

She wondered how he knew it was there. She raised her head a little and saw a red exit sign glowing like a beacon. They were almost out.

The girl's apartment was empty, everybody snapping on latex gloves. "Toss the place," Walczak said. "See if there's anything that connects her to Sarah."

"I think we know that," Hawkins said.

"What's your problem, Hawkins?" Hawkins was about to tell him when Richter came out of the bathroom.

"The girl is here by herself. No Sarah."

"How do you know?" Walczak said.

"No extra towels, and look around. No luggage, clothes and shoes all the same size." Richter went over and opened the fridge. There were bottles of water, a six pack of Heineken, some wilted vegetables, and a jar of mayonnaise. "Nothing here for guests," he said. "Yeah, she's alone." The others were looking at him like he'd spoken in Swahili. "What?" he said. "I did this for a living." The electric kettle whistled. "Shit. She must have just left."

Walczak spoke into his collar mike. "Owens? Have you seen anybody?"

"Negative."

"Are you sure? You've seen nobody at all?"

"I saw a black guy and an old lady."

Isaiah and Grace were almost at the end of the hall when they heard the tall woman shout, "Hey, you! Stop!" They burst through the exit door and onto the side street. Isaiah pulled on Grace's sleeve. "Come on. My car is this way."

"No!" She turned in the other direction. He couldn't do anything but follow her. Ahead of them, three men with guns came around the corner. Isaiah looked back. The tall woman was coming after them, a gun by her side, and the BMW was swinging out of the alley. They were no match for three armed men, but if they wanted Grace it was unlikely they'd shoot her. Their best chance was to go right at the lone woman. If Isaiah could distract her long enough, maybe Grace could get past the BMW and escape. He grabbed her by the sleeve again and pulled hard. "Grace, wait, we have to go back!"

Grace stopped. "Get in." The GTI was parked at the curb.

"Let me drive," he said. He had skills behind the wheel. Grace ignored him and got in the driver's seat.

"Get in," she said. She started the engine. The three men were closing fast, aiming their guns with two-handed grips.

"Halt right there!" the Latino man shouted.

Most people would have freaked out and stopped, but Grace slammed the car into gear, tromped on the gas, and drove right at them. They scattered, cursing and shouting. Isaiah glanced at the rearview mirror. The BMW was catching up fast. The GTI was no match for pure speed, but the GTI was lighter, more maneuverable. They might get away if they stayed on the side streets and made a lot of turns.

"Take a right here," he said. Again, she ignored him, went straight, and turned left onto Magnolia, a big wide street. "What are you doing?" he said. The BMW made the turn and was fast closing the distance. Grace spun the wheel, made a slick downshift, the rear end sliding around. She floored it, tires screeching as she turned into an alley. "At the end, go left on Seminole," Isaiah said. She turned right. Was she deliberately defying him? "Okay, there's a parking lot up here," he said. "You can cross it and—"

"I live in this neighborhood," she snapped. "Will you please shut up?" She drove like a professional, rowing expertly through the gears, drifting, double-clutching, matching engine speed with RPMs to keep the car balanced through the turns. Two minutes later, they were free and clear. She slowed down and drove at the speed limit.

"Suggestion?" Isaiah said humbly.

"What?"

"Maybe go to my place?"

The team reassembled at Jimenez's car. "Goddammit, Owens!" Walczak exclaimed. "How did they get by you?"

She looked at her boots. "Wasn't my fault. I wasn't expecting a black guy and I thought the girl was an old lady."

"That and you're loaded," Hawkins said.

"I ain't even close to loaded," she replied, reeling a little.

"Well, the girl's on notice now," Walczak said. "We'll never find her, and if she's in touch with Sarah, we'll never find her either."

"So we go after the black guy," Owens said, like it was just as well.

"Yeah," Jimenez said. "That should be easy. There's only four or five of them in Long Beach."

"Six," Hawkins said.

Richter was distracted, smoking and scanning the surrounding area. What the fuck was he doing now? Walczak thought. Since when did this dull, lazy asshole who spent most of his time with a burrito in his mouth get so goddamn smart?

"What are you looking for?" Walczak said. "Mexican food?" Richter didn't answer and kept looking around. "What is it, Richter?" Walczak demanded.

Richter smiled and nodded. "We're not out of it yet."

CHAPTER FOUR
Enchantée

The address in the note turned out to be a small shop Dodson had driven past many times before. The sign said ROYAL CUSTOM CUTLERY. There was an impressive display of knives in the window, all different kinds. There was no dust, dead flies, or chipped paint, like in every other shop on the block. A buzzer sounded and the door clicked open. Dodson didn't know what he was expecting but it wasn't this dude.

"Mr. Dodson, how good of you to come!" the man said in a booming, James Earl Jones kind of voice. He was of mixed race; white and something else darker.

He was not young and shaped like an avocado. He had a shiny face, a merry wink in his eyes, and a jet-black toupee that sat on his head like a nesting raven. "Would you like a refreshment? I have a variety of beverages. Water, soft drinks, coffee or tea." A jolly motherfucker, Dodson thought, but it was forced. There was something behind it that wasn't jolly at all. He was dressed like someone from another decade. A brown suit with really wide lapels and wide legs, a yellow polka-dot bow tie, and two-tone shoes with little perforations on the toe box.

Over the years, Dodson had learned to never enter a confrontation

69

on the defensive. If you came in weak, you'd be playing catch-up for the rest of the conversation. "Who are you?" he demanded.

"I, sir, am Chester C. Babbitt," Chester said, ever so pleased to be asked. "A purveyor of custom cutlery since 1998." He swept his arm over the shop. "I daresay there isn't an aficionado anywhere in the world, assuming he is serious, of course, who doesn't have a Babbitt in his collection." There were glass cases full of knives, all neatly labeled. Pocketknives, lockbacks, bowies, Japanese and American tantos, kukris and ka-bars. There were knives for butchering, carving, slicing, cleaving, skinning, and killing. There was also an array of axes, scimitars, sabers, and samurai swords. Anything with a cutting blade. Dodson was no expert but they were beautifully made, the handles crafted from exotic woods, mother-of-pearl, polished bone, brass, and steel.

"May I call you Juanell?" Chester said.

"No you may not."

"Fine, fine, no problem." Chester waved a hand like he was about to sing "Que Sera, Sera."

"What's this about?" Dodson said.

"Yes, I see, get right to it. Very good, Mr. Dodson. Rest assured, I understand the value of time. I can't remember who said it and I'm paraphrasing here—yesterday's the past, tomorrow's the future, but today is a gift. That's why it's called the present." He smiled winningly but Dodson just stared at him.

"Start talking, Chester, or I'm out the door."

"As you wish, as you wish." Chester inhaled deeply, his chest expanding a couple of inches. He began pacing and nodding, his hands clenched behind him like he was summing up the prosecution's case. "I happen to have knowledge of an incident that took place some years ago. You were living in an apartment with Isaiah Quintabe and your girlfriend, Deronda Simmons. Quite a young lady, if I do say so myself. Her hindquarters are quite famous around here, almost a tourist attraction." He waited for Dodson to laugh but got nothing. Chester picked up a throwing knife off the counter. It was made from a single piece of metal, the blade shaped like a spearhead, the handle with holes in it to reduce weight. The black finish made it seem more lethal. Chester turned it round and round in his fingers like a cheer-leading baton. He went on. "It seems that the three of you, as it were, conspired to rob a drug dealer named Junior, and, at some point, the operation took a—wrong turn, shall we say? To make a long story short, you had to be rescued by Isaiah, and, in the process, he shot Ju-nior and his bodyguard Booze Lewis, severely wounding both men. Are you with me so far?"

"Keep talking," Dodson said.

"Unfortunately or fortunately, depending upon one's point of view, this leaves you and your friends in a somewhat vulnerable po-sition, if you catch my meaning."

Dodson hated being jerked around, somebody trying to make him sweat.

"Look, muthafucka," he said. "You think you scaring me? I don't scare, you feel me?" He walked up to Chester, the twirling knife between them. "You gonna come at me, come at me, or you and your bow tie can go fuck yourselves."

Chester went so still it was like he'd been paused on a DVR. The wink in his eyes had gone, sweat trickling down his temples. His smile had turned into a talon. "All right, Mr. Dodson, let us talk terms." Only now did Dodson notice that Chester's canines were sharpened into dagger points. *This muthafucka is crazy.*

Ten minutes later, Dodson came stumbling out of the shop. As the door closed, he heard the throwing knife *thunk* into the wood. Shaken, he thought about screaming, but he was too cool to scream. He walked back to his car. He'd been in trouble many times before but nothing like this. What if Cherise found out? What if *Gloria* found out? She'd ride him like the number 9 bus.

71

But how did Chester know about the robbery in the first place? Dodson hadn't said anything to anybody and Isaiah was rock-solid. Dodson made a growling sound, his head about to detonate. "I'm gonna kill that bitch."

He called and said he was coming over. "Let me check my calendar," Deronda said. "I might be at a stockholders' meeting or getting some rims put on my car." Her new place was near the East Village, a high-rise, gleaming white with frosted windows and a fountain out in front. He rang the buzzer.

"Yes?" she said through the speaker.

"The hell you talking 'bout, *yes?* It's me, goddammit."

"You know what? I think I recognize your voice. You sound like that moron who sold his half of the business just before it went global."

"Let me in, girl, 'fore I climb up on your balcony and beat you to death." Dodson rode the elevator, looking at himself in a mirror etched with wood nymphs and climbing vines. The worry and lack of sleep were weighing his whole body down. He looked like a piece of raw liver hung on a hook. Deronda's apartment was on the seventeenth floor. He knocked, waited, knocked again, waited, and just as he was about to ram his fist through the peephole, the door opened.

"*Enchantée,*" Deronda said, with a mocking grin. She jangled with gold jewelry, her pink dressing gown long and flowing. She wore strapless heels, fluffs of pink feathers on them. Tony Montana had apparently decorated the living room; everything white, gold, shiny, or fringed. A bottle of Dom was in an ice bucket set on a coffee table that looked like a dragon. She poured herself a glass and took a sip. "Ahh, life is good, ain't it?" she said. "Oh, wait, I'm sorry. Your life ain't shit, is it?" She flounced down on the sofa and crossed her legs. "Now how can I help you today? Don't be shy. Are you lookin' for a job? I happen to have an opening for a dishwasher and I believe with your experience you might be a perfect fit. If you're interested, call my niece, Belinda. She's my new assistant."

Dodson suppressed the urge to strangle her. He handed her Chester's note. "What's this?" she said, eyes wide like a child was giving her a present. "Your curriculum visa? I hope there's no criminality on it. It might disqualify you from further advancement." She read the note and spilled her champagne. "Oh my muthafuckin' God."

"Who did you tell?" Dodson said.

"Nobody!" Deronda said, shrugging with both shoulders. "Why would I?"

"You know I didn't say anything and Isaiah wouldn't either. Spill it, girl, this shit is important." Dodson put his high beams on her until she withered in the heat.

She cringed. "I might have told Nona."

"*Nona?* That bitch got a mouth big as a damn bathtub and you told *her?*"

"Keep your voice down, Janeel is asleep," Deronda said. "See, here's what happened. We was in Vegas for a bachelorette party. Lisa was gonna marry Lester DuPont, why I couldn't tell you. Why would you hook up with somebody who drives a jalopy and can't take you nowhere unless he got a coupon?" Dodson made a growling sound. "Okay, okay," Deronda said. "We was partyin', see. We went to a couple of clubs, then we came back to the suite, right? So me and Nona was in the Jacuzzi—we was talkin', tippin' Hennessy, doin' our thing, and then Marlene came in with this fat-ass joint and we—"

"I swear to God, I'm gonna strangle you with my bare hands."

"Okay, okay. So me and Nona got to reminiscing, talkin' 'bout all the crazy shit we done, and the story about the robbery just kind of slipped out. I told her how we planned it and how the shit went wrong and how Isaiah shot Junior and Booze Lewis." Her voice got small. "I told her everything."

Dodson walked away three steps and came back. "I can't believe you did that. If I wasn't so terrified I'd throw you out the window."

"Who gave you the note?" she asked.

"Somebody named Chester Babbitt. A crazy muthafucka, owns a knife store over on Atlantic."

"How does he know Nona?" she said.

"Who gives a shit? He's gonna tell Junior if we don't do what he says."

"Junior's back?"

"Uh-huh, Booze is still with him and so is Michael Stokely. You do a search on *killa thugs with no conscience* and Stokely's name will come up two million times."

"You don't think I know that?" Deronda looked nauseated, a hand on her stomach. "So how much cash does this knife man want?"

"He don't want cash," Dodson said. "He knows I can't come up with anything and he knows the bank owns them food trucks."

"What about Isaiah?" Deronda said.

"What about him? He's scraping by like always. Louella Barnes is paying him with a reindeer sweater."

"I heard," Deronda said. "So what then?"

Dodson picked the Dom up by the neck and finished the bottle. He wiped his mouth with his shoulder and looked at her. "He wants us to rob Junior."

Deronda gulped air. "Rob Junior? You mean *again?*"

"That's what he wants."

"You mean if we don't rob Junior he'll *tell* Junior?"

"Uh-huh."

After the car chase, Isaiah took Grace to the house. She stood in the doorway a moment, looking around like it might be a trap.

Isaiah was self-conscious as she surveyed the minimal furnishings, polished cement floor, and tall bookshelves loaded with LPs. She smiled. *She likes the place!* he thought. No, it was the dog. How many times would he fall for that? Ruffin came bounding out of the hallway, deliriously happy to see his old pal.

"Hello, beautiful. How are you, huh? Yeah, I'm glad to see you too."

Isaiah went into the kitchen, prepared Ruffin's dinner, and came out with the bowl. Usually, the dog would come as soon as he heard the can opener, but he stayed with Grace, panting and mewling and trying to lick her face. She took the bowl from Isaiah and set it down in front of the dog. "Here you go, boy. Good, huh?" she said, happy to see him eat.

"Okay," Isaiah said, "let's talk."

She sat on the edge of the couch. He stayed standing, his hands in his front pockets. "Who were those people?" he said.

"The driver was Stan Walczak. I didn't get a good look at the others but I can guess who they are. They were with my dad at Abu Ghraib."

"Abu Ghraib," Isaiah said evenly.

"Dad was an MP. He didn't do any of the abuse. He was just there." She got out her phone, did some scrolling, and handed it to him. "He sent me pictures." There were group shots of the people who had chased them and other soldiers as well; eating MREs, lying around in their narrow cots, posing with cells behind them or standing in long concrete corridors. They all wore fatigues, but Walczak's looked new.

"I don't remember the other people's names," she said.

"What about that guy in the porkpie hat?"

"I've never seen him before."

Isaiah took her into the second bedroom he used as an office. He'd never realized how barren the room looked. A desk, a chair, a folding table with nothing on it, two file cabinets, and stacks of storage boxes. It looked like he was either moving in or moving out. There were only two personal items. A photo of Marcus and Isaiah mugging for the camera, and another of Mrs. Marquez holding up a chicken by its feet. Its name was Alejandro, named after her pendejo ex-husband. Isaiah got another chair and set it as close to his as possible without putting them on top of each other. They sat down at his laptop and did a search on Walczak.

Stanislaw Walczak was founder and CEO of Walczak Security Services International. The website said:

> WSSI provides consulting, informational and decision making services in support of our national security, intelligence and military operations. WSSI retains 17,000 employees all over the world and offers exciting career opportunities for former military personnel and security professionals. Our principal service areas are:
> - Command and Control
> - Intelligence Systems and Operations
> - Investigatory Services
> - Communications
> - Cyber Security
> - Readiness
> - Surveillance and Reconnaissance

"Jesus," Grace said. Isaiah tried not to echo the sentiment. She shook her head. "I don't understand. Why would Walczak be after me?"

"He's not, he's after your mom," Isaiah said. "He thought she was staying with you." Anticipating her question, he went on. "She has something Walczak wants and if he's personally involved, it's something important."

"Like what? Mom was an artist."

"Whatever it is, it probably came from your father." Either that, he thought, or your mother killed somebody close to Walczak. Grace was still gaping at the web page. It was as if she couldn't wrap her head around the enormity of her pursuer.

"This is too much. I can't let you do this."

"You're not letting me do anything," Isaiah said. "I took the case, I'll finish the case." The bravado felt good but he was almost as intimidated as she was. This was way deeper than he'd ever imagined. Walczak had huge resources at his command. Trained operatives, computer analysts, drones, satellite photography, military and law enforcement personnel, 17,000 employees, and an arsenal of every weapon imaginable. Walczak could take over France. Finding Sarah would have to wait, Isaiah decided. Keeping Grace safe was the first priority.

They took the dog for a walk and he gave her the leash. Ruffin was on his best behavior. "He's a great dog," she said.

"He's a weird dog," Isaiah said.

"Why?"

"He's a wimp, especially for a pit bull." Isaiah remembered the murderous struggle he'd had with Manzo, the gang leader threatening him with a gun, Ruffin watching distractedly, like they were two palm trees blowing in the breeze. "Once he walked away from a couple of pigeons squabbling. If Mrs. Marquez's Pomeranian barks at him he'll go back in the house. If somebody rings the doorbell, he'll bark, but only if it's somebody he knows."

"Every dog is different," she said as if he was attacking the dog's ethnicity. "Just like people."

"You ever have a dog?"

"A few. Linus was my favorite. He was a Cavalier King Charles with three legs."

"What happened to him?"

"Cancer," she said. "I think they catch it from humans."

At least they were talking about something other than the case, he thought, but she was only being polite, throwing him a conversational bone, not really into it. It was discouraging but he'd volunteered for this and had no right to expect more.

They arrived at McClarin Park. Old-fashioned streetlamps lined the main pathway and lit nothing but themselves, moths fluttering in the moons of amber. Around them and beyond were shadows within shadows, leafless trees like veins against a blue-black sky. A couple of old men, Mo Hopkins and Dancy Fitzgerald, were camped out next to the cement-block restrooms, arguing over a can of Colt 45.

"Don't worry," Isaiah said, sensing her hesitancy. "We come here all the time. You can let Ruff off the leash." She did and the dog went meandering, his nose skimming the grass like a metal detector as he disappeared into the dark. Isaiah felt safe almost anywhere in East Long Beach because he had ex-clients everywhere. If something was to happen here, Mo and Dancy would come running with the sharpened screwdrivers they kept under their layers of rank clothing.

Two people were coming up the path. Seb Habimana was a small, precise man who wore glen plaid suits and walked with a cane, the same cane Isaiah had snapped over his knee. It had since been mended, a brass coupling holding the two pieces together. Seb had lost a leg when he was a boy back in Rwanda. An enemy of his tribe had hacked it off with a machete. Years later, Seb returned the favor. The head of his cane was fashioned from his attacker's tibia.

"Is that who I think it is?" Seb said, an acrid smile disguised as warmth.

Isaiah felt the hate uncoiling in his gut. He clenched his fists. There was suddenly too much blood in his neck and face, his heart was slamming against his rib cage like a man trapped in a burning room. Grace felt it and looked at him.

"You okay?" she said.

Seb's flunky was with him. Laquez was bubble-eyed and brainless, his face scrunched up like he was thinking about philosophy or writing an op-ed. He was a vicious, cowardly kid. He'd stab you to death with an ice pick but only if you were sleeping. Isaiah had sent his brother to Folsom.

"Isaiah!" Seb said. "How are you? You're looking well." Isaiah didn't answer. Seb looked at Grace. "Where are your manners, Isaiah? Aren't you going to introduce us?"

"No, I'm not," Isaiah said.

"How you doin', baby?" Laquez said, leering at her. "What're you doin' with this punk-ass muthafucka?"

"Hi," she said faintly.

"What's up with the white girl, Isaiah?" Laquez went on. "Sistas ain't good enough for you? You know what they say, if it's white it ain't right."

Isaiah's gaze never left Seb's. "You're too stupid to live, Laquez, and if you provoke me I'll put you in jail just like your brother." Laquez buttoned up, his eyes retreating into their sockets.

"There are matters still to be resolved, Isaiah," Seb said. "I have not forgotten."

"I haven't either. Now get out of my way."

The air went out of the world. Laquez looked all too willing to step aside but Seb stood his ground, adjusting the grip on the cane, getting ready to slash. *Do it,* Isaiah thought. *Do it so I can stick it through your heart.* Ruffin appeared out of the dark. He sensed the tension and stopped, but it was enough to distract Seb. Laquez stepped behind him.

"Hey, man," he said, "why don't you keep that damn dog on a leash?" Isaiah shouldered past Seb, Grace trailing him out of the park.

They didn't talk for a while. Grace said, "Do you mind my asking what that was about?"

"Yeah, I do." They kept walking and as they neared the house, he said, "His name is Seb Habimana. He killed my brother." Grace stopped and put her hand on his arm.

"Oh, Isaiah. I'm so sorry."

He felt the anger rise in his throat, the hatred like bile. "And I'm going to kill him." He thought he'd learned his lesson about hate, but it didn't stick. He was bitter and vengeful and couldn't control it.

When they got back to the house, Grace said she had to go out again. "Just something," she said with a shrug. It was one in the morning. She'd nearly been kidnapped by a guy with a private army and now she was going out? "Don't go back to your place, okay?" he said. "They might be watching it."

"Right."

He left her some bedding and went into the bedroom. He didn't undress, left the light off, and lay down on the bed. He'd sent Dodson a text, saying he'd taken on a new case and they needed to talk. Might as well face the music. He thought about what Laquez had said about sistas not being good enough for him. A lot of people made a fuss about a black man dating a white girl. The implication was that you thought black women were an easier score or were too common, the equivalent of an economy car. White women were rarer and therefore harder to catch, and capturing one spoke to your manliness and was somehow poetic justice; a black man doing something he'd have been lynched for a few decades ago. Isaiah wondered how Laquez would have reacted if Grace was Chinese or Puerto Rican or Pakistani. Would their status as girlfriends diminish with the darkness of their skin? To Isaiah, race had nothing to do with it. He'd have been drawn to Grace if she was Martian or Mongolian. He thought about the lengths people went to find someone. Dating websites, speed dating, hanging out in bars, letting their friends set them up, and it was still more likely than not

80

you'd end up alone. Restrict your choices to your own kind and your chances for happiness went down exponentially.

It was almost dawn when Grace returned. Isaiah peeked through the blinds and watched her get out of the car. She had a duffel bag and a toiletry kit. She'd gone back to her place. So much for telling her what to do. She'd changed her clothes. She had on sagging, dirty jeans with holes in the knees and a T-shirt with oil stains on it. Her hands were dirty. After going to her place, she'd gone somewhere else, but at least it wasn't on a date.

He heard her come in, greet the dog, and take a shower. There was some rustling around in the living room and then it was quiet. A brooding light came through the blinds, caging Isaiah in bars of shadow. Grace was forty feet away, and for some reason that made him feel lonelier. Ruffin had stayed with her. There was something special between those two and he wished he could be part of it.

CHAPTER FIVE
She Had All the Power

Richter had come up with the obvious, gathering CCTV footage from businesses around the Edgemont, his boss pissed because he hadn't thought of it first. He had WSSI's document specialists generate five fake FBI IDs, and there were no problems getting the footage. People responded to the FBI. The team was gathered in Walczak's study again, working at their laptops, going through miles of tape. It was laborious and time-consuming. The guy who helped Grace could have come from any direction, and it turned out there were more than four or five black people in Long Beach. What the team remembered wasn't any better than civilian witnesses. It was embarrassing. *Is this the guy? No, he was fatter. No he wasn't. Bald? Get out of here. He had a mustache. No, that was a shadow. I'm telling you, he was an older guy. An older guy can move like that?*

"Listen. You're all wrong, okay?" Walczak said decisively. "I've identified a lot of people from video. Terrorists, in fact. This guy was thirties, five-ten, soul patch, tattoo on his forearm, sneakers and a light green shirt. I'm sure of it."

Richter countered. "Twenties, six feet, skinny, no facial hair, jeans, light blue shirt, Timberlands, and it was too dark to see any tats."

Walczak sneered. "We'll see about that, Sherlock."

It was evening when they found what they were looking for. The black guy was as Richter described down to the Timberlands. "Well, I'll be," he said, smiling at his boss. "I guess I just got lucky."

Walczak pretended not to notice that everyone was gleeful. He gestured dismissively. "Okay, okay. Can we get back to work?"

The black guy was in footage taken from a liquor store and a pawnshop a block and a half away. He was getting out of his car. It took three different snippets and a lot of enhancement to get the license plate number. His name was Isaiah Quintabe, an address a few miles from the Edgemont. He was some sort of neighborhood P.I. The articles said his nickname was IQ.

"I know him," Richter said. He remembered the case because Isaiah had embarrassed him. The Coffee Cup had been robbed. The camera wasn't working and the witnesses didn't remember anything except the guy was black and had a gun. Richter told the lady who owned the shop it was highly unlikely the perp would ever be caught. Besides, he thought privately, it was too penny-ante to bother with. A day later, Isaiah came into the station accompanied by two winos Richter hadn't interviewed. They identified the robber as one Spencer Witherspoon, a small-time criminal with a long record. The two winos swore by it and picked Witherspoon out of a lineup.

"You shoulda asked us," one of the winos said. "We was sittin' right across the street." Since then, Richter had heard stories about Isaiah's exploits and his reputation as some sort of wizard at catching the bad guys. He had much respect around the neighborhood.

"How do you know him?" Walczak said.

"From a case. He's a smart guy. Nobody to mess with."

"When was this?"

"Years ago."

"Then how does that help us now?" Walczak said, throwing up his hands. "Well? Do you have anything else irrelevant to say?"

"The guy gets paid with cakes and pies," Owens said. "I'd say he's nobody to worry about, right, Jimenez?"

Jimenez was surprised by the question. "What?"

"Okay. Tonight then," Walczak said, adding, "If that's okay with you, Richter."

Do you have anything else irrelevant to say? If that's okay with you, Richter. If they were on the street, Richter would have beat him to death with one of those yellow sneakers. He'd decided what he was going to do. Break the case himself. Find Sarah on his own and rub it in Walczak's face until it turned to shit. How to get started? He wondered. Isaiah was still the only point of contact but Richter needed to know more about him, things you couldn't Google. Who did Richter know that Isaiah knew? Spencer Witherspoon.

Lots of people thought Richter was still a cop and were happy to make a few dollars for giving up Spoon, the useless prick.

"Spoon, open up," Richter said, pounding on the door. "Police. Don't make me kick it down." The door swung open and there was Spoon; his face was bruised, one eye closed, his jaw lopsided, a giant bump behind his ear, his arm in a sling made out of a ripped towel, and he was leaning on a crutch.

"Where was the police when I needed 'em?" Spoon said.

"Finally got what you deserve, huh?" Richter barged in, looked around at the mess, and shook his head disgustedly.

"The maid took the day off," Spoon said. "How can I help you, Officer?"

"Isaiah Quintabe. What do you know about him?"

"Why should I tell you? You the one took me to jail." Richter kicked the crutch away and Spoon fell to the floor, howling. "Damn, man, the fuck's wrong with you?"

"Start talking."

"Help me up," Spoon said. Richter kicked his injured leg.

Spoon howled some more. "Okay, okay, man! What do you wanna know?"

"Everything. Details."

"Details?" Spoon said. He looked like thinking was new to him. "Well, I know Isaiah's at the Coffee Cup almost every day. I shoulda thought of that before I tried to rob the place."

"What time?"

"In the morning, when people usually have they coffee—no, wait. I seen him there at night too. Verna makes soup, sausage rolls, chicken pot pies. Too bad I can't go in there no more." Spoon told him about Isaiah's friends, Juanell Dodson and a girl named Deronda something. "If you don't know her you'd recognize her. Girl got a booty like she's towin' a double-wide." Spoon was useless after that. Even a few extra kicks didn't help his memory.

Richter went to the Coffee Cup. He talked to the lady who ran the place.

"Why do you want to know about Isaiah?" the lady said.

Richter told them he was a former client and he owed Isaiah a lot of money. He said he'd lost Isaiah's address and phone number but knew he hung out here sometimes.

"The guy really helped me, you know? I really want to pay him back."

"He comes in when he comes in," she said. "I don't keep track."

"Nothing regular, huh?"

"Sometimes on Wednesdays. Comes in after his workout, all sweaty and such, but that's hit and miss too."

"Please don't tell him about this," Richter said. "If I ever catch up with him, I want it to be a surprise."

Discouraged, he went outside. He looked and looked again. Right across the street, huddled in a vestibule, were the same two winos who had identified Spoon way back when. He walked over there smiling, trying to look friendly, a hard thing for him to do.

They shot him that *What are you doing here white man* look. Their names were Mo and Dancy. They slept in the park but came over here in the daytime because Verna gave them leftovers and a little money if they cleaned up the parking lot.

"Do you know Isaiah Quintabe?" Richter said.

"What you want to know 'bout him for?" Mo said, sticking out his chin.

He told them the same story he told the old lady. Then he gave them twenty dollars each to sleep in the vestibule instead of the park and to call him if Isaiah showed up. If they did he'd give them twenty more. "Remember. It's a secret."

At a little past midnight, Jimenez, Hawkins, Owens, and Walczak were in a van parked down the block from Isaiah's house. Walczak wondered how people could live here, stuck in a stucco cracker box with an ugly chain-link fence and no landscaping. The group was dressed exactly like a SWAT team: helmets, face shields, body shields, assault rifles, and Kevlar vests with POLICE stenciled on them.

"It's hot in here," Owens said. "What are we waitin' for?"

"Richter," Walczak said. "He's got the thermal imaging camera."

"Did you know he was like that?" Jimenez said.

"Like what?"

"Smarter than you." The others looked away so they wouldn't laugh.

The plan was to go through the front door with a Remington 870 door-breaching shotgun, yelling *Police, get on the floor!* Which should forestall any neighbors from calling 911. The targets would be Tasered immediately. If they ran out the back, Richter was waiting for them with a .44-caliber handgun and a .32 in the back of his pants. The targets would be subdued and bum-rushed into the van. In and out. Should take two minutes at the most.

* * *

Hawkins knew everyone assumed he'd be the first man in. He was always the first man in. Because of his size people thought he was bulletproof. If he was an actor, he'd be cast like that wobble-eyed bald-headed freak in *Friday*. He was scary just walking around. He was an all-state linebacker and defensive captain at UC San Diego. His degree was in athletic therapy and kinesiology and he worked as a physical therapist in Lynwood for a while. He hated it and got fired because he intimidated the patients and there were complaints that his massages were more like getting crushed by an avalanche.

He didn't know what to do with himself so he joined the army, and being an MP seemed like a natural fit. Not a drunk soldier on earth would fuck with him and who *wouldn't* obey his orders? He was smarter than the job but you can't have everything. He did some bad shit at Abu Ghraib but he didn't think about it. He could do that, keep things compartmentalized. It was like his mother's house and the room where his father had died. It was always locked and never talked about. The only thing he couldn't contain was his anger. He was angry all the time. Road rage was a hobby. Just the other day a guy cut him off and he tailgated the asshole for fifteen minutes, leaning on his horn the whole time. The only reason the guy got away was because he turned into the police station parking lot. Hawkins got into bar fights, ran over crows and stray cats, and scared his neighbors so badly they built a fence out of cinder blocks that was nine feet tall. But mostly he was angry at Walczak. This motherfucker not only gets everybody in deep shit, he comes out of it smelling like a rose in a garden of money. Hawkins worked as a campus security officer at UC San Diego, where people chanted his name every time he made a sack.

* * *

"I'm not going in first," Hawkins said. "You hear me, Walczak?"

"Yes, I hear you," Walczak said, "and nobody said you would. I'll go in first, okay?"

"That's big of you. Ain't nobody in there with AKs and IEDs."

"Then what do you want me to do?"

"I want you to go fuck yourself."

Out of the blue, Owens said, "How's everything going, Jimenez?"

He looked at her. "How's everything going? What kind of question is that?"

She shrugged. "Just askin'."

Richter came through the radio. "There's two people in the kitchen. One sitting, one standing."

"Well, let's go get this shit over with," Hawkins said. He looked at Walczak. "Lead the way."

"Why didn't you tell me before you took the case?" Dodson said indignantly.

"Because I don't have to ask your permission," Isaiah replied. Dodson was angry. *Too* angry, he thought, even for the situation.

"You ain't asking permission," Dodson said. "It's courtesy, not to mention a sign of respect. This is the same shit you did with Carter. Why the hell did you bring me on if all you was gonna do is ignore me? This is bullshit, Isaiah!"

"What's the matter with you? Did you have a fight with Cherise?"

"Whether I did or I didn't is none of your concern. How much we getting paid?" Isaiah hesitated. "Oh no," Dodson said. "Don't tell me, let me guess. A free haircut? A box of cornflakes? Some reindeer pants to go with that sweater?" Isaiah gestured at Grace's painting propped up on the counter next to the toaster. He hadn't decided where to put it yet. "What?" Dodson said. "The client's gonna buy you a new toaster?"

"The painting."

"*That?*"

"I like it."

"You *like* it? That ain't no reason." Dodson walked away three steps and came back to where he started. "Who's the client?"

"Her name's Grace," Isaiah said. "She's an artist."

"Nigga, please. Big Earl is a house painter. He ain't got but one eye, and he could do better than that. We talked about this, Isaiah. We supposed to be making money."

"And you're supposed to bring in big clients. What happened to that?"

"I told you, I'm working on it."

"Well, you better work harder because I'm taking the case," Isaiah said. His voice had a little too much *fuck you* in it. Dodson nodded, as if to say, *Is that how it is?*

"That's some low shit right there. That's wrong and you know it."

Isaiah thought about Marcus and how he would have handled this. He made people feel important, that their opinions mattered. It was one of the reasons everybody loved him and why he never seemed to be lonely. Isaiah couldn't get himself to apologize. Why should he feel sorry for doing what he'd always done?

"You got a thing for her, don't you?" Dodson said.

"A thing for—no, I don't," Isaiah said lamely. "She's just a client."

"Uh-huh, and you let her pay you with a painting? Who do you think you talking to? I know the fever when I see it."

"I don't have any fever," Isaiah mumbled.

"That's what you said about Sarita and nearly got us killed." Dodson was almost shouting. Isaiah looked at him directly.

"Look, I took the case, okay? I can't go back on my word."

"You gave your word to me too," Dodson replied. Isaiah knew he should apologize but he'd waited too long. "I'm out," Dodson said, and he walked out of the room.

"Here we go," Walczak said. He slid open the door of the van and slammed it shut again. "Abort! Abort!"

"What? Why?" Richter said from the radio.

"It's not Grace." A second black guy had come out of the house. He got in his car and drove away.

"Who's that?" Owens said.

"Grace must have taken off," Walczak said.

Richter said, "Or maybe Isaiah knew we'd find him and hid her someplace."

"He couldn't be that good."

"Why?" Jimenez said. "Because then he'd be smarter than you too?"

"Let's get the fuck outta here," Hawkins said.

Grace's first thought: this was a bad decision. In the daytime, the wrecking yard was familiar and felt as safe as a playground, but at night it took on a whole different character. Spotlights lit up the yard like an alien landing zone. Around the edges, stacks of crushed cars watched through squashed eyes, the crane a crippled dinosaur looming against the yellow moon. Isaiah appeared out of a shadow.

"Park around back," he said. "Behind the warehouse." He looked wide awake and eager. She thought about leaving but remembered Walczak's bleached teeth in her rearview mirror, bared and hateful. When she got out of the car, Ruffin came to greet her and then Isaiah led her into the warehouse. There was a loft she'd never noticed before. Grace followed him up the old wooden stairs, gray with age, splinters on the banister. *I'm going to sleep up there? I'd rather sleep in my car.* A low-wattage bulb hung on a wire, illuminating a cleared space amid the cobwebs, car parts, and miscellaneous junk. It was swept, mopped, and dusted clean. Cleaner than her apartment, she thought. There was a new futon, and bedding still in its packages. A lamp, a boom box, and a small TV were on a folding table; a space heater and a mini-fridge on the floor.

"I hope it's okay," Isaiah said.

"It's fine," she said, a little stunned. "Thank you." She wanted to say, *You did all this for me?* She didn't know what to do and stood there feeling stupid. He seemed to sense she was self-conscious, probably how he felt when he was looking at her paintings.

"There's a bathroom next to TK's office," he said. "It's got a shower and everything. Try not to go out. If you need anything, ask TK or call me."

"Okay."

"Ruffin's going to stay with you. He's good company."

"Thanks. That's really nice of you."

"I've got to talk to TK. You want to talk about the case later?"

"No, not tonight," she said. "I've got something to do." He looked like he was going to say something but didn't. He went down the stairs, Grace thinking he's *too* nice, he couldn't be for real. She took a closer look around. There were CDs for the boom box. A box of tissues. A can of pepper spray. There was also water, energy bars, and fresh fruit in the mini-fridge. There was even a wastebasket, the Rubbermaid sticker still on it. "I don't believe it," she said. Obviously, he liked her, and she had to admit, he was attractive—and cool, but not in a street way or a TV way. He had the kind of cool she liked. Quiet, thoughtful, sharp as a box cutter, no flash but you knew he was in the room, and thankfully, not into pop culture. Plain car, no gold chain, no studs in his ears. The CDs were all jazz and classical.

A stack of clean towels and two shopping bags were on

the futon. In one there was a new pair of jeans, a package of T-shirts, a denim jacket, socks, even underwear. Everything in *her exact size*. It moved her and she nearly started to cry. "Jesus," she said. The other bag held a toothbrush, toothpaste, a hairbrush, shampoo, conditioner, a shower cap, and a bar of soap—wait, it wasn't any old soap. It was the soap she used all the time, Dove. She scratched her pocket watch tattoo, something she did when she was confused or anxious. How could he possibly know that? When he was at her place he didn't go into the bathroom. Was it a coincidence? Lots of people used Dove. Did he recognize the smell? No, that was too much.

She realized he was taking care of her and she tried to think of the last time that happened. Maybe never. She'd had a few boyfriends who wowed her at first but eventually took off their costumes and revealed their fucked-up selves. There was the overcontrolling musician who'd lost a career-ending finger. She'd always thought that was why he was so good in bed, like he was making up for the lost appendage with a working one. Then there was the writer, brilliant and beautiful. He tried to commit suicide a week after they met but she hooked up with him anyway. He was like a pinball; lights flashing and bells clanging as he ricocheted from mood to mood. He wouldn't take his meds until he finished his book, which he never worked on because he was high all the time. When he'd drained her of every last giving, loving, maternal instinct she'd ever had, she left. There were others but they were no better.

"You get the love you think you deserve," Cherokee told her over and over again, but the insight was only a cluster of words, another homily, useless in everyday life. It reminded Grace of the escargot tongs her mother kept in a drawer with the butter knives and the soup spoons. She had to stay wary of Isaiah. He'd have a litany of issues like everybody else and she had a bunch of her own. No, she'd keep him at a distance. The last thing she needed was another unpredictable man in her life. She wasn't afraid of him, not in the least. She was afraid of herself.

Later, she went downstairs. TK and Isaiah were sitting at the rickety card table, talking and doing nothing. *He's waiting for me,* she thought.

"We're going to order some Thai food," he said. "Want to eat before you go out?"

"No thanks. Another time." She hoped he wouldn't ask where she was going, and thankfully he didn't. She drove away and saw him in the rearview mirror, frowning with curiosity. And something else too. What was it? She was trying to decide but he was gone now and she wished she'd driven slower and gotten a better look.

Sarah sat in the car and watched for Grace every day. She had her schedule down and was almost always treated with a look, however brief. Once, she'd nearly been caught, but fortunately, she'd been shielded by the rain. She'd named her daughter Grace for two reasons. Because it meant kindness and love and because she was a fan of Grace Hartigan, an abstract expressionist who hung out with Jackson Pollock and Elaine de Kooning. Sarah had become a fan of Hartigan when she saw one of her paintings titled *Grand Street Brides.* It depicted a group of mannequins dressed up in wedding gowns, which was pretty much how she felt about her marriage.

Tonight, she was at the Eastside Diner; their specialties, shitty coffee and greasy things on buns. If you sat in the corner booth and looked between the telephone pole and the gray car parked at the curb, you had an unobstructed view of the Edgemont. Sometimes, Sarah never saw her daughter at all, but even a brief glimpse created enough fantasies to last her until the next time. A Whole Foods shopping bag set off an entire lifestyle. *She eats healthy, of course she does. Nothing but fresh and organic and no gluten, not for my girl. She steams everything, snacks on raw vegetables. Look at her, how slender she is! She takes yoga or Pilates, maybe both. And she runs. In the morning, before I get here. No drugs, no alcohol, not like her mother. Oh, I WISH I could see her paintings!*

Arthur chided her. "Instead of making things up, why don't you just go talk to her?"

"I can't."

"Why?" Arthur said.

"Because she has every reason to hate me." Sarah looked at him, this dear sweet man with a frizz of graying hair, a white beard, and wise, gentle eyes. He was patient and she needed a lot of that. He sighed, shook his head, and went back to reading his book about the NSA.

Tonight was interesting, Sarah thought. Grace was accompanied by a young man and they went into the building together. Probably not her boyfriend. They were too stiff, too tentative. First date? Grace could do worse. The guy had a nice vibe and he didn't seem like another artist. Not flaky or smug. She wondered what they were doing up there. Maybe she was cooking for him. Yeah, something like couscous or Indian food, something hip and exotic. They were probably lounging on big pillows and talking about an art review in the *New York Times* or how he was crowdsourcing his independent movie.

Arthur signaled for more tea. "It's like waiting to see Bigfoot."

"Just a little longer?" She wanted to see if the young man was spending the night. "It's too early," she said.

"What?" Arthur said.

"It's too early in the relationship for sex."

"That's what I think too."

"There he is," Sarah said. The young man came out of the building, turned the corner, and disappeared. She was glad. *My girl's no pushover,* she thought. "I guess we can go."

"Hallelujah," Arthur said. They were waiting for the waiter to bring the check when the young man came jogging back, patting his pockets like he'd forgotten something, and ran into the building. There was some movement inside the gray car, parked not twenty feet away. Three men and a woman got out. Sarah immediately recognized them as military; the aggressive attitude, the implacable eyes, the calculated movements. They stood there talking conspiratorially, headlights from a passing car revealing their faces. Sarah was horrified. *She knew them.* She immediately turned away from the window, swallowed her heart, and hoped against hope they hadn't seen her. "Oh my God," she whispered.

"Sarah?" Arthur said.

She heard the group walk off and turned to look. They were making straight for the Edgemont. "What's wrong?" Arthur said. "Who are those people?"

Sarah barely heard him. She wanted to call Grace but didn't have her number. If she went out there they'd nab her. *Call the police!* No, she couldn't do that either. "Oh my God!"

"Sarah, tell me, what's going on?" Arthur demanded.

"Those are Walczak's people. They're after Grace!"

Suddenly, the three men who'd gone in came out with guns at their sides. They ran around the corner, disappearing into the dark side street. Moments later, Grace's little white car came ripping out of there. "Grace!" Sarah shouted. A big silver car appeared, its engine roaring as it sped after her—and there he was. *Walczak.* "Oh no, oh no!" Sarah said. "I'm so stupid, I'm such an idiot!" She was crying now, everyone in the place looking at her. Arthur rose and lifted her to her feet.

"We've got to get out of here."

Sarah was furious when they got back to the motel. Walczak was trying to get to her through Grace, her precious daughter. Had she gotten away? Of course she had. Chuck had taught her to drive like a maniac when she was in middle school and the young man was with her too. No, her daughter was fine, she was sure of it. Walczak, that vicious bastard. He had to be told, *Hands off Grace*. Arthur had warned her not to contact Walczak but she couldn't resist. She hated that bastard.

For the last ten years, she'd been a fugitive. It was harrowing, exhausting, and soul depleting. She'd almost turned herself in to the authorities a thousand times but the thought of prison was too terrifying. And then there was Grace. She couldn't let her down. So she scurried from one bleak town to another, working as a waitress or a bartender, living on tips and staying in depressing motels, never hanging around long enough to make friends. Because of the warrant, she was deathly afraid of being pulled over by a cop. She had to look like an average American nobody. She bought her clothes from the Goodwill, her shoes on sale at drugstores. She gave herself haircuts with a cuticle scissors. She drank too much and watched a lot of TV.

She thought this would be her life forever until one night she saw a story on the news about high-quality fake IDs from China. You could buy them online for two hundred bucks. Same card material, thickness, bar code, photo, font, even the hologram was perfect. They made them for twenty different states. She used her meager savings and bought the Florida license—a state where she'd never been. If a cop in any of the other forty-nine states scanned the license he'd come up with nothing. She relaxed a little. She decided to go where she'd always wanted to go, stay awhile, maybe make a friend or two. She got a job as a cocktail waitress, rented a studio apartment, and put a vase of marigolds on the tiny breakfast table.

One afternoon, she wanted something to read and wandered into the local bookstore and there behind the counter was a teddy bear of a man. When she said she didn't know what she was looking for, he asked her questions that led to her love of art and he showed her books by artists she loved and ones she'd never heard of, and he showed her biographies and autobiographies and books about expressionism, impressionism, romanticism, postmodernism, pop art, cubism, and futurism—all with the unassuming ease of someone talking about their garden or a pleasant day at the beach. He said he was yakking too much and that he did that sometimes and he offered to make up for it with a cup of tea. She accepted and that was the start of it. She had come to believe kindness was the most important quality a person could have, the paucity of it in her life making it all the more cherished. Arthur was not only kind, he was understanding and wise and gentle and she fell in love with him and told him everything and he said you will never ever be whole again until you see Grace and she knew he was right. So they made the long drive to California in his aging brown Volvo, listening to his awful collection of seventies hits, her guilt growing with every mile. Why hadn't she done this sooner? She was a wimp, that was why. Afraid of the warrant, afraid of Walczak, always afraid afraid afraid.

They were staying at the Holiday Inn in Phoenix and she was swimming for the first time in ten years, enjoying the cool pleasure of gliding through the water. She thought about the other pleasures she'd missed. Live music and drinks at the Old Corral, getting her hair washed, creating something beautiful with her hands, driving to Reno with Stephanie, eating horrible Cheetos and making fun of their husbands. And loving her daughter. The thought of her made Sarah cry. She was lifting herself out of the pool when the anger she had suppressed for so long came blasting out of her like an F-15 at takeoff. *Walczak.* Goddamn fucking Walczak. She hated reading about his success, his wealth, and she hated him for other reasons as well. When she got back to the room she told Arthur, "I want a million dollars."

"Me too," Arthur said. "What are we talking about?"

"I want Walczak to pay me a million dollars or I'll release the pictures." She didn't want to be greedy, but if she was going to be a fugitive for the rest of her life, she could at least be comfortable.

"That's nuts, Sarah. Do you know who he is? What he does?"

"Of course I do. Don't patronize me, Arthur."

"I'm not. I'm just saying it's impossible. Besides, we don't need a million dollars."

Her eyes spilled furious tears. "He ruined my life, Arthur! I spent *ten years* being homeless and lonely and afraid." She clenched her fists and shook them at him. "It's not about the money, don't you see? A million, ten million, I don't care!" She went to the window, stared at nothing, a malicious smile lifting her face. "He will *hate* this. He will *hate* being bested by a woman and *hate* that I've got something on him, that *he's* the victim now—and most of all?" Her smile broadened and she put her palms on the glass. "He's not in control." She laughed. "Oh, I *wish* I could see him! I'd give anything to watch the smugness wiped right off his stupid face and watch him go to pieces over his gorgeous wife and his perfect son! That would be the best thing *ever,* don't you think?" She went quiet, the merriment dissipating into darkness. "He took everything from me, Arthur...everything." She felt hollow, her voice resounding in the empty space. "He reduced me to nothing. Can you imagine what that feels like?" She looked sharply at Arthur, her eyes so searing it startled him. She spit out the words, *"And I'm going to pay that bastard back!"*

* * *

Arthur was an activist's activist. He protested against wars, police brutality, racism, and corporate greed. He'd demonstrated for civil rights, gay rights, the environment, and raising the minimum wage. One afternoon, he was making a speech to a crowd gathered at the border. They were protesting a new section of the wall that was under construction. He got into a shoving match with police. He was arrested on federal property so it was a federal crime and he got a thirty-day sentence. Arthur mistrusted authority to the point of paranoia. He'd read widely on police tactics, intelligence-gathering, espionage, data mining, surveillance, and countersurveillance.

The first thing he did was make more copies of the Abu Ghraib photos and put them in Dropbox, Mozy, and iCloud, and on an external hard drive he kept at the store. Next was the demand note.

"If we want to send him an anonymous email," Sarah said, "why don't we just go to Kinko's? Why are you looking at me like that?"

Arthur bought a laptop that would only be used for contact with Walczak and turned it on at public hotspots. He installed something called HTTPS and another thing called Tor. He signed up for an anonymous email account and did some other computer stuff, none of which she understood. After a lot of testing and trial runs, they finally sent Walczak a message demanding a million dollars in cash, more instructions to follow.

"This is going to be dangerous, Sarah," Arthur said. "Really dangerous. You can still back out, you know."

"No. I want that bastard to twist in the wind."

She remembered Walczak chasing Grace at the Edgemont. That awful man had brought her innocent daughter into his schemes of death. He had to be warned. One night, while Arthur was sleeping, she took the special laptop across the street to a café where they had a hotspot. She sent Walczak an email.

If you go anywhere near Grace again I'll release the pictures IMMEDIATELY and you will all GO TO JAIL!

Satisfied, she returned to the room, put the laptop away, and lay down next to Arthur. She was scared but excited. Life had pushed her around for all those years, life had all the power. Now she would do the pushing. Now she had all the power.

CHAPTER SIX
Mr. Brown

I saiah didn't have time to deal with Manzo's request so he called in the marines. It was early in the morning when two representatives from the Carver Middle School Science Club came to Isaiah's house. Sometime back, the club members were being bullied by a big kid named Rayo. Isaiah intervened, found an outlet for Rayo's aggression, and the problem was solved. Phaedra Harris, the new president of the club, was different from the previous office holder, who wore braces, carried a tuba case and a three-hundred-pound backpack. Phaedra wore a light gray business suit, a bright but fashionable ruby-red tote bag, and low heels.

"Good morning, Mr. Quintabe," she said, her smile as friendly as her firm handshake. "You probably don't remember me, but we met before. I was part of the committee that came to see you about Rayo."

"I do remember you, Phaedra," Isaiah said. "It's nice to see you again."

"We're dressing a bit formally today. The Academic Decathlon quarterfinals are this afternoon."

"Well, good luck to you."

Phaedra was obviously smart but not like the smart kids on TV.

She wasn't *acting* like an adult. It was as if she *was* an adult; poised, completely comfortable with herself, none of that uncertain awkwardness common to thirteen-year-olds. If it wasn't for her age, she could have hosted *Good Morning America.*

"I'm Isaiah," he said to her companion.

"Pleased to meet you, Mr. Quintabe. I'm Gilberto Cervantes," Gilberto said. "I have followed your exploits closely, sir. Very impressive, I must say."

"Call me Isaiah. And you can drop the sir."

"I'm afraid that won't be possible, sir. It's the way I was raised." Phaedra looked up at her forehead.

In contrast to Phaedra, Gilberto was formal and stern, his impatient brow seemingly a permanent fixture. But he was no geek either. No pudginess, thick glasses, or embarrassing haircut. He was handsome in his navy blue suit, his tie tied in a perfect Windsor, his wing tips polished and gleaming. And this wasn't a kid's ensemble. His pants weren't puddled around the ankles and his sleeves weren't too long. His clothes were tailored, his briefcase expensive. He looked like a shrunken tax attorney.

"Do you want something to drink?" Isaiah asked. "Water? Cranberry juice?"

"You wouldn't happen to have an espresso maker, would you?" Phaedra said. "I'm afraid I'm running a little slow this morning."

They sat in the kitchen, Phaedra sipping espresso, Gilberto sticking with his elaborate water bottle because of his high blood pressure. Isaiah told them about Vicente kidnapping his own daughter.

"That's a very serious situation, Mr. Quintabe," Gilberto said. "But I don't see a role for the science club."

"I need to find him, I need eyes and ears," Isaiah said. Phaedra was delighted at the prospect. Gilberto frowned like he'd missed a big write-off.

"I think we can accommodate you, Isaiah," she said. "I'm sure the club will be happy to help."

"I think you're being a little hasty, Phaedra," Gilberto said. "The membership might want to vote on it."

"No they won't. They'll go crazy and start calling themselves *agents* and *operatives*."

"Rules," Isaiah said. "This is about locating him. That's it. You will not get any closer than thirty yards and you will not—" He hesitated. Gilberto had a stylus and was taking notes on an iPad.

"Please go on, sir."

"You will not talk to him, contact him, enter his property, or make yourself known to him in any way," Isaiah said. "And if you find him you call me immediately. Is that clear?"

"Yes, that's clear," Phaedra said.

"I want your word."

"You have mine."

"It's understood," Gilberto said. "I have my faults but a lack of ethics isn't one of them."

Phaedra sighed. "Have you any ideas of where we might start, Isaiah?"

"His friends and relatives haven't seen him so I'm thinking he's gone to ground, probably with a woman."

"Typical," Phaedra said.

"What if he's left the city?" Gilberto said.

"Yes, that's a possibility, but it's only been a couple of days and gangsters aren't much for traveling out of the hood—and by the way, I'm paying you for this."

"That's not necessary," Phaedra said. "You've already compensated us more than enough. Getting Rayo off our backs was a huge relief."

"I'm afraid I don't agree," Gilberto said. "You may recall that in return for Mr. Quintabe's services we found Miss Myra's brooch."

"Oh, Gil."

"It's Gilberto. Never Gil."

"I'll pay each member of the club ten dollars an hour," Isaiah said. "I insist."

Gilberto allowed himself a small smile "Plus expenses? There may be transportation costs, meals, sundries and such, and of course, each member will keep scrupulous accounts. You needn't worry about that."

"I'm not worried," Isaiah said.

Gilberto glanced at his iWatch. "I'm sorry, Mr. Quintabe. But we should be going."

"I wish I could give you more to go on."

"Not necessary, sir," Gilberto answered, a little offended. "There's no need for concern. We'll handle it from here."

"*Sundries?*" Phaedra said as they went out the door. "Did you actually say *sundries?* You are *so* pretentious."

"I'm not pretentious, I just behave in a professional manner."

"What are you a professional of? The eighth grade?"

After the kids left, Isaiah decided to go to the wrecking yard. There was no need to, but he wanted to see Grace. He was getting in the car when he noticed a van parked at the end of the block, one he'd never seen before. It was a Ford Econovan, white, no signage, black bumpers, in need of a wash. A million of them out there. A foil sunshade was over the windshield. Why was it there? To save the plastic dashboard on a dented-up old car? A window was half open. Something you didn't do in this neighborhood unless you were in the car. Was he being watched or being paranoid? Nothing to do but test it out.

He went east on Broadway going the speed limit. The van didn't follow him but if these were the people at the Edgemont they were pros. They wouldn't make a mistake like that. They'd run a box on him. A different car would be behind him, which might be the white Lincoln four cars back. It was dirty. The windows too opaque to see the driver. A second vehicle would be trailing that one. They would switch from time to time so he wouldn't see the same vehicle in two different locations. Two more cars would be running on parallel streets, staying more or less even with him. No matter which way he turned, somebody would be there to pick him up, everybody in contact by radio. His adrenaline rose. He liked challenges and he enjoyed outwitting people.

He stayed on Broadway until he approached Los Alamitos. There was a fork there. Left and you merged onto Los Alamitos, right and you stayed on Broadway. The Lincoln was in the left lane and another car was driving side by side, a Nissan Rogue. Isaiah went right onto Broadway. The Lincoln peeled off, the Rogue staying with him. Not conclusive, lots of other cars made the same turn. He drove a ways and turned right on Shoreline Drive and into Shoreline Village, a touristy shopping area. He parked in the lot. It was almost full. The Rogue parked too but some distance away. Again, not conclusive and he wanted to be sure. He got out of the car and walked into the concourse. Foot surveillance was much harder.

When he was out of sight of the lot, he jogged to the Queensview Steakhouse. The dining room was on the second floor. He asked the hostess for a window seat and ordered a salad. He saw the tall woman from the Edgemont walking quickly through the crowd, rubbernecking. Yes, they were definitely tailing him. The woman stopped and talked into her collar mike. A few minutes later, her four colleagues showed up. They looked grim, talking a bit before they split up. Isaiah paid his bill, left the restaurant, and took the bike path back to his car. The surveillance was worrisome. It made it harder to see Grace, but getting kidnapped worried him more. If he didn't get caught alone and on foot he should be okay.

* * *

The team regrouped in the parking lot. The Audi was gone.

"He made us," Richter said.

Owens shook her head. "He didn't act like it. He was driving at the speed limit."

"That don't mean shit, woman," Hawkins said. "Why don't you shut up?"

The country girl smiled like Huck Finn with a Glock in his pants. "I don't believe I will. And if you want to make me, well, here I am."

"Why do you think he made us?" Jimenez asked.

"Why would a homeboy come here to shop?" Richter said. "He's not a tourist. He'd go to Costco or Walmart, not a place like this." A moment's pause, everyone wondering why they hadn't thought of it.

"Right," Walczak said like he'd known it all along. "We'll have a team meeting later. I'll text you." Everyone was already walking away. Owens was parked next to Jimenez.

"I'm going to get something to eat," she said. "Want to come?"

"No thanks," Jimenez said. He didn't look at her and got into his car. "I had a big breakfast."

Walczak drove to the office, wondering what his parents would think about the mess he was in. They were exacting and demanding in the extreme. He remembered them cross-examining him because he got a 94 on a calculus test. His argument that it was still an A only earned him derision and a curfew. His mother and father were both attorneys. They drove matching Jaguars, had their assistants buy little Stanislaw's Christmas presents, and exuded all the warmth of a grand jury subpoena. They didn't realize the worst thing they could do to their son was ignore him. A driver dropped him off and picked him up from school. A housekeeper who spoke little English made his meals but didn't read him stories or tuck him in at night. On Christmas Eve, his parents went to parties, his gifts piled up under the perfect tree, put there by people who did that for a living. He opened his presents alone, his parents hungover. On Thanksgiving, the housekeeper made him turkey sandwiches. She abused him when he took a bath and he defiled her in his dreams. He imagined himself living with the Yamamotos next door. He imagined himself living with the Brady Bunch, he watched the reruns all the time. He wondered what it would be like to be greeted by his mother when he came home from school or to play catch with his father. A real family had lived in his imagination for all those years and a family was all he'd ever wanted.

He called Patty. She and Noah would be back Saturday morning as planned. If Walczak had everything wrapped up by Sarah's Friday deadline, it should all work out. It was close, though. Too close.

"Stay another day or two if you want to," he said.

"Don't be silly," she said. "My parents are coming, don't you remember? They adore you, you know."

"I love you."

"I love you too."

Grace worried TK would treat her like a nuisance and didn't know what to expect when she came down from the loft, the dog leading the way.

"Mornin', Grace," he said. "Want some coffee? I ran out of sugar, but I got some of that powdered cream." She liked how he looked. A rangy, gnarled tree branch stuck into grimy coveralls and topped with the dirtiest cap she'd ever seen. His large eyes had a film over them as if at any moment he might start to cry, though she doubted he ever did. His smile was weary and amused, like there was nothing in the world you could say or do that would surprise him. They sat on rusty lawn chairs set up in the shadow of the warehouse. Ruffin was relieving himself on one of the wrecks.

"See that?" TK said. "He likes to piss on Japanese cars. He'll walk past a whole row of Chevys to piss on a Toyota." She sipped her coffee. It was good, tasted just like her own.

"As long as I'm here, is there anything I can help you with?" she said.

"Prob'ly not. Mighty rough work for a girl." She gave him a look. "What?" he said. "That ain't nothin' against your feminism."

"You've seen me work on my car."

"Oh, now, don't get all lezbo on me."

"*Lezbo?*" she said with a laugh.

"I got no trouble if you like your meat off the bone. It's the men who make me nervous. Two dicks in the same bedroom is one too many."

She helped TK dismantle a Dodge pickup. Her dad had taught her a lot about cars. When she was fourteen, he bought her the GTI on the cheap. It had been totaled in an accident and was registered as salvage. Between tours, he helped her rebuild it and she helped him build his own project. It was one of Grace's happiest memories. Working alongside her dad, handing him tools, talking about school, Mom telling funny stories about his growing up, stopping for an egg salad sandwich and a Coke and listening to him explain about timing belts, fuel pumps, injectors, and roller bearings and showing her how they worked with his nimble hands and strong eyes.

Once, she'd asked him why he'd joined the army. He said he was young and directionless and getting into trouble. He said his father told him over and over again that he would never amount to anything and he was afraid that might be true. He also knew he would never get anywhere by himself. He needed structure and limits and unyielding demands and that was what the service gave him. It forced him to be a man.

"One thing I learned?" he said. "Never back down, sweet pea. Fight for yourself because no one else will."

Her dad loved Steve McQueen. Sometimes, they'd stay in the garage, sitting in his car and watching McQueen's old movies on a laptop. Mom thought it was weird but it didn't seem that way. They watched *The Thomas Crown Affair, Tom Horn, The Getaway, The Great Escape,* and *Bullitt.* Especially *Bullitt,* sometimes twice in a row. The car chase through San Francisco was the best ever. Better than all the new movies with their special effects and actors that looked like they'd come straight from the spa. Every time they watched it, she'd ask him, "Think you could do that, Dad? Drive like Steve McQueen?" And every time, he'd answer her with a shake of his head and a playful smile. "No problem, sweet pea. No problem at all." She was too young to get a driver's license but he'd take her up to Kern Canyon Road in the GTI, a twisty stretch that wound through the foothills all the way to Miracle Hot Springs. He showed her how to drive *fast.* He said she had talent, that she could drive professionally, but she had no interest in it. She did it for him. She missed him so much. She ached for him.

After her mom fled Bakersfield, Grace stayed with her grandmother but the old woman's health was failing and she was nearly blind. Child Services placed her in a foster home. Gordon and Margaret Markle were empty-nesters, their two sons off at college. They lived a hundred miles from Bakersfield in Fresno, somewhere between a small town and a big one, the truck route running through it, arid except for green patches of almonds, grapes, and tomatoes and vast poultry farms, thousands of chickens imprisoned in warehouses rank with ammonia and hormones. Margaret was scrawny, cheerful, and energetic. She sold real estate and was forever loading and unloading FOR SALE signs in and out of her car.

"It's going to be great," she said like she was showing Grace a finished basement. "We're going to get along fine, aren't we?"

Gordon was also scrawny, cheerful, and energetic. He had a gap between his front teeth and big eyes that reminded Grace of Mickey Mouse; wide open and continuously delighted. In another context, he'd look high. Gordon was an accountant for a grain company. He worked from home a lot and whistled off-key while he crunched numbers on his laptop.

Grace's room was upstairs. It was pleasant and had a view of cattle munching on hay bales. She liked to listen to them moo. School was school, boring and unending. The boys said nasty things, the girls stayed away. She spent most of her time in her room, reading, drawing, and crying.

Margaret was at an open house and Grace and Gordon were sitting in the breakfast nook. He'd made ice tea and his special tuna sandwiches. "Did you notice the dillweed?" he said. "I like a little relish in it too. Margaret hates it, of course."

"It's good," Grace said, wishing she could spit it out.

"So the social worker told me you're an artist," he said.

"I'd like to be."

"Hard way to make a living," he noted. "You should have a backup plan."

"I'll think about that, Mr. Markle."

"Mr. Markle is my father," he said like he'd made that up himself. "Call me *Gordo.* Everybody does. Hey, I want to show you something." They went out to the garage and he ushered her in with a warm hand on her back. He'd converted the place into a workshop where he made things out of leather. For some unknown reason, orange cowhide seemed to be his favorite, burned, stamped, carved, and gouged with garish designs. Different-size daisies, stars, and happy faces on a ladies' purse; lassos, spurs, and anatomically incorrect horses on a man's belt. They were among the ugliest things Grace had ever seen.

Gordon beamed. "Beautiful, huh?"

"Yeah, really," she said. She wondered who would put down real money for an orange wallet sewn with leather shoelaces.

"Marketing's the problem," he said with a serious nod. "When I find a distributor they'll go like hotcakes, don't you think?"

"Yeah, sure."

He smiled knowingly. "You want the purse, don't you? Here, take it."

"No, I couldn't."

He thrust the purse into her hands. "I insist. The kids at school will love it."

Fresno days were longer than Bakersfield's. She couldn't believe she'd only been with the Markles a month. She had to get out of there. *Had* to. She hid the hideous orange purse behind a dumpster before she went to class. One day it went missing. Grace was happy to be rid of the thing but as soon as she came home Gordo said, "Hey, kiddo, where's the purse? I thought it was your favorite."

Escape seemed unlikely. She had no money and her only living relative was Uncle Alex, who wore suspenders and wasn't all there. *Home,* she thought. *I have to go home.* I can be where Mom and Dad used to be. I can listen to their voices and talk to their ghosts.

Gordon made the time even more interminable. He took her to the mall and tried to buy her clothes but she refused. He insisted on playing badminton with her to keep her figure trim. He wanted to talk about her love life. "Got a boyfriend?" he said.

"No."

"No hot guy at school you've got an eye on?"

"No."

"I bet they've got an eye on you," he said, Mickey's eyes ogling her. He bought her art supplies. "I know you really like art," he said solemnly. "I want to encourage you all I can." He put his hand on her shoulder and squeezed it. "I *get you,* kiddo. I really do. You ever need to talk, I'm here." She didn't need help with her home-work but he helped her anyway, leaning over her, his face near her hair. She could have sworn he was smelling her. "It's good to have a friend, don't you think?" he said.

"Yeah. It's great."

She tried to keep away from him but he was always there. When she cleaned the kitchen, when she went outside to draw or read. When she did her laundry or vacuumed the living room. Some-times, he'd knock on her door and say, "I made lunch for you," or "Let's go for a drive," or "Hey, there's something great on TV." She had to accept a few of his invitations, she was living in his house, af-ter all. He complained about Margaret. *She's always busy. She doesn't listen. She's letting herself go.*

They were in the breakfast nook having another tuna fucking sandwich. "She's a good person," he said. "But she's not fun, she's not easygoing, she doesn't know how to chill." He put his hand over Grace's. "Like you." Grace learned Margaret's schedule, leaving her room when Margaret was around and skulking about when she wasn't. Gordon was perfunctory with his wife and when she nagged, which was frequently, he'd sneak looks at Grace and roll his eyes.

Another oppressively hot day in Fresno; the smells of cow dung and alfalfa hung like drapes in a barn. Margaret was in bed with her allergies and Gordon ushered Grace into the garage, that hand on her back again.

"What are we doing, Gordon?" she said. "I have homework to do."

"It's Gordo. Remember?" He rubbed his palms together. *"Okay,"* he said, like at last he could get rolling. "I just wanted to show you a few things." He found a scrap of cowhide and held it up to her like a theater ticket. "This is *vegtan*. Veg because it's dyed with vegetable dye and tan because it's tanned. Do you know what tanning is?"

"Yeah, I do."

He seemed not to have heard her because he went right on with his spiel. "Tanning means it's treated with chemicals, so it doesn't rot and smell bad, and let me tell you, this stuff stinks to high heaven." He kept talking and gesturing too much. He's nervous, she thought. This was a pretext for something. He blathered on awhile before finally, *finally,* getting to it. "Okay," he said decisively, "that's enough of that."

"Great."

"Hey," he said, brightening. "Why don't we have a little party?" He went into the fridge and brought out a bottle of premade margaritas. He poured two drinks into plastic cups and gave her one.

"Our little secret, right?" he said, a creepy twinkle in Mickey's eyes.

"I don't drink."

He looked astounded. "You don't? Oh come on now. Don't be a stick-in-the-mud. I thought you kids liked to party."

"No, really, I don't drink." Gordo kept smiling like she would change her mind but she didn't respond.

"Okay," he said with a disappointed shrug.

She asked for a lock on her door but he never got around to it. She installed a dead bolt herself but he removed it, saying it was a fire hazard and he needed access to the room in case of an emergency. Grace asked Margaret about it. "Don't ask me," she said, "that's Gordon's department."

Margaret was at the hairdresser when he showed Grace the metal box he kept hidden under the workbench. He looked like a kid with a hidden stash of candy. "Look what I've got," he said. He opened the box with a key. "Come on over here. Don't be shy." He held it close so she had to stand shoulder to shoulder. There were tidy stacks of cash bound with rubber bands. "My mad money," he said like it was buried treasure. "Margaret doesn't know about it. How much do you think is in there?"

"I don't know."

He grinned proudly. "Going on five grand. I put a little in every month. Been doing it for years." He nudged her, Mickey's eyebrows going up and down. "What do you think of that?"

"It's great."

"You know what? Margaret's going to a conference next week. Maybe you and me should take a little trip. How about it, huh? San Francisco, say? It's a great place. We'll have fun."

"I have school."

One afternoon, he barged into her room unannounced. She was sitting on the bed in boxer shorts and a sports bra reading. "Woops," he said. He grinned, put his hand over his face, and peeked through his splayed fingers. "Sorry." He backed out of the room, taking his time as he closed the door. "Hey. Want to go get a burger?"

That's it, she decided. That's enough. She heard her dad's voice. *Never back down, sweet pea. Fight for yourself because no one else will.* It was Tuesday. Margaret would be home around five. At four-thirty, Grace went into the garage and left the door open. She sat on the workbench, swung her legs, and waited. Gordon came in. "Oh!" he said, like he hadn't watched her from his office. "How you doin', kiddo?"

"Hi."

"What are you doing in here?"

She looked directly at him. "Waiting for you."

He smiled and said in ascending notes, "You look like you're up to something."

She gave him her mischievous smile. "Do I?" She slid off the bench. "I wonder what that could be." He stood close and breathed into her eyes.

"You're really cute, you know that?" She gave him the direct look for another two seconds and said gaily, "Take some pictures of me!" She gave him her phone.

"Great idea," he said.

114

She unbuttoned the top two buttons of her shirt and vamped, hand in her tousled hair, her lips pooched out.

"Beautiful," he said. "Very sexy."

"Booty shot!" She turned around, stuck out her butt, and looked seductively over her shoulder.

"Very nice, *very* nice," he said, taking picture after picture.

"Let's take some selfies!"

"Great idea!"

He pulled her in until their heads were touching. They grinned like idiots. "How's that?" he said.

"Take another one," she said. She stuck her tongue out like she was going to lick his ear.

"Oh, that's great!"

"You do it." He obliged her, his tongue feathering her earlobe.

"Want that drink now?" he said, with that creepy twinkle.

"Our little secret?" she said, twinkling back. He got out the booze and poured the drinks. They sipped, looking at each other over their cups and smiling. It was quiet except for the cows calling to each other. There was sweat on his forehead. If Minnie saw Mickey's eyes, she'd put on lingerie and get out the condoms.

"Okay!" he said, like it was time to take action. Manfully, he tossed his cup aside and did the same with hers. "Come here." He pulled her in for a kiss. She leaned away.

"I don't think so," she said.

"What?"

"I said I don't think so." She pushed his hands off her and stepped back.

"Why?" He was truly surprised. "I thought we could have a little fun."

"Fun for who, Gordo? Me or you?"

"Both." He thought a moment and sneered. "Oh, I get it. You're a little cocktease, aren't you?"

"I wouldn't say that. But I am curious."

"Curious about what?" he said, his tone a little harder.

"About why a forty-seven-year-old man is trying to seduce a fifteen-year-old girl." His turn to step back.

He scoffed. "Nobody's trying to seduce you."

"You thought you had me pegged, didn't you?" Grace said. "A loner, no parents, the new kid at school. Naturally I'd want a substitute father, and why not good ol' understanding Mr. Markle? The friendly authority figure who lets you call him *Gordo*." She huffed. "You thought I didn't notice you looking down my shirt? That I didn't know why you asked me about my boyfriends? That you wanted to know if I was fucking yet? And what's with all the touching? You don't touch Margaret half that much, and by the way, she's a much nicer person than you'll ever be."

"Margaret has nothing to do with this," he said stiffly.

"Did you really think I'd be impressed with your five thousand dollars? What a doofus." She chuckled. "You know what was really lame? Giving me the art stuff because you really *get me*." She clutched her chest melodramatically and looked at him like a starving kid in India hoping for a tuna fucking sandwich. "It was so, so moving. Honestly, Gordo. It was."

"Are you having fun? Because this is getting boring."

"What was that other bit? Oh yeah. Taking me into your confidence, telling me your little secrets. Was that supposed to make me feel grown-up and special? Because it didn't, Gordo. I'm a kid but I'm not a moron—and *San Francisco*? Really? What were you thinking? That I'd eat a shrimp taco on Fisherman's Wharf and get horny?" Gordo was staring at the floor, his arms around himself, lips pursed and nodding. She looked at him with loathing wonderment. "What is it you really want? Do you want to be in charge, is that it? Be the man of the world and teach the innocent virgin a thing or two? Blow her mind? Give her her first orgasm?"

He shook his head and put his palms out. "Okay, Grace—"

"It's a fantasy, right? I'm the pretty girlfriend you never had in high school or the bitch that gave it up to the cool guys but not to you? Or maybe you're just a dirty old man who wants to see some teenage tits."

"Are you finished?" he said like what she'd said was nothing of consequence.

"This shit is fucked up and pitiful, Gordo. *You're* fucked up and pitiful and do you want to know why?"

"Why?"

"Because it makes you a pedophile."

His head jerked back and he wagged it like a ratchet wrench. "What? No! Now really, Grace, that's over the line."

"You want to fuck a fifteen-year-old kid and *I'm* over the line?" She went up to him and hooked a finger inside his shirt, her face inches from his. "Do you know what the law calls it, Gordo? They call it sex with a minor. They call it statutory rape."

"That's it!" he said, pissed off. He grabbed her arm and yanked her toward the door. "You're outta here." She twisted away.

"Get off me, asshole." It was almost five o'clock. They heard Margaret's car pulling into the driveway.

"I wonder who that could be?" Grace said.

"Oh shit!" Gordon said. He hurriedly closed the door and locked it, Mickey's eyes wild and unseeing. "Okay, okay. Calm down."

"I'm as calm as I could be," Grace said calmly.

"Gordon?" Margaret called out.

"I'm going to go out there and you stay here," he said. Grace kept her gaze on his as she unbuttoned the rest of her buttons. "What are you doing?" he said. "Don't do that!" He was sweating dark circles under his armpits; a cowlick popped up all by itself.

"Gordon!" Margaret said sharply. "Where are you? I need you." Grace's shirt was all the way open, her sports bra visible.

"What do you think, Gordo? Hot, huh?"

Gordon looked like a T. rex had stuck its head in the garage. "Cut it out!" he said.

"Gordon?" Margaret said, annoyed now. "Are you in there?"

His voice went up an octave. "J-just a minute, honey."

Grace said, "I'm in here too, Mar—" Gordon clamped his hand over her mouth. She laughed at him with her eyes.

"Shut up," he whispered. "Are you crazy?"

"Gordon?" Margaret said. "Is somebody in there with you? Answer me!" Grace peeled his hand away from her mouth.

"Better answer her, Gordo."

"Uh, no, honey. I, uh, I have the game on. I'll be out in a minute, okay? I'm doing something."

"You sure are," Grace said. Margaret tried the door, rattling the knob.

"Why is the door locked?"

"Could you give me a minute, *please?*" Gordon said. "I'm busy."

"Busy with what?" Margaret said heatedly. "Oh God, you're not doing *that* again, are you? You are so disgusting." They heard her walk away.

Gordon shook his forefinger like a maraca. "That wasn't funny, Grace. Not funny at all! Now I'm going in the house and I better not hear a word about this ever again."

"Sorry, Gordo," she said. "We're not done yet. I haven't told you what I want."

"What you want?" He paused a moment and sneered. "Oh, I get it. This is a shakedown, is that it? Well, it's not going to work. I'll tell Margaret you tried to seduce me, I'll tell her you're a slut and you fucked all the guys at school."

She hopped on the bench and swung her legs. "You're forgetting about the pictures, Gordo. The ones we took a few minutes ago?"

"You bitch!" He grabbed her phone. "What's the passcode? And don't fuck around, I'm serious."

"There is no passcode. You need a fingerprint—and please don't break the phone. Everything backs up automatically." Gordon paced in a circle, running his hands through his hair.

"You bitch, you goddamn bitch." He stopped, trying to gather himself. He ran his hands through his hair again and sucked in a sharp breath. "Okay. What do you want?"

"Money," Grace said. "All five grand. Now."

"Out of the question. I worked hard for that money. I'll give you five hundred." He glanced worriedly at the sports bra. "No, make it a thousand. And that's final."

"You know who could settle this?" she said thoughtfully. "Margaret. Tell you what. Let's go see what she thinks." Gordon stood there, slumped and humiliated, Mickey's eyes sliding down his Dockers and onto his deck shoes. Grace took the metal box from its hiding place. "Say, Gordo. Do you think I could have the key?"

She turned sixteen the day she took the bus back to Bakersfield with five grand in her backpack. She promised her Uncle Alex she'd give him the house if he would take care of everything until she came back. Then she got the GTI out of the garage, locked the door with a heavy chain and padlock, and drove the hell out of town at a million miles an hour.

Three years went by before she returned. She signed the house over to Uncle Alex so he could sell it. "What are you gonna do with all the furniture and stuff?" he asked. She was staying in Cherokee's one-bedroom apartment, where she had half a closet, a drawer in the bathroom, and a bookshelf all to herself. Everything in the house had to go. There were piles and piles of books, some

Sarah had read to Grace while they swayed in the porch swing. She donated those to the library, the furniture and clothes went to the Salvation Army. Everything else went to the dump. It was torment. There were favorite coffee mugs, letters in shoe boxes, photo albums, a wooden burro from a vacation in Mexico, pots and pans, dishes, lamps, collections of knickknacks, two TVs, Christmas lights, a stereo, the bed her parents slept in, the blankets that kept them warm. She put her mother's favorite nightgown and her dad's coveralls in a garbage bag and piled it in with the rest. She couldn't bear the thought of anyone else wearing them. There were a million other things, meaningless now that they were gone. She wondered why the stuff had mattered at all and why they'd squandered so much of their time on life's detritus instead of each other.

She'd always believed her mother was alive, but her dad was gone forever. His belongings were the only evidence that he'd existed and that he'd loved her and that they'd watched Steve McQueen movies together in his car. She had to keep something of his, a talisman, an enduring lucky charm. She had to keep *him.* There was only one choice. It would be a hardship but she would make it work. She had to.

It took an hour and a half to strip the Dodge pickup down to the frame. Grace sat next to TK in the crane and watched him working the levers and pedals as easily as riding a bike down a bike path. A disk-shaped electromagnet was suspended by chains from a thirty-foot boom. TK deftly lifted the five-hundred-pound engine block out of the pickup. Grace was nervous, hugging herself.

"What's the matter with you?" TK said.

"I don't like that thing. I feel like it's gonna yank me out of here by my belt buckle."

"It's strong, all right. But you're safe. Just don't stand underneath it with a metal plate in your head." TK swiveled the boom around and set the engine down between two others as gently as a fresh egg.

Later, they were back in the lawn chairs, drinking cold beers and eating takeout pizza. "So there's these three old men, you see," TK said, "and one of 'em says, 'Sixty is the worst age there is. You feel like you need to pee and nothing comes out.' And the second old man says, 'That ain't nothin'. When you seventy you can't even take a dump without eatin' a bran muffin.' And the third old man says, 'You boys don't know about trouble 'til you're eighty. I pee and take a dump every morning at exactly six a.m.,' and the first old man says, 'Well, if you can do all that every morning at six a.m., what's your problem?' And the third old man says, 'I don't get up 'til seven.'" Grace spit up her beer and laughed for the first time in recent memory. It felt good. It felt great. "Okay, your turn," TK said.

"My turn for what?"

"To tell a joke."

"I don't know any jokes."

"Everybody knows at least one joke," TK said. "Now, come on, girl, out with it. I'm putting a roof over your head. You owe me."

Given all the other things that were happening, Grace felt a surprising amount of pressure. "Okay. Here goes."

"Lay it on me," TK said, leaning back in his chair.

"What did the elephant say when he came down to the riverbank and saw Tarzan naked and doing the backstroke?"

"I don't know."

"How in the hell do you breathe through that thing?"

There was a moment of silence and then TK busted out laughing and so did she. She wanted to thank him but didn't know how.

TK handed her another beer. "Isaiah said you're an artist."

"Yeah, I paint," Grace said. The pizza had bacon on it and there was cheese melted in the crust. It was *really* good.

"What do you paint?"

"My feelings, memories, dreams."

"Feelings, memories, and dreams, huh? Y'all should paint mine. You'd need a canvas as big as the sky. If you don't mind my asking, who are you hiding from?"

"It's a long story," she said, "but they're scary people. If you ever want me to go, just say the word."

He lit a Pall Mall, squinting as he exhaled. "Shoot, girl, scary ain't nothin' to me."

TK told her he grew up in Fontana, about sixty miles from LA. At the time, it was an industrial center because of the steel mill. "They let us black folks work in the mill, but we always did the dirtiest work and lifted the heaviest loads." When TK was a toddler, a family friend named O'day Short started building a house in the white section of town. TK's dad helped him out. "The Klan came around and threatened O'day, told him to get the hell out," TK said. "He reported it to the sheriff, but he told him to get out too. The goddamn chamber of commerce wanted O'day out so bad they offered to buy the place. He turned 'em down flat."

A few days later, TK's father was just arriving at O'day's house when it exploded into flames. O'day, his wife, and their children were killed. TK's father got blown into a ditch. He suffered third-degree burns that crippled him for the rest of his life. "Fire department said it was an accident," TK went on. "Said O'day was lightin' some kinda lamp. Shoot. What kinda lamp blows up like a goddamn bomb? They had one of them arson experts come out and he said somebody did it on purpose—and you know what the DA did? He closed the case."

TK's family moved to Long Beach because there was work there. His mother was a maid to some of the local businesses, including a used car dealership. At nine years old, TK was washing and waxing cars for ten cents an hour. There was a black mechanic who let him help out. Changing oil and tires and flushing out radiators. He learned to use tools. He learned to love cars. Then one afternoon, out of necessity, he used the salesmen's bathroom. The owner strapped him with a fan belt until he bled. He got fired and so did his mother.

"I worked on cars for twenty-five years 'til I could afford this place," TK said. "Never made as much as a white man for doing the same work and never *met* a white man who was as good as me."

"I believe it," Grace said.

"I've had the gangs climbin' over my fences, thieves pointin' guns at me, cops shakin' me down. There was a real estate fella wanted this land. Sent his thugs over here trying to intimidate me. I introduced them to my friend Mr. Brown and they never came back."

"Who's Mr. Brown?"

The wrecking yard was in a desolate area. People who didn't want to pay the landfill fee used it as a dump. Bums stayed warm around trash can fires. People abandoned their tires and appliances. Dead bodies were found here. Isaiah drove into the yard. He was worried about Grace, wondering if she and TK were getting along. There were other things weighing on his mind. He'd done some research and what he'd discovered was as bizarre as it was disturbing.

Grace's father, Chuck, had been involved in a long-standing feud with a next-door neighbor, a truck driver named Kyle Munson. The feud had started small. Who was responsible for trimming the tree that hung over the fence, your dog crapped on my lawn, could you keep the music down please, the property line is here, not there, and like most conflicts between men, it turned into a contest for virility and control. There were loud arguments. Threats were exchanged. Once they got into an out-and-out brawl. Munson got the worst of it. The police came and arrested them both.

One night, a masked gunman attempted a home invasion. Chuck tried to fight him off and was killed. Sarah escaped unharmed.

Grace, not named because she was a minor, was asleep in an upstairs bedroom. The next day, Kyle Munson was shot to death in his garage and within hours of that, Sarah fled for parts unknown and a murder warrant was issued for her arrest.

Initially, the police thought Munson was the one who broke in and shot Chuck, but he'd been on a long haul to Des Moines when the shooting occurred. Police speculated that Chuck's murder was random and that Sarah had retaliated against the wrong man. No wonder Grace didn't want to talk about it, Isaiah thought. Who'd want to relive that ordeal, expose that horror show? It said a lot about her too. Why she was the way she was.

Isaiah parked next to the GTI. He panicked when he heard the gunfire. He scooped up a tire iron and ran toward the sound and as he came around the mountain of tires, he saw Grace and TK. He was teaching her how to shoot skeet with a Browning pump-action, 12-gauge shotgun he called Mr. Brown. Grace was working the target launcher. TK had the gun in position and a Pall Mall dangling from his lips.

"Pull," he said.

Grace pressed a button and an orange clay disk zipped over the yard as fast as a fleeing dove. TK fired, hardly moving the gun, the disk exploding like a saucer hitting a sky-blue wall. He hit the next seven in a row as casually as flipping pancakes.

"Jesus," she said. "You make it look so easy."

"I been at it a long time. Not a whole lot to do out here."

"Are you a hunter?"

"No," he said, "I'll eat a bird but I don't want to watch it die. Your turn."

Grace had trouble loading the gun, fumbling with the shells. "What'd I tell you?" TK said impatiently. "Push the shell *down* and then in." When the gun was finally loaded, he helped her get it in the proper position, pressing her cheek against the stock and lifting her elbow. "Okay now, you been shootin' too early, when the target ain't nothin' but a blur. You want to shoot when it comes into hard focus." He pointed at a spot in the sky. "Right about there—no, no, don't aim at it, don't you listen?"

Isaiah smiled. TK had talked to him the same way when he was teaching him how to drive. "You point the barrel about halfway between the launcher and the focus point," the old man said. "Let your eyes follow the target, the gun will follow your eyes, you understand?"

"Yes," she said curtly. "I understand."

"Keep your movement short and smooth, and turn your shoulders, not the gun. Like a cannon on a battleship. You ready?" She nodded.

"Pull," she said. She missed five in a row. She was frustrated, her movements getting jerkier, the stock coming off her cheek. Every time the orange disk escaped into the yard she said *Ahh shit.* Isaiah knew the feeling. He always expected to be good at something right off the bat. "And I'm not a *lezbo*," she added.

"Maybe not," TK said, "but you're acting like a girl. Now stop all that moanin' and bitchin' and settle down. You know what to do, so do it."

She sulked a moment, took a deep breath. "Pull." She hit the next three in a row. She was astonished. "Did you see that?"

TK laughed. "I sho' did. Makes you wonder if Annie Oakley was a lezbo." Grace let out a whoop and they high-fived. Isaiah was envious. He wished he could make her feel that way.

"Hi," he said cheerily, trying to match their mood. She smiled wanly, like she'd bumped into him at a survivors' group.

"Want to join us?" TK said. "You'll be up against a real sharpshooter."

"No thanks. I'm not much for guns."

"The dog don't like gunshots," TK said. "I'm gonna go see where he's at." He left, walking quicker than usual. Grace unloaded the gun, Isaiah looked at the dirt.

"What are we gonna do about my mom?"

"Keep looking."

"Where?"

"There's nothing in the present," he said. "So we've got to look back." Grace sighed.

Laquez had come to the wrecking yard looking for an alternator. His elderly Corolla had died one of its many deaths. The broke-down piece of junk needed an alternator. Laquez knew what it looked like but not what it did. The problem was, Corollas were popular. Not a lot of them made it to the wrecking yard. It was Laquez's favorite car to steal when he was into that. Now he was taking the bus to work— if that's what you could call it; being Seb's flunky, running all over the damn place, picking up money, smurfing from bank to bank, taking his ugly-ass suits to the cleaners and washing his Jaguar only to get yelled at and told he was stupid. There was no way to please that little Zimbabwe motherfucker. The other day, he'd hit Laquez with that goddamn cane, the third time in three weeks. That thing left a mark that hurt for days. Sometimes he imagined creeping up on Seb, wrapping some piano wire around his neck and yanking it tight. Be fun, watching his disrespectful face puff up and that one leg kicking around.

Laquez stumbled to a stop and almost shouted. A goddamn pit bull ran by chasing a goddamn ground squirrel. He hated them things. His brother's dog, Cisco, chased him up a tree and nearly bit his ass off. Lately, Laquez had been wondering about his future. Was this going to be his life? Fixing his fucked-up car, sleeping on his stepsister's sun porch, and working for a crazy African? It was better not to think about shit like that. It didn't do nothing but make you feel worse than you did before.

He spotted a Corolla that was about the right year. With any luck, there'd be an alternator in there that wasn't corroded to shit. Then he saw Isaiah and that white girl from the park. He ducked down but didn't know why. They were standing near the warehouse, talking, the girl not happy, Isaiah being all quiet and spooky like he usually was. A funny place to bring his girlfriend if that's what she was. Laquez had never fucked a white girl but he'd like to. His dick game was off the grid, although he hadn't many chances to play it with a white girl or anybody else. He watched Isaiah get some groceries out of the car and they went into the warehouse together. Were they living there? No, Isaiah had his own crib. Had to be the girl. Now why would somebody like that be holed up in a wrecking yard? She was on the run. No other reason made sense. Laquez thought Seb might want to hear about this. He called him.

"What is it?" Seb said. "I'm very busy right now."

"Well, you might be busy," Laquez replied, "but you won't be too busy for this."

The winos called. Isaiah was at the Coffee Cup. Richter hurried over there. He was sitting in a booth at the very back, eating something and brooding like he'd lost his best friend. Richter paid off the two winos and told them they could go. He sat in his car and waited. The more he thought about that fucking Walczak, the angrier he got. The shit he said: *Get out of here and I mean now! Well, open the goddamn door. Are you a cripple? Don't just stand there like an idiot, do something! That's the worst idea I've ever heard. No, you dummy! That's not what I asked for at all!*

Walczak would have dinner in a restaurant and make Richter wait in the car for hours. Or at the office. Or the gym. Or anywhere at all. He'd tell him to run down to the store, seven miles from the house, and get him some gum. He'd tell him to make coffee and then complained about it. Once, he made Richter clean the swimming pool. It made Richter grind his teeth while he slept. He couldn't wait to shut that asshole up and humiliate him in return. He had to think of something cool to say when he brought Sarah in. He practiced some lines. *Yeah, it's me. You remember, the guy with the big stupid mouth? Think I should go clean the pool now? Why don't you run along and let the professionals handle it? You know, people who know what they're doing? Everything's under control, Balzac. Go play tennis or hit a golf ball.*

Isaiah couldn't finish his chicken pot pie. He couldn't stop thinking about Grace; about where she went and why she was so mysterious. You don't act like that if you're going to fix a radiator. She had to be meeting somebody, but why so late? Why? Did her lover have a night job? Did he work the late shift at Jiffy Lube? It was driving Isaiah crazy. *He had to know.*

He drove over to Hanover, a side street near the wrecking yard. If Grace went out, she'd have to pass him. He turned out the lights but kept the engine running. He waited, alternately excited and embarrassed, but the longer he sat there the worse he felt. This was an invasion of privacy. She trusted him and here he was, actually stalking her. This was wrong. Flat-out wrong. She drove past him. He put the car in gear and went after her.

Richter followed him well back. Isaiah was so hot on the girl's trail he wasn't paying attention. Age-old story. Jealous boyfriend, girlfriend that's sneaking around. Richter hoped he wouldn't kill her. Maybe knock her around a bit. Soften her up. Richter felt like himself again, chasing a perp, master of his environment. A cop doing what he was supposed to do.

Isaiah almost turned back a couple of times but the bloodhound in him was baying at the moon. Eventually, Grace ended up someplace so mundane it was almost a letdown. A tidy house with a tidy lawn in an ordinary residential area. It was set back a ways from the street under a copse of trees. Grace took some clothes and the toolbox out of the car and unlocked the garage door. She went in and closed the door behind her. The light went on. Isaiah was so excited he was vibrating and his palms were sweaty. Okay, he thought, it was a garage and she had tools. She was working on a car. But why? She already had a car. So the question was, *whose car was it?*

He had to see. He got out and walked past the garage. The windows were opaque. He'd have to look in through the door. He crept toward it, blood pulsing in his throat, his ears humming with adrenaline. He was usually hyperaware in situations like this, but his focus was on the garage door. He crept closer. He heard her working, tools clanking.

"Fuck," she said.

There was only one way to see her. Did he have the nerve? What if she caught him? He couldn't imagine the embarrassment. It was an old door and hadn't quite closed. He peeked through the narrow opening. The only thing he could see was the back end of a car under a car cover. She was working in the engine bay. He'd have to step inside to get a look. He felt a whole new kind of anxiety, worse than any life-threatening situation he'd ever been in. He put one finger on the door and started to push. He smelled cigarettes and then someone hit him over the head and again across the ribs. He cried out and fell to the ground.

Grace heard the sound. She looked up from the engine bay and the guy with the porkpie hat came in with a police baton.

"Make it hard for me and I'll hurt you," he said.

"Good luck with that." She picked up a ball peen hammer. She thought about screaming but Cherokee's parents weren't home. And she hated the idea, this asshole thinking he could scare the helpless girl. He came closer and she stepped around the car. He looked fierce and happy, like he was coming off the bench for the first time. He grinned.

"Want to play ring-around-the-rosy?"

It occurred to her: *Get in the car and lock the door.* Not easy. She'd have to lift the car cover and where were the keys? On the workbench in plain view. *Shit.* He moved, she moved. They were looking at each other over the trunk. Porkpie glanced at the door. "Walczak, she's in here!" Grace turned her head and that's when the son of a bitch threw the goddamn baton. It glanced off her temple.

"Fucker!" she yelled. She dropped the hammer, and just like that he was on her. He punched her in the stomach. She'd never felt pain like that before, like something inside her had imploded, and the shrapnel cutting off her windpipe. She bent double and choked for breath.

Isaiah was conscious but couldn't get up. His rib cage was glowing hot and his head was covered with a scalp of pain. He could feel the damp grass on his face, smell the dirt, taste the blood running into his mouth. He heard struggling. Then he saw Porkpie. He had Grace duct-taped and slung over his shoulder. She saw him for a millisecond, her expression saying, *What are you doing here?* Porkpie looked around furtively and hurried to his car, parked a distance behind the Audi. *Get up, Isaiah. You have to get up!* He struggled to his knees. Porkpie was fussing with his keys, trying to open the trunk and hold on to Grace at the same time. *Get up, Isaiah! Get the fuck up!* He was on his feet, vision blurry. Porkpie was closing the trunk. Isaiah staggered toward him. *Get him! Get him before he drives away!* His legs wouldn't obey. Porkpie was in the car, starting the engine. *Get him, Isaiah! Get him!* He was almost there but tripped and fell. Porkpie sped off so fast he banged a wheel into the curb, something coming loose and clattering.

Isaiah got in his car and started the engine. He had blood in his eyes from the scalp wound. He wiped it away and went after them. He was driving by rote but his rote was better than most. His reflexes were slower, but he knew where the gears were, he still had clutch feel and he knew how to get around a corner. Porkpie was driving a Lincoln Continental and he'd gone south on Bitterman. Isaiah reasoned he wouldn't take side streets to wherever he was going. He'd get on a main drag. In this case, Anaheim. Isaiah's inner GPS knew the shortest way to Anaheim wasn't via Bitterman. He took a more direct route, reached Anaheim, and as he approached Bitterman, the Lincoln appeared. He started to call 911, but the pain in his ribs made him drop the phone. "Dammit, Isaiah!" he shouted.

He had to concentrate on driving, Porkpie had some skills of his own. He turned off Anaheim onto Fitzhugh, a street that went into the foothills. Isaiah caught a red light and there was traffic. By the time he made the turn, the Lincoln was gone. He floored it, screeching around a slow curve, arriving at a four-way intersection. *Which way did he go?* Isaiah looked left. Narrow street, streetlights on the corners, rows of expensive houses on either side, the light eventually dimming to where you couldn't see the end. Had Porkpie gone into a garage? No, he didn't live here. The houses were too upscale.

Isaiah had been told numerous times that he had eyes like a hawk and he knew that to be true. He could scan a room, a city block, or a crowd of faces the way a peregrine could fly over a vast, brushy landscape and find that silhouette, that twitch, that shadow, that gleam of an eye, and spot the tiny ground squirrel that was the same color as the rocks it was hiding between. Way off in the dark distance, he caught the tiniest speck of light. Odd because it was in the middle of the street. He got his binoculars from the glove box and looked. It was a yellow reflector on a yellow sign. Some of the letters were missing. First, there was a blank, then an O, blank, A, T, blank, R, blank, U, G, blank blank blank blank blank, E, and one last blank. It was like *Wheel of Fortune.* It took him one second to figure it out. "Not a through street," he said. It was a dead end. He couldn't see any side streets but that didn't mean there weren't any. Still, the odds were the car hadn't gone that way.

He looked straight ahead. Same same. Houses, lawns, driveways, and then darkness. He saw a guy in a suit carrying boxes to and from his car. He might not have seen a Lincoln Continental going by but he would have noticed a car that was speeding. Two little kids were playing on the lawn.

"It's way past your bedtime," the man said. "Your mom's gonna kill me." Isaiah drove up, saw the man nearly dropping the box. He had that *Oh shit, it's a gangbanger* look on his face.

"Sir?" Isaiah said. "Did you happen to see my friend? He's really drunk and driving too fast. I'm afraid he'll kill himself."

"Nope," the man said, already turning away.

"Are you sure?"

"Yes, I'm sure. Let's go inside, kids."

Go right, then, Isaiah thought. He made the turn but now what? He was on Colter. Colter stayed upscale until it reached the south end, where the neighborhood demographics descended into minimum wage. He drove fast and when the houses got raggedy, he slowed down. Empty land on his left. On his right, a long straight-away of houses, sheer darkness behind them. House after house. Could be in any of them. He could hear TVs and see people through the windows, their cars as shabby as the area. Maybe he'd get lucky and see a Lincoln Continental parked in a driveway. He crept along, getting more afraid for Grace. Porkpie could be beating her. Raping her. Or worse. The houses could have been cloned. *Which one? Which one? For God's sake, gimme a fucking break.* He stopped. The hawk eyes had blinked. He'd missed something. He backed up and stopped. Every house had a light or a TV on except this one. It was a warm night. The windows had screens but they were closed, the drapes drawn. Did the occupant want privacy or had he gone away? But the house was *too* dark, Isaiah thought, and Porkpie would need light. Isaiah got out of the car and slipped around the side of the house. No light. Around to the back. A light on there? No. He went to the other side of the house. Also dark. The basement had transoms. They were dark too.

Grace wasn't there.

Richter had taken her to his old house, the one he lived in before he hooked up with Walczak. What a shipwreck, he thought, and he wondered how he'd put up with it for all those years. The air was funky and compressed. The filthy shag carpet hadn't changed and neither had the sink crusted with brown rust or the swaybacked sofa where he watched Dodger games and fell asleep drunk. He would have opened a window but they were painted shut.

The girl was a stubborn little thing. Wait'll she sees what's coming for her, he thought. He had knocked out more teeth, broken more noses, and crushed more faces than anyone else in law enforcement. He was known for it. The guys called him Knuckles. *Maybe lighten up some, Knuckles. What did you do to him, Knuckles? Ease up, Knuckles, don't you think he's had enough?*

He decided to play Good Cop first. He took off the duct tape, sat her down at the kitchen table, gave her water, and asked if she had to go to the bathroom. She was relieved but sullen, rubbing her wrists and glaring.

"Look," he said with his best sympathetic smile, "you've been through a lot and I'm sorry for that. Walczak and the other guys get a little carried away. Iraq did something to their brains." She was looking at him like he was week-old roadkill. Fuck, he wanted to hit her. If this didn't work he'd use the electric cattle prod, eight thousand volts, enough to knock a steer sideways. It was lying right on the counter but she hadn't glanced at it. Probably never saw one before. Affably he said, "All I want to know is where your mother is hiding. I'll ask her a few questions and that's it. That's all I need."

"I don't know where she is," Grace said. "I'm looking for her too."

Grace had seen cattle prods when she was living with Gordo. She'd made friends with the cows in the field next door and she hated those fucking yahoos in their wife-beaters and big belt buckles who liked to hurt more than herd. A cattle prod was right there on the counter. A two-pronged fork that housed the electrodes, a long, yellow plastic handle with a box at its base to hold the battery. Was that her fate? Getting the shit zapped out of her, writhing and screaming on the floor?

"Okay," Porkpie said like they were starting over. "Your mother drops out of sight for ten years, and you're telling me she doesn't contact you? That's not believable, Grace. You're her daughter. You must have talked to her."

She tried to keep the condescension out of her voice. "Isaiah is an investigator. Do you think we're hanging around together for fun? I hired him to find my mother because I don't know where she is. That makes sense, doesn't it?"

He smiled. "I'm not buying it. He's your boyfriend."

She was losing her patience. "Jesus. Do you remember what happened at the garage? Isaiah was creeping up to spy on me, right? Well, let me ask you. Would my *boyfriend* have to sneak up on me? No, he'd say, 'Hi, honey, it's me.' Isaiah is a detective and I hired him to find a missing person."

Porkpie tried to seem unruffled but it wasn't working. He yawned and lit a cigarette. To bide for time, she thought, come up with something to say. Then it struck her. *He didn't make me wear a mask. What's he going to do when we're done here, turn me loose?* He was going to kill her and the realization made her nauseous. She needed some time herself. *How do I get to that cattle prod?*

"Could I have a hit off that?" she said.

He offered her the pack. "Want one of your own?"

"No, a couple of drags will do me fine." Who would kill someone when they were sharing a cigarette?

Isaiah was frantic. The houses were all the same. The Lincoln would be garaged by now, so what was he looking for? *Think, Isaiah, think! What do you know about Porkpie?* He lived in the neighborhood. *What else? What else?* He was a smoker. *What else?* The Lincoln was new but filthy. He was a slob. *What else?* This was an out-of-the-way neighborhood. Did Porkpie commute all the way to WSSI and back? No, he lived elsewhere, so he hadn't been home in a while. *What else?* Nothing. *What else what else? Think, Isaiah. For fuck's sake, think! Anything! Random! Stream of consciousness!* A beer drinker? Yes. Newspapers or online? Newspapers. Pride of ownership? No. His house would be like his car. What did he do for a living? Military? No. Didn't have the bearing. A cop? He had the swagger and Walczak had cops on the payroll. And that stupid hat. It was the same kind Gene Hackman wore in *The French Connection. This isn't helping. What else what else what else?*

They were almost done with the cigarette. She scratched her tattoo and noticed Porkpie was wearing a Dodgers pin. "You like the Dodgers?"

"Yeah. I've been a fan for decades. I'm talking Tommy John, Steve Garvey, Matty Mota, all those guys."

"My dad loved the Dodgers," she said. A full-dress lie. "But I don't get it. What's so great about baseball?"

Porkpie smiled, warming up to it. "It's the all-American pastime. It's simple. Run, hit, catch. Anybody can play. But when you see the pros, you get the beauty of it." He shook his head wonderingly. "A great double play, a one-handed catch, a player beating a throw to home." He looked off at a diamond in the sky. Then he threw his arms out wide and cried, "Safe!" He laughed.

She smiled appreciatively. "Wow. I guess I never saw it that way." Porkpie's expression changed. He looked at her, embarrassed that he'd taken the bait. He lit another cigarette. *I've got to get that cattle prod.*

The houses were running together because Isaiah didn't know what he was looking for. He was insane with fear, his T-shirt stuck to his back, his heart on full auto. Through instinct more than anything else, he stopped and got out. The house was rundown. The gate hung by a single hinge, flyers stuck in the chain link fence. Either the guy didn't give a shit or he hadn't been home. The yard was strewn with beer cans and cigarette butts. Definitely a slob. There were lights on, but Isaiah couldn't hear a TV, mandatory in a neighborhood like this. Was the guy busy doing something else? Isaiah got closer and saw something over the doorbell. A metal logo screwed into the wood. The words were rusted over. NO SOLICITORS, maybe? BEWARE OF DOG? Instinct again. He tiptoed up the stoop and rubbed off the rust. The logo was colored blue and gold and shaped like a parking meter. LONG BEACH POLICE DEPARTMENT.

"Can I have a cigarette?" she said. "I guess I do need one." He slid the pack and lighter across the table. She took one and lit it. They smoked in silence, eyeing each other through the lazy curlicues of smoke. The chatter was gone, the pretense was gone. The only sounds were surges of canned laughter and the occasional car going by. It was humid and close. She was sweating. There was nothing left except the inevitability of her death. His gun was in his shoulder holster. She imagined him reaching for it, aiming at her, and pulling the trigger. How long would that take him, two seconds? Porkpie looked more powerful than overweight. A neck like a fire hydrant. Hairy hands. Could she get to the cattle prod and stick him before he shot her? No, not possible. She tried to read his face. Tight jaw and tired eyes, like they'd seen everything, like they'd seen too much. *He doesn't want to do this,* she thought. He was drawing it out, giving her as much time as he could. He leaned back in his chair as if to gain distance, to disconnect. Drops of sweat trickled down his temples, his face sodden with resignation. He could have been a prisoner in front of a firing squad. She could feel the pendulum slowing down...slower...slower...stop. He tensed and flicked his cigarette away. The time had come.

She thought about pleading, begging for mercy, but she felt herself getting angry. Who was this fuck, this shit, this inhuman son of a bitch about to take her life? *Who was he?* He was allowed to kill her? Murder her like Walczak had murdered her dad? No. *Fuck you, you shit. You will not take my life.* She leapt to her feet, upending the table on him; he fell backward, the table on top of him. She got to the counter and grabbed the cattle prod. He couldn't see her and fired blindly. BLAM BLAM BLAM! She ran from the kitchen and out the back door.

Isaiah heard the gunshots. "Grace!" he said. He sprinted around the side of the house and saw Porkpie galloping off into the dark, waving a gun. *He's after her. He's going to kill her.* Isaiah ran. His ribs hurt and pain pounded on his brain, but he kept going. He lost them in the dark. He stopped and listened. He thought they were to his left. He ran through brambles. He couldn't see. He tripped on a rock and fell down. He got up, stopped and listened. He couldn't locate them. They were getting away. He shouted, "Grace! I'm here! I'm here!"

"Isaiah!" she called back. More gunshots. BLAM BLAM. He saw the flashes. He ran. *If you killed her you're dead. If you killed her you're dead.* He was getting close to where he saw the gunfire. He stopped. It was so quiet you could hear the air molecules brushing against your eardrums. He heard rustling at his two o'clock. He thought about rattlesnakes. He crouched and edged toward the sound. He saw a bulky silhouette and the outline of the hat. Porkpie was turning in one direction and then another, looking, listening. *Stay where you are, Grace. Just stay where you are.* Isaiah had to get behind the guy. He hunched over and moved heel-to-toe, easing up when his foot touched a twig or a leaf. Porkpie was fifteen, twenty feet away, hard to tell in the dark. Isaiah was even with his shoulder. He had to keep moving. Porkpie heard him and whirled around, the gun in a two-handed grip. Isaiah went still. He breathed through his nose, small breaths, his T-shirt a wet rag. A few terrifying seconds went by. Porkpie turned away and moved off into the dark, disappearing again.

"Shit," Isaiah whispered. He had to find Grace before Porkpie did, but all he could do was lurch around in the dark. Take the high ground, he thought. There was a pile of boulders. He'd get a better view from there, but he'd also be easier to spot. He clambered up like a slow-motion gecko. He peered over the top, scanning, scanning, the hawk eyes keening. He saw movement. Slight. More like something going from dark to darker. More movement a little farther away. Hunter and prey? Which was which? He got down from the boulders and army-crawled in that direction. He stopped. That amazing quiet again. Movement. A short quick burst. He crawled some more. Someone tore off running and someone bigger gave chase. Isaiah ran. He couldn't see them, only hear their footsteps, their scrambling. He heard Grace cry out. She'd fallen. He visualized her curled up in a ditch, her ankle broken, brittle with fear, Porkpie grinning, creeping toward her, finger on the trigger.

He had to do something but he didn't know where they were. He picked up a rock, threw it. "Over here, asshole!" he shouted. He hit the ground just ahead of the gunshots. BLAM BLAM! "You missed!" He rolled behind a log. BLAM BLAM BLAM! Local cops carried Glocks with a ten-shot magazine. Porkpie was out of ammo. Isaiah was about to move when he heard a new mag click into place. *Shit.* What was Porkpie doing now? *He wants to get Grace, but he knows I might attack him.* Grace was injured and not likely to go anywhere. *Porkpie's coming for me,* he decided. *Lead him away, not too fast or he'll go back for Grace.* He moved, shaking a bush and turning abruptly, flipping over rocks, trying to make Porkpie think he'd taken a position. He waited. No gunshots. He waited. Still nothing. Panic snatched away his breath. He was wrong. *Porkpie's going for Grace!* His instincts or God guided him, because he didn't trip and he didn't fall down. "Grace! Grace! I'm coming!" he shouted. Porkpie stepped out of the dark and shot at him. BLAM BLAM. Missed by a grain of sand. Isaiah heard the bullets zip past him. He dived and rolled but couldn't get up fast enough. Porkpie's doomsday silhouette was coming toward him, not hurrying, knowing it was all over. Isaiah got up. "Shoot me, motherfucker," he said. *If Grace gets away I don't care.* Porkpie raised the gun—and Grace appeared wraithlike, waving a stick. *A stick?* Porkpie turned but not in time. She poked him with it. *What's she doing? He's going to shoot her!* Porkpie screamed like a flaming baboon. He twisted around, shooting as he fell, BLAM BLAM BLAM BLAM, Grace and Isaiah, arms around each other, hobbling into the night.

CHAPTER SEVEN

I Am Satiated Beyond My Concepts

Juanell had gone out and the baby had finally fallen asleep. Cherise was exhausted, eating a Yoplait, a poor substitute for the quarts of strawberry ice cream she inhaled when she was pregnant. Didn't matter. All that was over with and soon Micah would be growing up and she'd miss the time when he was a baby and made little gurgling noises and laughed when she made a funny face; when he was a miracle and God's gift and bless his Holy Name.

Her mother came in, fussing and criticizing like she always did. What was it this time? Juanell left the refrigerator open. Juanell forgot the Pampers again. Juanell is drinking too much. She was the same way when she was vice principal at Carver Middle School. Students and teachers alike stayed out of her way.

"Do you know what Juanell did?" Gloria said. "He left the toilet seat up and there's hair in the shower drain. That man is like some kind of wild heathen. He's not even civilized."

"Mama, he lives here," Cherise said.

"Why are you always making excuses for him? You listen to your mother, she knows a thing or two. Take your thumb off a man for five minutes and all you'll end up with is a bum sleeping in your bed. That's their true nature. Lazy, shiftless, and completely unreliable. Look at your father, ups and runs off with some half-wit barmaid."

You gave him plenty of reasons, Cherise thought. "And you think Juanell might do that too?" she said.

"He might, or something worse."

"You know that's not true."

"No, I don't," Gloria replied. "I don't know that at all, all those women he meets at the food truck. Probably giving away chicken as we speak."

"Juanell doesn't need fried chicken to seduce someone," Cherise said, "and if he was cheating I'd know. He couldn't hide something from me if he was a flea on Isaiah's dog," Gloria replied.

"That's what I thought with Josiah. And look how that turned out."

"Why are you always on him, Mama? You know I love him. Why can't you accept him?"

Gloria raised her chin as if the moment required more gravity. "You are my treasure, Cherise," she said, "and I always wanted you to have a man that deserved you. Somebody who would treat you right and give you everything." Her voice trembled, tears lingered on the edge of her eyes. "Somebody who was like Josiah before he married me."

"Oh, Mama," Cherise said. She hugged her and held on.

"Oh, stop it now," her mother said, stepping away. "I've long since forgotten about all that. Would you like me to make you some lunch?"

Cherise knew, of course, that Juanell had sold his half of the truck to Deronda and that he'd partnered up with Isaiah. Did he really think he could keep that a secret in a neighborhood where people knew if you were getting food stamps and that your husband was messing around with a half-wit barmaid? That he had lied to her made her angry, but she felt bad for him too. She knew he wouldn't—*couldn't* stick with the food truck. Selling fried chicken was as dignified as anything else, but it wasn't for her Juanell. The swaggering, smiling, ever-confident, ever-fearless man of her dreams was turning into a dreamless worrier, wrapped up in paying the bills and little else. Cherise also knew about Deronda's success and that made her feel worse. Her husband, who always thought he had all the angles and knew all the moves, had outmaneuvered himself, and now here he was, struggling to support his family and keep his pride intact at the same time.

And something else was bothering him. Something unusual, something disturbing, not part of the usual rat race issues. She'd given him openings. *Are you okay, baby? You seem worried about something. Are you catching a cold? Is there something on your mind?* But he'd passed it off as too many hours in the truck or Deronda getting on his nerves. Cherise had gone back and forth with herself, but in the end, she decided to let him come to her. If she didn't trust him, what was the point?

Deronda drove the Miata along Anaheim. She kept the top up so she wouldn't mess up her hair. She was going to meet Dodson at a club called Night Out. She couldn't believe this shit with Chester and Junior. All that nonsense happened years ago and here it was again biting her in the ass. The past never passed, did it? She thought about her son, Janeel. He was conceived in a bathroom stall at an underground club in Compton. She couldn't remember the guy's name or what he looked like and she was glad for that.

When she found out she was pregnant, she thought it was the worst day of her life. The fuck was she gonna do with the goddamn baby? Her nights would no longer be her own. There'd be no more smoking weed or swillin' back Seven and Sevens or partying with Nona and them. Her lineup of baby daddies would disappear as fast as her belly grew. She thought about getting rid of it but her father said he'd disown her. She didn't believe all that stuff about a baby changing your priorities. How could a little thing like that turn you into somebody else? But when the baby arrived, it was like God had tapped her on the shoulder and shed his grace on thee. She loved to watch Janeel get out of the car and walk his little self into day care. Or lie on the floor with him and wonder at his tiny fingers building something unrecognizable out of Lego, and she loved cozying up with him on the sofa reading *Who Was Harriet Tubman?* more than he did. She was proud of how she'd finagled the loan and built up the food truck business. She wasn't some down-and-out homegirl working at Rite Aid and feeding her son mac and cheese out of a box. She was a businesswoman, she was *somebody,* and her son would be somebody too and he was the *only* reason why she had done what Dodson told her and got dressed up like the ho she used to be. A satiny, thigh-length, steeply cleavaged dress, stiletto heels, glitter in her lip gloss and eye shadow. Her dad said her perfume smelled like a fruit basket exploded in a candy factory.

She grilled Nona and finally got the truth out of her. It was Christmas, and Nona's family had gathered at her mother's house for dinner and to pass out presents. After the ceremonies were over, the young people went out into the yard to party. It was a warm night, everybody was drinking, having a good time and swapping stories. Nona didn't have any stories so she told everyone about Deronda, Dodson, and Isaiah robbing Junior. One of the listeners was her cousin Sylvia's husband, Chester. Sylvia was a strange woman who had a little money from an inheritance, which gave her time to be a voodoo queen. She dressed all in white and walked around like Whoopi Goldberg in *Ghost.* She also sold *gris-gris* charms, which usually amounted to no more than a dried-out chicken bone. She also passed herself off as a practitioner of *hoodoo,* the equivalent of a Chinese herbalist. Her handful of patients said her concoctions never did anything but give them cold sores and constipation.

She met Chester when she went into his shop looking for a ceremonial dagger. She collected them. Nona liked to say she used them to cut up more *gris-gris* charms from her next three-piece at Popeye's. Sylvia knew instantly that in a past life, she and Chester had been vampires together in New Orleans. His sharpened canines were proof of their relationship. Three weeks later they got married. The ceremony was conducted by an old lady who was something like a high priest or a witch doctor. There was a lot of drum beating, chanting, and African-type dancing that went on for hours. Nona said Chester danced like a polar bear with a Hula-Hoop. She went home when the old lady brought out a snake.

Unfortunately, Sylvia's vampire heritage didn't save her from falling off the pier in Rainbow Lagoon and drowning. She and Chester had gone out for a late-night walk. Chester, who grieved for a week, two on the outside, found himself a widower and the sole owner of Sylvia's condo. Perhaps out of loneliness, he continued to appear at family events, no one wanting to tell a man who made knives for a living and had teeth like a coyote that he creeped everybody out.

"I'm sorry, Deronda," Nona said. "But that's how it happened. Did I cause some kind of problem?"

"No, this ain't no problem," Deronda said. "This is a goddamn disaster."

Dodson and Deronda entered Night Out, which was somewhere between a small club and a big bar. From Junior's perspective it made sense as a hangout. Too small and it had no cachet. Too big and Junior would be lost in the crowd. There was the usual dance floor, the usual DJ and ear-shattering rap music, the atmosphere dense with alcohol, weed, and sex.

"Brings back memories, don't it?" Dodson said.

"Yeah," she replied. "And not all of 'em are good."

144

Junior was holding court in the VIP area; a cluster of plush sofas, oversize ottomans, and low tables enveloped in pink light and haze from a fog machine. It looked like heaven on a sitcom. Junior was seated on a sofa, no doubt drinking his favorite drink, Parks Punch. It was a ghetto cocktail made up of vodka, Crystal Light lemonade powder, margarita mix, and Coca-Cola. Deronda couldn't think of a nastier combination. Seated next to Junior was Booze Lewis. He'd always been big and muscled up but now he looked like a giant bullfrog in a leather jacket and a Kangol cap.

There were the usual bunch of hoes and hangers-on, drinking and partying and trying too hard to look like they were having fun. Deronda remembered herself in that same scene, laughing too loud and buying cocktails she couldn't afford.

"I only met Junior once or twice," Deronda said. "What am I supposed to do?"

"Find out where he keeps his money," Dodson said.

"That's crazy. He might not even remember me."

"Tell you what. Walk over there backwards and see if his memory comes back."

Deronda made her way over to Junior. He looked the same, like a pug with cornrows, his sunglasses too big for his tiny head. He was dressed nice if you liked shiny green track suits, colossal gold chains, and four diamond studs in each ear. She wondered if he could hear straight.

She forced herself to smile. "Whassup, Junior?"

"And who might you be?" he said like he was offended. "Are you and I correlated or do we coexist in separate realities?"

Junior talked that way because he thought it made him seem smart, but to Deronda's ear, it sounded like he'd swallowed a dictionary sideways. She sat down next to him and crossed her legs. "You remember me. I'm Nona's friend, Deronda. I met you at a party and then at that club, the one over near the freeway?" Junior glanced at the burnished thigh bridging the space between them and looked her over again.

"On second thought," he said. "I do believe I retrospect our assignation. You was walkin' away and I retained an image of your morphology."

"That was me." She was tired of people talking about her booty, if that was what he was referring to. What was so fascinating about a hump on your back? If it was all that exciting they should go to the zoo and look at the damn camels.

"May I requisition a drink on your behalf?" Junior said.

"You may," Deronda said, edging a little closer. Before she could tell him what she wanted, he snapped his fingers at a passing waitress.

"Could you convey a Parks Punch to my counterpart?" he said. "And one for my eminence as well." The waitress blinked twice and moved off.

Booze was too wasted to say anything and sat there like one of the sofa cushions. Junior's phone buzzed. He looked at the caller ID, got up, and walked off a ways. She was starting to lose her nerve. Yes, she'd been with a long list of dog-ass losers but the idea of spending time with this little monster was beyond the beyond. She was about to get up when Michael Stokely and three other thugs showed up. Stokely was the former enforcer for the Crip Violators and scarier than ever. He wasn't as big as Booze but he was harder, more indestructible. You knew if he took off his shirt all you'd see was a stack of cinder blocks. He had evidently done some more time, his brown skin nearly black with prison tattoos, which hadn't lightened his mood any. He had the same look he'd always had, like he came here to kill somebody with malice of forethought. His three homeboys looked like they were at a casting call for merciless brutes. *These are the people who would come after you if Chester spilled the beans,* Deronda thought. The waitress brought the drinks. She took a sip and almost spit it out.

Junior came back and she turned on her brightest smile. "I missed you," she said.

"Please excuse my audacity. Business matters frequently demand my inattention."

"No problem. I understand completely."

Junior gave her his serious face, which was slightly better than a pug in heat. "Are you aware that in my opticals, you are the delineation of sexuality?"

"Thank you, Junior," Deronda said. "I am gratified by your commendation." *Two can play this game.*

"The adulation pertains to my selfhood." He put his hand on her knee.

"On no, the reimbursement is all mine," he said. She put her hand on his.

"I am satiated beyond my concepts."

She was getting queasy. It was easy to get Junior to hit on her but the only way to find out about his money was to go home with him. She finished her drink. "Junior, could I get another one of these?"

It was late. The lone lightbulb cast a pensive halo over the loft, darkness all around it. Grace was sitting on the futon with her arms around her knees, Isaiah standing with his hands in his front pockets. Neither had mentioned their night with Porkpie. Isaiah had saved her life and she had saved his and without acknowledgment, they knew this bond, this connection—so extraordinary and intimate—should forever be a secret.

At the moment, she was annoyed and giving him a hard time again. "How can I remember any more than I already do?" she said. "And I still don't get why looking into the past is going to help us find my mother." Isaiah knew why she was resisting but he had to get on with this.

"Just go with me on this, okay? It doesn't pan out, we're no worse off. Who was your mom's best friend?"

"There's no point in answering that question."

Isaiah believed in the adage *The best predictor of the future is the past,* but having to explain everything was a little insulting. He was a pro, that's why she'd come to him. "Grace, you hired me to do a job. Get out of my way and let me do it." Still, she pushed back.

"My mom's been missing for *ten years.* Those people are long gone."

"Grace," he said, not fucking around anymore. *"Who was your mom's best friend?"*

She was stunned for a moment. "Stephanie," she said. "I don't remember her last name. She was an artist too. She was a real ditz, but I think that's why Mom liked her." Grace got out her phone and showed him a picture of a woman about Sarah's age. She was wearing a Mad Hatter's hat, an orange sarong, and a bikini top, a Rubik's cube on a chain around her neck, mischief in her owlish eyes. She was sitting on a bright orange bicycle with a tail of long feathers like a peacock.

"I have no idea what that's about," Grace said.

"Does the color orange mean anything to you?" Isaiah asked. She shook her head. He went on. "Do you remember anything specific that involved your mom and Stephanie? Anything? It could be random."

"Um, yeah, sort of," she said. "I remember they went on trips together. I guess it sticks out because it pissed off my dad. Mostly what I remember is him yelling, her crying, and a lot of slamming doors."

"What was your dad angry about?"

"I don't know. I must have been what—seven years old? Oh, these are some of Mom's art pieces. She worked in different media." She showed Isaiah a short animated video of a strip club. It was intentionally blurry, ghostly strippers onstage, men watching and waving dollar bills. With startling suddenness, a stripper leapt at the camera, coming into sharp focus. She was

148

banshee-like and aiming a gun right at you. "Mom was angry a lot," Grace said.

Another photo showed a miniature house, a perfect house, like an ad for a real estate development called Oak Lane. It was painted all beige, even the doors and windows, and you could imagine that the rooms inside were beige and the people in them lived beige lives. "Yeah," Grace said. The house nearly filled the frame, but around it you could see it was set on a flat desert plain. Isaiah indicated a tiny, flea-size speck at the very edge.

"Do you see that?" he said.

"Yeah. Looks like dust on the lens."

"You said your mom and Stephanie took trips," Isaiah said. "Where did they go?"

"I don't know, but..." She showed him four photos of a van parked under the carport. In two of them, Sarah, Stephanie, and a guy in a straw cowboy hat were mugging for the camera. The women were in bikinis. In the second, an older guy in an orange T-shirt was on top of the van, arranging water cans. The sliding door was open, the orange bicycle with the feathered tail inside. In the fourth, the older guy was leaning against the bumper reading a newspaper. You could make out part of the headline: 37 GO. The rest of it hidden in the folds.

"Who took these pictures?" Isaiah said.

"I got them off my mom's phone."

"Do you still have it?"

"No. I tossed it a long time ago." Grace was restless and edgy, but he persisted. There were two words painted in orange on the side of the van. EVER AFTER. They were crude, like a sign for a garage sale.

"Ever After," he said. "What does that mean?"

"A band? A book title? A new kind of Ecstasy?" She was fucking around and Isaiah gave her a look. With a sigh, she did a quick search, Isaiah watching her small hands manipulate her phone. "There's a movie about Cinderella called *Ever After,*" she said dryly. "Is that what you're looking for?"

Isaiah let that go. "What else did your mom and dad fight about?"

She shrugged. "I don't know. Ordinary stuff—oh, there was Mom's friends. Dad hated them." She showed Isaiah a photo of Sarah, Stephanie, and a bunch of scruffy, happy people in the backyard, building something out of two-by-fours and plywood. There were tools, a sawhorse, buckets of paint, a couple of window frames, and building supplies scattered around.

"What were they building?" Isaiah said.

"Beats me."

She felt scrutinized. He knew her underwear size and what brand of soap she used, for Christ's sake. What else did he know? It was unnerving. He made you choose your words carefully and read between your own lines, and when he asked you questions, he listened *hard.* Another thing that hadn't happened in a while. Who actually paid attention these days? Who did she know that wasn't always waiting for their turn to speak? He was persistent too. He kept coming. There was no way to back him off. Should she tell him what happened? There was a part of her that wanted to but no, out of the question. She hadn't told anyone, not even Cherokee, and it wasn't any of Isaiah's business, no matter that he was trying to help her. It was obvious he cared for her, but he was keeping his feelings in check. She felt oddly ambivalent about that. It was a relief, but it made her anxious too. A sign her resolve was leaking. Forget it, she thought, maybe in some other life. Right now, she had to find her mom. There were important things they had to talk about.

TK called up to them. "Hey, you two? I ordered some Chinese food. Come on down and eat." She colored a bit, TK calling them *you two* as if they were a couple. If Isaiah noticed he didn't let on. They sat around a rickety card table next to TK's office. There was pork chow mein, egg rolls, beef with broccoli, and lemon chicken. They ate off paper plates and drank beer with frost on the bottles, Ruffin snorfling around for tidbits. Isaiah liked the way Grace dug right into her food, eating like a construction worker. He was far more fastidious.

"You guys making any progress doin' whatever it is you're doin'?" TK said.

Grace shrugged. "Some, I guess." Isaiah felt the words like a flu shot.

Grace and TK chatted about finding another catalytic converter for the GTI and if TK had seen *Transparent.* No, he said. He saw the commercials and preferred *The Walking Dead,* where the zombies were either men or women.

They talked about an incident that happened in a down-and-out section of North Miami. Charles Kinsey, a behavior therapist, was retrieving a patient, an autistic man who'd left the group home. Both men were African American. Officers encountered the pair while searching for a suicidal man who reportedly had a gun. The patient didn't have a gun—he had a toy truck that was clearly visible. The officers ordered the two men onto the ground. The patient was sitting, Kinsey was lying flat on his back with his hands in the air. Kinsey begged the officers not to shoot, telling them repeatedly that he was a therapist and that his patient was autistic and didn't have a gun, he had a toy truck. Inexplicably, an officer shot Kinsey. The officers put three pairs of handcuffs on him, rolled him over and left him there bleeding for twenty minutes.

"Bet that shit don't happen in Palm Beach," TK said.

Isaiah was envious, how TK and Grace could talk so easily while his conversations with her were like trading bricks.

"Okay, it's time," TK said.

"Time for what?" Isaiah said.

151

"Time for you to tell a joke."

Grace smiled and put her chopsticks down. "Tell a joke?" Isaiah said. "I don't know any jokes."

"Grace already told hers," TK said. "Now it's your turn." They looked at him expectantly. The pressure was terrible. He was the unfunniest person he'd ever known. The last time he'd made someone laugh was when Mrs. Marquez saw him fall off the roof and land in the bougainvillea.

"Well?" Grace said, obviously enjoying this. Thankfully, he remembered a joke a thief had told him on their way to the police station. He cleared his throat.

"Did you hear about the two guys who were arrested for stealing a calendar?"

"Can't say that I have," TK said.

"They both got six months." Isaiah smiled, hoping to encourage them, but they sat there like their portraits.

After an interminable pause, Grace said, "Good one." Then she excused herself and said she had to go. She drove away. He stood there, watching her turn signal blink. Why couldn't she let him in on it? For fuck's sake, he'd saved her life.

Deronda went home with Junior. His cologne was so strong it left a film on her skin. He hardly paid attention to the road, talking constantly, kicking the shit out of the English language. "Welcome to my reverence," he said as he opened his front door. Deronda thought she'd walked in on Sonny Corleone beating a man with a garbage can lid but it was the huge TV. She considered her place colorful and rambunctious but it was a nunnery compared to Junior's living room. There was more chrome than a dealership for lowriders and more zebra hide than she'd seen on the Discovery Channel. The sofa looked like the dominant stallion.

"Please. Make yourself convenient," Junior said. He killed the sound on the TV and put on some Drake, the lyrics about being bigger than you've ever done it.

"Could I use the bathroom?" Deronda said.

"Down the hall and make a starboard on your left."

The bathroom looked like James Brown and Lady Gaga had done each other's hair and makeup. Deronda counted six different kinds of tile in six different colors. The shower head looked like an airplane engine. "Oh my muthafuckin' God," she said. Right there on the counter was a shiny black dildo that must have been cast from a mastodon or the Lincoln Memorial. She turned on the tap and called Dodson. "I can't do this," she said. "Even if I break him off a piece he's not gonna tell me where his money's at."

"He don't have to tell you," Dodson said. "It's there in the house. You know he's not gonna let his cash out of his sight. Search around for it."

"Search around for it? Where? In his sock drawer?" But Dodson had already ended the call. Junior knocked on the door.

"What's happening in there? I hope you're not having trouble with your rectal operations."

"No, I'm fine," Deronda said. "I'll be out in a minute." Wait a second, did he say *rectal* operations? Was he out there taking the cap off a family-size tube of K-Y? Oh hey-ell no. She'd kill herself before she let that happen. The problem was, she couldn't look around unless he was asleep, and he wouldn't fall asleep until she had exhausted him—which she was perfectly capable of doing, assuming she didn't beat him to death with that dildo.

She took a bunch of deep breaths, pulled the hem of her dress down, and went back to the living room. Junior was lounging on the sofa in a shiny red-and-gold bathrobe that was quilted like a puff jacket. He was still wearing his sunglasses, his bony legs were crossed, his uncut toenails like mussel shells. He patted the space next to him.

"Ensconce yourself and let us celebrate our amalgamation," he said.

She sat down and he put his arm around her. "You have a beautiful place, Junior," she said. "I've never seen anything like it."

He smiled at her like a pig on garbage day. Suddenly, he pulled her close and kissed her. Junior was a notorious womanizer. You'd think he'd know how to kiss instead of ramming his tongue into her mouth. It felt like a nightcrawler wriggling down her esophagus. She pulled away before she choked. He started groping her, nibbling her neck, whispering nonsensical nothings in her ear. He slipped his hand under her skirt and slid it up her thigh. She clamped her hand over it. "I'm sorry, Junior. I should have told you this before, but I'm on the rag and I bleed like I been stabbed in the cooch."

"That is certainly a fiasco on your part," he replied, "but there are other mechanisms for gratifying your due diligence." She was trying to figure out what that meant when he said, "Get on your knees, bitch."

CHAPTER EIGHT

Praise God

Richter was pissed, Sarah's daughter getting him to let his guard down. He'd see her bleeding out of her ears before this was over. And that goddamn Isaiah. He was a fucking menace. The problem now? If he couldn't find Sarah he needed another way to fuck over Walczak. The officious dimwit was giving him shit again.

"Flyers?" he said, incredulous. "That's your idea, Richter? You want to put up *flyers?* Why don't we beat on bongos or send up smoke signals? Ridiculous!"

"You want people to look for Grace, don't you?" Richter said. "How else can we let them know in that neighborhood? Robocalls? Your technology is useless here."

The whole team waited, Walczak in the hot seat once again. He mumbled, "I'll have the office make them up."

They came out nice. On brightly colored paper with a photo of Grace from her website. The caption, HAVE YOU SEEN THIS GIRL? $5,000 REWARD.

"We'll have everybody in the area looking for her," Richter said.

"Yeah," Jimenez agreed. "Poor people are into rewards."

"I still don't think they'll work," Walczak mumbled.

* * *

Isaiah drove through the neighborhood, tearing the flyers down. The crew was following him again. By now, they knew he was deliberately eluding them and they tried different techniques. They used rental cars, changing their silhouettes with caps and wigs and different kinds of sunglasses. They changed the formation of the follow cars. They'd put a GPS tracker on his car, which he found and threw in a passing garbage truck. And then one morning, they were gone. Had they given up on him? Did this mean they'd found Sarah? Maybe. Isaiah drove into a parking garage, wound his way up to the top, and immediately went down again. If they were tailing him he'd see them on their way up. Nothing. He drove down long isolated straightaways. He walked into crowds, checked window reflections, and took selfies to see who was behind him. He called TK to see if Grace was okay and everything was fine. Had Walczak caught Sarah? Was that why they no longer needed to follow him? To be sure, he drove over to the West Ocean Condos, one of the tallest buildings in Long Beach. Twenty-nine stories. He followed the FedEx man inside, took the elevator, and got out on the roof. He looked over the parapet and saw a four-rotor industrial drone about ten stories down, hovering over the building entrance waiting for him to come out.

He went back to his car. He drove to a culvert near his house. He parked, climbed the fence, and walked into the big drainpipe. He had to stoop and his sneakers got wet. Eventually, the drainpipe fed into the LA River. The drone operator would anticipate where he was going and hover over the exit while Walczak and his team watched the entrance. Isaiah went a couple of hundred feet and found an escape ladder. It led up to a manhole cover that opened into an alley. He'd found it when he was running from two Asian Boyz with guns. He climbed up the ladder and took the bus to the wrecking yard. He'd come back for his car later.

The team was pissed off and frustrated. They met at La Frida, where Richter said the carnitas were the best he'd ever had and the salsas were homemade. Walczak wouldn't eat Mexican food with somebody else's mouth. He could feel everyone blaming him, the CIA hotshot deked out by some homeboy gumshoe. He got the blame and that fucking Richter got the glory.

"I told you he was smart, didn't I?" Richter said.

"Yes, Richter, you told us," Walczak said wearily. "You're a fucking genius, okay? You're a goddamn fucking Einstein that makes me coffee and washes my car." Richter shrugged and went back to his carnitas. The others looked away, probably wondering why an ex-cop would put up with this shit.

Owens held up her empty margarita glass. "Over here." Everyone looked at her. "It's only my second."

"The money drop is Friday," Walczak said. "We have to find Sarah and Grace before then and need I remind you that your necks are on the line too?"

"Well, you're in charge, Mr. CEO," Hawkins said. "Tell us. What's the plan?"

Walczak sipped his ice water and wondered if the help here washed their hands. A protracted pause. Forks clinked, there were chewing noises and the occasional throat clearing. Walczak felt the tension rise, everyone expecting him to say something and knowing he was out of his depth. Richter and the fucking Mexican were smirking and eating at the same time. They loved torturing him. They knew it was an impossible task, finding two people in a city of millions, assuming they were in the city at all.

"We're waiting," Jimenez said, still with that fucking smirk.

Owens smiled loopily over her margarita. "Hope it's not too complicated. We country girls are simple folks."

"I have to think about it," Walczak said.

"Think about it?" Hawkins said. "What have you been doing all this time? Daydreaming about your polo ponies?"

Jimenez wiped his mouth with a napkin and threw it down on his plate, the way he did it telling you he had something to say. "There's a way to find them," he said.

"Oh really?" Walczak replied. "Are you some kind of clairvoyant? You can see them in your crystal ball? You can read their minds?"

"I don't need no crystal ball and I don't need to be no mind reader." Jimenez picked at his teeth with a thumbnail. "I don't need to be nothing but me."

Dodson was in line at Mickey D's. Nothing like a Filet-O-Fish and a Shamrock Shake to ease your worries. Deronda hadn't come through. She said when Junior pushed her head into his lap she grabbed his sack and twisted it like a rusty faucet. When she got home, she washed her hands with bleach and disinfected the steering wheel in her car. She said she'd never put her fingers in her mouth for the rest of her life.

How did this happen? Dodson wondered. How had his life come down to something as fucked up as this? It hadn't started out this way. He'd been a good kid. A smart kid. He remembered being eleven years old and bringing home a report card with a solid B average and getting hugged by his mother and sister and high-fived by his father, who was home on leave. Joining a gang had never occurred to him until his father retired, came home from Afghanistan with two Purple Hearts, and got a job drinking full-time. A literal gloom fell over the house. His father liked the lights low or no lights at all. He'd sit in the La-Z-Boy, sipping cheap vodka with the TV on and the sound off. Maybe that was what his brain was doing, Dodson thought, reducing the world to crazy images. An easier place to leave behind.

Dodson's father had been his hero, but now he barely spoke and when he did it was usually in anger. Someone else was to blame for everything. His drinking, his rages, his joblessness, the solid B average that was steadily declining. Dodson's mother was a shadow, as if making herself tangible would set her husband off. Dodson was afraid of him and wondered if it was his fault that everything had changed.

Dodson spent more time out of the house with his new friends, some local hoodrats who smoked weed, got into fights, jacked people, stole anything that wasn't under the direct gaze of a security guard. They only went to school when there wasn't anything else to do. Dodson joined the Crip Violators, a gang that sold dope, got into shootouts, and went to adult prisons. In an infamous gun battle with the Locos, a bystander named Flaco was shot in the head and suffered brain damage. He was ten years old. Dodson felt responsible. He quit the gang and began his career as a hustler.

He partnered up with Alonzo and worked out a Ponzi scheme. They sold shares in housing developments in Tustin that paid twenty percent. You could even visit one. The manager was in on the scam. Eventually, some unhappy investors went to the police and Dodson did a bid in Vacaville. It's one thing to watch prison documentaries on MSNBC. It's a whole other trip to be there, locked up with a thousand or so ruthless felons, most of them gang members; sleeping in bunk beds lined up like used cars and wiping your ass with toilet paper that still had wood chips in it and eating a corn dog, frozen succotash, and an orange for lunch. Dodson saw an inmate make a pizza out of a food packet from home. The crust was made from crushed Doritos and ramen seasoning. The ingredients were put in the empty Doritos bag, water was added, and everything was smushed into a dough and rolled out with a plastic shampoo bottle. You cooked it by putting the bag under your pillow for fifteen minutes. When it was done, you topped it with squeeze cheese and summer sausage you cut up with your prison ID card and wah-lah, pizza. Not exactly Domino's but it was the best in the California prison system.

When Dodson got out he went to stay with his parents in Oakland. His father was sneering and self-righteous but still in the La-Z-Boy, drinking vodka with the TV on and the sound off. Dodson's sister Lavinia was off to college. His mother was overjoyed to see him. She cooked him his favorite meals and fixed up a room for him and asked him what he was doing. He said he was back in school taking classes to be a paramedic. She probably didn't believe him, but the idea of it made her happy. He didn't tell her about Vacaville.

He'd been there a week when his father said, "You can't stay here, you know. You're a grown man and I got enough mouths to feed."

"I never intended to stay," Dodson said. "I just came by to see how y'all were doing."

His father sneered. "We're doing fine—and now you can go back to your paramedic school."

Dodson borrowed some money from his mother and returned to East Long Beach. He partnered up with Alonzo again. They tried to rob small-time drug dealers like Omar Little did on *The Wire,* but they weren't Omar Little on *The Wire* and usually got shot at before the robbery even started. Dodson fenced stolen goods he bought from junkies and sold fake Social Security cards and cars that weren't his and Gucci handbags that weren't real. He made money, but it wasn't sustainable and the fear of going back to the joint was scarier than ever. He'd never really had time to think about what he was doing or where he was going, always caught up in the fight for survival. He went to stay with his Auntie May, temporarily he told her, until he got a job. But slouched on her velvet sofa surrounded by dark furniture and the smell of potpourri, without weed to smoke or liquor to drink or money to party with, there was nothing else to do *but* think. Truth be told, he was running out of energy for the game. Maybe it was time to retire. There's no such thing as a new leaf, he thought. Turn yourself over.

He went to see a friend of Auntie May's, a man named Cosell who ran an employment service. The waiting room was crowded, noisy, and full of people whose résumés could fit on a Post-it.

"Correct me if I'm wrong," Cosell said, "but you've *never* held a regular job?"

"When I was in high school I waited tables in a restaurant," Dodson said.

"For how long?"

"Three days. They caught me stealing tips."

"And since then you've been—"

"I was in pharmaceuticals for a while," Dodson said, "and after I got out of the joint I was straight-up hustling." It sounded pitiful when you said it out loud. He went on, "Look, I know I ain't the best prospect you ever had, but I'm quick, I pay attention, I can read people, and I could sell a Confederate flag to the niggas on my block. All I need is a chance." Cosell leaned back in his chair and seemed to think about it. Dodson got up to leave. "I appreciate your time."

"Don't be in such a hurry," Cosell said. "There are all kinds of people who are looking for an experienced hustler. You'd be surprised."

The next day, Dodson became an employee of Pinpoint Marketing Services, a telemarketing operation located in the windowless basement of an office building. Operators with headset mikes and desperate faces were pitching with smiling voices, the din filling the room. The supervisor, Casper Agnew, was a sullen, pockmarked white boy with a curved snout like a sandpiper and a collection of polo shirts with logos nobody had ever seen before. An ox, a shoe, a fire hydrant, a sprig of poison sumac. "This job is not hard," he said like he couldn't believe anyone would think it was. "All you have to do is read the script. If the customer asks a question, read the script. If he says he wants to think about it, read the script. If he says he has to ask his wife—"

"Read the script," Dodson said.

"You catch on fast, I like that," Casper said. Dodson couldn't tell if he was kidding or not. "Okay, let's say you get somebody on the phone," Casper continued. "The first thing you say is—" He was suddenly ecstatic, the transformation was Oscar-worthy. "Congratulations, Mrs. Smith! You've won the California Starlight Sweepstakes Grand Prize and you are the owner of a brand-new Mercedes convertible!" In an instant, Casper was sullen again. "Like that, you know? Like you're really happy for them."

"And all they have to do is pay shipping and handling?" Dodson said.

"Shipping and handling are included, but there is a three-hundred-and-forty-nine-dollar import tax. The cars come from the factory in Germany."

"If you don't give 'em something isn't that mail fraud?" Dodson said.

"It would be, but we're legit here," Casper said like he almost believed it. He nodded at a stack of small boxes containing brand-new Mercedes toy cars. "They're real craftsmen over there, don't you think? And look, people are going to give you all kinds of sob stories about why they can't spend the money. I lost my job, I'm living on food stamps, I'm at my mother's funeral—doesn't matter. Be merciless, and whatever you do don't let them off the hook."

"I've never let anyone off the hook in my entire life," Dodson said.

"A lot of rookies say that, but when the chips are down and some old lady is crying about eating cat food for dinner they fold like a Denver omelet."

"You don't know me yet," Dodson said. "But I don't fold."

Dodson made hundreds of calls but mostly got voice mail and hang-ups. He would have done better if he wasn't restricted to the script, and his commissions weren't much more than he'd make flipping burgers. All of the people he scammed were elderly. Many of them couldn't remember entering the sweepstakes because they never had. "You're Bessie May Atkins, aren't you?" Dodson would say. "At 4455 Grove Avenue? Well, I have your application right here in my hand and by the way, did you have a color preference for the Mercedes?" Then they'd say something like *Oh my goodness, my memory isn't what it used to be* and then they'd tell you their credit card number, going slow so you wouldn't miss anything. There was one old dude named Ezra Sanders who thought he'd be smart and asked for a picture of the car. Casper was ready for situations like this. He had a photo of his own Mercedes draped with colorful streamers and a program on his laptop for adding titles. This one said: CONGRATULATIONS TO GRAND PRIZE WINNER EZRA SANDERS! Ezra sent the money via Western Union.

Dodson hated the job. It wasn't any different than what he was doing before: taking money from people who couldn't afford it. The definition of a street hustle. He felt even worse about himself. He didn't belong here. He wasn't a loser like the rest of these bums. He was special, he just didn't know what his specialness was. He thought about going back into the crack business but that took more blind determination than he had these days.

It was the end of his shift and Dodson made his last call of the day. He tried to drum up some enthusiasm and dialed.

"Hello?" the voice said. A young man from the sound of it. Something off about his speech.

"Matthew Bunce?" Dodson said. "Is this Matthew Bunce of 338 Latimer Drive?"

"Yeah, that's me."

"Matthew, this is Ted Rogers from the California Starlight Sweepstakes and I have wonderful news! You are this month's grand prize winner and the proud of owner of a brand-new Mercedes convertible!" There was a crashing sound, followed by arms and legs getting tangled up in a table or a chair. "Are you all right?" Dodson said. "Matthew, can you hear me?"

"Sorry," Matthew said. "What did you say before? I won a prize?"

"Yes, you did, Mr. Bunce. You won the *grand* prize. A brand-new Mercedes convertible direct from the factory in Germany!" There was a pause. "Hello? Are you there?"

"I'm not allowed to drive a car," Matthew said.

"You're under sixteen?"

"No, I'm nineteen and four months."

Dodson was starting to get the picture. Matthew's score on the Stanford-Binet was a little below average. So what? he thought. A mark was a mark and he was working on commissions.

"We've got all kinds of other prizes," Dodson said, going off script. "Is there something else you want? We've got iPads, PlayStations, TVs, all kinds of stuff." He could hear Matthew breathing, tense, like he didn't want to say it. "What is it, Matthew? You can tell me."

"A dog. I want a dog."

"We got all kinds of dogs," Dodson said, smooth as heavy cream. "Big ones, little ones, any kind you want. Do you have a credit card?"

"No."

"Well, I'm sorry, Matthew. There's a mandatory canine documentation fee and we only take credit cards."

"Oh, okay," Matthew said. Dodson was about to hang up when Matthew added, "I can sign checks now. I have a trust fund but

I'm only allowed to write one if Nana can't because of her arthritis. Nice talking to you, Ted."

"Hold on there, Matthew," Dodson said. "Did you say *trust fund?*"

"Yeah, that's where we get our money. Nana says it's a lot."

"You know what? We got some new dogs that just came in." Dodson put his hand over his mike and said to the operators around him, "Bark!" They looked at him, puzzled. "I got a live one! Bark, goddammit! *Trust fund.*" The operators started barking like a pack of strays. "You hear that, Matthew? You can have any one you want." Drawn by the commotion and the words *trust fund,* Casper and the other operators drifted over. Dodson put the call on speaker.

"Do you have a beagle?" Matthew said excitedly. "A brown-and-white one?"

"Wait a second, let me see," Dodson said. "No, that's a Doberman... that's some kind of sheepdog—wait, there's one. A beagle, Matthew, and it's brown and white!"

"Oh my God, oh my God!" Matthew exclaimed. Casper was frowning, like he might put a stop to it.

"Now tell me about this trust fund. You said you can write checks?" Dodson asked.

"Uh-huh."

"Is Nana home all day?"

"Yeah. Except when she goes to play bridge."

"When's the next time she's playing?"

"Tomorrow," Matthew said. "The driver picks her up at three o'clock."

"All right, listen closely now. According to the contest rules, this has to be a secret. Break the rules and you don't get the beagle."

"Don't worry, Ted," Matthew said solemnly. "I'll keep it a secret from everybody."

Dodson gave him instructions about writing the check and made him write them down.

"I'll call you back tomorrow at ten after three," Dodson said.

"Okay, Ted. I'll talk to you tomorrow!"

The call ended. Casper and the operators broke into applause. "Sorry I didn't stick to the script, Casper," Dodson said. "I hope you don't mind."

Casper shook his hand. "You're the best salesman I've ever had."

Dodson couldn't sleep. He should have been excited, but all he felt was an overwhelming sense of doom, like he was standing on the edge of the Empire State Building and his reward was on the pavement a hundred stories below. He got up, watched TV, read the paper, and drank some of Auntie May's Chateau LaSalle Pink Sauternes. He fell asleep as the sun came up.

At 3:10 that afternoon, Dodson called Matthew, the operators gathered around, Casper standing by with his cell phone.

"What's up, Matthew?" Dodson said in that breezy way he had. "How's everything?"

"Have you still got my dog?" Matthew said.

"Yes, he's right here and he can't wait to see you." One of the operators panted and mewled. "Is your nana gone?"

"She just left."

"Do you have the check?"

"Yes, Ted, I have it."

"Read it back to me," Dodson said.

"I made it out to Pinpoint Marketing Services," Matthew said proudly. Dodson made him spell it. Matthew continued. "Five-zero-zero-zero-zero dot zero zero. Then I signed it at the bottom." Dodson and Casper had argued about the amount. If two people could live off the trust fund and they had a driver, there had to be big bucks in there. On the other hand, if the check was too big, the bank might question it and call Nana.

"You did good, Matthew," Dodson said. Casper was on his cell talking to somebody. He nodded. "Okay, Matthew," Dodson went on. "A man's gonna come to the door and I want you to give him the check. I'll drop by later and bring you the dog."

"Nana said not to open the door for anybody."

"It's all right, we're friends, aren't we?" Dodson said. There was a pause. "Matthew, are you okay?" He heard sniffling. Matthew was crying.

"I don't have any friends," he said. "But now I'll have my beagle...and you."

There was a sudden emptiness in Dodson's chest, like an earth mover had rolled through and shoveled out his heart. The doorbell rang. "That's him, Matthew," Dodson said, his voice notably softer.

"Okay, I'm gonna open the door now." The chain rattled, a door opened.

A man's friendly voice said, "Hi, you must be Matthew. I'm Ted's buddy. He told me all about you. Is that check for me?"

"Should I give it to him?" Matthew asked. Dodson sat there, looking down at his hands. He'd negotiated a fifty percent commission. Casper grumbled but twenty-five grand was good money for one phone call.

"Answer him," Casper breathed. "What's wrong with you? *Answer him!*" Dodson didn't move, the operators holding their breath, urging him on with their eyes.

"Ted?" Matthew said. "Are you there?"

The man said, "Come on, kid, hand over the check. You want the dog, don't you?"

"Ted?"

"Close the door, Matthew," Dodson said.

"What the hell are you doing?" Casper said, the operators muttering their alarm.

"Close the door?" Matthew said. "But you said—"

Dodson cut him off. "I said close the door, Matthew."

"Are you crazy?" Casper said.

167

"Hey, stop fooling around and gimme the check," the man demanded.

"SHUT THE GODDAMN DOOR!" Dodson roared. "DO IT NOW, MATTHEW!" The door slammed.

"You don't have to be mad at me," Matthew whimpered.

"I'm not mad at you," Dodson said. "It was my fault, that was the wrong man. Now tear up the check and throw it away."

"What about my dog?"

"I'll get back to you," Dodson said, and he ended the call.

"You're fired." Casper looked up at the ceiling tiles for an explanation, and then he walked away. The operators dispersed and went back to reading their scripts. Dodson got up, put on his hoodie, and left.

The house was a two-story traditional in Bixby Knolls. A young man with Down's syndrome opened the door and saw the cardboard box set on the stoop. Wary, he opened it and cried out joyfully as he lifted the beagle puppy into his arms and hugged it. Dodson waited until Matthew went back inside, and then he drove away.

That was the end of it. The end of the game. And for the first time since he was eleven years old, Dodson thought about the future. What would he do next week, next month, next year, and the years after that? All he saw was himself in rags, begging for change and living under a bridge. He felt pitiful and stupid. He *was* pitiful and stupid. The swaggering, too-cool hustler that the ladies loved and that was always flush, reduced to living in his Auntie May's second bedroom, cleaning her house and cooking her supper. He went out but only to fool her into thinking he was looking for a job. The whole time he was convinced people knew he was menial and useless. It went on like that for weeks. Auntie May was getting suspicious, Dodson feeling pressure to the point where he was going to leave and live on the street. Then he met Cherise and his orbit reversed and he spun off into deep space as uncertain as he'd ever been; Cherise guiding, encouraging, and yelling at him until he crash-landed in a life he'd not only never imagined but had never occurred to him. He was a husband and a father with a loving wife and a beautiful baby boy and all of it was threatened by Chester fucking Babbitt.

Cherise was taking a bath. Her mother had gone home and Dodson was carrying Micah in his arms. He smelled like milk and Motherlove. Dodson couldn't believe the baby was so tiny and fragile and seemed to weigh less than his seahorse pajamas. For all the trouble it took to get him here he should be a full-grown man with a job and a driver's license.

"How you doin', kid?" Dodson said in his inside voice. "You don't worry 'bout nothin', you hear me? Your old man got it all under control. Ain't nothing he can't handle. I faced down nig— people ten times worse than Chester. You watch and see. I'll take care of everything."

Dodson was already in bed when Cherise came out of the bathroom wearing nothing but her wedding ring and toenail polish. He was about to say something, but she shushed him and slipped under the covers. Over the next hour and a half, Dodson said *Praise God* so many times she had to tell him to stop. Afterward, when they were breathing normally again and the sweat had dried, she said, "Did you enjoy yourself, Juanell?"

"Did I *enjoy* myself? I'm not sure. I don't remember nothing but gunfire, a couple of tsunamis, and floating up to heaven."

"Would you like that to happen again?" she said.

"Yes, I would."

"Then tell me what's been troubling you or the next time you float up to heaven it'll be for real."

Dodson explained about Chester, the blackmail, and Junior.

Cherise looked at him for what seemed like a long time. "You are incredible, Dodson," she said, not in a nice way. "You are really incredible."

"Yes, I know."

"Did you tell Isaiah?"

"No."

"Why not?"

"I messed up and I want to fix this on my own."

Cherise sighed. "I know you better than you know yourself, you know that, don't you?"

"Yes, I know," Dodson replied regretfully.

"The reason you haven't told Isaiah is because you don't want to bring up that shameful part of your history. Isn't that true?"

"Yes, that's true." He crossed his eyes and saw himself laid bare. A cheap watch with the case removed, all his moving parts in the open for Cherise to criticize and tinker with. She rolled over on top of him, the warmth of her titties on his chest.

"You are my everlasting love, Juanell, but sometimes you're so stupid I want to pound a nail in your head. Now I want you to call Isaiah, do you hear me? Chester could endanger me and endanger our baby. Is that what you want?"

"No. But I want to talk to Chester one more time," Dodson said.

"And right after that you'll call Isaiah?"

"I will. I promise."

She wiggled around a little. "You up for another round?"

"Can you imagine?" Phaedra said as she and Gilberto entered Isaiah's living room. "That horrible boy, Malik, had the nerve to say I wasn't black enough."

"What did you say?" Gilberto asked.

"I said I was as black as midnight in Muddy Waters's basement and furthermore, wearing big white T-shirts and overpriced sneakers and following every sentence with *Know what I'm sayin'?* didn't qualify him as anything but a lemming."

"Well, for once we agree. Of all the people, Malik gets to define who is and isn't black? If it was up to him, being black would mean singing the national anthem as a rap song and throwing up gang signs at your graduation—oh, good morning, Mr. Quintabe."

"Good morning," Isaiah said. "How did the quarterfinals go?"

"We came in second place. Thanks to Phaedra's boyfriend, *Greg.*"

"Oh, will you give it a rest?" Phaedra said. "My God, Greg missed *one* question."

"No. He missed *the* question. What do you see in him anyway?"

"He's smart, cute, and quite an athlete. He's been swimming competitively since he was seven. Does that answer your question?"

While Isaiah made the espresso, Gilberto said, "We have a number of things to report, sir. Like everyone these days, Vicente left a trail of footprints on social media. He doesn't have his own Facebook page but his organization—"

"It's a gang," Phaedra said. "Sureños Locos 13 is a *gang.*"

Gilberto ignored her and continued. "There are lots of photos of the *gang* smoking marijuana, showing off illegal firearms, and so forth. Most of the comments referenced Vicente's personality and its similarity to female pudenda, or were threats on his life. However, we did find a number of entries made by a girl named Josefina Soto. They were all in the same vein. Vicente is hot, Vicente has a nice body, did you know I don't have a boyfriend etcetera, etcetera, and at one point they agreed to hook up. We think Josefina could be harboring Vicente."

"According to her page," Phaedra interjected, "Josefina is single, parties a lot, and—"

"She works at Subway," Gilberto reinterjected. Isaiah thought they were worse than him and Dodson. Gilberto continued, "There are seven Subway restaurants in the Long Beach area. We'll have the correct one identified by the end of business today."

"How?" Isaiah said.

"There's a teachers' conference. We're getting out of school early. Subway employees work two shifts. Eight to three and three to eleven. A club member will arrive at each restaurant a little before three. Whether Josefina is leaving or arriving, we'll see her."

"Smart," Isaiah said, smiling. "Remember the rules, okay? You see her, you call me. Nothing beyond that."

"Not to worry, Mr. Quintabe," Gilberto said. "Your rules will be obeyed and no laws will be broken."

As they went out the door, Phaedra said, "Did you actually say *no laws will be broken?*"

"Excuse me, I forgot. You and *Greg* are regular outlaws. I think I saw your wanted posters in the post office."

"And what's with the *end of business?* What business?"

"*My* business, thank you very much," Gilberto said. "And by the way, would you like to study at my house tonight?"

"Sorry, I can't. Greg and I are robbing a bank."

There was something else on Josefina's Facebook page that Phaedra and Gilberto hadn't discussed with the other club members. In one of the pictures, Josefina was sitting on a parking block behind a Subway restaurant, smoking and giving the finger to the photographer. In the background, you could see the top of a billboard advertising a movie, *Guardians of the Galaxy.* That billboard was right across the street from the restaurant on Long Beach Boulevard. The only question now was whether Josefina worked mornings or evenings. They waited across the street.

"We should have told the others," Gilberto said. "This isn't fair."

"It's our case," Phaedra replied. "We should get the glory."

Gilberto didn't reply. A little after three, Josefina came out wearing her uniform and a look on her face like she'd just escaped a flogging. She walked north on Long Beach Boulevard.

"I'll call Isaiah," Gilberto said. Seeing Josefina in the flesh made him anxious.

"What for?" Phaedra said. "We don't know if Vicente is staying with her or not. Oh look, she went past the bus stop."

"And that's important because—"

"What's the matter with you?" she said. "Are you not eating carbs again? It means she's walking home. We can follow her."

"I don't think so," Gilberto said, actually taking a few steps back. "Remember the rules? We take no action without Mr. Quintabe's expressed permission."

"No action vis-à-vis Vicente," Phaedra said. "Now don't be such a tight-ass and come on."

"I'm not a tight-ass—and that's a very vulgar expression."

Josefina led them to a small clapboard house with a sheet of plywood over the front window and a dried-out lawn. "She makes minimum wage so it can't be her place," Phaedra said. "Her parents', most likely."

"Good, we've got her address. We can call Isaiah now and let him take over."

"We don't know if Vicente's in there or not. Why waste Isaiah's time? I'm going to stay awhile. If you want to go, go."

"Did I say I was going?" Gilberto replied. "No, I didn't, and in the future, I'd appreciate it if you didn't put words in my mouth." They watched awhile, bored and restless, self-conscious about being out in the open. It was a sweltering day, Gilberto complaining that he hadn't applied sunscreen.

"My skin is very sensitive," he said defensively. "And this is turning out to be a big nothing." Josefina came out of the house and walked off down the street.

"Great, she's gone," Phaedra breathed. "It's time to take action."

"Action? What action?"

"There are no cars around and as far as I can tell, no one is home. I'm going to take a quick look-see."

Gilberto was flabbergasted. "A look-see? A *look-see?*"

"Will you please stop repeating what I say?"

"The things you say are so nonsensical they bear repeating, and we are *not* taking a quick *look-see*. This is a clear violation of Mr. Quintabe's rules and furthermore, someone might be in there sleeping or watching TV. We have no way of knowing."

"I need a lookout." Phaedra eyed him like a promising candidate.

Gilberto was resolute. "No. I refuse and that's final."

"Okay, suit yourself. I'll call Greg."

Phaedra had two packages of Oreos and a box of Fig Newtons under her arm, Gilberto reminding her that he was recording them as an expense. She rang the bell. "Hello?" she called out. "I'm selling Girl Scout cookies. They're on sale, fifty percent off." No answer. She smiled brightly into the peephole. "I said they're fifty percent off!" No answer. She glanced back at Gilberto, standing nervously behind a palm tree. "I'm sorry, I got that wrong," she went on. "They're actually *seventy-five* percent off! You can't beat that, now can you?" Again, nothing. She trudged down the stoop. "This is very disappointing."

"Can we go now?" Gilberto said, coming out of hiding. "I have a test to study for."

"The computer science test? My God, you could *give* that test. Wait, I want to check something." She went back up the stoop and turned the doorknob. "It's open!"

Gilberto was aghast. "That means someone's home!"

"Josefina forgot to lock it."

"In *this* neighborhood?" Gilberto said. "People put locks on their cats. Don't you get it? Someone's home!"

"I want to take a look," Phaedra said. "All I need is a clue, like a child's toy or something."

174

"No. I draw the line. Call Greg if you want to, but I'm not going."

"Fine, stay here," she said, hesitating a moment before adding, *"Chicken."*

They crept in together. "This is positively the most idiotic thing I've ever done in my short but accomplished life," Gilberto whispered. "This could cost me a scholarship, a career—my neck."

"Shut *up,*" Phaedra whispered back.

"We need a cover story."

"For what?"

"For why we're in someone else's house," he said.

Phaedra handed him the cookies. "Say you're a Girl Scout. If you see someone coming, whistle."

"Whistle? Did you say—"

"Gilberto!"

Phaedra tiptoed into the hallway. She hadn't been this unnerved since she rode her bicycle without a helmet all the way home from Gilberto's house. A clock was ticking. It was obnoxiously loud. Cautiously, she approached a doorway. Ever so slowly, she peeked in. There was a messy bed and unisex laundry but no indication of Vicente or a child. She crept forward to another door, took another peek. A woman as old as the pyramids at Teotihuacán was asleep in a rocking chair, her chin on her chest, unpleasant stains on her robe. Phaedra went on, past a bathroom that smelled of shampoo and Lysol. That damn clock was getting louder, ticktocking her nerves to bits. Any second she expected to hear Gilberto whistling, assuming he hadn't wimped out and gone home. *Oh my God, I'm sweating.* She never sweated. She didn't even wear deodorant. She hesitated. What if Vicente returned? He was a member of the Sureños Locos 13. *A gang.* This was a stupid idea, she decided, but there was only one more door. Take a look or leave while she still could? She'd come this far, she thought, and she wasn't about to let Gilberto win the day. She peeked in and gasped. "Oh no," she said. She turned around to run but the old woman was standing right there in her gray bathrobe and hazy eyes and her lips curled in over her toothless gums. Phaedra yelped and nearly jumped out of her pumps.

The old woman rasped, "Qué haces aquí?"

"Sorry," Phaedra said as she blew past her. "I'm all out of cookies."

CHAPTER NINE
Tell Them Everything

It was late and Chester and Sylvia were on the pier in Rainbow Lagoon. It was high tide in a high wind, breakers crashing against the pier, hissing as they retreated into the dark; the damp air smelling of salt and the tar on the pilings. There was no one around, the businesses closed up tight. The area looked like it was waiting for a hurricane.

"I'm freezing!" Sylvia said, clutching her white rabbit-fur jacket to her throat. "I want to go back!"

Chester's teeth were chattering. "N-not now, my love, just a little l-l-longer. The fresh air is b-b-bracing, wouldn't you say?"

"This is ridiculous!" Sylvia shouted. "I'm going back!" Chester was leaning over the railing. He pointed. "Look, darling, it's Ichthys!" Ichthys, Chester had learned, was the pagan fish symbol for the Great Mother Goddess and represented the outline of her vulva, and goddesses of any kind were always of interest. He didn't know how Sylvia got herself over the railing, but there she was, plunging headlong into the black, undulating sea, flailing her arms and yelling something that sounded like *Fuck you, Chester! A curse on your—*

Chester got an equity loan on Sylvia's condo, remodeled the

shop, expanded his inventory, and did more advertising, but the uptick in revenue was hardly worth the trouble. And then the police opened an investigation into Sylvia's accident. Two homicide detectives called Chester in for questioning.

"Why did you decide to go for a walk in the middle of the night?" the bald one asked.

"My wife and I were vampires in another life." Chester grinned to show his teeth. "The night is our milieu."

"Uh-huh," said the second bald detective. "Well, how did five-foot, one-inch Mrs. Vampire manage to fall over a chest-high railing?"

"She wanted to see Ichthys."

They grilled him for three hours. He thought he was pretty convincing, but when they directly accused him of killing Sylvia he asked for a lawyer. The cheapest defense attorney he could find was a grubby little shyster who advertised on bus benches and had a grubby little office on the wrong side of Seventh Street. Nevertheless, for a murder case he wanted a ten-thousand-dollar retainer and promised there'd be more costs if they went to trial. Chester didn't have ten thousand dollars and that's when he remembered Nona telling the story about Deronda, Dodson, and Isaiah robbing Junior. A record search revealed their financial situations. Not promising, but Isaiah was a neighborhood icon with a reputation for being clever, creative, and relentless. Chester didn't want to deal directly with someone they called IQ, so he went to Dodson, who would naturally tell Isaiah, and Isaiah would come up with a plan.

But now Dodson was stalling so Chester called the wretched little termite in for a meeting. Chester looked around at his creations, each its own sun, reflecting his artistry, his mastery of the craft. He could hardly stand to sell them. The knives weren't his children exactly, but they were extensions of him, pieces of his genius the public was privileged to buy. Sometimes he refused a sale because the buyer didn't appreciate how fortunate he was to own a Babbitt, or the guy wanted *something to have around* or was the kind of reprobate who would toss the knife into a tackle box with his bobbers and cheese bait.

The shop was Chester's world. His blood and guts. His very soul. And now this murder case threatened to take it all away. He'd have to sell his inventory on the cheap, close the store, lose the condo, lose everything. He'd be nothing again, like he'd been all his life. The weirdo who wore a bow tie, had a knife collection and no friends. If Dodson and his crew didn't succeed in robbing Junior, he would go berserk, like the time he beat a man nearly to death and cut off his pinkie finger with the same knife the man was trying to steal. When Chester knew he was going to prison he had his canines sharpened. Nobody wants a blow job from a man with fangs. He spent twenty-eight months in Folsom locked up twenty-three hours a day. "Never again," he said.

Dodson drove over to the knife shop, thinking about what he would say. He had only served a bullet at Vacaville, but he'd met more than a few crazy motherfuckers like Chester. Most of them were cell warriors; mad killas out on the yard but cowards face-to-face. Time to give this boy a ho check, Dodson thought. See how woke he was. See if he had some spine. He entered the shop. The air conditioning was off and it was hot. He felt claustrophobic this time, like he'd walked into a mouthful of silver fillings.

"Hello, Mr. Dodson!" Chester boomed. "What a pleasure seeing you again! I hope you bear good tidings."

"I don't," Dodson said, belligerent.

Chester turned somber. "I see."

"This shit is impossible, Chester. We don't know where Junior keeps his money and he's not gonna tell us."

"What does Isaiah say?"

"He doesn't know what to do either. None of us hang with Junior and his money could be anywhere." Dodson sat on a stool, unwrapped a cherry sucker, and put it in his mouth. "You a dippy muthafucka, you know that? You was in the joint, wasn't you? I bet you was netted up in there too. Kept you in the ding wing with the rest of the lame ducks." Chester reacted indignantly to the prison slang. He'd definitely done some time, Dodson thought, probably for biting somebody with those coyote teeth.

Chester started pacing around with his hands behind his back. "This is very disappointing, Mr. Dodson. Very disappointing indeed."

"That's too bad, Chester, 'cause I ain't doing this shit and neither is anybody else. You need to face reality, son. None of us got no real money so unless you come up with a two-hundred-and-fifty-month payment plan you shit out of luck." Dodson let the sucker click around in his mouth. Chester was getting pouty like a spoiled rich kid used to getting his way.

"Those funds *must* be obtained!" Chester said. "I will accept no excuses!"

"You need to exit that bus," Dodson said. "It ain't goin' nowhere."

"*Yes it is!*" He actually stamped his foot.

"The fuck are you, six years old?" Dodson got off the stool and stepped in close enough to see the underside of Chester's chin. "Look here, Chester. You and your knives don't scare me. I'm a *homegrown* nigga, I'm gangsta to the bone. I took down muthafuckas worse than you with my left hand. You want to tussle with me you better have something better than a shank in your hand."

Chester's pout had turned to anger. His face was shiny, his eyes were overcast and thin as razor cuts. "I find myself in a predicament, Mr. Dodson," Chester said. "I'm backed into a corner, and as such, I have nothing to lose." Chester moved to one of the displays and reverently selected an axe. It was like an oversize tomahawk with a broad, evil-looking blade. "This is a Dane axe. The Vikings used them to great effect when they were destroying villages and setting fire to the villagers." Dodson backed up a few steps, calculating how fast he could get to the door.

Chester launched himself into a martial arts demonstration, his movements precise and surprisingly graceful, grunting from the effort, the clownish figure transformed into a trained warrior. He slashed, thrust, decapitated, and disemboweled, stabbing and bashing with the butt of the handle and spinning it like a pinwheel. "I realize...I may seem...ridiculous," he said between breaths, "but appearances...can...be...deceiving.... But I...do not...accept...your...excuses, sir....I...do...not...accept them...at...all!" Chester's bow tie was coming loose, sweat dripping off his nose; the hairpiece was tipped sideways. "You...*will*...comply...Mr. Dodson...do...you...hear me?...You have...no...other...option!" Chester was getting more frenzied, the canines glazed with spit, the eyes leaving tails of light like a comet. "Those...who have...under...estimated me...have met...with consequences...they did not...anticipate!" Dodson's bluster had turned into horror. Chester hadn't been in the ding wing. They kept him in ad seg with the serial killers that stabbed you fifty-seven times before they ate your lips off. Chester stopped and panted like a werewolf. "I will not cease...Mister...Dodson....I...will...give...you...no reprieve...until I...have...destroyed...your life AS YOU ARE DESTROYING MINE!" He swung the axe, slamming it down on a display case, the glass exploding, the blade cutting through the metal frame and cleaving through the shelves right down to the floor. "NOW GET OUT OF MY SHOP! GET OUT OF MY KINGDOM!" Dodson fled, running to his car and driving away so fast he sheared the side mirror off the car in front of him. As soon as he was a safe distance away, he called Isaiah and set up a meeting at the wrecking yard.

"What's this about?" Isaiah said. "I thought you weren't talking to me anymore."

"I didn't think so either," Dodson said. "But a lot of things have changed."

Grace was working in the warehouse when two kids came meandering in. They were arguing and didn't see her at first.

"That's what you get for making fun of my look-see," the girl said.

"Oh, I'm sorry," the boy replied. "I suppose *Greg* doesn't worry about his personal safety. He's too busy polishing his swimming trophies."

"You're jealous, aren't you?"

"Oh please. Why would I be jealous of someone who spends half his life underwater?"

Grace liked them immediately. They were different, oddballs, which she definitely related to. "Hi. I'm Grace. Isaiah's friend."

"Gilberto Cervantes." He shook her hand vigorously. He was dressed like an attorney on his day off. A pink polo shirt, khaki slacks, and polished cordovan loafers. "A pleasure to meet you," he went on. "As they say, any friend of Isaiah's." Grace tried not to stare. The kid had tassels on his shoes.

"Hi, I'm Phaedra," the girl said. "Phaedra Harris." She smiled with all the confidence of a motivational speaker. She was dressed casually, but her handbag cost more than three weeks of groceries.

"What can I do for you?" Grace said. "TK isn't here, but I can help you if there's something you need."

"We're meeting Isaiah," Phaedra said.

They sat around the rickety card table. Gilberto had his own fancy water bottle and sipped from that. Phaedra tasted TK's coffee and grimaced. "I don't mean to be rude, but what is this?"

"She's a coffee snob," Gilberto said, rolling his eyes.

"Says the kid with the three-stage filter in his water bottle."

"What are you guys doing for Isaiah?" Grace asked.

Gilberto lowered his voice and smiled ruefully. "I'm afraid that's confidential."

"We've been watching someone for him," Phaedra said.

"Don't you believe in confidentiality? Really, Phaedra."

"Ignore him. He's fussy. I put a fingerprint on his briefcase."

Grace could hardly keep from laughing. The kids were cute, but as much as they tried not to be, they were still kids.

"If I may ask," Gilberto said, "is your relationship with Isaiah personal or professional?"

"For God's sake, Gilberto," Phaedra said.

"He's helping me," Grace said.

Gilberto nodded sagely. "Ah, a client. Say no more."

Isaiah parked the Audi and hurried into the warehouse. He was relieved when he saw Grace. She looked like she was enjoying herself. You had to be a kid or a dog, he thought. "Hi. Sorry I'm late."

"It's okay. I've made some new friends," she said.

"What's happening with Vicente?" he asked the kids.

"First let me say—" Gilberto began.

Phaedra broke in. "I saw luggage. Two loaded suitcases, a duffel bag, a child's backpack, and a box full of toys. Vicente is leaving town."

"You went inside his house?" Isaiah said.

Gilbert frowned. "Yes, she did, Mr. Quintabe. I urged her not to, but she insisted and I accompanied her for protection purposes only."

Isaiah was angry. "You broke your word, and if something had happened to you, it would have been my responsibility. Didn't you get that?"

"I'm sorry, Isaiah," Phaedra said. "I lost my head. It's

inexcusable." She was terribly embarrassed. Gilberto looked at her, indignant and pitiless.

"What are you going to do, sir?" he asked.

"I'm not sure. I have to think about this, but you're done now, and I appreciate your help."

"It was very nice meeting you, Grace," Phaedra said.

"Same here," Gilberto agreed, as if he really had to think about it. "We'll invoice you, sir, and I hope you've learned your lesson, Phaedra."

"Yes, I have learned a lesson," she replied. "The next time I need help I'll call Greg." Grace and Isaiah watched them, still bickering as they left the yard.

"He really likes her, doesn't he?" Grace said.

"Likes her? How can you tell?"

"He doesn't know how to express it, so he..." her voice trailed off, "...does what he knows how to do." An excruciating moment went by, the kind where you don't know what to do with your face.

"I have to go," Isaiah said. "Another case." He hurried away. She thought about him. He could have met the kids at the house but he'd met them here instead. She knew why, but she wanted him to say it. *I came here to see you.*

Isaiah drove to Josefina's house. He parked the car and waited. He heard music from inside. A while later, Vicente showed up with a little girl and a bag of groceries. Josefina met them at the door. She didn't acknowledge the girl, who quickly slid past her. She kissed Vicente and took the bag of groceries and closed the door. What now? Isaiah thought. There was no way to strong-arm Vicente or sneak the child out. "God, I'm stupid," he said aloud. He could figure out complicated problems and resolve complicated situations, but sometimes he was so busy being clever he didn't see the obvious.

He made a call and a short while later, Manzo, three Locos, and the girl's mother showed up. They rang the bell. When Josefina opened the door, they barged past her into the house. There was a loud argument. Fifteen minutes later, everybody came out again, the girl in her mother's arms. At last he'd accomplished something, but he was still wired up.

He thought he'd keep his semiregular Wednesday appointment with Ari, his Krav Maga instructor. Physical exhaustion might do him some good. Maybe he'd get some sleep.

If it was exhaustion he wanted, Ari delivered. Punch after punch, kick after kick, combination after combination, until Isaiah was all sweat and burning thighs.

He was getting back into his car when they came at him from all directions.

"Get this, muthafucka," the black guy said. Isaiah got in a few punches but they Tasered him and the next thing he knew he was hooded, his hands were zip-tied, and he was lying in the back of a van.

"*Finally,*" Walczak said. "Good job, guys." He raised his hand to high-five but nobody responded. He pretended he was scratching his head.

"How'd you know he'd be here?" Jimenez said.

"One of my sources," Richter said, with a lazy look at Walczak. "She told me he works out on Wednesdays and he comes in all sweaty. The gym couldn't be too far away and this place was right around the corner."

"Very cool."

"You guys take care of this," Walczak said. "I've got to go back to the office."

Jimenez grinned. "This is the part you're good at."

"Fuck you, Jimenez."

Judging from the turns and the cruising times, Isaiah figured they took the 710 to the 405 and then to the 5. After that, he lost track.

"You're in big trouble, Sneaky Pete," the black guy said. "You want to make this easy on yourself? Tell us where they are."

"I don't know where they are," Isaiah said. "They went off on their own."

"Then why were you evadin' us, asshole?" the tall woman said. "You think we're stupid?"

"I'm afraid of you. Who wouldn't be?" These guys were from Abu Ghraib and Isaiah had a pretty clear idea of what they were capable of. It scared him. Really scared him.

It took over an hour but they finally got where they were going. They hauled him out of the van and dragged him up some stairs, and when they reached the landing, the black guy beat him up, more terrifying with the hood on because you couldn't see the punches coming. You could tell he was enjoying it, saying, *Ooh shit, how did that feel, Sneaky? Watch out now, here comes another one. Why you makin' all that noise? That wasn't even a hard one.* When he was done, Isaiah was bleeding, groaning, and lying on the floor.

"That's just a taste," the black guy said. "The real shit ain't even started yet."

When they took off the hood, he was in a large supply closet, stripped of everything but a table and two chairs. No distractions, no escape, nothing to do but ponder your fucked-up situation. He knew they would try to humiliate him and establish control so he wasn't surprised when they made him take off his clothes and stand there naked. It *was* humiliating. He felt so vulnerable he wanted to confess. He didn't cover his genitals. He wouldn't give them that. He was thirsty. He hadn't had a drink in hours. The Latino man and Porkpie were seated at the table. The black guy was leaning against a wall with the tall woman.

"Pretty disappointing there, Sneaky," the black guy said. "You might have to turn in your black card." The tall woman laughed, harsh and braying. The Latino man kept Isaiah waiting, leaning back, his hands behind his head, looking at him like he was a stain or something floating in the toilet bowl. Porkpie was sitting next to him.

"How you doing, sport?" he said. He was going through Isaiah's wallet, examining each item as if it was a smoking gun. License, credit card, Vons Club Card, a receipt, Social Security card. He held them up to the light like they might be counterfeit. A small thing but it felt like a violation. Isaiah knew what to do. *Accept the situation.* Being outraged and making demands was useless. He had to convince them he was beaten, but at the same time staying alert and looking for a way out.

"Sit down," the Latino guy commanded. Isaiah carefully took a seat across from him. "Tell us where Grace and Sarah are and it's over," the Latino man said. "Simple as that."

"I don't know where they are. Really, I don't," Isaiah said.

The Latino guy was glaring like he'd been insulted. "Keep that shit up, okay? And I swear to God you'll be fucking sorry." The tall woman was prowling around behind him, smacking her palm with a police baton. He understood they had complete control over his body. What he had to do was keep his mind from coming apart. That's what they wanted. To break him down.

"Are you thirsty?" the Latino guy said. Isaiah didn't respond. They were trying to condition him, get him used to answering questions. "Are you thirsty?" he asked again. Another pause. "Answer my question. *Are you thirsty?*"

"Yes, I'm thirsty."

The Latino guy put a bottle of water on the table. "Would you like a drink?"

"Yes, I would."

"Go ahead, drink." Isaiah took the bottle and gulped. Never turn down food or water. "That's enough," the Latino guy said. "Put the bottle down." Another control technique. He tells you to do something and you do it, get you in the habit. His tone got harsher. "Where's Sarah and Grace?" The Latino man's bulging arms were covered with tats. Gang signs, lurid women with gigantic breasts, and snarling creatures aiming guns.

"I'm telling you, I don't know," Isaiah said.

"Liar. You're a fucking liar."

The woman was standing behind him, still slapping that baton against her palm. She poked him with it, fucked with his ears.

"Why are you being an asshole?" the black guy said. "You could be home right now, listening to your record collection and hanging out with Dodson."

Porkpie found a small photo booth snapshot of Marcus and a young Isaiah, grinning and goofing around. "Your brother, right? Marcus? This is the dumb fuck walked into the street and got hit by a car. What a stupid way to go." He held Isaiah's gaze as he folded the picture around his finger, squeezed it in half, then in quarters, and dropped it on the floor. *It's only a picture. Keep your cool.*

"Good thing he's your only family," Porkpie added. "Nobody complaining when they find your body." Porkpie was telling him they knew everything about him, that they owned him.

The Latino guy was leaning back—no, coiling, getting his feet under him, ready to launch himself. *Here it comes,* Isaiah thought.

"Well?" the Latino man said.

"I don't know anything."

"LIAR!" He leapt across the table and slapped Isaiah so viciously his head went back and forth like a door slammed shut so hard it opened again. The shock was as bright as an exploding sun, the pain sizzling like a third-degree burn. It hurt but he'd been hit harder with a closed fist. *Hold on for Grace. Hold on for Grace.*

"I swear to God, I don't know!" he yelled.

"Tell us right now, motherfucker." The black guy came off the wall and stood over him like a looming tornado. "Or I'll put you in so much pain you'll beg me to slit your fuckin' throat."

"You think we're messing around?" the tall woman said. She slipped the baton over his neck and yanked it under his chin. He *grrrr*ed and tried to pull it off but she was strong and had the leverage. His head was swelling, his throat buckling, he couldn't breathe. He kicked away from the chair and she dragged him backward, the baton getting tighter, the blood cut off from his brain, his eyes about to mushroom out of his head. He was going to pass out.

"Enough," the Latino guy said. The woman loosened the baton and let Isaiah fall to the floor, holding his throat and gasping. The black guy lifted him by his armpits and sat him down in the chair again.

"You getting the picture?" the Latino guy said.

Time to give them something, Isaiah thought. It was hard to speak. His throat was scuffed, his neck was sore. "After you chased us, we went to my house," he said. Porkpie was watching him closely, looking for signs he was lying. Isaiah cautioned himself. *Don't close your eyes, don't touch your face, don't pause.* "We stayed there awhile, talking," he went on. *Keep your head still, blink normally, look left.* "And they decided the safe thing was to get out of town, so they took off. The whole point was to hide, so why would they tell me?" His inquisitors feigned weariness and disappointment, and Isaiah knew they were going to torture him no matter what he told them.

"Okay," the Latino guy said. "Don't say we didn't give you a chance."

They took him into the stairwell and handcuffed him to the railing. His wrists were behind him and raised above his waist so he had to stand up or dislocate his shoulders. They left him there. He couldn't tell how much time went by. There was nothing in the world but his pain and helplessness. He couldn't stand up anymore but as soon as he bent his knees, the pain in his shoulders doubled, tripled, and he thought he heard his muscles tearing. *For Grace for Grace for Grace for Grace,* but even his mantra receded in the torment. He cried out, "Please! Please, untie me! Please!" He'd never begged before. It was its own kind of torture. He hung there in the quiet and the smell of dank cement. He screamed, "PLEASE HELP ME! PLEASE!" But no one came. He fell into a stupor, his body daggered with pain. Time crawled by, half dead, barely moving. The pain blotted out thought, emotions, memory. Self. He screamed and screamed until he couldn't hear himself anymore, moaning now, mouth open and drooling. When the black man and the tall woman appeared, he sobbed with relief. She grinned.

"What do you say, Sneaks? Ready yet?"

Isaiah wanted to answer but his mouth was so dry he couldn't open it. They dragged him back up the stairs and through the office, deliberately banging him into chairs and tables. They threw him into the supply closet again and put a hood over his head that was soaked in hot sauce. He screamed, his eyes blistering, every breath a flame down his throat. He writhed and choked, trying to shake the hood off, but it enclosed him, encased him, a coffin full of mustard gas. He thought he was going to die. The men were yelling, but he could barely hear them. *Where are they? Where are they, motherfucker!* Over and over and over again. The tall woman kicked him with her cowboy boots, the pointed toes digging deep.

"What do you say, Mr. IQ? Feel like talkin' now?" she said. The others began stomping him, going for his groin, his hands, his head. One of them was taking it easy, pulling back on his kicks a little. Was it Porkpie? Why would he do that? Isaiah covered up and they kicked his thighs and back.

"PLEASE STOP! PLEEEASE!" he screamed.

The only thing holding him together was the thought of the crew working on Grace. Beating her, assaulting her, breaking her fingers, breaking her art. He was disintegrating, his rational mind a formless smear, nothing but the need for the pain to stop. He would tell them everything. He would give up Grace. He couldn't take it anymore—and then, miraculously, they stopped, everyone breathing hard. The black guy put his huge boot on Isaiah's throat.

"For the last time, asshole, where are they?" he said. Isaiah moaned. *TELL THEM EVERYTHING!* He opened his mouth but couldn't shape the words. He vomited.

"I need another beer," the woman said.

They removed the furniture and put on some hate rock so loud it became part of the pain. They left him alone again. The air conditioning was turned up high, it was freezing. They were letting him stew. Letting him think about the next round, the dread building until it overwhelmed him. He passed out.

When he awoke, he was still curled up on the floor, shivering, the hate rock filling every part of him that wasn't wracked with hurt. They weren't there and that gave him a moment's relief. *Have they gone? Please, tell me they're gone.* But they came back. The thought of more pain made him hysterical. He began twisting and writhing and babbling incoherently. He couldn't remember what they wanted to know. The Latino was talking on the phone. The black guy took off the hood and taunted him, the woman poured her beer on the floor. He opened his mouth and tried to catch some of the drops. They asked him again about Grace and Sarah and when he wouldn't answer the black guy got fed up.

"Then enough of this bullshit," the black guy said. He hauled Isaiah up and slammed him against the wall. "You think this is bad, asshole? This is nothing. This is a day at the beach. This is Disneyland!" The black guy put his massive hand around Isaiah's jaw and squeezed so hard Isaiah thought his gums would snap. "NOW START TALKING MOTHERFUCKER OR I SWEAR TO GOD I'LL CUT YOUR GODDAMN DICK OFF AND HANG IT AROUND YOUR NECK!" The same massive hand gripped

Isaiah's forehead like a grapefruit and banged it into the wall. "DO YOU HEAR ME? DO YOU FUCKING HEAR ME?" Isaiah couldn't hear him anymore. There was only his hot breath and his bloodshot eyes and his teeth bared like a carnivore and the pure, unadulterated hatred. Isaiah had reached a kind of resigned calmness, like there was nothing more they could do except kill him and that would be a relief. From somewhere not in his conscious mind, he decided he'd given them enough of his dignity. No more begging or cowering or crying. No more fear. Death was death. He looked at the black guy blankly, even while his head was thumping against the drywall and the pain was everything.

Porkpie appeared at the door. "Hold it, hold it, Hawk. You're gonna kill the guy."

The black man stepped back. Isaiah fell to the floor and felt a small measure of victory. Then he thought of revenge.

"Fuck it," the Latino guy said. He said to the woman, "Owens, find a table where we can lay him down. Did somebody bring a bucket?"

"It's in the van."

"Get it. Fill it with water. And see if you can find a towel too." The black guy let Isaiah go and he slumped to the floor. "You gotta admit. The guy's pretty tough."

"What's this asshole's name again?"

"Isaiah. They call him IQ."

The black guy and the woman left. The Latino guy's phone buzzed. "Yeah?" He listened a moment and ran out of the room.

CHAPTER TEN

Boom Boom

The team got numerous calls about the flyer. All of the callers were obvious liars, throwing in some detail they thought might apply to a white girl. *I seen her at the store, buying some kind of fresh vegetables. Yeah, she was driving one of them 'lectric cars, don't even have to put gas in it. She was at that bar over on Vernon, had some kinda blue martini with an umbrella in it.* The African man who called was polite, calm, and obviously educated. He knew things they hadn't put in the flyer, like the pocket watch tattoo and the shirt Grace was wearing. What convinced them was that he'd seen her with Isaiah. He said he'd met them at a bar in Long Beach.

"This better not be bullshit," Jimenez told him.

"I can assure you, it is not," the African man replied.

Seb sat in his booth, waiting. He thought about Isaiah and his white girlfriend and he hoped the men who had put up the flyer would hurt them very badly. Seb had been in love with a woman named Sarita. He had followed her here from another continent. She was his dream woman and proof he was worthy of love. She was the bridge between a small-time criminal and a man with stature and respectability who could hold his head up anywhere.

Isaiah had robbed him of all of that. Seb felt it like his missing leg; something not there but throbbing with pain. Five thousand dollars would be very useful right about now. Business had dropped off precipitously. He simply didn't care anymore, and money-laundering was not an enterprise where one could afford to be lax. He didn't attend to his clients the way he should have. They complained they couldn't reach him, a serious charge when you're holding a felon's illegal cash, and some of the account totals were less than what they should be. Clients with guns came to collect, and Seb took money from other accounts to pay them. He had become slovenly, shaving less often, not wearing a tie, his mortgage payments six months behind. And who was the cause of this? *Isaiah*. That intolerable busybody, that insignificant pest had destroyed everything. He would pay, Seb had vowed. He would pay dearly.

Four men and a woman entered the bar and strode down the aisle. They looked like a slow-motion shot of the bad guys on their way to the showdown, coming right at you, frightening and determined.

"Good afternoon," Seb said pleasantly. "I'm pleased you could make it. Would you like something to drink?" They stopped at the booth, looked at him, sizing him up, a small man in an old-fashioned suit, smoking an English cigarette, a fancy tea set arranged in a grid in front of him. He heard the woman mutter, *He's a faggot*.

"No, we don't want a drink," the white man in the tennis sweater said. "Where's the girl?"

"If you don't mind, I'd like to see the money first." Seb knew he had the upper hand. These people were frustrated. Whatever the reason, the girl was important to them. The white man threw a thick envelope down on the table.

"We have the money, asshole," he said. "Where is she?"

"While I am sure you are men of honor," Seb replied, "we are unknown to each other. I would like to see the money, please."

The black man pulled a gun. "Tell us motherfucker and tell us right now!"

Seb replied calmly, "Come now, there is no need for that. The situation, as I see it, is this. You want assurance that I am telling the truth and I want assurance that you will not take your money back."

"Three seconds, motherfucker." The black man grabbed Seb's wrist, turned it over, and stuck the gun barrel into his palm.

"He'll do it, ese," the Latino guy said. "No shit."

With his off hand, Seb took a sip of tea. "I was hoping we would discuss this in a reasonable fashion." The black man knocked the cup out of his hand, the delicate porcelain shattering against the wall.

"One," the black man said. Seb dusted the debris off his coat.

"It is unfortunate that all too frequently we must resort to violence. Let us be reasonable."

"*Two.*"

"You are making an unwise choice," Seb said. "The resulting bloodshed would hardly be worth it." Seb was looking past them. They turned their heads. Sahid, the bartender, was aiming an AK-47 at them, a prostitute named Millie was doing the same with an Uzi. Laquez came out of the hallway with his bulging eyes and stupid grin. He was aiming two pistols sideways like an idiot.

"Whassup, muthafuckas?" he said cheerfully.

Seb removed his hand from the black man's grip. "How about this? One of you will verify that the girl is where I say she is. Then he will call you. When you are satisfied the young lady you seek is at the location, I will keep the five thousand dollars and you can do what you will. In the meantime, you will disarm and stay here as my guests. Are you quite certain you won't have a drink?"

Isaiah had lost consciousness again and when he woke up, he was alone. He didn't hear voices. He put his ear to the floor and didn't feel any footsteps. The hate rock and the air conditioner were off. They'd forgotten to put the hood back on and the door was open. They'd left in a hurry, which meant they had located Grace. He had to call her, warn her, but it was impossible. He was bleeding from the nose and ears, his swollen eyes were like looking through a windshield hit by a flying bird. Blood from the earlier beatings had caked, new blood sheeting over it, adding thickness and shine. A cracked rib pierced his organs. He was sure his arms had separated from his shoulders, the nerves and ligaments dangling loose. His brain had become a separate entity; a power station run amuck, sending crackling jolts of pain to every receptor cell in his body.

He had to sit up. He leaned against the wall and gave it a try, twisting around, lifting himself. He thought his body would explode, his guts splattering on the walls. He made sounds he'd never made before. But he was sitting up. His head was bowed, his breath like a death rattle, blood and drool dripping onto his naked thighs.

He knew how to get out of a zip tie. First, he had to bring his wrists underneath him so they were between his knees. He had long arms and that made it easier than it might have been. It was excruciating but he did it. Now he had to slip his wrists under his feet so they'd be in front of him. *Oh motherfucking shit* that hurt. He paused to let the pain dissipate from extreme to less extreme. He thought he would pass out again. Standing up was next. He got on his knees first and leaned against the wall. Then he got his feet underneath him and pushed himself up, his shoulder sliding up the wall. He was standing up but so unsteadily he nearly fell down again. He breathed and drooled and tried to catch his breath. He urged himself to stay conscious.

Now the zip tie. The first part was counterintuitive. He grabbed the tag end of the tie with his teeth and pulled it even tighter until the strap was cutting into his wrists. Theoretically, if you put your wrists over your head, puffed out your chest, and brought your wrists down into your midriff with enough force, you wouldn't break the strap, but you would snap the tiny locking pin inside the housing. Theoretically. He waited until the pain subsided some. He took more deep breaths but they hurt too. Then he raised his wrists as high as they would go and brought them down with everything he had. He nearly blacked out and would have toppled over if he hadn't leaned into the wall. But the locking pin had broken. His hands were free. The pain came in huge spasms. He grunted in time with the spasms and vomited again. He staggered to the door. He saw his clothes and cell phone strewn on the floor. He took two steps toward them. Then his knees gave out, his vision went black, and that was the end of the world.

Dodson was early for his meeting with Isaiah. He drove into the wrecking yard and saw a white girl working under the hood of a smashed-up Civic. "Are you Grace?"

"Who are you?" she replied warily. She had a socket wrench in her hand and gripped it tighter.

"Juanell Dodson. I'm Isaiah's partner."

"I didn't know he had one."

"Would you mind doing something with that dog so I can get out of the car?"

"No, I don't think so," Grace said.

TK came out of the warehouse. "It's okay," he said. "It ain't nobody but Dodson."

"Go on, Ruff," she said, and the dog trotted into the warehouse like he was glad to get away from the riffraff.

"How you doin', Dodson? How's the baby?" TK said.

"Baby's doing fine," Dodson said as he got out of the car. "Cherise sends her love."

"Tell her I send it back."

"So you're really Isaiah's partner?" Grace said.

"Yes, I am."

TK was incredulous. "Wait a second. Did you say his *partner?*"

"That's right. We work together now."

"Well, good for you, boy," TK said, nodding and smiling. "I thought you was still dealin' crack." That got a look from Grace.

"No, I'm not dealing crack. I gave that up a long time ago."

TK took his cap off and scratched his head. "And then—what was it? You was running some kinda Ponzi scheme, weren't you?" He chuckled. "Yeah, half the neighborhood was after your hide."

"I gave that up too," Dodson said, hardly moving his lips. Grace was looking at him like a new species of insect.

"And there was something else you was up to," TK said.

"No, I wasn't."

The old man snapped his fingers. "I remember! You was sellin' counterfeit Gucci handbags out the trunk of your car!"

"I'm legit now, aight?" Dodson said irritably.

"So what is it you actually do for Isaiah? You some kind of secretary?"

Richter watched the wrecking yard with binoculars. He saw Grace and called Walczak.

"She's here."

"Anybody with her?"

"An old man and some homeboy."

"Are they armed?"

"Not that I can see."

"We're on our way."

The team arrived in a van and a rental car. Jimenez turned on the

TSJ vehicle-based military jammer they used for protecting convoys from IEDs. It would prevent anyone from calling in or out of the yard but the radios would still work.

Jimenez nodded. "Let's go."

The sun was fierce and they'd moved into the shade of the warehouse. Dodson and TK were arguing about whether or not Dodson was Isaiah's secretary. Grace was hunched down, giving Ruffin a bowl of fresh water. They heard engines at full throttle and saw a van and another car speeding through the gate. Grace stood up. "They're here for me," she said.

"Who is?" Dodson said.

"They'll kidnap me—and you too."

"Me? The fuck did I do?"

"Run!" She gave Dodson a shove and he took off. TK shot her a glance.

"Go on, girl. You know what to do."

Grace ran into the warehouse, made a quick stop in TK's office, and ran out the back entrance. She zigzagged through the piles of fenders, transmissions, and engine blocks and circled around the mountain of tires. She arrived at the perimeter fence but she'd forgotten about the double helix of razor wire coiled across the top. "Ah shit!" she said. She dialed 911 and got nothing but a howling noise. She heard the men coming.

A gravel road was the main thoroughfare through the yard. Dodson sprinted about sixty yards and had to stop. His lungs were failing, he had a stitch in his side. The van was speeding after him. Dodson turned into a narrow aisle between the tall stacks of cars. Stumbling and panting, he made his way along. He heard the van's doors slam open and running footsteps. He heard a man with a Mexican accent say, "Well, go after him. I'm too big to get in there." Dodson kept going, looking for a place to hide. You'd think it'd be easy, but the cars were crumpled, their roofs caved in, broken glass like sharks' teeth, doors bent in half, their side mirrors hanging by wires. He squeezed and sidled deeper into the aisle, cobwebs clinging to his sweaty face, his lungs sucking in rust and dust.

A woman said, "I see him! He's moving!" Dodson tried to sidle faster but the aisle was getting smaller. And smaller.

TK was lying on the ground. He tried to block them from chasing Grace and one of them hit him as they went past. His head hurt but it would take more than that to keep Thomas Marion Kahill from getting up again. He took a quick glance at the man who'd stayed behind. He was milling around, restless, jingling the change in his pockets. Had to be a cop, his gun in a shoulder holster, cheap suit, pleats in the pants. Tired of waiting, the cop got back in his car and turned on the radio. A Dodgers game. The cop could still see him but he'd have to chance it. If Grace and Dodson couldn't get over the fence, they'd have to come back here to the front gate. TK started to crawl.

Grace ran through the German section, looking for a hiding place. She was sweating, exhausted, her pursuers not far away. She could hear them yelling at each other to check this and go that way. One of them was Walczak. She saw the battered Passat where she'd met Isaiah. Thinking it might be good luck, she got inside. The backseats were missing and she crawled into the trunk. The lid didn't fit anymore, light around the edges, a jagged hole the size of a cop's badge where the metal had rusted through. The first things she saw were two shadows on the weedy ground, long and thin, aliens or giant grasshoppers, getting closer, fuller, shape-shifting into men who wanted to kidnap her and kill her mom. Walczak came into view. He paused and took a careful look around, his gaze moving and stopping, moving and stopping, moving—and stopping on the Passat, or was it something else? Could he see through the hole? She scooched back. The trunk was stifling and stank of rotting upholstery and gasoline, the sweat like a coating of grease. She'd picked up Mr. Brown in TK's office. It was as heavy as an anvil and hard to maneuver in the enclosed space.

Walczak came right toward her, gravel crunching under his feet. The hole went dark. He was a foot away. She heard him take a deep breath, like he was either weary or had at last found his prey. She barely had room for the gun barrel. She aimed it at the hole. Was she really going to shoot him? Blow him apart with a shotgun? She put her finger on the trigger and waited for the trunk to open. *Fight for yourself, sweet pea.*

"Anything?" Walczak said loudly.

"Nope," the other man said even louder. "But she couldn't have gotten far. We were right on her ass."

"She could have gone into the stacks."

"That's where I'd go."

They moved off. Grace waited—and waited. She heard nothing but sparrows chirping. She wanted to stay hidden, but it was so hot she thought she would faint. Ever so carefully, she crawled out of the trunk, trying not to clank the gun on something. She gradually raised her head so she could see over the side windowsill. Walczak had only moved to the perimeter of the section. The loud talking was meant to bring her out of hiding. The black man was creeping from car to car, looking inside and going on to the next. In a minute, he'd be at the Passat. She crawled out on her elbows, the gun held in front of her, keeping the car between her and her pursuers until she couldn't go any farther without being seen. She got up and ran into the stacks.

"There!" Walczak shouted.

The aisle had ended. Dodson was stuck. He looked back through the tangle of wrecks and saw the woman. "I see him!" she yelled.

She raised her gun and fired off a couple of shots, but she didn't have the angle, the bullets ricocheting and punching holes in the cars. This ain't no kidnapping, Dodson thought, this bitch is trying to kill me! Where to now? Up to this point, he'd been moving between the stacks, the cars piled like scrap metal pancakes on either side. There was nowhere to go now except between the cars themselves, lined up front to rear. He had to go back toward the woman before he found a crevasse wide enough. He edged himself in and inched along sideways, shimmying and squeezing past bent bumpers, open tailgates, dangling chrome strips, and tangles of wires, the crevasse getting narrower or wider depending upon the position of the cars. The woman reached the crevasse and shot at him again but there was too much in the way.

A man's voice shouted, "What's happening?"

"I almost got him!"

Dodson kept going, dead thirsty, cutting his hands on metal edges and broken glass, his pants and shirt ripped open, blinded by sweat, the smell of rust and gasoline making him sick. The crevasse ended. He had nowhere to go. The woman was getting closer. She saw him and kept coming. She'd have the angle soon. Dodson's path was blocked in all directions. There was nothing else to do but wait for her to kill him.

Grace ran into a long aisle between the stacks. She could see that it ended in open space. All the hiding places were obvious. Walczak was coming. There was an aisle that branched off the main one. It went about forty feet and dead-ended. She took a position at the back and waited. Walczak and the other man would run right past her from left to right. They'd be going fast, sprinting, and they might or might not be close together. She made sure there was a shell in Mr. Brown's chamber and the safety was off. The eight rounds were loaded with birdshot but at this range the spread might not cover both of them. Two shots then. *Boom-boom.* Something she hadn't practiced with TK. She tried to remember what he'd said. *"You been shootin' too early, when the target ain't nothin' but a blur . . . you want to shoot when it comes into hard focus. . . . You point the barrel about halfway between the launcher and the focus point."* She'd hit three clay targets in a row but that didn't mean she was good. It meant was she lucky. She racked the slide. *"Turn your shoulders, not the gun. . . . Let your eyes follow the target."*

She was afraid but eager. If Walczak wanted this mysterious *thing* so badly he'd hunt down two women, then he'd wanted it that badly when she was fifteen years old. Walczak was the home invader. *Walczak had killed her father.* "Come on, motherfucker," she whispered. *"Come on."* She heard the men breathing harshly and their pounding footsteps, they were going all out. She brought the stock up to her cheek and raised her elbow. They were almost in view. *Focus, Grace. Two shots. Boom-boom. Just like that.*

The black man ran past. BOOM! She shot behind him. He was partially hit. He screamed, his forward motion carrying him out of view. Walczak was trailing him. He tried to stop but stumbled into the open. Grace swiveled and fired. BOOM! Too slow. He'd already scrambled back to safety. *"Ah shit!"* she said. She could hear the black guy moaning.

"I'm gonna fuck you up, bitch."

"Come and get me, asshole."

"Grace?" Walczak said. "Put the gun down and we'll talk."

"Is that what you told the detainees?"

"Tell me where Sarah is."

"Fuck you, you prick." She was glad she was here, in this moment, wreathed in blue smoke, a shotgun in her hands. Tears of rage pooled in her eyes. She wanted to kill this fucking bastard so bad it felt like a desperate hunger or unbearable pain. "I know you killed my dad. I know it was you, you worthless piece of shit." She fired a round in his direction. BOOM! Metal whanged, glass shattered. Her face ran with tears and mucus. "YOU TOOK MY DAD AWAY FROM ME!" she screamed. She fired again. BOOM! Her voice came down, guttural, a growl. From a wolf. From a demon. "I'm gonna to kill you, Walczak. I'm gonna shoot you until there's nothing left but a puddle of shit." It wasn't a promise or even a threat. It was a fact, like death itself.

"I'm calling in the others now," he said. "We outman you, outgun you, and you'll be surrounded. Do yourself a favor and give us what we want."

"Never." There was no chance of killing him now and she was trapped in a cul-de-sac with twenty-foot stacks of cars fencing her in. She thought about being tortured and never seeing her mom again. She thought about Isaiah. She had to escape but the cars were too jumbled and overlapping to get through. *Now what, Grace?*

Dodson waited. The dust and sweat had turned to mud, blinding him, plugging his nose. He could see the woman through the labyrinth but she still couldn't get a shot.

"Oh, I got you now, you goddamn coon," she said.

He hadn't heard that in a while. What a fucked-up way to die. Shot by a racist in a wrecking yard. And why? For some girl who couldn't paint for shit and was paying them with one of her shitty paintings. He thought about Cherise and how she'd react when the police told her they'd found her husband dead in a pile of junk. He thought about leaving Micah fatherless. He thought about their grief. He thought about his own. Panic rose in him and spilled over the top. He made a wild sound of pure anguish and terror. "I've got to get out! I'VE GOT TO GET OUT!"

The redneck bitch laughed. "You ain't goin' nowhere, boy."

A man shouted, "Walczak's got her cornered. Let's go!" Dodson saw the woman going back the way she came. He heard the van's doors open and close, tires kicking up gravel as it sped away, leaving Dodson's resurrection in its wake. He was cleansed with relief and began to move. He had to get home. Home to his loving wife and his beautiful baby boy.

Grace was climbing a twenty-foot stack of cars, finding one meager foothold and then another like she was rock climbing. She was trying to keep quiet but metal creaked and bits of glass tinkled as they fell. She'd stashed Mr. Brown in one of the cars. There was no way to carry a shotgun and climb at the same time. The others had arrived and she heard them talking with Walczak, making plans: how to surround her, how to close in. She was halfway up the stack. Careful, careful, don't hurry, be quiet, be quiet. She was slick with sweat, her shirt drenched, her tongue was stuck to her palate. She'd cut her hand on a shard of glass, the blood running down her arm. She could see the top of the stack, only four cars to go—and then her foot slipped and she nearly fell. She grabbed on to a side mirror that came off and she nearly fell again.

"She's moving," Walczak said. "Cut her off!"

She regained her footing and heard Walczak bounding across the cul-de-sac and leaping onto the stack beneath her. She got to the top and hopped from roof to roof until she reached the edge. The path below was clear. She clambered down and ran.

Walczak landed moments after her. He caught up easily and tackled her. She tried to scramble away but he stood her up and backhanded her viciously. "You fucking bitch!" It infuriated him, how much trouble she'd caused. "Where's Sarah? Where is she?"

"Fuck you!" She windmilled girl punches. He slapped her again. "Coward! Coward!" she screamed, blood and spit flying out of her mouth, her hatred so intense it surprised him.

"Tell me where she is!" he shouted. He got her in a wrist lock, bent it back to the breaking point, and put her on her knees, but she kept screaming *Coward* and *Fuck you*. "Tell me, goddammit, or I'll break it off! Where's your mother? Where's Sarah? TELL ME RIGHT NOW YOU STUPID CUNT!"

Grace screamed and screamed but wouldn't give up. Walczak didn't actually see the dog until it was leaping through the air with its jaws open and its lips pulled back over its fangs. He hadn't been hit that hard since he was on the practice squad at USC and got run over by a two-hundred-and-sixty-pound defensive end. He couldn't reach his gun because he was curled up with his hands beneath him so the dog wouldn't bite them off. "Get him off me! GET HIM OFF ME!" he screamed. But she didn't. She let the dog maul him while she kicked him again and again. She stopped, panting, glowering down at him.

"Who's the cunt now?" she said. She gave him one last kick and then ran off with the dog.

Walczak moaned and wailed. His Italian tennis sweater had been reduced to strands of bloody cashmere. He'd lost a shoe, his wallet was ripped in half, the credit cards riddled with teeth marks. He'd been bitten multiple times, his wounds pulsing. He tried to find his collar mike but the dog had ripped it off. "Help," he said to a Subaru with no doors. "Somebody help me."

"Eighth inning, two men on, Uribe's up," Vin Scully said in the voice of summer and happier times. Fucking Uribe, Richter thought. Fifteen seasons in the majors and hitting over .300. You'd never know it by looking at him. He weighed as much as Richter did and looked like he should be pushing a hot dog cart. How does that happen anyway? One guy grows up in a shack somewhere in Hasta Luego or East Peru, hits baseballs for a living and ends up making fourteen million a year. Another guy works on the shithole side of LA, takes killers and drug dealers off the street, makes fifty-two grand a year and gets booted off the force for an accident. What the fuck was that all about?

"A swing and a miss and Uribe strikes out for the second time today," Vin Scully said. Richter knew they were going to kill the girl and her mother and for what? To save Walczak and those other assholes from what they fucking deserved? Richter also realized he was putting himself in harm's way. If this thing went bust and the law got involved, he could be sent to prison with a bunch of motherfuckers he'd either jailed, beaten, robbed, or all of the above. The only reason to hang in was to rip Walczak off. And fuck the rest of them. He owed them nothing. He had always wanted to go to Switzerland. The streets were clean and it was cool and crisp and there were lots of trees and mountains and no gangbangers, earthquakes, or smog. He could get lost there. He could learn to ski.

"Will you look at that?" he said. Grace was running directly toward him, a dog galloping alongside her. She didn't see him because of the reflection off the windshield. "Oh, this is too good," he chuckled. That prick Walczak was out there running around like an idiot and the wily old veteran ends up with the girl. That asshole would never hear the end of it. Richter decided he'd wait until she was real close, then get out and give her a whack. The dog? Put a bullet in its head and that was that. He drew his gun. She was forty yards away, thirty, twenty-five—he heard the clattering growl of a diesel engine. It took a moment for it to register because he was focused on the girl. At first, he couldn't tell where it was coming from, the sound bouncing off all the cars. The engine noise got louder, metal on metal screeching, a chain clanking. He glanced in the rearview mirror and saw the old man in the cab of a backhoe. Richter didn't react immediately because the girl was getting closer and the backhoe was moving so slowly. What an idiot, he thought. Did Gramps really think he could sneak up on him in a rig like that? Richter was reluctant to move the car, it might spook the girl. He decided to chance it, the backhoe was inching along and the girl was ten yards away. Five. He started to get out of the car, but in the same instant, his gun was yanked upward, out of his hand, and something slammed down on the roof so hard it jolted the whole car. "What the fuck?" he shouted. He couldn't believe it. The goddamn car was *levitating,* and that's when he realized the rig wasn't a backhoe, it was a goddamn crane with a goddamn magnet! The boom was up so high he hadn't seen it. He opened the door, but the car was already fifteen feet off the ground and rising. He tried to pull his gun off the roof but the boom swung the car around wildly and dropped it on the ground, the impact so hard the windows shattered and the airbags went off. Richter was bounced out of his seat, banging his head on the roof, something crunching in his neck. Even with his face smushed into the airbag he could hear the old man and girl woo-hooing.

CHAPTER ELEVEN
Train Wreck

Walczak, Hawkins, and Richter went to the emergency room. Owens and the fucking Mexican didn't have a scratch on them. Richter had damaged his fourth and fifth vertebrae and had to wear a neck brace. Hawkins's right side was pincushioned with birdshot. Walczak felt like he'd fallen into a tree shredder. He was lying facedown on a gurney. The nurse who was dressing his wounds was a black guy with tats and dreadlocks and he was almost as big as Hawkins. Whatever happened to those nice, white, female nurses? The ones named Betty or Dot who treated you with prim efficiency and tried to make you comfy? Who wants to be looked after by a guy who looks like Bob Marley's bodyguard?

"How you doing, sah?" the guy said. "I nevva seen nuttin' like dis, mon. Dis dog g'wan mess you up good, ya?"

"Thanks for telling me."

"Watcha do ta dis dog make him bite ya like dis?"

"I was attacked."

"Ya mussa dun sumpin' mon. Most dog smatta dan ya tink."

Walczak hated being here. He could hardly stand up so this oaf had actually held on to his arm while he took a piss. FUCK he hated that.

Walczak had enjoyed working for the CIA. He liked that it was select and special, which made him select and special, and he liked that it was secretive and even Patty couldn't know what he did. He liked that he could find out anything about anybody and, if he was careful, use it however he wanted. Frame the guy, get him fired, get his family and friends to turn on him, ruin him financially. Put his whole life in jeopardy. It wasn't so much that he enjoyed being above the law. What gave him pleasure was that he *was* the law. The CIA had great volumes of rules and regulations governing its operatives, but once you were out in the field, you fulfilled your mission in whatever way seemed pragmatic. Owens could do an amazing impression of a good ol' boy comedian who wore a Cornhuskers cap and a flannel shirt with the sleeves cut off. The guy had a catchphrase. *Get 'er done!* Walczak adopted it as his slogan.

After Bob Marley's bodyguard left, a doctor came in. "How are you feeling, Mr. Walczak?" he said. For fuck's sake, the guy was a goddamn Pakistani, maybe even an Iraqi. Walczak watched him closely. Maybe this guy knew who he was and would accidentally give him a shot of cholera or hepatitis C.

"I will give you a tetanus shot and some medication to reduce the pain," the doctor said. "The nurse will give you instructions on how to keep your wounds clean."

In two days, Walczak was supposed to hand Sarah a million dollars and he was trying to get used to the idea that he might have to pay it. She'd never live to enjoy it, he thought. She had no idea of the assets he had at his command. A moth wouldn't be able to get in or out of the drop area without being tracked, netted, and stripped of its wings. His revenge would be molecular. He would torture her protons.

Following the revelations about prisoner abuse, Walczak was relieved of duty and sent home to Langley. He was declared nonoperational and sent to see the Company shrink. He thought therapists were supposed to be neutral, but it was clear from the start what she thought of him. She said he lacked empathy and that he was unable to put himself in someone else's shoes. That he couldn't feel for other people.

"Of course I can feel for other people," he replied. "I have as much empathy as anybody else."

"Then how could you act with such cruelty at Abu Ghraib?" she said.

"You can call it cruelty, I call it a necessity. We gathered important intelligence. Intelligence that saved American lives." He knew that was iffy, but he wasn't going to give this smug cunt with her pearls and degree from Harvard one fucking thing.

"That's debatable," she said, "but let me ask you this. Many of the detainees were noncombatants, and the reports say you tortured them anyway. Why?"

"How do you know they're noncombatants until you torture them?"

She shook her head. "So it's all about expediency."

"Yes," he said as if it was obvious. "Getting the job done."

"In a civilized society, we have to make moral choices. Not just expedient ones."

"Society isn't civilized."

"What if the things you did to the detainees were done to your wife and son? How would you feel about that?"

Walczak shrugged. "I'd feel the need to kill the people who did it, if that's your point."

"When you were beating a detainee or hanging him in a stress position, didn't you feel bad about it?"

"No, I didn't."

"Why not?"

"I don't know. I just didn't."

"And yet you say you have empathy." She leaned back and tipped her head sideways.

"I do have empathy," Walczak said.

"For who?"

He shrugged. "Ordinary people."

"Do you realize your behavior was universally condemned by ordinary people all over the world?"

"Yes, I'm aware of that."

"And?"

"And—I don't care."

His answer was part bluster and part stubbornness. He cared. You'd have to be a complete sociopath not to care and he was sure he wasn't one of those. But whatever compassion he had left was buried beneath layer upon layer of sedimentary mayhem that made up his past. Every new cruelty pushed the one beneath it deeper, every beating suffocated another, every scream drowned out the one that came before it. He had come to feel that each act was a thing unto itself. A one-off, an anomaly, and therefore forgivable.

During his years at the Company, he made a lot of connections in government, the military, the intelligence community, and private industry. When he started to build his business, he thought Abu Ghraib would mark him as a pariah, but he wasn't looking to do business with Bristol-Myers or Walmart. In his world, they appreciated a nonempathic, expedient SOB who didn't feel the suffering of others and would do anything to *get 'er done.*

WSSI protected corrupt dictators and suppressed democratic movements. It assassinated rebel leaders and stole high-tech know-how for the Chinese. It guarded Russian gangsters, shipments of illegal arms, and entire military installations. It carried out black ops and secured black sites. The company worked so closely with the US government it was hard to tell where one left off and the other began. The two entities made policy together. They shared databases and technology. They shared secrets. Edward Snowden? What a joke. His revelations hadn't done anything to protect privacy. Your personal data was no safer than a lawn ornament. WSSI could tell you what porn you watched, the amount of your last overdraft, and the results of your colonoscopy. It could print out your passwords, start your car, watch you take a shower, and listen to you fart. It could map the ruins of a lost city, sniff out chemical weapons, and locate underground missile sites.

It had made Walczak a rich man. There were a Bentley and several Porsches in the garage. He had a private helicopter and a new Gulfstream. He owned houses in LA, London, and Abu Dhabi. His closets held half a million dollars' worth of clothes. He was a member of seven country clubs, he owned racehorses and had a multicultural legion of beautiful women who wanted him in their beds. So fuck you, Langley. Did you hear me? *Fuck you.* But none of it was helping him find Grace and Sarah.

They were the worst kinds of targets. No sightings, paper trail, or phones that could be traced, family and friends who either didn't know anything or wouldn't tell. No patterns or predilections that would lead to a location. He was desperate. Sarah could exhume the whole putrid mess and the thought of it terrified him, all that savage debauchery erupting out of the grave like bloody fingers in a slasher movie, its grip around his throat, throttling him with shame.

He envisioned the photos appearing in the *New York Times* and on CNN. He could see the media outrage metastasizing to every country in the world, his name synonymous with cruelty, depravity, and perversion. The most excruciating part. His family. The business was earth and he was Atlas. His family was his only true source of happiness, and the only people he knew who still saw him as a patriot, a hero, and a great human being. He loved family outings, soccer games, holidays, barbecues in the backyard. He even wore a chef's hat and cooked the hamburgers to perfection. He enjoyed the screaming kids, flying Frisbees, the big game on, everybody sitting around, talking and laughing, enjoying themselves, enjoying him. He was everyone's pride and joy. The one who'd made it big. A star on the world stage. That goddamn Sarah. There was no jungle, mountain range, coral reef, sand dune, hidey-hole, or unknown corner of the planet where she could not be found. He had to get those photos back and destroy every copy in existence or they'd be hanging over him like a guillotine for the rest of his life. Suppose Sarah was hacked or she showed them to somebody who showed them to someone else or she released them anyway? The thought of his darling wife Patty seeing him rape a helpless woman made him sick. The thought of his precious son Noah knowing his father was a monster made him want to die. He'd never been so afraid. Not when the desert night was lit with tracer rounds and the mortar shells exploded so close you thought you were finished and you could hear your fellow soldiers screaming and dying in the rubble. None of it frightened him more than the revelation of his beastly heart.

He called Patty just to hear her voice. They small-talked. She put Noah on the phone and he went on about a new video game and how Grampa was deaf and Grandma made cookies that were so bad he fed them to the dog and the dog threw up.

"I love you, Noah," Walczak said.

"I love you too, Dad. See you soon."

In the morning, Walczak caught a cab home from the hospital. He took more Demerol and lay on the bed trying to find a position that didn't hurt. Failing that, he went cringing and limping to his study. Might as well do something useful. He got out his laptop and scanned his emails. There was one from Sarah.

If you go anywhere near Grace again I'll release the pictures IMMEDIATELY and you will all GO TO JAIL!

He thought a moment and grinned. He couldn't suppress his elation. He punched the air and shouted "YES!" Sarah had made a huge mistake. He immediately called Jimenez.

"What's up, Balzac?" Jimenez said.

"It's Walcz—get everybody together. I think I have something." He hung up and laughed. He couldn't wait to spring it on Richter, shut him down for once, and that fucking Mexican too. Walczak was bleeding through his bandages. He thought about Sarah and Grace and what he'd do to them. He'd invent new atrocities that would take a long time. He'd lynch that dog and make them watch.

Isaiah stumbled through his front door wearing only his pants. He fell down, more blood and bruises than human. Grace put her hand over her mouth to stifle her scream. She ran to him and put her arms around him.

"I'm taking you to the emergency room."

"No. That's where they'll look first."

"Where then?"

Mrs. Marquez was a neighbor. She was also a nurse and a good friend. She took him to her sister Elena's house in Lakewood. Elena worked in an old folks' home and the two women looked after him better than any hospital. They propped him up with pillows, iced down his bruises, applied first aid to abrasions, put his arms in slings so he wouldn't have to carry them, and loaded him up with Vicodin. Mrs. Marquez hooked him up to a fancy electrostimulation machine she borrowed from work to help him heal faster. Grace was there the whole time, watching intently, like she wanted to help but didn't know how. He liked that a lot. The pain was still bad and at Mrs. Marquez's insistence, Isaiah called Raphael, who delivered a half ounce of something called Trainwreck. A hybrid, Raphael explained. Mexican and Thai sativas bred with Afghani indicas.

"Go easy," Raphael said. "This shit'll make you high as the

fucking sky." Isaiah was reluctant to smoke something called Train-wreck, but Mrs. Marquez said the doctors she worked for used it, sometimes on themselves.

Elena said, "No ser un debilucho." Which, judging from the look on her face, meant something like *Don't be a pussy*. Isaiah didn't want to be a pussy in front of Grace so he nodded. Elena expertly rolled a joint, and for the first time in his life, he smoked weed. He didn't feel anything for a while, the women watching him like he was about to give birth. Ten minutes later, or maybe it was an hour, he started to feel a calmness he'd never felt before—but also isolated and removed, like he was looking down on himself from the ceiling. His vision went from 720p to 1080, but the colors were off and too bright. The sound of the TV was clearer, but nobody had turned it up. The pain was there but distant and muddy.

"How are you?" Mrs. Marquez said. The women were smiling at him, and suddenly, that seemed incredibly funny. He burst out laughing and so did they, their glee making him laugh even harder. Eventually, everyone calmed down, but they were still looking at him.

"You know what?" he said. "I'm hungry." They broke into hysterics again, laughing and laughing until his stomach hurt and his injuries throbbed and he couldn't laugh anymore. Grace was smiling at him almost affectionately. The weed made him loose and brave. He wanted to kiss her.

Dodson and Deronda came over. "I'm sorry I've gotta do this now," Dodson said, "but I fucked up, or should I say *somebody* fucked up, and we in a situation we don't know how to get out of." He told Isaiah about Chester, Junior, and the blackmail.

Deronda looked at Grace suspiciously. "Who are you? You're not his girlfriend, are you?"

"No, I'm not," Grace said, like she didn't want Isaiah to hear her.

"Tell me about Junior's place," Isaiah said quickly.

"His crib is over on Minden, behind the Shop 'n Save," Dodson said. "I took some pictures." He gave Isaiah his phone. The photos showed a small nondescript house, well maintained with the usual chain link fence and burglar bars. No alarm box because nobody in the hood paid attention to them. The doors were formidable. Solid-core from the look of them and overlaid with a grid of cast iron security bars. The dead bolt was a high-quality Medeco that couldn't be picked, bump-keyed, or drilled. The two old friends exchanged a look.

"You thinking what I'm thinking?" Isaiah said.

"Yeah, I believe I am."

"What?" Deronda said. "What are you thinking?"

"You don't remember?" Dodson said, smiling. "I'm surprised at you."

It took a moment before it came to her. She smiled back. "Y'all was crazy then and you crazy now." They talked and came up with a plan.

"You two will have to do the heavy lifting," Isaiah said.

"Who two?" Deronda said, alarmed. "You mean me and Dodson?"

"I can be there but that's about it."

"Lord have mercy," Dodson said.

"We gonna need more than mercy," Deronda added.

When they were gone, Grace sat in silence for a long moment. She looked at him.

"What?" he said.

"You were the Battering Ram Bandits?"

Isaiah knew that the investigation, if that was what you could call it, was getting more random and directionless. People thought he was infallible, but in situations where there were no leads and scant information he'd get stuck just like the police. He was frustrated and pissed off about his other agenda too. Knowing Grace.

His probing had revealed little about her. It was like unearthing a million-year-old fossil. A slight mistake and the whole thing would crumble into dust.

Even though he was asking the questions, he felt like she was the one getting the answers, patting him down with her artist's eyes. Was she getting angry about the lack of progress? Was she suspicious, thinking maybe he was drawing this out? *Was* he drawing it out? No. He wanted to find her mom, please her and see what happened. She did seem a little more comfortable with him, or maybe not and he was just hoping that was true. The only time he'd been relaxed with her was when he was high. Being high all the time had occurred to him and he wished he could make her laugh when he was sober. He wanted to tell her that she was safe with him, that he'd rather get hung in a stress position than hurt her. He felt her sadness. He wanted to erase it, smooth it over, heal it, even though he knew that was impossible. Her father had been murdered and her mother had abandoned her.

When Marcus was killed, Isaiah didn't think he'd feel anything but sadness ever again. He worried that he meant nothing to Grace, that he was just a way of finding her mother. A tool, like a hammer or a saw, and the more he thought about it, the more likely that seemed. He couldn't think of a reason why she would be attracted to him over and above the case. When the case came to an end, he'd probably never see her again. He tried to imagine a way of convincing her to stay but nothing, absolutely nothing, came to mind.

He was lying on his side, dozing. He woke up but didn't open his eyes. He could hear the TV murmuring from the living room. He could smell onions and cilantro and the remains of the weed. He smelled Dove soap. He felt the air move and a warmth beside the bed. Grace was there. Doing what? he wondered. If she was working on her laptop he'd hear it. Was she reading? Sleeping? She took a slow breath and exhaled the same way. No, she was awake. Just sitting beside the bed. It felt eerie, even threatening, someone there when you were at your most vulnerable. He opened his eyes a hair's breadth, his vision blurred by his lashes. He could make out her waist, the top of her jeans, and her knees. She was turned toward him. She's watching me. Don't move. Don't even twitch. He felt an urgent need to swallow, but it would give him away. His nose itched, his legs were in an uncomfortable position, his breathing was shallow and he couldn't get enough air. He was about to feign wakefulness when she stirred and stood up. She paused. Was she still looking at him? And then he felt the back of her hand brush his face so lightly he thought he might have imagined it. A trill of high notes shivered through him. He wanted more than anything to look at her and smile and say he wanted her and everything would be okay. He opened his eyes, but she was already leaving, her back to him as she turned into the hall. Could he have done it? He wondered. Told her how he felt? Yes, he could have, *should* have, he decided.

Or maybe not.

He was up, dressed, and reading the paper when she returned with a cup of coffee and her laptop. Had she really touched him? Why? Was it affection? Did she want him to wake up and say something? Did she want him to kiss her? Did she want him to— Shut up, you idiot. You're dreaming. She was probably brushing lint or crumbs off his face.

"I was just thinking about something," she said, handing him the coffee. "In that picture, my mom and Stephanie were wearing bikinis, right? Obviously, they were going to the beach. And remember those water cans on the roof of the van? If they had to bring their own water, it had to be someplace isolated."

"Okay," he said.

"Mom liked to party, so maybe she was going to a beach where the cops don't bother you and you can camp, build a bonfire, drink, do what you want. She was always doing stuff like that."

He took the tiniest sip of coffee and his tongue winced. He'd seen her make the brew, the brown crystals like something mined from the center of the earth.

She showed him a map of California on her laptop. "Look at this," she said. "We lived in Bakersfield—that's here. If you wanted to get to the beach, you couldn't go direct because the air force base takes up this whole part of the coast."

"Okay."

"You'd have to go around it to here, Gaviota State Park. Scott, my ex-boyfriend, is a professional surfer. He says there's a party beach just south of there. It's really isolated and it's the closest one to the house. Maybe that's where Mom was going in the pictures. Maybe she's there now."

"Yeah, maybe so," Isaiah said. He knew this would go nowhere but didn't want her to feel bad.

"I think we should check it out," she said.

"You mean go there?"

"Yeah, it's only a three-hour drive. If we leave now, we can be back in the morning."

"Sure," he said. "Sounds great."

She had no idea why she concocted the story about the beach. One minute she was writing an email to Cherokee and the next, she was looking at a map of the California coast. And what was that she said? It's the closest one to the house? God, he must think she was an idiot. And why had she touched him? She couldn't help it, that was why. She'd lied to him too. Scott was a motorcycle mechanic who couldn't swim. Was she trying to make herself more attractive? Look, Isaiah, see what cool boyfriends I had? How embarrassing. Isaiah wasn't exactly a great catch himself. He was lonely and isolated and didn't have any social skills or a social life to use them in, but that was true for her too. Pathetic things to have in common. But Isaiah was also gentle and sweet and there was a basic decency about him. What do you do with someone who doesn't want to control you, undermine you, or use you for an emotional kickball? He was into her, that was obvious, and somehow she knew if she rejected him he would continue the case until the end. He was—what's the word? Honorable. She hadn't known anyone like that since her father. She wondered if that was part of it; her feelings for Isaiah a cog in some complicated Freudian backstory. Couldn't you just care for someone because they were gentle, sweet, and good? She knew she shouldn't be thinking about him. A relationship wasn't possible. Isaiah was a curious person and if they ever got together he'd find the fracture where she'd split in two and he'd wonder how it happened and go looking in the wrong half and see the ugliness she couldn't let anyone see and she'd have to get away from him and there'd be more pain and sadness and she was carrying enough already.

She knew they weren't making progress on the case. She sensed his anxiety and wanted to tell him not to worry, that she knew he was doing his best. But how do you talk to a man like that? He was *so* withholding. He hadn't said a single thing about himself. He didn't brag about his cases or tell stories about the bad guys he'd faced down or recite a list of accomplishments. Every man she'd ever known had done all of those things, sometimes in a single conversation. She wondered what would happen when the case ended. Could she really let him go? She could already feel the loss. Maybe there was a whisper of hope—for herself. For the two of them. *No, Grace. Don't be an idiot. Don't be a stupid idiot.*

And yet.

Grace said she had something to do before they left for Gaviota. Isaiah watched her leave the house. She had the toolbox and was wearing her dirty clothes. She was going to that damn garage again. *Oh my God* he wanted to know what was in there. Maybe TK sold her some parts. He called TK at home.

"Yeah," he said, "she came in but I didn't have what she wanted. Told her she had to buy it online."

"What did she want?"

"An intake manifold for a Ford 390 FE but I couldn't help her. They stopped making 'em in seventy, seventy-one, something like that."

Isaiah wondered why Grace was working on a forty-year-old engine. Building a hot rod, maybe, like a hobby? A gift for Cherokee? She's entering a car show? He had to stop thinking about it. It was making him crazy . . .

Grace didn't get back to the house until after ten. She showered, changed, threw some things in her backpack, and just like that they were heading out of Long Beach on the 710, destination Gaviota State Park. She drove. She hadn't got all the grease out from under her fingernails, her hair was still wet.

They crossed the LA County line. He couldn't believe this was happening. They'd be in the car together for three hours going and three hours coming back and if they weren't returning until morning it meant they would stay there *overnight*. It was disappointing she was so matter-of-fact about it. No, this wasn't a move on her part, she was just trying to find her mom. He glanced at her sideways. Her eyes were emotionless and glued to the road, her hands firmly on the steering wheel. She was almost grim. He envied her. At least she had something to do. He was the guy. It was up to him to start an interesting conversation but he didn't know what to say, and as the road signs sped past, a tension crept into the car until there was no room for anything else but a queasy smell he thought might be coming from him. *Say something, Isaiah.* He ran through a list of subjects but they were all dumb, bordering on *Do you have any hobbies?* He'd never felt so inept in his life, and despite the thrumming engine, the car seemed to get quieter. The slightest movement was as loud as a belch. He cleared his throat like he was going to speak but didn't, which only made it more imperative that he say something. Ten minutes, twenty minutes, half an hour went by without a word. There was nothing about the scenery to comment on, the freeway was the freeway. He had to clear his throat again but forced himself not to. He felt lonelier the farther they drove, like the wall between them had grown impenetrable and they would remain in their fortresses forever. They were all the way to Santa Barbara before she said, "Do you mind if we take the long way?"

Isaiah didn't know what the long way was but he shrugged and said, "Sure."

The long way was Highway 154, a two-lane road that went east and north, away from the ocean, winding and looping its way through the foothills. There weren't any towns and it was too dark to see anything, brush and scrubby trees texturing the blackness. Grace drove fast. *Really* fast. The headlights lit nothing but the beginning of the next bend, but she steered into them headlong, no clue of what was coming. A sweeper, S turns, a hard switchback. A dead end. She braked into every apex perfectly, downshifted and accelerated all out, the tires screaming as they slid, the rear end drifting out wide, sometimes to the yellow markers, a cliff on the other side. Isaiah held on to the armrest, his back pressed against the seat, his body leaning back and forth like a windshield wiper as they went through the turns. He nearly said *Slow the fuck down, are you crazy?* but he held it in. He thought she might be grandstanding but there was nothing on her face except a focused calm and the absolute certainty she could control the car. And then he realized *she was enjoying herself.* The long way was for bliss, not showboating. When they reached the valley floor she said, "Sorry."

He was wriggling the underwear out of his crack, sweat drying on his scalp. "No," he said, trying to sound cool. "It was fine." The road was flatter and straighter and she drove like a normal person. The pumping adrenaline gradually dissipated and the tension returned. Two lonely people sitting next to each other with nothing to say. A couple of centuries went by and she said, "Do you mind if I put on some music?"

"No, not at all." He worried she would play some obscure band from Seattle called Filth Monger or ask him if he'd ever heard the Zoo City Boyz play live at the Adderall Club but when he heard the opening bars of "My Girl" he grinned and they both laughed.

"Greatest song ever written," she said.

"How did you get into Motown?" he asked.

"I had a friend, Lacey, and she had her dad's old albums. I liked them more than she did. I lip-synced with Diana Ross, did the dance steps and everything."

"Sorry I missed that."

"You didn't miss much, believe me," she said. "I never told anyone I liked Motown. I don't know why it was a secret. And then punk came along and I fell into that. I'm glad those days are over."

They swayed in their seats to David Ruffin's soulful crooning. Grace murmured the lyrics at first, but then she rolled down the window and with the wind for cover, she started to sing—to herself at first, but by the time the song got to I—guess—you'd—say for the second time, she was belting it out like Isaiah wasn't there, joy and relief in her voice like she'd just been released from prison. And then, for the first time ever outside the shower, he opened his mouth and sang and shared the same joy and relief and he was sad when the song ended but "Sugar Pie Honey Bunch" came on after that and "Superstition" after that and "Tracks of My Tears" after that and they sang and sang with her hair fluttering in the night air and her pale green eyes sparkling as they sped along the highway, the darkness wrapped around them like a cocoon, and he thought it was the best time he'd ever had in his life.

It was after midnight when they reached Gaviota. Their silences were comfortable now but crackled with anticipation. He'd expected there'd be a motel or two, but there was nothing.

"What should we do?" she said.

"Sleep in the car?"

They parked on a side road under a eucalyptus tree. They went to pee in the bushes and came back to the car. They put the seats back, ate energy bars, drank FIJI Water, and looked at the sky through the sunroof, a gray wash backlit by the moon. They dozed awhile, and when he woke up, the music was off and he was a little damp from the mist. He glanced at Grace. She had dozed off too, a soft netting of shadows on her face. Even in her sleep, she seemed troubled, as if she was waiting for an order to evacuate. His eyes trailed down her delicate arm, pausing a moment on the pocket watch tattoo, sliding over her wrist to her small hand clutched in his. He held on until dawn, feeling like a voyeur, greedily watching her until a spangle of sunlight opened her eyes. She sat up, her hand withdrawing from his. She didn't acknowledge the separation and he wondered if she had taken his or he had taken hers.

"Good morning," she said.

"Good morning," he said.

A stand of cypress trees marked the beginning of the trail that zigzagged down to the unnamed party beach. They picked their way along the side of a bluff, sneakers slipping on the dirt, a long fall if you stumbled. This wasn't Isaiah's habitat and he was nervous without a sidewalk underneath him. His ribs were taped up and his other injuries limited his mobility. He was hurting and stifled his grunts. He took tiny steps and used his hands to stay upright.

"Are you okay?" Grace said. She had stopped and was looking back at him.

"Yeah, yeah, I'm fine." He hadn't glanced up until now. The sun was glinting over the horizon, a mist rising from the steel-blue sea, gentle foam breakers like a smile around the bay. Seagulls sailed by, complaining about their privacy, the breeze so refreshing he nearly lost balance.

"Amazing, huh?" she said.

"Yeah, amazing."

There was nothing on the beach. Not a person, a tent, or a campfire. "Well, I guess Mom's not here," she said wryly. "Sorry."

"Don't be. We had to find out, didn't we?"

"Want to go down there anyway?"

They sat in the sand, the briny air filling their lungs, the sun warming their souls. She had her arms around her knees, her eyes closed, her face up to catch the sheer goodness of being alive. It was both thrilling and perfectly natural when he took her hand. She looked at him and smiled and he felt like the curtains had parted and the Wizard was God.

Reluctantly, they decided to leave. Grace lingered a bit and found a sturdy stick of driftwood. "What's that for?" he said. As they climbed the trail, she stayed in front of him, reaching back with the stick to pull him up the steeper parts. Ordinarily, he'd have been embarrassed, but this was more like a connection, dreamy vibes moving through the old wood.

They stopped for Belgian waffles in a Danish-style tourist town called Solvang. She said if she didn't paint or draw every day she felt guilty and he said he felt the same way about his work. The price of obsession, they decided. They both thought the best part was when you were *in it* and you weren't aware of anything else, not sitting on your own shoulder kibitzing and criticizing. She squinted at him.

"You knew my mom wouldn't be there, didn't you?"

"Yeah, I guess I did."

"Why? Because it was stupid?"

"No. Because the two men in those pictures were wearing hiking boots. Makes it hard to walk around in the sand."

"You're getting me back for the joke thing."

"I wouldn't do that. I'm not that kind of person." This was fun, he thought. He'd never bantered before. He told her about her coffee.

"You're kidding."

"No, I'm straight-up serious. I'd rather drink a cup of dirt than whatever it is you've been making."

"It's the coffee, right?" she said hopefully. "The instant?"

"No. I've had instant coffee. You must be doing something wrong. Do you follow the directions?"

"You mean boiling water and adding the coffee?" she said. "Yeah, I follow the directions."

"From now on, let me make the coffee," he said, like there would be more mornings together. Their eyes met.

"Okay," she said.

The drive back was different in the daytime, less clandestine but still exciting because it seemed normal. Two people who liked each other had gone to the beach and now they were going home. Grace didn't have any more Motown so Isaiah played some of his music. *The Atomic Mr. Basie,* the Count and his band swinging so serenely it made you want to skip down a country road, and Louis Armstrong's *Potato Head Blues,* as tasty and joyous as anything ever played by men with horns, and George Shearing's "Little White Lies," Shearing's fingers moving over the keys like a butterfly flitting from dandelion to sunflower to peony to poppy.

Grace drove and listened to the music and thought about her mom. How their relationship had been much more than just getting along okay and the usual mother-daughter bullshit. Sarah was always affectionate and she encouraged Grace to be independent. She let her daughter solve her own problems and take the consequences of her mistakes. She never said *It's cold outside, Grace. Please take a jacket*. Instead, she let Grace go outside, feel the cold, and regret not taking a jacket. If Grace had a choice between doing her homework and watching TV, Sarah didn't say *Homework time, Grace*. She let Grace skip the homework, go to school, and be embarrassed. But she was always there to help and was effusively happy when Grace accomplished something. She didn't push. She stood at the finish line shouting encouragements. And as Sarah grew as a person, she made sure Grace did too. She talked to her daughter about ideas and books and art. She never said *Isn't Michelangelo amazing?* She said what she enjoyed about him, she showed her *own* interest. It wasn't a teaching moment. It was a shared experience.

And Sarah let her daughter make decisions. When Grace started wearing embarrassingly short skirts, Sarah said she couldn't control what her daughter did outside the house, that she could hike up her skirt as short as she wanted to. Sarah said she had done things like that to get attention from boys. The question was, what did Grace want attention *for*? Sarah never pried, never said *Do you want to talk about it, Grace?* She talked about herself. She confided, in an age-appropriate way, and always tried to understand instead of judge. Who wouldn't confide in someone like that? They were close because Sarah let her daughter come to her.

Their only serious point of conflict was her father. Sarah was a different person around him. Quieter, more acquiescent, inclined to say nothing instead of something. But as she came into her own the marriage deteriorated, Grace felt she had to choose sides, dividing her time like a parent with twins. She loved her mother. She respected her and trusted her and would have crossed the Sahara or caught a dragon for her. When she left, she took the world with her.

Elena was home when they got back from Gaviota. Grace was disappointed. She wasn't ready to take Isaiah to bed but she did let her eyes linger on his before they went off to their separate rooms. As she got ready to shower, that familiar, reflexive voice of ambivalence bled into her hopefulness. She was always ambivalent. Nothing in her life had ever been black-and-white. The people who said there were no gray areas were simply ignoring them. The ones who said *Go for it* had never been haunted by her demons or slogged through the muddy swamp of complications that were sure to arise.

Something always prevented her from getting what she wanted. In this case, it was her. Check that. It was always her. Was she really going to let Isaiah go? He was smart, compassionate, sexy—and something else. What was the word? *Tender.* She'd never said that about man nor beast. Maybe, she thought, things would be different this time. Maybe *she* would be different and they could make something good together. "Yeah, that could happen," she said as she stepped into the shower. But as the warm water cascaded down on her face, the same face she'd held up to the sun and felt the breeze coming off the steel blue sea, she got angry. Why should she be controlled by all the shit in her past? Why should she always get in her own way? She deserved a life beyond her fears. "Jesus, Grace," she said. "For once, just go for it."

CHAPTER TWELVE
Bad, Bad Leroy Brown

They were gathered in the study for another stupid meeting. It bored Richter shitless, how Walczak could turn one goddamn paragraph into the Gettysburg Address. Look at him, with his homo tennis sweater and his homo haircut and his indestructible smile, those fucking teeth like a row of shiny sugar cubes. He was messed up from all the dog bites, cringing and wincing every time he moved, everybody enjoying the shit out of it.

"Sarah's email *says*," Walczak said, putting a finger in the air, "'if you ever try to hurt her *again*.'" He looked at the crew like they were schoolkids. "Do you know what that means?" He waited a moment, building up to it. "It means—"

"Sarah was there," Richter said. "She saw what happened. She was somewhere around the Edgemont." Walczak's face folded in on itself and his teeth got darker.

"That's right," he said, hitting the *t* hard so it sounded like *tuh*. He glared at Richter through his homo tortoiseshell reading glasses, his lips in a straight line. "Thanks for pointing that out."

The crew busied themselves like illegals in a sweatshop, looking through the CCTV footage again, focusing on the places with a line of sight to the Edgemont. Richter's punishment for stealing

230

the boss's thunder was to *maybe go patrol the grounds now.* Patrol the grounds for what? A Stealth silverfish couldn't get past the trillion-dollar security system.

Early on in his career Richter was part of the Rampart CRASH Division, where seventy cops were busted for thefts, robberies, beatings, and payoffs. He squeaked by with a suspension only because there was no direct evidence and no witnesses who hadn't left town. He was transferred to the Seventy-seventh Street Division in Inglewood, where he terrorized the lawless and the law-abiding alike. Eventually, his notoriety caught up with him. Internal Affairs was sniffing around. He reminded a few of his connections that he knew where the bodies were buried and got a job on the Long Beach PD. He toned down the extracurricular stuff. He was tired of all the drama.

It was luck how he met Walczak. His partner was out sick and he was by himself. He got a call about an assault, an officer in need of assistance. The altercation took place in a parking lot outside the offices of Walczak Security Systems International. Two employees, both ex-military, had gotten into a brawl and both were seriously injured. Richter knew something was wrong the moment he arrived. A passerby, not the company, had called 911, and they'd brought in a private ambulance and their own doctor. They wanted to keep this to themselves. Richter heard opportunity knocking on his savings account.

He told the officer to secure the scene and met with WSSI's chief of security, Milton something, one of those clean-shaven guys with a buzz cut, a T-square jaw, and a suit previously worn by a Greyhound bus or a rhinoceros. Milton explained what happened, trying to be offhand, his military-speak getting in the way. *The subjects were acquaintances . . . the incident took place at approximately twenty-three hundred hours . . . they were roughhousing and an altercation ensued.*

"Really, Officer," Milton said. "We'd rather handle this in-house."

"What you'd rather do doesn't really matter, one guy's got a crack in his skull and the other guy's got broken ribs and a dislocated jaw."

"Nobody's pressing charges."

"They don't have to press charges," Richter said. "I can." Which wasn't true but it sounded good.

"Is that really necessary?" Milton said. "I don't know if you know anything about us, Officer, but WSSI is a worldwide company with—"

"Yeah, I know, you're like Blackwater."

"No, we're not," Milton replied, like he was denying he had syphilis. "But we do the same kind of work. Obviously, a fight between employees would not be good publicity."

"You mean it wouldn't be good publicity after five of your *employees* got indicted for shooting a bunch of civilians in Mosul?"

Milton was rattled now. "It was a confusing situation. They were mistaken for hostiles."

"What about the woman and the baby?" Richter shot back. "Were they mistaken for hostiles too?" Richter knew that companies like WSSI hired ex-cops all the time and if their personnel department chose people who mistakenly shot moms and babies he'd fit right in. He looked at Milton and nodded thoughtfully. He put away his notepad. "So let me see if I have this straight. Two of your employees were walking out to their cars. One of them fell down and bumped into the other guy and he hit his head on the pavement. Do I have that right?"

"Yes, you do, Officer," Milton said, trying to cover up a smile. "That's exactly how it went down. Here. Take my card."

A few weeks later, on a blistering day in July, Richter arrested an elderly bag lady. She was drunk and threatening people with a screwdriver. He put her in his unmarked car and left her there while he went to a motel and got a blow job from a hooker in exchange for keeping her out of jail. He hung out for a while, drinking beer and watching the last three innings of the Dodgers game, at which point he was hungry so he walked over to In-N-Out and had a couple of cheeseburgers with double meat. By the time he got back to the car, three hours had gone by. People were pounding on the car's windows; 911 had already been called. The bag lady was a sweaty mess, hair plastered on her anguished face, a curled hand slapping feebly at the window, barely breathing in her two sweatshirts and man's corduroy coat. When he opened the door the smell made the whole crowd step back. "You left me," she gasped. "You left me here to die."

She needed a new kidney and Richter was fired. He thought he could shrug the whole thing off but of all the fucked-up shit he'd done in his life, that was what wormed its way into his dreams; that he'd nearly killed an old lady because he was a lazy asshole.

An article about the incident appeared in the *Long Beach Press-Telegram* and six days later he got the call from Milton. The so-called job interview took place in a bar at the Hyatt Hotel. Milton drank club soda, Richter ordered eighteen-year-old Glenlivet, a double.

"According to what I have here," Milton said, opening a file folder, "in April 2007, you got a complaint about loud music. According to your incident report, the suspect, a minor, allegedly behaved in a threatening manner and you defended yourself with your flashlight, resulting in the suspect suffering severe head lacerations."

"Look," Richter said, "the guy played varsity football and he had a weapon."

"He was on the golf team and he had a TV remote. And later that same year, you allegedly harassed an administrative assistant, repeatedly referring to her butt as a *turd cutter.*"

"Come on," Richter scoffed. "She was always flaunting it, wore those tight skirts. When she walked it was like juggling basket-balls. Anyway, it was her word against mine."

Milton continued. "In September of 2008, you were suspected of taking seventy-one thousand dollars from a drug dealer."

"They never proved a thing."

"But somehow, you were able to buy a new Lincoln MKX."

"How do you know that? Nobody knew about that."

"In October of 2009," Milton said, wearily turning the page, "you were suspected of demanding sexual favors from a woman you'd pulled over on a traffic stop."

"She was driving erratically and she was a prostitute."

"She was parked in the Walmart parking lot and she was an em-ployee." Milton went on. "In May of 2012, you allegedly accepted payoffs from a man whose street name was the Counterfeit King."

"I was working for him off-duty and he had a print shop. Where did you get my personnel record?"

Apparently, disgraced cops who'd been on their college wrestling teams and scored 97 percent on the firearms qualification course were hard to come by. WSSI brought Richter on as a "security ana-lyst" at a salary of $72,500 a year plus benefits. He was glad to have a gig, but gladder still to put his past behind him. Almost behind him. Something random would set it off. A wobbling fan, a truck backing up, a stoplight changing from yellow to red. He'd smell the stink first. Then he'd see the runny gray eyes sliding off the old lady's face, her skin cracked and dirty, loose brown teeth in her rot-ting mouth. And that hand. That fucking hand. Sooty, like she'd stuck it in a chimney, a blackened bandage around her thumb, blotches of red on her shredded nails. Sometimes he thought he heard it, tapping on the window, scratching on the door.

Richter's first assignment for WSSI was surveillance on a scien-tist named Garrison Lew. Lew worked at a pharmaceutical com-pany and was suspected of stealing company secrets. His contract stipulated he could only be fired for cause and the company didn't have enough evidence to take action.

"What am I supposed to do, catch him in the act?" Richter said.

"No," Milton said. "You're supposed to make him stop."

Richter broke into Lew's house, waited until he came home, and gave him a Maglite shampoo just like he'd done to that little fuck the golfer. Then he sat Lew down in the dining room, gave him a digital tape recorder, and told him to list everything he'd stolen, when and where. When Lew refused, Richter rinsed and repeated until he got a full confession. Then he gathered up Lew's watch, wallet, laptop, and loose cash and told him, "Quit your job. I mean tomorrow. If you don't, I'll come back and stuff you headfirst into a sewer pipe."

Sometime later, Walczak called him into his office, which was more like a hotel lobby with an ocean view. "I need a personal bodyguard," he said, not looking up from the papers on his desk. "Do you think you can handle that?"

"Yeah. I'm pretty sure I can."

"There might be additional duties."

"Additional duties are my specialty."

Walczak let him live in the guest house, gave him an expense account, a new Lincoln, and use of the company hookers. There was nothing to complain about except Walczak himself. What a monumental prick. He was everything that was wrong with rich people: arrogant, entitled, always showing off and throwing his weight around, and he was an evil motherfucker to boot. Compared to him, Richter was John the Baptist or Peter the Great or one of those other saints his mother was always praying to. And Walczak knew Richter had no place else to go so he abused him with impunity. Who'd want a washed-up cop who suffocated an old lady and got fired by an internationally known security company? He'd be back in his fucked-up house eating SpaghettiOs out of the can.

The only way to get out of this with his pride intact was to fleece that monumental prick for every dollar he had.

Richter was permitted back in the inner sanctum but wasn't allowed to touch the laptops, which were reserved for the professionals. He was falling asleep when Owens said, "I got it," pleased she'd finally done something right. She'd found a segment of footage from a diner across the street from the Edgemont. It showed Sarah and a man coming in, taking a booth by the window. They saw the action with Grace and Isaiah and left. Unfortunately, the lighting was dim and the camera had been there since the nineties so the image was poor quality. The man was black, looked to be in his fifties, little square glasses, an unkempt mess of graying hair, a full beard and a T-shirt draped over his paunch that said BAD, BAD LEROY BROWN.

"He looks like a black Jerry Garcia," Jimenez said.

"Who's Jerry Garcia?" Owens said.

"Sarah and Jerry are a couple," Richter said. "If we find Jerry we'll find Sarah."

"Isn't that obvious?" Walczak said, pissed that he hadn't said it first. "For Christ's sake, Richter, is that what I pay you for? Telling us things we already know? Why don't you go wash the car or something."

The facial recognition system at WSSI marked where rigid tissue and bone were most apparent, it delineated the curves of the eye socket, nose, and chin, and it took measurements of depth and axis. These things are unique and don't change over time. Collecting that kind of data was illegal in California, but the Feds had a database with thirteen million people who had committed federal crimes. If Jerry was in there, maybe they could identify him. Maybe. Even after enhancement, the shot of Jerry's face was blurred and pixelated. The beard didn't help either.

Predictably, the results were disappointing. The system came back with over a thousand possible Jerrys spread out all over the country. Even after eliminating the ones who were dead, in jail, or obviously the wrong guy there were still over three hundred and fifty left.

They were in the study again. Walczak frustrated, out of ideas, hoping somebody besides Richter had one.

"What happened to the bar?" Owens said. All the liquor had been removed.

"We're here to work, hayseed," Hawkins said. "Maybe drink some white lightnin' when you get back to the barn."

"Why don't you go write a rap song," she replied. "Something you people are good at." Hawkins stood up. Owens stood up.

"Could you please control yourselves?" Walczak said. "Kill each other after this is over."

"So what's next, boss?" that fucking Mexican said. "You got some other kind of high technology you want to lay on us? Some other kind of recognition? Armpits? Feet? I got a real distinctive foreskin. It's got freckles on it."

"Fuck this," Hawkins said. "I'm going home."

"No, we're not finished here," Walczak said.

"Oh yeah? Well, *I'm* finished here and I'm going home."

"Let's back it up a second," Richter said. "Sarah was on the run, right? Maybe she—"

Walczak glared and interrupted. "Richter, discuss these things with me first, will you? You work for me, remember?"

"Sure, no problem." Richter sat there, said nothing, and fiddled with the end of his tie, everybody waiting, wry smiles, wondering what Walczak was going to do. He looked like he was holding in a massive fart.

"Okay," he said, without moving his mouth. "Go ahead."

"Like I was saying, Sarah was on the run, right? She can live anywhere she wants and people who have a choice usually go by three things. Where they can find work, the kind of people they like, and the weather. What did Sarah do for work before the artist thing?"

"Waitress, bartender," Walczak said.

"No help there. What kind of people did she like?"

"Artsy types, musicians, writers, useless fucks who lie around and complain about the government."

"You can find them people anywhere," Owens said.

"Yeah, but Sarah's *deciding* where to go," Richter said. "She can pick and choose. What about weather?"

"Sarah hated cold weather," Walczak said. "Anything below eighty degrees was winter as far as she was concerned."

"That eliminates the Deep South, anyplace east of the Rockies," Richter said. "Alaska, Oregon, Washington, and Northern California. That leaves Southern Cal, Nevada, New Mexico, Arizona, Utah, Texas." Jimenez glanced at Hawkins. *Do you believe this guy?*

"You're stretching it," Walczak said. His blood pressure made his eyes flutter, his butt wounds were bleeding again. "You might as well say Saudi Arabia or Europe."

"Think about going on vacation," Richter said. "If you want to go somewhere you've never been before you do it by reputation. If you like hot weather and an artsy crowd you don't go to Farmington or Steamboat Springs."

"There's Austin, Taos, Santa Fe," Jimenez said. "Nothing I know of in Arizona, Utah, Nevada, or the rest of Texas."

"Austin," Walczak offered grudgingly.

"What about here?" Hawkins said. "That bitch could be living down the block and we wouldn't know it." Owens was frowning, trying to think of a suggestion. "Don't bother," Hawkins said. "If we want to buy a horse we'll ask you."

"Cut it out, okay?" Jimenez said. "It's time to go to work."

They went over the list of Jerrys. There were two in Austin, one in Santa Fe, one in Taos, seven in the Bay Area, one in Silicon Valley. They decided to nix LA for now, reasoning that Sarah wouldn't plant someplace so close to Walczak. They drew straws for who went where.

"Santa Fe?" Owens complained. "What's in Santa Fe?"

"Good Tex-Mex and a lot of turquoise jewelry," Jimenez replied.

"This is a really long long shot, you know," Walczak said, thinking, *I'm not taking the blame for this.*

"You got any better ideas?" Richter said. Walczak had no comeback.

Everyone got up to go but Jimenez just sat there. "Why don't you just pay her the million?" he said. "It's not like you can't afford it." The others muttering and nodding in agreement.

"You don't know that cunt like I do," Walczak said. "Sarah hates me and for good reason too. She won't stop. She'll release the pictures anyway. Trust me on this one. She wants my ass, not the money. If she's not dead we're fucked." The others looked at each other as if to say, *Do we believe him?*

"Let's get to it," the fucking Mexican said.

Walczak glared at Richter. "If this turns out to be a waste of time? I'll kick you out on your ass and you won't be able to get a job as a crossing guard. Do you understand?"

"Yeah, I do," Richter said.

When the ex-cop left the room, Walczak could have sworn he was smiling.

Sarah met Stan Walczak at a memorial service for a friend who'd been blown up by an IED. Chuck went off to carouse with his old buddies, leaving Sarah and Walczak time to talk, go to lunch, and get a motel room. The affair lasted several months. Walczak was handsome and sophisticated. She knew he was at Abu Ghraib but he denied torturing prisoners. He said if he had he would have been fired and she wanted to believe him. Walczak had also seen the world and he appreciated art and music and he ate his pasta al dente instead of cooked into mush and he drank wine instead of beer. At the same time, Sarah's marriage was falling apart. She was about to file for divorce when Chuck told her he had incriminating photos from Abu Ghraib and that he intended to blackmail Walczak. He'd always hated that pompous asshole. Sarah was horrified by the pictures but didn't want Chuck to go through with it. She knew that if Walczak did those things at Abu Ghraib, he'd have no problem killing her husband. Or her. She devised a plan. She and Chuck shared a password manager. She'd get the passwords and delete all the pictures in the cloud accounts. Then she'd tell Walczak what she'd done and he would drop the whole thing. Chuck would be furious but that was a lot better than getting himself killed. What she didn't know was that Chuck had already sent the demand note.

It never occurred to her that Walczak would stage a home invasion. She knew it was him the moment he came through the door. Chuck went for one of his guns and Walczak shot him in the back. During the commotion, Sarah grabbed Grace and fled. Afterward, she realized she'd just witnessed a murder and she was the only person who could link Walczak to the crime. If both she and Chuck were dead, the cloud accounts would lapse all by themselves. When Sarah left Bakersfield, she was fleeing Walczak as well as the police.

Sarah told all this to Arthur in a sobbing confession. He didn't judge, saying she'd had no idea what the affair would lead to and that Walczak had killed Chuck, not her. She loved him for that. But now, in their cramped room at the Travel Inn in Burbank, she was frustrated with him. He'd been humoring her about helping extort Walczak, hoping she'd back out on her own as the deadline drew closer.

"Don't do this, Sarah," Arthur said. "It's either a death sentence or a jail sentence. It simply won't work."

"It won't work if you keep saying it won't," Sarah said sharply.

"You don't seem to know what you're up against. Walczak's people are ex-CIA and -FBI. They're professionals. They've dealt with this kind of situation dozens of times with drug cartels and terrorists, and they have the technology, all the latest. They'll see us coming from a mile away. Ten miles away!" He softened, pleading. "Forget this, Sarah. For God's sake, let's just go on with our lives."

She glared at him, fierce. "He made me live like an animal and you want me to go on with my life? He murdered my husband! He murdered Grace's father!" She put her face in her hands and wept. Arthur breathed a deep sigh.

"I'm sorry," he said, "but it can't be done. That's all there is to it." Sarah left. Arthur brooded. She stayed away for hours and returned with a bottle of wine and a kiss. They hugged and held each other for a long time. Wearily, lovingly, and in true Arthur fashion he said: "Okay, if that's what you really want, I'll help you."

When they were writing the demand note, Arthur said to give Walczak until Friday. It would give them time to plan the money drop.

"The idea is to keep them scrambling," Arthur said. "To sow confusion and never let them rest." After he wrote down a few things, he and Sarah studied maps and spent a couple of days driving around the area, scouting routes and locations and figuring out the timing. They went shopping at a prop store, bought a few throwaway phones and a junker from an old man at a wrecking yard.

Afterward, they ate bad sushi and drank good sake. They were somber and hardly spoke. It felt like the day before the invasion.

"Do you think it will work, Arthur?" she said.

"Yes," he said unconvincingly. "Yes I do."

* * *

Hawkins, Jimenez, Richter, and Walczak went to see their Jerrys but none was the one they wanted. Wrong height, age, build, hair, or facially just not the same. Owens had gotten pulled over for DUI and was stuck in Santa Fe. The money drop was today, and the team was waiting in Walczak's study. Walczak was still in pain and so was Hawkins. Richter looked ridiculous in the neck brace. Like kids had buried him in the sand with his head sticking out. The call came in at three in the afternoon.

"It's me, you shit," Sarah said. "I should forget about all this and turn you in."

"But you won't because you want the money," Walczak said. He'd drawn a million dollars in brand-new one-hundred-dollar bills from his personal accounts and it *really* pissed him off. "I want some reassurances here. How do I know you won't keep a copy of the pictures?"

"I *will* keep a copy. What you're paying for is my promise that I won't release the pictures publicly. I'm going to give you instructions now, are you listening?"

Oh my God, he wanted to jump through the phone and strangle this cunt. "Yes, I'm listening."

"Buy a Samsonite suitcase," she said. "Are you writing this down? A Samsonite Omni PC Hard Spinner in Caribbean blue. Nothing else, do you understand?"

"Yes, I understand."

"You have ninety minutes to get the suitcase and drive downtown."

"Where downtown?"

"I'll call you in ninety minutes." She ended the call.

"Two cars," Jimenez said. "Walczak and Richter will pick up the suitcase."

"Why?" Walczak said.

"Because. You're too fucked up to do anything except drive and Richter has done this kind of shit before." Another smirkfest.

Walczak pretended not to notice. "My techs will handle the drones from the office. They'll know what we're doing but not why. As soon as we've got Sarah cornered they'll return to base."

"What's all the bullshit about a suitcase?" Hawkins said.

"They'll try and switch it," Richter said.

"You mean they're going to take our suitcase, give us theirs, and we're not supposed to know about it. That's stupid."

"Don't forget, they're amateurs. One way or another they'll fuck this up."

"You got one of those GPS things for the suitcase?" Owens said.

"No, I don't," Richter answered. "I'm an idiot."

Ninety minutes later, Walczak was sitting in his car, talking on the phone with Sarah. "We have the suitcase and we're downtown," he said.

"Is it the right one, the Samsonite?" Sarah said.

"Yes, it's the right one."

"Go to the seven hundred block of Main. The Windward Mall. Take the suitcase and wait in the rotunda."

Main was a one-way street. Walczak pulled into the passenger drop-off. "See you later," Richter said.

He got out of the car with the suitcase. Walczak stayed put. There was no place to park here or on the other side of the mall so Hawkins and Jimenez went into the parking garage. Hawkins would stay with the car, Jimenez would enter the mall on the second floor. He'd stay out of sight and see if he could pick out Sarah or Jerry. Walczak's techs were given photos of the two of them. Drones would be circling overhead. Six of them.

Richter sat down in the rotunda and put the suitcase beside him. He heard Jimenez through his earbud. "Touch your chin if you can hear me." Richter touched his chin. "I'm on the floor above you. I can see the whole place from here."

Richter waited. It was a weekday, nothing special going on. Shoppers with shopping bags, people in the food court eating bad Chinese food. More amateur bullshit. They should have done this on a weekend when the crowds were bigger and it was easier to get lost.

"You're not going to fucking believe this," Jimenez said. "At your two o'clock, a Mexican guy just came in, he's got the exact same suitcase. These people are clowns."

Richter almost laughed. He saw the guy, small and brown, wearing an Angels baseball cap. He didn't seem especially nervous, more uncertain than anything else, like he wasn't sure he was in the right place. He sat down not thirty feet away. Richter's phone buzzed. "Yeah?"

"Leave the rotunda," Sarah said. "Take the suitcase with you. The exit is to your right. *Go now.* I'm staying on the line." Richter glanced up at Jimenez and shrugged with his palms up. He went out the exit.

"He's leaving," Jimenez said. "East exit. The Broadway side."

"Who's the Mexican guy?" Walczak said.

"A decoy," Jimenez replied. "We just got suckered."

"FUCK!" Walczak shouted. "Did you hear that, Richter? It was a fucking decoy!"

As soon as Richter got outside, Sarah said, "There's a cab stand in front of you. Take the first cab and tell the driver to go straight up Broadway."

"How far?" Richter said.

"Until I tell you to stop." She ended the call.

"I'm in a cab, heading south," Richter said.

Walczak shouted, "SHIT!" Jimenez was caught flat-footed, stuck in the mall, and Richter had gotten into a cab on the street *behind him.* Walczak was going to make a U-turn but the goddamn street was one-way. He drove fast up the block to the next intersection.

If he turned left he'd be driving parallel to the cab but that street was one-way too. "FUCKERS!" he shouted. He'd have to turn right and circle the entire mall to catch up with the cab. "Where are you, Hawkins?"

"I'm just leaving the garage," Hawkins said. It was rush hour. The traffic was almost at a standstill. They'd have to play catch-up. Jimenez was catching a cab and would be even farther behind.

"Tell me you've got them," Walczak said to the tech.

"We're all over them, sir," the tech said. "The drones are flying in a hexagram formation at different altitudes. There's no chance they can get away and the GPS signal is strong. Oh, sir? The cab is cutting across a parking lot and it's turning into an alley. I think it's a planned route. They're bypassing some of the traffic."

"Dammit, DAMMIT!" Walczak screamed. He honked his horn uselessly at the line of cars in front of him. Walczak, Hawkins, and Jimenez had made up some ground but were still a ways back.

"Sir?" the tech said. "The cab has stopped in front of a parking garage on the twenty-one-hundred block of Nelson Avenue. It's a hospital."

"I'm getting out of the cab and heading into the parking garage," Richter said. "She told me to walk up the ramp so I'm walking up the ramp. Where are you?"

"Too far away to help," Walczak said. "Fuck this up and you're fired."

Sarah waited in the old clunker. She had parked it on the second floor in a row of other cars. The car barely ran but Arthur said all it had to do was start up one more time. She was hunched down in the front seat, turned around so she could peek beneath the head-rest. Walczak's man would walk right past her. She had told him to hurry, but obviously he wasn't. He was waiting for Walczak and the others to catch up. She and Arthur had taken a test drive from the mall to the hospital at the same time of day. It took them seventeen minutes. Walczak should be six minutes away. "Hurry up," she whispered. She was barely breathing and she'd never heard her heart thump so loudly or felt it so insistently. Suddenly, there he was, the man with the porkpie hat walking neither fast nor slow, carrying the Caribbean-blue Samsonite, his eyes sweeping back and forth, sometimes glancing behind him. "Oh my," she whispered. He looked silly with the neck brace, like he was resting his chin on the edge of a pool. He went past her, and when he turned the corner to the next ramp she started the car.

Richter walked up the ramp on high alert, figuring Sarah and Jerry would be in a car and had some slick way of getting out of the garage. But they didn't know about the drones. He heard tires squealing. "Yup, just like I thought," he said. "She's here."

Sarah pulled up next to him in a Buick Skylark, white with a rattling engine and a temporary spare tire. Stupid, Richter thought. They should have gone with something more anonymous. Sarah's window was closed and the door locks were down so he couldn't reach in and grab her by the throat. "Hello, Sarah," he said, stalling for time. "How are you?" He heard the trunk latch clunk.

"In the trunk," she said.

"Walczak never said you were hot. Do you have a boyfriend?"

"Do it now or I'm leaving!"

Richter walked slowly around to the back and put the suitcase in the trunk. He hadn't even closed it when the car took off with a lurch and drove away, the trunk lid bobbing up and down.

"She's got the case and she drove up the ramp," Richter said. "She's in a white Buick Skylark, old one, license plate Abel Baker seven one five one."

"Got it," the tech said.

"Where are you, Walczak?"

"Three minutes away."

Sarah drove up two floors and there was Arthur, standing next to the brown Volvo. "We did it," she said as she got out.

"Not yet," he said. He took the suitcase out of the Buick's trunk. "Hurry up and get ready." He glanced at his watch. "We've got three minutes."

Richter ran up the ramp, the bolster-size burrito he'd had for lunch slowing him down. He was holding his sides and gulping air when he found the Buick, the empty suitcase on the ground beside it. The GPS tracker was useless now. "They're gone and they left the suitcase," he said. "Where are you?"

"I'm here," Walczak said. "Jimenez and Hawkins too."

"The drones are all over it, sir," the tech said. "It doesn't matter where they come out. We'll see them."

"I think they switched cars," Richter said.

It was twenty after five. There was only one way in or out of the garage. Lots of people were getting off work, a line of cars stacked up at the kiosk. Sarah and Jerry hadn't planned for that, Walczak thought, as he walked up the line, eyeballing the drivers and peering into the backseats. Richter was coming down the other way. Arthur would be behind the wheel, thinking he was Tom Cruise in *Mission: Impossible 12,* not knowing they knew what he looked like. Sarah would be hiding in the trunk, dreaming about how she'd spend the money.

Walczak wondered how long he'd have to waterboard her before she gave up the photos. Ten, fifteen seconds tops but he'd keep it going another fifteen minutes or so just for the pleasure of seeing that bitch drown.

Jimenez was sitting in the Denny's across the street from the hospital's main entrance. Hawkins was watching the second entrance. The drones were up there, circling at low altitude, people pointing at them and giving them the finger.

The techs were told to watch for baseball caps and sunglasses. The movie star disguise that never worked. Sarah was thin, blond, and fair. Jerry had a beard and a belly on him, impossible to hide. Even though the money was in hundred-dollar bills, it would have to be in something large, a different suitcase or a duffel bag.

"Where are you, Sarah?" Walczak said as he continued along the line of cars. "Where arrre youuu?"

"I think we've got them, sir!" the tech exclaimed. "We've got visuals on both. They're wearing caps and sunglasses."

Walczak laughed. "Didn't I tell you?"

"Sarah's got a carry-on suitcase, the black guy's wearing a backpack. I think they're going to take separate buses."

"Jimenez? Come pick me up," Walczak said.

"On my way," he said.

"That stupid bitch," Walczak went on. "I can't wait to beat that cunt to death and spit on her grave."

"Hold it, sir," the tech said. "I'm sorry but it's not them, false alarm."

"Are you sure?"

"Yes, sir. It's definitely not them."

"FUCK!"

At 6:05 there were only a half dozen cars in line at the kiosk. Walczak and Richter went up and down the ramp and checked the cars that were still parked. Nothing.

"Anything, Jimenez?" Walczak said.

"Nothing."

"I got nothing here," Hawkins said.

"Sorry, sir," the tech said.

By 6:30 there were hardly any cars left and people were coming out of the hospital in ones and twos. "They couldn't have gotten away," Walczak said. "It's not possible."

"They could be waiting us out," Jimenez said. Before Walczak could give his okay, Jimenez brought everybody in.

"I'll give the orders, Jimenez," Walczak said.

"Well, you're too fucking slow. And I'll do what I want."

They checked the cafeteria, hallways, bathrooms, common areas, and waiting rooms. Nothing. The drones were running out of battery and had to return to base.

They regrouped at Denny's, people looking at the four pissed-off men who weren't eating or sitting down.

Walczak could see Patty's brilliant smile as she came in the door and Noah running into his arms, happy to see his dad. "We're not done," he said to the crew. "I'm not letting that bitch hold those pictures over my head forever. We have to track her down."

"Count me out," Jimenez said. "It'll never end."

"You should have paid her the million in the first place and we could have skipped all this mess," Hawkins said.

"What if Sarah comes back for more?" Walczak argued.

"She won't," Jimenez said. "Nobody would go through all this bullshit again."

"We can't let her get away with this," Walczak insisted. "She's a danger to all of us."

"No, she's not," Jimenez said. "I'm going."

"Richter?" Walczak said, asking for support.

"She's one and done," Richter said.

Walczak shot cruise missiles out of his eyes. "I don't accept this. I don't accept this at all. We *have* to do this!"

"Why?" Hawkins said. "Because you tell us to?"

Walczak thought a moment. "No. Because if we catch her, you can have the million dollars."

249

That shut everybody up, looks being exchanged, Hawkins rubbing his chin. "You might have something there."

"That's what I thought," Walczak said.

"Do I get a cut?" Richter said.

"You mean for fucking everything up? No. And you're an employee. You're on salary and lucky to get that." Walczak headed for the door. "I *still* can't believe they got away."

When Arthur and Sarah were discussing plans for the money drop, Arthur took a long look at the Abu Ghraib photos.

"How can you stand to do that, Arthur?" Sarah said. "They're hideous."

"Yes, they are. And that's in our favor." Arthur explained that because the photos were so hideous it was unlikely Walczak would add anyone else to the team. That meant they were only dealing with the five of them and not WSSI's 17,000 employees. "We've got to pick them off one by one," Arthur said. "And they'll probably use drones."

Hours before Walczak's team got to the mall, Arthur hired a laborer to take an identical suitcase and sit in the rotunda at a specified time. Arthur said his sister needed it and he couldn't wait for her. He showed the guy that the suitcase was empty and paid him twenty dollars. He said his sister would pay him twenty more, thinking he wasn't really cheating the guy. He'd get a free suitcase.

Walczak was told to arrive at the mall's south entrance, which was on a one-way street. He would probably stay put, otherwise he'd have to park several blocks away or in the garage, where he'd be stuck. There would be a second vehicle and maybe a third, but the lack of parking would present them with the same problem and they'd be temporarily out of the picture. Because Sarah had asked for a specific model of suitcase, Walczak would think they were going to make a switch, and that would make foot pursuit a priority. One or more of the team would leave the vehicles and watch from inside the mall. When Sarah instructed the guy with the suitcase to leave the mall and get into a cab, that would—*should* leave them behind. In the meantime, Walczak wouldn't have the option of making a U-turn. He'd be facing the wrong way and the other vehicle or vehicles would have to play catch-up. When the cab reached the hospital parking garage, the guy with the suitcase would—*should* be alone. Which, amazingly enough, happened. When Sarah was hiding in the junker and Porkpie came walking up the ramp by himself, it seemed like a miracle.

Once Porkpie put the suitcase in the Buick's trunk, she drove up a couple of floors and parked next to Arthur's brown Volvo. She peeled off the coveralls she was wearing over her clothes while Arthur removed the money from the suitcase, eliminating the GPS tracker that was no doubt hidden inside. Arthur had specifically wanted hundred-dollar bills instead of twenties. They made a smaller package. Two minutes and twelve seconds later, they crossed the walkway into the hospital. He kissed her and told her he loved her, and they went their separate ways.

Walczak's techs diligently watched the drones' live feed but neither they nor Jimenez in the Denny's across the street picked up on the woman with her hair tucked under a mousy brown wig coming out of the hospital's main entrance. She was wearing blue scrubs, reading glasses with no lenses in them, and a prosthetic around her waist that made her look fat. Her thin lips were thickened with lipstick, her pale skin darkened with spray-on tan, a stethoscope around her neck, and lifts in her shoes. She was also walking amid a crowd of other people in blue scrubs who were leaving for the day, something they always did at five o'clock in the afternoon. At the exact same moment she appeared, so did a short, pale, blond woman wearing a cap and dark glasses whom Arthur had hired to carry a suitcase, walk fast, and get on the bus. He gave her a hundred bucks and told her they were shooting an independent movie.

Hawkins was in his car parked across the street from the hospital's second entrance, but neither he nor the techs noticed the clean-shaven man in blue scrubs who was carrying a medical bag and wore a fake nose and a girdle to hide his paunch; his wild hair cut short and darkened with dyed eyebrows to match. He was also walking amid a crowd of other people in blue scrubs who were leaving for the day, something they always did at five o'clock in the afternoon. At the exact same moment he appeared, so did a rotund black man wearing a false white beard and wig and carrying a large backpack whom Arthur had hired to walk fast and get on the bus. He gave him a hundred bucks and told him they were shooting an independent movie. And neither the drones, the techs, nor Walczak's team saw Sarah and Arthur meet up at the Motel 6 in Burbank or drink a bottle of Veuve Clicquot as they danced around the room throwing the money into the air.

Arthur wanted to be sure they were in the clear, so he decided to wait a few days before he gave up the passwords. Walczak was getting what he wanted so there was no need for him to pursue Grace. But no contact with her. Not yet. Wait until things cool down. They left the brown Volvo in the parking garage and found a near-new Chevy Tahoe on Craigslist. They bought it for cash and hit the road at sunrise, Arthur singing "Bad, Bad Leroy Brown" so loud she tried to make him hum. They stopped in Fresno for supplies. Camping equipment, bicycles, food, water, sunscreen, a new bikini for Sarah.

"I can't wait to see you in that," Arthur said as they got back on the highway.

"The view isn't as good as it used to be but I think you'll be impressed."

"I already am. We'll hit Reno sometime tomorrow afternoon."
She was giddy. "I can't believe it. After all these years. Finally!"

"Life begins today, my love," but in the dark files of Arthur's accumulated wisdom, he knew Walczak wasn't done.

Bad, bad Leroy Brown, baddest man in the whole damn town...

CHAPTER THIRTEEN

The Battering Ram Bandits

Dodson and Deronda went to the storage locker where the teenage Battering Ram Bandits had made their plans, stored their stolen goods, and fought each other for control. There was nothing much there. Boxes of old records, tools, scrap lumber, and networks of dusty cobwebs.

"Dang, this place is nasty," Deronda said.

"There it is," Dodson said. The battering ram was leaning against a wall. The dark metal was rusted in places and crusted with oxidation. It looked like an abandoned torpedo.

"I seen the police knock down doors with them things," Deronda said.

"Swing it right and you can knock down a house. You gotta help me, you know," Dodson said.

"Help you? Uh-uh, not gonna happen." She folded her arms across her chest as if that made it final. "Last time I swung something was when I tried to hit my brother-in-law with a meat mallet."

"You got anything happening today?"

"I gotta get back to the food truck. My daddy's covering for me."

"Then tell him you'll be late. You gonna be busy for a while."

"Busy doin' what?" she said.

"Practicin'."

They found a condemned building with broken windows and streamers of yellow caution tape flapping around. Dodson snipped through the chain link fence with a bolt cutter and they went around to the back, Deronda stepping gingerly through the chunks of cement, broken glass, and coils of moldy dog shit. "I hate this already," she said.

They reached a fire exit. The door was hefty and sheathed in metal. "Okay," Dodson said. "Take your end of this thing. No, not like that, you not lifting weights. Pick it up sideways." Grudgingly, she obliged him, taking hold of the front handle while he held on to the back. "We're gonna swing it back and forth," he went on, "get a rhythm, like you're on a swing at the playground. When we got it up to speed, we swing extra hard and we hit it right there." He indicated the dead bolt. "Okay, hold on tight now. We're gonna do a few warm-up swings, then I'm gonna say one, two, three, and on three we do it. You got that?"

"Yeah, I got it," she said, sulking. "This ain't exactly rocket science." They took some warm-up swings. "Dang, this thing is hurtin' my back."

"Shut up, goddammit. Here we go. One...two...THREE!"

Deronda swung but let go of the handle, the momentum ripping the ram out of Dodson's hands. The ram banged into the door and dropped to the ground with a clank. Deronda hopped away like the thing was on fire.

"The fuck you doing, girl?" Dodson said. "You supposed to hold on to it!"

"It's too heavy."

"Too heavy my narrow black ass. I seen you throw a bowling ball at Lamar Wiggens and knock him down like a tenpin."

She stamped her foot. "See, I knew this would happen. I broke a nail." She held it up like she'd lost a finger.

"Michael Stokely's gonna break every bone in your body if we don't make this happen. Now pick the goddamn thing up and let's do it again."

Four tries, two arguments, and another broken nail later, they finally managed to knock the door down. "See?" he said. "This shit works if you do it right." Deronda was sweaty and scowling.

"I gotta go pick up my son from day care."

"Since when does day care let out at ten-thirty in the morning? Pick your end up. We gotta find another door."

Grace entered Royal Custom Cutlery with an earnest, curious look on her face. An interested buyer. Chester Babbitt smiled broadly. "Good afternoon!" The volume and depth of his voice were startling. She was more excited than afraid. She liked being part of this. She liked helping Isaiah.

"Good afternoon," she said, trying not to react to his weirdness. *A bow tie? Jesus. Are those his teeth?*

"And how may I help you today, young lady?"

"Just a penknife. My dad says Babbitt knives are the best in the world. He could never afford one so I want to get him one for his birthday."

Chester beamed. "Well, that's very kind of him. Please, come this way and let's see what we can find."

As he led her to a display case she said wonderingly, "Your shop is amazing. Did you make all of these yourself?" *Stop looking at me like that.*

"I did indeed," he said with feigned humility.

"That's incredible!" She hated being girly-silly but it was part of the plan. With too much ceremony, Chester opened a display case and brought out a velvet-covered tray arrayed with five pocketknives in various sizes.

"How much is the little one?"

"One ninety-five," he said, as if he could hardly believe it was so inexpensive.

"Wow. That's a lot."

"Would a twenty percent discount help?" He smiled magnanimously.

"Oh, that would be great!" she squealed. *Stop looking at me like that!* Chester put the knife in a monogrammed box and the box in a velvet monogrammed bag. "That's beautiful," she said. "Do you have a card?"

"Of course, take several."

"Thank you so much, Mr. Babbitt. My dad will be thrilled!"

"The pleasure was all mine." He bowed. "Do come back anytime."

She left the shop happy. She could hardly wait to tell Isaiah.

Chester closed up and thought about the girl. He should have gotten her name. She was a tasty little thing. If she returned maybe he'd take a nibble. Sadly, she was a mere distraction from the matters at hand. Chester had sent multiple texts to Dodson. Do not disappoint me, Mr. Dodson. The consequences will be severe. I am expecting good news and only good news. Think of your family. Dodson and his friends could not fail. They wouldn't be *allowed* to fail. Collection agents were calling. His landlord was starting eviction proceedings. His first court appearance was next week and the lawyer was demanding his retainer. Chester was well aware Dodson might hold back some of the money. It was a given. But Chester had a bottom line. A hundred thousand dollars. Any less and he'd tell Junior about the robbery anyway. It would serve them right. Why should they get to be happy?

Grace drove over to Cherokee's parents' place. They let her use the garage. She was pretty sure Isaiah wouldn't follow her anymore.

She parked and went in. She liked working late. It felt private and intimate, which was how it should be. She rolled back the cover until the front end of the car was exposed. It thrilled her every time but it made her sad and remorseful too, sometimes to the point of tears. The car was only a collection of metal parts but it meant much more than that. The fun, the closeness, the fantasy that something inanimate could give you attitude and coolness and you'd be a badass too. Grace didn't believe in heaven but she did believe in *presence;* that when a loved one passed, they left an essence within you that needed honoring and celebration or it would die and evanesce forever. The intake manifold was heavy. She fitted it into place and went to work.

It was quiet at Elena's house. Isaiah was pleased with Grace's mission to the knife shop, but they had a ways to go before all the pieces of the plan were in place. He hadn't told Dodson and Deronda about it. No need raising their expectations. Now he was in bed trying to gather himself. The torture had lasted less than a day, but it had affected him more than he'd anticipated. He had a hyped sense of danger now, like he had to be vigilant all the time. He was afraid.

The memory searches with Grace were going slowly, and unlike TV detectives, Isaiah needed time to consider, assemble, and formulate. It was like looking at the stars. At first, they seemed random, scattered helter-skelter by the Big Bang. Only when your mind connected that star to this one and this one to that one could you say, *That's a bear, that's Gemini, that looks like a soup ladle.* At the moment, all he had were stars.

He got a call from Dodson. Junior was at a club and looked like he'd be there awhile. Isaiah put on his shoes and walked in measured steps down the hall. Grace was coming the other way. She smelled like motor oil.

"What's going on?" she said.

"Junior's at a club. I've got to go help Dodson."

"I want to go," she said. "I owe him. I nearly got him killed."

"No, not a good idea."

"Why?"

"It's too dangerous."

She tipped her head sideways and looked at him thoughtfully. "So it's not too dangerous for you, Dodson, and Deronda, but it's too dangerous for the white girl?" He started to reply, but the words evaporated as soon as they hit the air. People had given him dirty looks before but nothing like the withering pale green laser beams burning a hole through his skull. He swallowed hard. "Yeah, sure, come along," he said. "We could use the help."

For the first time since Dodson bought the car, the stereo was off. He and Deronda were waiting for Isaiah in the parking lot at Shop 'n Save. Dodson didn't get scared too often but he was scared now. He'd rather get a beatdown from Michael Stokely than put his family at risk but that was what he'd done. He hoped that goes-around-comes-around shit wasn't true. God had a long list of crimes he could punish him for. Another first. Deronda was sitting there quietly, not bitching or accusing or talking shit about somebody. She was probably thinking about little Janeel. How he'd be affected if she was badly hurt or dead. There was no one to take care of him but her father, who was pushing seventy. Chester called.

"Hello, Mr. Dodson," he said, that Dane axe in the big voice. "Are we making progress?"

"Yes, we are," Dodson said. "Isaiah has come up with a plan and we're about to get to it right now."

"I hope you're not lying to me."

"That's the straight-up truth. I want to get this over with same as you." The call ended.

"Was that him?" Deronda said.

"Uh-huh," Dodson said.

"Is he as crazy as they say?"

"No. That boy is off the crazy scale altogether."

"We gotta do this, Dodson," she said, her eyes on her child's future. "Failure is not an option."

Isaiah and Grace arrived in the Audi. Deronda was incensed. "What's she doing here?" she said.

"She came to help," Isaiah replied, without much behind it.

Dodson was pissed too. "Help how?" he said like Grace wasn't there. "She gonna paint Junior's living room? The bitch almost got me killed!"

"What you shoulda brought is a couple of bloodhounds instead of Barbie Doll here," Deronda said.

Before Isaiah could go to her defense, Grace said evenly, "You're looking for Junior's money, aren't you? I'm another pair of eyes. Do you really want to pass that up?" Dodson and Deronda looked at each other, conceding with their silence.

"What's happening with Junior?" Isaiah said.

"He's still at the club," Deronda answered. "My sister's watching him. She'll text you if he leaves. I gave her your number."

"The fuck we waitin' for?" Dodson said. "Let's get this show on the road."

They drove to Junior's place in the Audi, Grace behind the wheel.

"You let her drive your car?" Deronda said. "She must be your girlfriend."

"No, she's not," Isaiah said.

"No, I'm not," Grace said at the same time.

"When we get there," Isaiah said hastily, "check for seams in the drywall, loose tiles, floorboards, and hatches in the ceiling. Does Junior have kids?"

"I hope not," Deronda replied. "That's all the world needs is more Juniors."

"I mean did you see a kids' room in the house?"

"No. Why?"

"It's a thing they do these days. A stuffed animal. Under the baby's mattress. When we get there, Dodson, take the kitchen. Grace, take the bedroom. There's probably a closet in the hallway. Deronda, take that."

"Why does she get the bedroom and I get the closet?" Deronda said.

"She's an artist. She sees things."

"What about you?"

"I'll look around."

Junior used to live in a condo in Bluff Park until Isaiah shot him and Michael Stokely in the hallway outside Junior's door. Since then, Junior had declared Caucasian neighborhoods too dangerous and had returned to the hood and the house where he was raised. Grace parked in the alley and they piled out of the car. Isaiah went into the trunk and equipped everybody with a screwdriver, a box cutter, and a small flashlight. They crept across the backyard like a herd of cats, Dodson and Deronda carrying the battering ram. The back door looked more invincible than it had in the photos, the grid of security bars thicker and more solid. Only the lock plate and the Medeco dead bolt were exposed.

"How do we get through the bars?" Grace said.

"We don't," Isaiah said. "If they hit the dead bolt hard enough, it'll rip right out of the doorframe."

Deronda and Dodson got in position with the ram. Isaiah had duct-taped the tongue of a sneaker over the business end. It would mitigate the noise but only a little. There was a moment of tense quiet, the teammates looking at each other. *Do or die.*

"You ready?" Dodson said.

"Fuck yeah I'm ready," Deronda said fiercely. Her game face was frightening. "Let's knock this muthafucka down."

They swung the ram, getting their rhythm, Deronda generating more speed than Isaiah could have if he was fit. Dodson said, "One...two...THREE!" There was a loud crash, the forty thousand pounds of force ripping the Medeco right off the wooden frame. There were grins of relief and elation. Isaiah raised his hand for quiet. They listened. Loud noises weren't uncommon in the hood; sirens, screams, fights, gunshots. Most were ignored unless they didn't stop. Who wants to stick their nose in somebody else's mess when you've got messes of your own? Isaiah nodded and they went inside.

Deronda's sister, Kalista, hadn't been out on the town since she'd started working at the food truck. It felt good to be at a club, dressed up slinky, swiggin' back Seven and Sevens and playing lookie-loo with the bruthas. *What's Cecil doing in here? This ain't no place to recapture your youth. You better go home and watch* The Price Is Right. *Oh no, don't be lookin' at me, you popeyed muthafucka. My shit ain't even in your hemisphere. Wait a minute, wait a minute, this brutha here look just like Denzel. Look at him, tryin' to check me out on the hush-hush. Don't be so shy, baby. Come on over here and buy Kalista a drink.*

She glanced over at Junior in the roped-off VIP area. *That's some daffy shit right there. Since when is a drug dealer a very important person? Da-yem, he's ugly. I seen better faces in a fish tank. Is that Michael Stokely? Why that nigga ain't dead or locked up is a muthafuckin' mystery—ohh shit. Here come Denzel! Yeah, baby, get your fine self over here. You and me is gonna party.*

Isaiah and the others froze when they saw Junior's decor. Deronda said, "It's something, ain't it?"

"Jesus," Grace said. "What's with all the zebra skins?"

Everyone dispersed to their assignments. Isaiah toured the house, getting the feel of the place, imagining himself as Junior with some cash to hide. He would have to visit his money frequently so Isaiah checked the carpet for worn spots in unusual places. He examined the edges and corners to see if any had been lifted. Nothing. He decided to focus on the rooms with hard floors.

The laundry room first. The washer and dryer were too obvious but he looked them over anyway. There was dust on the dryer control panel. The washer was open, a few clothes and a bath towel in the drum. Something under them? No. Anyplace else? No. There were no hollow spots in the walls or removable floor tiles.

He checked on Deronda and Grace and gave them instructions. *Move the bureau. Check the underside of that table. Take the trash out of that wastebasket. Behind the mirror. That plant is artificial. See what's under it.* He didn't need to tell Dodson anything. Dodson was a former drug dealer and had hidden more dope than Scarface. Isaiah moved Deronda to the living room, and she went to work slashing the couch to pieces with the box cutter. "Where's your money, Junior? You can't hide it from Deronda. She can *smell* money, she can *feel* money, she can—"

"Be quiet," Isaiah said. He was getting more and more anxious. If Junior hid his money somewhere else they were screwed. He eyed the drug paraphernalia on the coffee table. Rolling papers, a couple of bongs, baggies of weed, and a platinum lighter with Junior's initials engraved on it. Isaiah pocketed the lighter.

Denzel's real name was Robert, which Kalista preferred over those ghetto names. Her friend Jamonica had named her son Tylenol, a migraine of a child if there ever was one. Kalista had to admit, Robert had some savvy; not pushy, asking her about herself, not counting the drinks he was buying and paying for them with an American Express Gold Card. They danced a couple of times. He had below-average moves but at least he didn't do anything embarrassing like moonwalk or spin around on his head. At the moment, they were standing at the bar. He was leaning in close, whispering something about the curve of her neck, his warm breath sending jingle bells through her body. She was about to take this juicy brutha back to the crib when she glanced over his shoulder and sucked in a sharp breath. *Junior and his crew were gone.* "Oh shit."

"What?" Robert said.

"Stay right there, baby. I'll be back before you know it." Kalista hurried through the crowd, panic like acid reflux welling up in her throat. A huge security man stood at the entrance to the VIP area.

"Did Junior leave?" she asked him.

"Uh-huh."

"When?"

"A while ago. He got a phone call and busted on outta here. From the look on his face I'd say somebody's gonna get the hell beat out of 'em."

Isaiah searched the bathroom. He went through the drawers, the toilet tank, under the sink, the ceiling, the floor, the plumbing fixtures, and the drains. He flinched when he saw the dildo. There were two stacks of clean towels on a shelf wrapped in blue paper. Nothing in those either. Frustrated, he returned to the living room. Deronda was still slashing at things, stuffing spilling out of the furniture and floating around the room. He stood there visualizing everything he'd seen like a reel of microfiche, reexamining each frame for discrepancies. When he got to the laundry room he paused. The dryer had dust on the control panel. It hadn't been used, but there were clothes and a bath towel in the washing machine. Why use the washer and not the dryer? And why wash a towel when you had them delivered by a laundry service wrapped in blue paper? His phone buzzed. A text: JUNIOR'S ON HIS WAY!!

A car came roaring up. The doors burst open and four homicidal brothers got out.

"Oh my muthafuckin' God," Deronda said. Isaiah darted into the hallway and shouted in a stage whisper, "Dodson, Grace, let's go! Junior's here!" They went out the back and raced across the yard, Deronda muttering *Oh shit oh shit oh shit,* Dodson helping Isaiah along. *There was something tricky about that washing machine,* he thought.

"Dodson, drive," Isaiah said as they clambered in. "Where's Grace?"

"I don't know," Deronda said.

"I thought she was with you," Dodson said.

Isaiah nearly lurched out of his seat. *"You mean she's still in there?"*

Junior's neighbor had called him when she saw the gleam of a flashlight in his bedroom window. Junior and the crew came busting through the front door, guns drawn, halting when they saw the wreckage. "Oh shit!" Junior said. "My domicile has been exfoliated! Excavate the premises!" The fellas looked at him. "Search the goddamn house!" The fellas ran off in different directions. Junior sprinted straight to the laundry room.

Grace didn't know Isaiah had already searched the laundry room, and she hadn't heard him because the door was closed. She was feeling through the stacks of towels when she heard a man yelling and what sounded like the marines storm-trooping through the house. She looked around. There was no place to hide.

Junior yanked the laundry room door open, saying, "If my assets have been diversified I will coagulate every nigga in the neighborhood!" He couldn't remember being this outraged since that bitch Deronda almost tore his nuts off. He went directly to the washing machine. He lifted the spindle and the whole barrel came out with it. Underneath was an Adidas bag. He unzipped it and rifled through the bundles of bills, counting it out loud. All sixty-seven grand was still there. "See there," he said, pleased with himself. "This is the aftermath of deliberating with my mentality."

When Grace was ten years old, she had participated in an extracurricular program called Odyssey of the Arts. The students wrote poetry, performed scenes from *Duck Soup,* painted their dreams, sculpted their nightmares, and did a form of dance called Expressive Movement that combined ballet, jazz, Hula-Hoops, and gymnastics. Grace was a standout, cavorting about in pink spandex, doing the splits and twisting her body parts into curlicues, the other kids jealous because she was naturally flexible—which came in handy as she contorted herself into the dryer moments before Junior arrived, babbling some kind of nonsense about coagulating niggas. She was curled up like a fetus in a metal womb, the door open slightly but enough for him to see her if he looked. *Would* he look? She was relieved when he went straight to the washer. She could hear him lifting the lid and something else that clanked and made him grunt. Then he unzipped a bag. He babbled some more craziness about deliberating with his mentality, then the sounds went in reverse and he closed the lid. Grace's back was killing her, her neck was cramping up. *Leave, Junior! Leave already!* But he didn't. Instead, he made a call.

"What do you mean who is this?" he said. "Are you disqualified from deencryptin' your caller ID? What do I want? I want you to dispatch yourself to my constabulary on the double. I need you to deodorize my ambiance. What do I mean? I mean get your fat ass over here and clean my goddamn house! Oh, you will if you ever want to ingest my weed again—and bring Laeesha with you."

Junior left, but two girls were coming over to clean the house, which would no doubt include the laundry room.

* * *

Grace called. "Are you all right?" Isaiah said.

"I'm in the laundry room," she whispered. "I think the money's in the washing machine."

"Don't worry about the money. Stay quiet. I'll get you out of there in a couple of minutes." Isaiah ended the call.

"Did you just say don't worry about it?" Dodson said. "I need that money, Isaiah."

"I know you do."

"Then why'd you tell her that?" Deronda said.

"If they hear her and go in, they'll kill her. Do you want that on your heads?"

"Forget it, you're right," Dodson said. Deronda looked like it was a fifty-fifty call.

"What are you gonna do?"

"Talk to Junior."

"*Talk* to Junior? How? You got a translator that speaks gibberish?"

Junior looked him up and down when he came to the door. "And who might you be?"

"Isaiah Quintabe."

"That name has no validation with me."

"They call me IQ."

"Your initials don't clarify your job description."

"Your neighbor said you got robbed," Isaiah said. "I thought I could help."

"Junior DeWitt don't need no help. Now I suggest you exit my domicile while you still have the capacity to relocate your ass on outta here."

Michael Stokely appeared. "I heard of him. He's some kinda private detective. He helped out my homeboy Cheesy."

Isaiah entered the living room he'd been standing in a few minutes ago, the group eyeing him skeptically. "I'll look around first. Do you mind if I do this alone? I don't want the crime scene contaminated."

"If you're wasting my time your oblivion is irrefutable," Junior said. "And we might kill your ass too."

Isaiah wandered from room to room, not really looking at anything, pleased that it had worked out this way. It made things a lot easier. He texted Grace Get out now, and he heard her go out the back door. He returned to the living room.

"Did you discover anything irrelevant?" Junior said.

Isaiah paused a moment, blinked. "As a matter of fact I did." He took two items out of his pocket and handed them to Junior. "Do you recognize these?"

"No, I've never perceived them in my entire life-span."

"Well, they were in your house."

Grace drove away from Junior's, Deronda seated next to her with the Adidas bag on her lap, Dodson and Isaiah in the back. Deronda unzipped the bag and looked inside. "Check this out. Must be a million dollars in here." She tipped it back so Dodson could see it.

He took a quick glance. "I'd say that's sixty, seventy thousand, around in there. I hope that's enough to make Chester happy."

"Grace?" Deronda said. "I'm sorry for what I said. You stuck your neck out for us and I owe you big-time."

"No you don't," Grace said with a soft smile.

"You sure we gotta give all the money to Chester?" Deronda said. "How would he know if some of this fell out the car?"

"Can't be too much or he'll know," Dodson said. "How much you think, Isaiah?"

"When are you supposed to pay him?"

"Tomorrow. We could stall him."

"Then do that. Let's wait for a bit. See what comes up."

When they arrived back at Shop 'n Save, Deronda gave Grace a hug. "Thank you, baby. You ever need something you let me know."

"I will."

"Talk to me for a minute, Isaiah," Dodson said. Isaiah walked him to his car. "This shit ain't over," Dodson said. "Even if we pay Chester he'll be back for more." He read Isaiah's look. "You got a plan, don't you?"

"Yeah, but I'm not sure it'll work."

"I gotta get home. We'll talk about it, okay? How you doin' with Grace?"

"I don't know."

"Get used to it," Dodson said. "I been with Cherise for a while now, and she surprises me every day. I'll see you later—partner."

Two a.m. Isaiah peeked through the blinds and saw Grace in her dirty clothes, putting her toolbox into the GTI. He was resentful. All he'd done for her and she couldn't let him in on it? He'd had enough. He was going to go out there and demand to know what was going on. He was putting on his hoodie when Grace came in.

"Hi," she said.

"Hi," he said.

"I want you to come with me."

Neither of them said a word on the drive over. They got out of the car and she held his hand as they walked toward the garage. He felt like he was about to open Tutankhamen's tomb or get a first look at the Holy Grail.

"I guess you've been wondering what I've been doing," she said.

"A little," he said with a quick shrug.

She opened the door and turned on the light. There was the car with a cover over it, the one he'd seen before. "I've been working on it a long time," she said. "I've got things left to do but it's mostly there. Want to take off the cover?"

He went to the front of the car and pulled the cover toward him, slowly, enjoying the drama, Grace rigid with anticipation. It felt like there should be a soundtrack. The cover slid over the roof, down the windshield, over the hood, puddling on the floor. He recognized the car. A '68 Mustang GT, racing green with black wheels. It was beautiful but it didn't answer any questions. He walked around it, examining every part carefully. If the body had been restored you couldn't tell. Seamless surface, perfect paint. Every inch of chrome gleaming, every detail of the interior showroom-new. The car looked familiar but he couldn't put his finger on it.

"Where have I seen this before?" he said.

"It's the Mustang Steve McQueen drove in *Bullitt.*"

"You mean the actual car? Couldn't be."

"Everybody thought there were two of them," Grace said, "but there were really three. They needed one for the scenes, one as a spare, and one for rehearsal. A collector has the first one, Fox Studio is restoring the second, and this is the rehearsal car. They crashed it before shooting started."

"How do you know it's the real thing?" he said.

"Fox. Their name is on the registration." The car suddenly seemed bigger and brighter. "Nobody knew it would be valuable so it was sold for parts."

"How did you find it?" he said.

"I didn't. Dad did. He was stationed at an army depot up near Herlong for a while. When he was on leave, sometimes he'd go to San Francisco. He was in a salvage yard looking for—I don't know what it was, but somehow, he found the car." She smiled like she

270

was seeing her dad tell the story. "He said it was a miracle, like magic, like the car had been waiting for him." Her eyes brimmed with tears, her voice broke. "It was his dream car. He loved it so much." She bowed her head. "He loved it so much." Isaiah went to her and held her and she wept.

CHAPTER FOURTEEN

The God of Freedom

Grace entered the knife shop. Chester was wearing a bib and had what she hoped was tomato sauce clinging to his fangs.

"Hello again!" he bellowed. He went for a hug and she couldn't escape. He folded her into him, his body squishy and massive, reeking of a cologne that smelled like dead muskrats in an orange grove. She kept her hands on his hips to keep his groin from touching her. Finally, he let go. "You're looking quite lovely today, my dear. Tell me, how did your father like the knife?"

"Oh, he loved it! He said it was the best present ever!"

"Are you here to get him another?"

"No, I'm afraid not. I'm actually here to ask you a favor."

"Ask away!"

"I was hoping I could take some pictures?" she said in her meekest voice. "Dad really wants to see the shop."

Chester was ever so pleased. "Why, certainly!"

Grace took a few shots of the displays and Chester posing with his wares. He looked like a salesman for a tribe of Vikings, holding that battle axe. He insisted on taking selfies, his ponderous arm around her. It reminded her of Gordo.

"Chester, would it be okay if I took some pictures of your workshop?"

"Why, of course!" he said with a gallant sweep of his arm. "Right this way." They went into the back. There was a long workbench. Scattered about were unpolished blades, tools, grinders, rivets, handle materials, and other stuff she didn't recognize.

"Wow," she said. "So this is where the magic happens."

"Magic indeed." He held his lapels with both hands and looked off at a legacy that was apparently on the ceiling. "I believe it's a form of alchemy, hellfire transforming the very earth itself into boiling flames and the boiling flames into unyielding steel that will last through the millenniums and stand forever as a testament to the artistry of its maker." He blathered on. Grace took pictures and feigned attentiveness, one eye casting around for the perfect spot. She let him talk until she couldn't stand it anymore. She glanced at her pocket watch tattoo. "Oh heck. I'm late. Dad will be thrilled with the pictures."

"I was only too happy to oblige," Chester said. He walked her out, that big feverish mitt on her back. "I have a thought. Perhaps we might have lunch together. The Souplantation has a wide variety of salads and the clam chowder is scrumptious."

"Oh, I can't today," she said with feigned regret. "How about I call you tomorrow?"

"Excellent, excellent, I look forward to it."

As soon as Grace got out of the shop, she shivered to get the cooties off and hurried to her car. *Jesus,* he was creepy. She called Isaiah.

"How'd it go?"

She beamed through the phone. "I think it went fine."

"Good. We'll see what happens."

Grace went back to the house and showered to remove any trace of Chester. She wished Ruffin was there, but Elena made them leave the dog at TK's. She thought she'd help Elena cook dinner, but as she approached the kitchen, she heard Elena on the phone, arguing with her boyfriend. He lived in Temecula and rarely came to see her.

"Don't say you miss me," Elena said. "Knock on the door and tell me you have tacos."

Grace wanted no part of that conversation so she went into the living room. Isaiah was sitting cross-legged on the floor. He had printed out Sarah's pictures and they were spread out in rows. Grace sat down next to him and felt a zing as their knees touched. He didn't acknowledge her. He was deep in the zone, she knew that now. He was rearranging the photos like a street hustler working a shell game. He stopped. She waited. He indicated the four pictures of the van parked under the carport.

"These were taken on different days," he said. She couldn't tell if he was talking to her or to himself.

"Why would it take more than one day to pack?" she said.

"No, I mean they're separate trips."

"Are you sure? Everybody's wearing the same thing. Same bikinis, the man's wearing the same orange T-shirt."

"The T-shirt is a little more faded in this one," he said. "And look at the van's registration tags. They're different colors. Blue, yellow, red. I still don't get this," he said, tapping the words on the side of the van. EVER AFTER.

"What does it all mean?" she asked.

"It looks like your mom and her friends went on this trip every year, someplace special, like an annual event, but by the time you were a teenager, she'd stopped going. Why do you think?"

"My dad, maybe. He thought her friends were hippies and he hated hippies."

"I think they went there." Isaiah put his finger on the picture of the miniature house that was painted beige and set on the desert plain. Grace tried to make the connection but couldn't.

"How can you tell?"

He indicated the picture of Sarah and her friends building something in the backyard. "That's what they're building," he said. "The little house. See the cans of paint? They're the same color beige— and see this?" He shifted his gaze back to the photo of the house and the tiny flea-size speck at the edge of the frame.

"What is that?"

"It's the tip of a feather. From this." He tapped the photo of the orange bicycle with the long tail feather stowed inside the van.

"Oh my God, you're right!" she said, taken more than ever with this quiet man with his quiet ways. "But how do we know Mom's gone there now?"

"We don't, but maybe—" He zoned out again. She watched his eyes moving slowly over the photos centimeter by centimeter. "Here." He tapped the photo of the guy reading the paper, part of the headline visible. 37 GO.

"Thirty-seven go?"

"I think the rest of the line is *thirty-seven gold medals.* The Olympics." She was stunned.

"You follow the Olympics that closely?"

"The date on the headline is August. I can't think of anything else that would fit." She did a search on her phone.

"You're right," she said wonderingly. "The US won thirty-seven gold medals at the 2000 Games. But I don't see how that's connected to Mom."

"The Olympics take place in August, and it's August now."

Grace summed it up. "Okay, so every August, my mom goes on this trip to the desert until my dad stops her, but now that she's free to do whatever she wants she's gone there again?" It was a reach and even if he was right, California was full of deserts and so was the whole Southwest. Isaiah's shoulders slumped. He blew out a big disappointed breath, his sense of failure palpable.

"It's okay," she said. She put her hand on his shoulder. He stiffened. Damn, she thought. She'd embarrassed him. He didn't look at her.

"I've got to go to my place," he said. "Pick up a few things."

"Can I go with you?"

No one was watching the house. As soon as they came in, that familiar feeling of loneliness and isolation overcame him. He wondered if she felt it too. "Could you grab some of Ruffin's food?" he said. "The kitchen, the cupboard on the right."

He went to the bedroom and packed some stuff in a duffel bag. He knew where everything was and left the light off. He hurried, feeling like she might leave if he wasn't there. Even in the dark, he could see her painting as clearly as if it was propped up on the kitchen counter next to the toaster. He went still. Something was edging into his consciousness. He couldn't identify it, not even vaguely, but he knew it was urgent. Pivotal. Revelatory. Good or bad, he couldn't tell, or even if those labels applied. He could see pieces now, vague and unknowable, drifting around in an endless void. Slowly, they moved toward each other, and with that came a growing anxiety that made the progression even more momentous. The pieces massed together and conjoined, breathtaking in their scope and meaning. It was as if an exploded sun had reassembled itself, its shards and fragments returned to their proper places, its shining form filling the emptiness with light. He didn't move for fear it would fall apart. He understood Grace's sadness. He understood her real secret. He was startled when her arms reached around him. He looked down at her small hands resting on his chest and felt her body pressed against him. She turned him around and kissed him and he kissed her back and everything was fine.

She awoke the next morning and smelled good coffee and toasted bread, the warmth of him lingering like something aged and precious on the tongue. She yawned and sat up. Her painting was on the wall in front of her. At the studio, it was part of the atmosphere, blending in with everything else. Here, it was stark and shocking, her nightmares exploding out of the canvas like the maw of an incubus, engulfing her in its wet heat, laughing as it feasted on her newfound confidence, grinding it into the ridiculous fiction it was. She put her head in her hands. "I'm so stupid! *What am I doing?*" She went to the bathroom, washed her face, and waited until she calmed down. She joined Isaiah in the kitchen and she could tell from his expression he felt the change in her.

"You okay?" he said.

"Yeah, yeah, I'm fine." He gave her coffee and she held the cup like an offering. She sipped in the strained silence. She wanted to reassure him, say *We can still be friends,* but that sounded fucked up no matter who said it or how. She tried diverting him back to the case. "About my mom? I know you did your best." He turned away. She'd embarrassed him *again.* When they got to Elena's, he went straight inside.

Grace watched TV with Elena. The program made no sense or maybe it was her. She worried about Isaiah, wondering if he was beating himself up. Or hating her. Finally, she couldn't stand it anymore and knocked on his door. He didn't answer, but she could hear him talking to himself. She went in. He was standing in the middle of the room, staring at a darkened window.

"Reno," he said.

"Reno? What about it?"

"Your mom got a speeding ticket in Reno. In August of 2000." That frightening memory again.

"Well, it's the desert," she said. She hesitated. Did she really need to keep challenging him? She had to. She had to find her mom. "But if they went camping, why there? There are way better places to go than that."

He turned away from the window and looked at the floor. "The bicycle," he murmured. "The bicycle...the bikinis...the hat...the house." She could hear his gears whirring and wished she could get inside his head and watch them work. He said, "Your mom was going someplace where you can ride an orange bicycle with feathers on it, wear bikinis and silly hats. Someplace where you'd put a little beige house in the middle of nowhere. Does that mean anything to you? Do you associate any of that with Reno?"

"No. I'm drawing a blank."

"Damn," he said. He put his hands in his front pockets. They heard Elena calling them for dinner. "I'm going to wash up," he said, and he left the room.

Grace remained there, thinking, her forehead wrinkled. She wanted to help, to make his theory work. Sparks in her memory were trying to ignite, the tinder stubbornly resisting. "What *is it?*" she said. It was agonizing. Spark. Spark. Spark. Another spark. And then...

A flame!

She ran to the bathroom and pounded on the door. "Isaiah, open up!"

He came out. "What? Are you okay?"

With her eyes open wide she said, *"Burning Man!"*

Owens got out of the Santa Fe city jail feeling older, dried up and derelict. She had a total of nineteen texts and voice mails from Walczak telling her to check out her Jerry and get her drunk ass home. She bought a bottle of Grey Goose, got a motel room, and had a couple of pick-me-ups. She drank a lot, but she didn't think she had a problem. Yeah, sometimes she binged and stayed in her apartment blotto for a couple of days, but that was only once in a while. Her favorite thing used to be getting functionally drunk and going to Knott's Berry Farm. It was nothing like the ranch she'd grown up on, but she liked it anyway. The rattling stagecoach with horses that smelled like alfalfa, the buildings made of old wooden planks. She liked to pan for gold, everybody looking at her because she wasn't seven years old. People saw her uniform and said thank you for your service. There were *Peanuts* characters everywhere. She got banned from the park for offering Snoopy a slug of vodka from her water bottle. Owens worked behind the bakery counter at Vons, putting lemon tarts and banana cream pies into the display cases and spelling out HAPPY 70TH GRANDPA on birthday cakes. Her supervisor, Tina, called. A total bitch, her enormous belly a storage tank for a lot of the inventory. She wanted to know where in the world Owens had been for the last few days. "A better hell than yours," Owens said. "And by the way? Fuck you."

Owens volunteered after 9/11 because she wanted to help her country. She wanted to make a difference. Be a patriot. Then she got over there and what she was doing felt disconnected from anything to do with country or patriotism. It was like the house was on fire and you were somewhere pulling weeds. And that was what she brought back with her, that disconnectedness. The feeling that you had separated yourself from the human race and now you were something apart and broken and alone. She wanted Jimenez. Who else would have her? No normal man could know what she'd done and not leave in disgust.

The Grey Goose gave her a boost. She cleaned up and went to see her Jerry. His real name was Arthur Freeman. He owned a bookstore called Turning Pages. It was funky and cramped and stank of incense. Books about politics, war, and dead photographers were on the front table, a yellow Lab slept on the floor, yearning in yips. Owens meandered around and found what she was looking for above a table of close-outs: a framed photograph of Arthur, shaking hands with Michael Moore. There was no doubt about it. Arthur was Jerry and Jerry was Arthur. Same hair, beard, paunch, contours of the face. He was definitely the man who was with Sarah that night in the diner.

Owens approached the faggot mincing around behind the counter. Red hair, a Jewfro, a name tag that said I'M CAMERON. ASK ME ANYTHING!

"Good morning," he said brightly. "How can I help you today?"

"I'm an old friend of Arthur's. Is he around?"

"No, I'm afraid not. He went on vacation."

"Went with Sarah, did he?"

Cameron smiled at the familiarity. "Yes, as a matter of fact. They took off yesterday."

"Where'd they go?"

"I'm sorry, I can't tell you that."

"Are you sure? We was supposed to get together."

"Well, you know Arthur," he said with affection. "That's the way he is."

Owens went to her car and waited until closing time. Cameron came out, rolling his ten-speed—what else? She followed him to a coffeehouse—where else? And then to an old adobe apartment building, as funky as the bookstore—of course. She put on a ski mask and latex gloves and followed him as he walked his bike up the stairs. When he opened his apartment door, she said, "Hey." He turned around. She stuck a gun in his face and said, "Say one word and I'll shoot you in the mouth." She gestured with the barrel and they went inside.

"Take anything you want," he said. "Just don't hurt Peaches." Alarmed, Owens glanced around quickly and saw a marmalade cat, sitting on the arm of a chair, twitching its tail.

"Get out your phone," she said. "Put in the passcode and give it to me." He did as he was told. "Now stand over there, face the wall, put your hands on your head, and lace your fingers together." She went through the emails and texts.

"It's okay, sweetheart," Cameron said to the cat, who wasn't the least bit upset. "Everything's fine."

Owens saw what she wanted and pocketed the phone. "Turn around."

He did. He had that familiar look of impending death. "You're not going to kill me, are you?"

"No, you're safe." She threw a vicious right and knocked him unconscious. Peaches yowled and scrambled under the couch. Owens went out to her car and called Walczak.

"Well?" he said.

"They went to Burning Man."

"Burning Man? What the hell is that?"

You had to drive through Reno to get to Black Rock Desert, where the Burning Man festival was held. A seven-day affair that was way more than a festival. It was an entire metropolis, a pop-up population center on a vast desert plain of nothingness, not a tree, a bush, or a fire hydrant anywhere in sight. The website said it was... *a culture of possibility... a network of dreamers and doers.* A blogger said it was like Woodstock, the Rose Bowl parade, Halloween night in Hollywood, and the world's biggest rave all rolled into one. Isaiah had asked Dodson to help and he was happy to get away from Chester fucking Babbitt.

Grace drove at top speed while Isaiah and Dodson looked at photographs of the festival.

"Damn, man, this is some dippy shit right here," Dodson said.

There were tens of thousands of people gathered in an area as big as San Francisco. *Acres* of parked cars and RVs were neatly arranged in a huge U of concentric half-rings. Within the rings there were what they called *camps.* Groups of people banded together to create their own Xanadus of canopies, tents, exhibitions, art installations, performance stages, water dispensaries, and chow lines. The camps had names. 1001 NIGHTS, 17 VIRGINS, VILLAGE NOT FOUND, 7 DEADLY GINS, FIRST BANK OF BRC.

In between the U's arms was the Playa. An immense space, a desert unto itself, too vast to walk across in the intense heat. Everyone had bicycles or drove some kind of strange vehicle. Here and there, like bizarre oases, were harem-size canopies, geodesic domes, outlandish sculptures as big as buildings, and structures for which there were no names. An imperial road, wide enough for the Roman legions, led down the center of the U, into the desert and up to the Burning Man: a massive wooden stick figure, 155 feet tall, held upright by steel cables strong enough to withstand the powerful dust storms. It might have been a Nazca line character come to life or a totem for an ancient tribe of islanders, its eyeless gaze looking out over an endless sea of sand. A daunting place to find one woman, assuming Sarah was there at all. Isaiah had no idea how he'd approach it.

As they drove, he glanced at Grace several times, hoping for some sign that things between them were all right, but her gaze never wavered from the road. He wondered what had happened. Was the sex that bad? It didn't seem to be. From his perspective it was intense, passionate, and beautiful. He thought it might be something else he'd done, didn't do, said or didn't say. He hated that he was so inept at this. Okay, maybe she was distracted because they were on their way to find her mother. That had to be it. Who wouldn't be distracted? He'd stick with that explanation for now.

Dodson called Cherise and reassured her he'd be okay. Even through the phone you could hear her mother saying something about Earl Cleveland never running off to the desert. Dodson and Cherise went on talking about moving into a bigger apartment and taking the baby to the doctor, their closeness and partnership self-evident. Somehow, that raised the tension in the car, as if Isaiah's needs and Grace's rejection of them were on full display. They stopped in to get gas and buy bicycles and a bumper rack to keep them on. Isaiah said he could drive and Grace gave him a battened-down smile when they switched seats.

"You okay?" he said.

"Yeah, I'm fine," she said, her voice as blank as the washed-out sky. He took the wheel, and she contented herself watching the blur of drab scenery go by. Fresno, Merced, Stockton.

"Want to listen to some music?" he said.

"No thanks."

He reached across the cup holders and tried to hold her hand but she curled up to sleep. He was distraught but kept it in.

Cameron woke up. The pain in his head thumped. His vision was off-center and he couldn't keep his balance. Terrified, he found Peaches and hugged her, bleeding on her fur. "Are you all right, baby?" The woman who assaulted him was the same one who came into the store and asked about Arthur. He called Arthur repeatedly but all he got was his voice mail. And then he remembered. There was no cell service at Burning Man. "Oh, Arthur," Cameron said.

Arthur and Sarah held hands as they rode their bicycles side by side. They were in the Playa and the sun was setting, the raw desert dyed purple and gold, mutant vehicles gliding past. A psychedelic trolley car, a snail clad in armor plating, a ship made of scrap metal, merry-go-round horses prancing on the deck. Some of the huge art installations were burning, set ablaze to acknowledge that life is fleeting, live it while you can. They looked like pagan bonfires or a village in Vietnam set ablaze by the invaders. Arthur glanced at Sarah, the flames illuming her face in shimmering amber. She was beaming. She was joyous. More alive than he'd ever seen her. They smiled as they rode past a caravan of teapots and a grove of glowing tulips tall as trees.

"I'm free," Sarah said. "I'm free."

* * *

Owens was gloating when she arrived at Walczak's house. She'd found the real Jerry. "What have you been doing all this time?" she said. "Pickin' lint out of your belly buttons?" She grinned at Hawkins, who replied with an *I'll deal with you later* glare.

Walczak thought about taking the company helicopter but it would have to make a fuel stop and was slow compared to the jet. They landed in Reno, rented a van, and joined the bumper-to-bumper traffic. Thousands of people were heading to see the final ceremony, the burning of the Burning Man.

Jimenez and Owens were sitting in the backseat, the road noise covering their voices. "The fuck are you doing?" he said. She had her hand on his thigh.

She pulled her hand away. "Nothin'. I ain't doing nothin'."

"Don't they have some kind of VIP service?" Walczak said, honking the horn.

"No, they're very democratic," Hawkins said. "They don't give a fuck who you are."

"That's a shame, it really is. One of these days, somebody's going to have the balls to make America great again. You wait and see."

"What's that supposed to mean?" Hawkins said. "All you rich white men will run the show? Leave us niggas out all over again?"

"What *is* your problem, Hawkins?"

"My problem is you, motherfucker."

"Well, what exactly?" Walczak said. "What *exactly* is your beef?"

"My beef is this. We all did some dirty shit over there, but the only one who came out of it with anything is you."

"And whose fault is that?" Walczak replied. "All us rich white men who held you back? The fact is, I made my way and you didn't. That's nobody's fault but your own."

Hawkins was about to get into it when Richter said, "There's a cop up there. Pull over."

A highway patrolman was sitting on his motorcycle, waving the traffic along. Walczak stopped and flashed his fake FBI ID. "Officer, we've got a situation."

Photographs of Burning Man were one thing, but nothing could have prepared Isaiah for the reality of being there. It could have been a rodeo for circus performers or a circus for rodeo clowns or Comic-Con on amphetamines or Mardi Gras on Jupiter or all of the above. *Hordes* of people were dancing to a pounding techno beat or juggling bowls of goldfish or riding bicycles that looked like scorpions or plodding around on stilts flapping angels' wings or playing in a marching band of women wearing white wigs, white makeup, and white choir robes.

"You people are crazy," Dodson said.

"You people?" Grace said.

"You see any bruthas out here?" They looked around. Not a black or brown face anywhere.

"Think of it this way," Grace said. "You guys have more sense."

The costumes made Stephanie's hat seem like a plaid shirt. There was a ball gown, a gas mask, and deer horns made from tinfoil. There was a ringmaster's tailcoat, a thong, and fireman's boots. There was a parrot's bill, pasties, and an overcoat of blinking Christmas lights. There were hundreds of near-naked bodies and glittery body paint and Mad Max goggles and hair extensions in peacock colors and masks—of monsters, werewolves, wild beasts, politicians, superheroes, emojis, cartoon characters, and faces for which there were no names, the whole scene lit up with a blazing array of strobe lights, neon lights, light sticks, bonfires, and the eyes of people on Ecstasy. Set farther back into the desert stood the Burning Man. Towering and majestically uplit, the God of

Freedom, its silent imperial voice commanding you to come forth and worship. The massive crowd was starting to move in that direction. The witching hour was at hand. Isaiah, Grace, and Dodson stood there, overwhelmed. It was like watching the great migration of wildebeest crossing the Serengeti. Locating Sarah was no more likely than finding the one with a spot under its chin.

"I'm sorry," Isaiah said.

"It's okay." Grace wiped a tear away with her knuckle and they joined the crowd.

Sarah and Arthur were in the second row closest to the Man. Sarah had never seen anything so awe-inspiring in her life. She clutched Arthur's arm and said, "Oh my." The ceremony started with a fireworks display, great gushers of sparks screaming and exploding against the black sky, the glowing sparks floating back to earth like heaven's fairy dust, the multitudes oohing and ahhing like they'd never seen fireworks before. As the display got louder and brighter, the crowd went berserk with anticipation, the din crashing against your eardrums, becoming almost unbearable, and then, all at once, the Man erupted into towering flames. They reached into the heavens, singeing the moon and spreading a quavering orange radiance across the Playa, the crowd screaming and laughing and whooping, cupping their hands around their mouths so eternity could hear them, and Sarah and Arthur hugged and kissed and cried.

The highway patrolman escorted the team onto the grounds and now they were walking through the weirdest shit any of them had ever seen.

"What's wrong with these people?" Walczak said. "Are they all on drugs?" The crowd was returning to the camps to party, the fading glow of the Burning Man in the distance. A naked, sweaty, immensely overweight man with a penis head and the head of a puppet on his penis came riding by on a unicycle.

"That offends me," Hawkins said. He stuck his foot in the spokes and the man careened into a canopy and the whole thing came crashing down, hippies running everywhere. Jimenez and Owens howled. Richter was bent over double laughing.

"WILL YOU STOP FUCKING AROUND?" Walczak screamed. The group stopped laughing but only because the wind had picked up and the air was choked with grit. They pulled their shirts up over their noses.

"Check your radios," Walczak yelled over the racket. "We'll lose each other in this mess."

"Do you know where we're going?" Jimenez said.

"Yes. It was in Arthur's emails."

The ceremony was over. Isaiah, Grace, and Dodson moved with the crowd back to the camps. Grace was looking around like she was in a life raft, lost at sea, searching the horizon for salvation. It was heartbreaking. Isaiah had let her down again. He'd failed. When they got back to Long Beach, she'd disappear and remember him as an incompetent fool who'd led her astray and was lousy in bed. He was trying to think of something to say when he realized he was feeling sorry for himself. He'd given up, too preoccupied with Grace to *do his fucking job.* He refocused; images, conversations, and printed words rolling past on the backs of his eyelids, his mind picking out stars of data he could connect into a constellation.

He saw the pictures of Sarah and Stephanie in their bikinis posing in front of the van. There was some connection between the picture and what he was seeing now, something the same but not the same, like sneakers and hiking boots. What was it? *Think, Isaiah, think. Try to remember. What was it? What was it, goddammit?* He remembered their arrival here, their shock at seeing the place and walking dumbfounded through the camps. GENITAL PORTRAIT STUDIO, CAMP BE BOTHERED, EMBASSY FOR EXTRATERRESTRIALS. He stopped and said, "Ever After."

"What?" Grace said.

"The words on the van. Ever After. *It's the name of a camp!*"

They got directions and mounted their bikes. Dodson pedaled, Isaiah sitting on the handlebars. Grace raced ahead, standing on the pedals, grim and unstoppable, sweat darkening her shirt. "Mom is here. I know she is."

Walczak's team trudged. The dust was blowing even harder and Camp Ever After was way the fuck over on the other side. They needed transportation. They tried to buy bicycles, but for some stupid reason, they didn't use money here. There was some sort of fucked-up bartering system. Walczak tried to trade his Rolex but no one believed it was real.

"Fuck this," Hawkins said. He gestured at a tent set a ways off from the others. You could see silhouettes through the fabric, a four-seater golf cart covered in seashells parked in front. Jimenez and Hawkins went in together. They surprised three naked people writhing around on an air mattress. "Gimme the key to the golf cart," Hawkins said.

The skinny white guy with the dick shaped like an ear of corn stood up. "Get out of here. You can't do this."

The bald-headed girl with three nose rings and a tat of the Japanese war flag dawning out of her pubes said, "There's security here, you know."

"We can have you arrested," the girl with the hairy armpits and a bush like Madagascar declared. They Tasered all three of them, found the keys, took their water and kerchiefs for their faces. They piled into the golf cart, Hawkins standing on the running board. They asked around. Camp Ever After was thataway. It took forever driving through the rabble but they got there. The so-called camp was just a random area marked off from its neighbors by the orientation of the tents. It was a fucking melee like everywhere else, everybody partying like a giant meteor had just passed through the stratosphere. The team checked their radios again and split up.

Walczak drew the kerchief up over his face, grit in every crease and crack in his body, the cacophony unceasing. There was no chance they'd find Sarah in this shit storm. She could be standing right next to him wearing a testicle mask or driving around in a shopping cart full of snapping turtles. A whoosh of flames made Walczak duck. It was a goddamn fire-eater. The guy was carrying a torch and blowing solvent onto the flames, a burst of them billowing into the air, people gawking like this had never been done before.

He shouted at the wind. "I HATE THIS FUCKING PLACE!"

They arrived at Camp Ever After, exhausted. Massive numbers of people were partying. "I'll take the left side," Grace said. "Dodson, can you take the right?"

"I'm on it."

"If we haven't found her in an hour, meet back here," Isaiah said. Grace and Dodson moved off. Isaiah remained, turning in a circle, doing his hawk-eye thing. If Sarah was visible he'd see her. He blinked. Walczak was coming right toward him. He was pissed off, sweating, his tennis sweater soiled with dust, his grimace gleaming unnaturally. "You're in a lot of trouble," he said, "but I guess you know that."

"You are too." Isaiah hated evil motherfuckers like Walczak and Seb, their rot and stink an infectious corruption like leprosy on a child. Irrationally, he wanted them to acknowledge what they were, what they'd done, and how the world would be a better place if they had never existed. "What does Sarah have on you?" Isaiah said.

"Pictures of you torturing and killing helpless people who couldn't fight back? That's what you did, isn't it? Tortured and killed helpless people who couldn't fight back?"

Walczak smirked. "Keep talking, asshole."

"I'm curious," Isaiah went on like he was asking about lawn care. "How do you feel when you look back on all that? Do you think you were a hero? That you were courageous? That you were serving your country?"

Walczak stepped in close. "I'm going to kill you, Isaiah. I'm gonna kill you *slowly.*"

"Let me put it another way," Isaiah said. "If your family knew what you did, would they be proud of you? Would *anybody* be proud of you? When those pictures come out, will you be proud of yourself?"

"Listen, you fuck," Walczak said. "Spend your measly million bucks while you can because you don't have much time left."

"What's *wrong* with you?" Isaiah said earnestly. "Sarah beat you out of some chump change and now you have to *kill* her? That's not a rational response. That's what a crazy man would do. That's what a sociopath would do. Don't you have any perspective on yourself? Don't you see what you are? You're a useless degenerate, Walczak. A creature, like a leech or a cockroach, but at least they serve a purpose. Why don't you do mankind a favor and go somewhere and die?"

"Don't ever let your guard down," Walczak said. "Not ever in your life."

"You have a false impression of me," Isaiah said.

"Do I? And what's that?"

"You're under the impression that I'm afraid of you."

Walczak heard something in his earbud. He reacted sharply and turned away. "Meet at the cart," he said as he ran off. *They found Sarah,* Isaiah thought. He hobbled after Walczak but couldn't keep up and watched him thread his way through the crowd and converge with the others at a golf cart. He'd never catch them. Reflexively, he reached for his useless phone, despaired a moment, and went to look for Grace.

Arthur and Sarah whirled around in a mad waltz, laughing and making out. The crowd was dancing wildly. Joints were passed and people were dipping their cups into a garbage can full of lethal-looking punch, not even lemons or oranges floating in it. The dust was picking up, but they were used to it now. Arthur got winded and sat down at a picnic table and she sat on his lap.

"Isn't this wonderful?"

"Yes, it is. It's the best."

"Thank you, Arthur. Thank you so much." She kissed him hard on the mouth. He broke it off. "What's the matter?" she said. He pointed with his chin. Through the crowd, they caught a glimpse of Walczak and his team gathering at a golf cart. The Latino man was pointing in their direction. "No, it can't be!" Sarah cried.

"Easy, my love. Stay calm. We've got to get to the car." He took her hand and they hurried to their bicycles. "We're going to be okay. We're going to be fine."

Grace made her way through the frenzy of partyers, searching desperately for her mother's face, her mother's love, the ten years they'd lost forever. The crowd was so huge, the music so loud. A wave of hopelessness overtook her and she stopped, irrationally angry at Isaiah. He was supposed to find her mom. He *said* he would find her mom. But here she was, wandering around blindly, stupidly, with absolutely no chance of—"Jesus Christ."

There was Sarah. Grace couldn't believe it. It had to be an apparition or a trick of the light. She blinked and stared but it was her mom all right, riding off on a bicycle with a heavyset man.

291

Like a punch to the heart, Grace felt the long days of hope and despair, of wanting and wishing, of saying her mother's name aloud when she woke up and when she went to sleep. A decade of emotions exploded out of her. "MAAAAHM!" she screamed. Ecstatic, she started to run but slowed and recoiled in horror. Walczak and the others were in a golf cart speeding after them.

"Oh no! Oh no!"

The cart swerved around a group of revelers and smashed into the fire-eater, his torch flung onto a tent. Walczak tried to keep driving but the crowd was angry, grabbing the cart and rocking it back and forth and screaming at the team. The team screamed back, threatening and shoving people away. More people were massing, trying to see what was happening. Grace fought her way through them, screaming *Maaahm, Maaahm!* The fire-eater's torch had set a tent on fire and what was probably a propane lamp exploded. Not chaos, but pure mayhem broke out, some of the crowd pushing in to help, others panicked and pushing to get away, the fire leaping from tent to tent, people slapping at the flames with blankets and dousing them with water bottles, dark smoke billowing, everyone screaming and shouting while the flames grew and grew, fanned by the wind.

A bunch of young guys, fueled by alcohol, were brawling with Walczak's team. The giant black guy was enjoying himself, grinning as he punched faces and kicked groins. The Latino guy was judo-flipping his opponents but getting hit repeatedly, bloodied but strangely patient, as if it would all end soon. Porkpie swung wildly, the tall woman whacking people with a police baton. Walczak was workmanlike, downing one attacker after another as if he was unloading a truck. People were throwing rocks and cans of food and chunks of firewood, the team with arms over their heads. Grace was joyful and screamed her delight. Her mom was getting away! And then Porkpie drew a gun and fired into the air. BLAM BLAM BLAM

BLAM. The mayhem was a game of croquet compared to the flat-out craziness that detonated. The entire area broke apart, people streaming between the flaming tents, dragging their friends along, hands over their faces, choking on the black smoke.

"Oh no!" Grace shouted. "Please, no!" The golf cart was free and speeding into the desert night, the crew screaming at their prey. Grace chased them, but the cart was far ahead, its taillights like dying embers, getting dimmer and dimmer. "Don't you hurt her! DON'T YOU HURT MY MOM!" The taillights disappeared, swallowed by darkness and the whorls of storming dust. Grace fell to her knees. She screamed and beat the desert floor with her fists and wept. And then Isaiah was there, kneeling beside her.

"They'll get her," she sobbed. "Walczak will get her and kill her!"

"No, he won't," Isaiah said. His voice was as hard as Chester's battle-axe. He picked her up and said, "Let's go."

CHAPTER FIFTEEN

Gravity

The team had caught up with Sarah and Arthur on the fringe of the parking area where there were no lights and no people. A few well-placed zaps and a punch to Arthur's solar plexus ended the brief struggle. The money was in their car, packed in two medical bags. They'd only spent forty or fifty grand.

"That's nothing," Walczak said.

"Oh yeah?" Hawkins said. "Well, you better write a check for nothing as soon as we get back."

The team headed to LA in the rented van, their captives tied up, duct tape over their mouths. Walczak flew back, saying for a million dollars he deserved it. Jimenez hunched down next to Sarah and ripped the tape off her mouth. She was conscious, panting, her head lolling around.

"You stupid bitch," he said. "Why would you do something like this? Didn't you know what you were up against? You could have avoided the whole thing if you'd minded your own fucking business." He was drinking one of Owens's beers. He held the cold bottle to his head. "Okay, here's the deal. You tell us what we want to know and you can walk."

"No we won't," Sarah rasped. "As soon as you're done with us you'll kill us."

"Yeah, but we can kill you fast or kill you slow. Slow is fucked up. It'll take *days* for you to fucking die. From hunger, thirst, whippings, the cattle prod. We'll hang you over a fire and lock you in a trunk with your own shit."

"He ain't fucking around, girl," Hawkins said. "I seen him do all that shit."

Sarah didn't reply and Jimenez slapped her hard. She cried out and sobbed, Arthur straining to get loose, saying *mmmff mmmff* into the duct tape. Jimenez leaned in close to her, trying to sound earnest because he was. "Tell us what we want to know. I swear to God it's for your own good." Sarah kept her lips pinched together and said nothing. "Don't say I didn't give you a chance," Jimenez said. He put the duct tape back over her mouth and got up.

"Did you tell her that if she don't fess up we'll kill Grace?" Hawkins said.

"Oh yeah. We'll kill Grace."

They underestimated Arthur, lots of people did. He was a paranoid hippie, a soap box liberal, another raving radical who had his picture taken with Michael Moore. Yes, he was all of those things, but he would not go quietly when the State came to get him. He would not go quietly when the right-wing militias came to get him. He had survival gear and freeze-dried food in his basement. He had an assault rifle he knew how to use. He had a tactical knife strapped to his calf.

Arthur had always longed for a cause he'd be willing to die for, but government overreach, Fox News, and mortgage-backed securities never seemed like enough. But Sarah was. She was leaning against him, whimpering, tears dripping over the duct tape and falling into her lap. She was always thanking him for bringing her back to life, but it worked both ways. Arthur had watched his wife die in a hospice, all twigs and empty eye sockets. His brilliant son, a master carpenter, died of a heroin overdose. Arthur had found him sitting on the toilet, the needle still stuck in the blight of purple tracks on his arm.

Arthur sincerely believed in his causes, but his grief made him rabid; fighting with cops, brawling with neo-Nazis, and sneering at death threats, glad he'd provoked them. Sarah had soothed his sorrow and filled his loss with love. She changed his diet, made him exercise and take his blood pressure medicine. They went to concerts and took long walks and cooked each other meals. They cuddled and laughed and made love. He was happy for the first time in years. Walczak was going to kill Sarah the minute he got the passwords but they'd have to climb over Arthur's dead body to do so. He had to keep her alive as long as he could, and if he lost his life in the process so be it. He could feel the knife in its sheath and the sweat under the Velcro straps. Be patient, he said to himself. They'd take him for granted and let their guard down and when they did, they'd be sorry.

Grace drove to the Reno airport while Isaiah used his phone to find a pay site and get Walczak's address. Dodson was asleep in the backseat. Grace kept glancing at Isaiah, waiting for him to say something. He let the silence go on. He was resentful. Here he'd been risking his life and *she* was going to shut *him* out?

"Could you tell me what you're thinking?" she said. "What we're going to do?"

"I don't know yet," he said, though he'd already sketched out a plan.

They left her car in the long-term lot and took a flight back to LA. Every seat was taken. Isaiah and Grace sat together, Dodson a few rows away. The seats in coach were built for legless anorexic people. Every once in a while, their elbows touched and were quickly withdrawn. The filtered air, the chemical smell of ballistic nylon, and the closeness of the cabin made Isaiah feel trapped, the whine of the engines heightening the tension like a drum roll. For the first time since they'd slept together, she looked directly at him. "Thank you for doing this," she said.

He shrugged. "Part of the job."

"Where do you think they are?"

He hesitated, like he was tired of the whole thing. "Walczak and his people probably got here on the company jet, but they wouldn't take Sarah and her friend back the same way. They'd have to get past airport security. They're driving. Walczak probably flew."

"Our flight takes an hour or so," Grace said, "and it's what? An eleven- or twelve-hour drive back to LA? We'll get there ahead of them."

"Yeah, we'll have some lead time." She waited for him to go on but he didn't.

"How will we know where they are?" she said.

He tried to look indifferent. "I don't know."

"You're being deliberately mean."

"No, I'm not," he said, raising his voice a little. "If I don't know I don't know." She fumed, he sulked. They hit some turbulence. The cabin was too hot and he was getting motion sickness and starting to sweat. He knew he was being an asshole but couldn't help himself.

"Look," she said carefully. "I can't handle everything right now, okay? It's too much for me. Could we just put the rest of it on hold until we're done with this?"

"Sure," he said, like it didn't matter one way or the other. She looked like she was about to hit him.

"Then could I *please* know what's going on?"

"There's only one way to find out where they're taking Sarah and her friend," he said. "Walczak has to tell us."

They took an Uber back to Isaiah's house and picked up the

Audi. Predictably, Walczak lived in an exclusive community in Newport Beach where nobody parked on the street and private security cars prowled like predators. They cruised past his mansion, a massive brick fortress surrounded by high ivy-covered walls. The driveway was gated and ran alongside a pasture of lawn before it reached the front door. The grounds were lit, lights were on in the house, the silver BMW parked in front of the garage. That the property was protected by state-of-the-art technology went without saying. Isaiah was wracked with misgivings. This was the only way he could think of to find Sarah, but it was more than dangerous. He could tell Grace he was calling it off but she'd be furious and do something rash on her own. They pulled over to the curb. "You don't have to do this," Isaiah said.

"I'd think twice about it myself," Dodson said.

"Thank you for everything," she said.

"Well, don't make it sound like we not gonna see each other again," Dodson said. "We'll catch you on the upside."

"If something happens to me? It's not your fault." Isaiah had too much to say so he didn't say anything. Grace was looking at him, "Isaiah..." She wavered, something of consequence teetering. "I'll see you later." Isaiah and Dodson got out of the car and she drove away.

Walczak was at his desk, talking on the phone with Jimenez. The team was still a couple of hours away.

"What's taking you so long?"

"The van is a piece of shit and the cruise control is set on eighty. What else can I do?"

"Any problems?"

"None so far. I'll call you when we're closer."

The call ended. The buzzer from the front gate sounded. Walczak looked at the security monitors and saw a car waiting at the front gate, the driver in shadow. He got on the intercom. "Who are you and what do you want?"

"It's Grace." Walczak stood up from the desk. *What the hell is she doing here?* Didn't she know this was suicide? She was up to something.

"Is Isaiah with you?"

"No, I'm alone. I want to make a deal for my mother."

He smiled. She'd seen them at Burning Man. She knew they had Sarah. This was perfect. Whatever Grace said could be cross-checked with what Sarah told them and between the two they'd get the truth. Still, he was suspicious. There had to be a catch to this. "Leave the car there and walk up the driveway."

He pressed the button that opened the gate and watched the security monitor. Grace walked slowly along the cobblestones. She looked utterly defeated, like every step brought her closer to the grave. She was carrying her handbag. He'd have to watch that. He went to the door with a gun in his hand. He opened it. She was forty feet away. He aimed the gun. "Stop right there and don't move." There was nobody behind her and the motion sensors would have picked up anyone else on the property. "Lift up your shirt and turn around slowly—stop there." He looked her over. "Put your hands on top of your head and lace your fingers together. All right. Back toward me."

As soon as she entered the foyer, he said, "Drop the bag." He closed the door with his foot, grabbed her by the collar, and shoved her into the wall. "Hands on the wall, feet spread." He kept the gun ready with one hand and frisked her with the other, squeezing her tits for good measure and letting his hand linger on her crotch. She was clean. "Turn around." She did and he backhanded her with everything he had. She cried out and fell to the floor. "Sic that goddamn dog on me, you fucking cunt? You're lucky I don't kill you right now." He dumped out her bag. The usual stuff. No weapon and nothing that could be used as one. Maybe this was legit. Maybe not. He stomped on her cell phone and hauled her to her feet. He pushed her down the hall and into the study. "Sit." She sat in an armchair. She was quaking and sniveling, her head down, arms folded across her chest. "Start talking," he commanded.

"You'll make my mom tell you everything and I will too. You'll know where all the copies are, so you can let us go. We won't say anything because there's no proof you did anything."

He thought about that. "Have you seen the pictures?"

"No, and it wouldn't matter even if I did. I just want this to be over."

"You know I can kill you both anyway."

"Yes, I know that, but why commit two murders if you don't have to?"

She was making sense, he thought, but he would kill them anyway. He wanted to punish them for all the shit they'd put him through. Isaiah and his friend were goners, of course. Jimenez, Hawkins, Owens, and Richter would have to go too. Any of them could withhold copies. One by one, they would be dealt with. A suicide, a car crash, a house fire, a robbery gone bad. Walczak knew people who did that kind of thing for a living.

"Could I please go to the bathroom?" she said.

He thought a moment. He didn't want to watch her piss and there was nothing in there she could weaponize unless she was going to stab him with an electric toothbrush. Besides, she was a trembling mess, holding herself and rocking back and forth like she was retarded. He nodded at his private bathroom. "Leave the door open. You come back here with so much as a bar of soap and I'll kneecap you." Grace got up and stumbled into the bathroom. He heard her pee, flush, and wash her hands. Stupid, he thought. Like being sanitary was important before you died.

Grace took a deep breath and came out of the bathroom, holding herself tightly, head bowed, trying to make herself look small and helpless. She was beyond scared, in some other state of paralyzing emotions. Walczak sneered at her, restraining his murderous urges. She waited for permission to sit down. He nodded. She took the same chair, keeping her arms around herself and rocking back and forth. Walczak put the gun in his belt. He found a legal pad and a pen, came over, and tossed them in her lap.

"The copies. Where they are and the passwords. Your mother's doing the same thing right now. If they don't match you're fucked."

"And then you'll let us go?"

"And then I'll let you go."

She nodded submissively, unfolded her arms, and pointed the small can of bear-strength pepper spray at him and pushed the button. He howled and grabbed his eyes. He staggered around, coughing and choking. He drew the gun, fired once, but the pain was so great he dropped the weapon on the floor. Grace shot another long spray in his face. He screamed and stumbled wildly toward the bathroom. He ran into an end table and crashed to the floor. She took the gun and aimed it at him. "Stay on the floor or I'll shoot you. I'll shoot you and make you beg for your life."

"Please, please let me wash my eyes! I'm going blind!"

"I'm glad, asshole. You don't deserve to see." She sprayed him again at close range until the can was empty. He was dripping, screaming, twisting around. She found the button that opened the front gate and then ran to the foyer to let Isaiah and Dodson in.

The three of them had discussed the plan on the drive back from the airport. "We want him to let his guard down," Isaiah said. He had envisioned every move Walczak would make and how she should respond. When she went inside the house she'd take her bag with her. Anything that could be used as a weapon would have been removed. Pen, nail file, anything. Walczak would immediately make her assume the position, then he'd empty the bag, find nothing, and feel as if he'd eliminated a threat. A search would come next. Isaiah had watched the cops frisk dozens of suspects. The cop would run his hands over the neck, shoulders, armpits, waist, legs, and inside the thighs but routinely skipped the forearms because they were up in the air or against the wall. That was why he'd taped a small can of bear-strength pepper spray just beneath Grace's wrist, the can hidden under her long sleeve. The spray produced 5.3 million Scoville heat units. A habanero pepper contained a paltry 100,000. Isaiah instructed her to keep her arms wrapped around herself so Walczak would get used to seeing her that way and not wonder what was in the hand she had clenched under her armpit when she came out of the bathroom. And if she was pitiful enough and submissive enough and could convince Walczak that she was too helpless to pose even the slightest threat, he might put the gun down when he got her something to write on. "Pick your moment," Isaiah said, "and spray him until you run out of spray."

"And don't hesitate," Dodson added. "Commit. All or nothing."

Walczak was still blubbering about washing his eyes out. Grace found a wooden chair in the hallway and brought it into the study. She and Dodson bound him to the chair from shoulders to waist with the roll of duct tape Isaiah had brought in from the car.

"Where are they taking Sarah?" Isaiah asked.

Walczak's eyes were swollen. His face was red and slimed with tears and snot. "Really? You think I'm going to answer that?"

"One more time. Where are they taking Sarah?"

"I'm not telling you shit."

Isaiah looked at Grace as if to say *We tried, didn't we?* They tipped the chair over on its back. Walczak was looking up now, his legs in an L.

"What are you doing?" he said. When he saw Grace and Dodson bring in a mop pail and a soup pot full of water, the realization slapped him as hard as he'd slapped Grace. "Wait a minute! Hold on a second!"

"Get ready, son," Dodson said. "'Cause karma's about to kick your ass."

Isaiah had seen video of people being waterboarded, but he didn't realize how violent it was until Grace was pouring the water into the towel Dodson had stretched tight over Walczak's face. In seconds, he was wriggling and squirming and bucking like a mummy trying to bust out of its wrappings, crying out between sputtering gurgles.

"Damn," Dodson said. "I almost feel sorry for him."

Grace was seething, demonic. Unleashed. She dumped more water on him. "You killed my father, you fuck! YOU KILLED MY DAD!" Isaiah was afraid Walczak would dry-drown and stopped her.

"Okay, I'll tell you, just please, no more," Walczak sobbed. He told them the team was taking Sarah and Arthur to the company airplane hangar at the Santa Monica airport. "I swear it's the truth! I swear!" He broke down and blubbered.

"How do we know he ain't lying?" Dodson said.

Isaiah pondered that a moment. "I should have thought of this before." He went to the desk and found Walczak's phone. "What's the passcode?" he asked. Walczak didn't answer. They were out of water but Grace started kicking him and screaming *Murderer* and *Piece of shit* and *I'm going to kill you.* Dodson looked at Isaiah but he said nothing and watched. He'd have done the same thing to Seb.

"Okay, okay!" Walczak bleated. He was hysterical and sobbing and drooling and bleeding. He gave up the passcode. His texts revealed the crew's real destination was WSSI's training facility in El Segundo.

They drove away from Walczak's house, Grace still apoplectic with fury, her fists and face splashed with blood. "I want to kill him. I want to go back and kill him."

"I know." Isaiah thought about killing Seb every day. That the wretch was still walking around on the earth was an outrage he could barely stomach.

Dodson looked at Grace and shook his head. "Girl, you ain't nothin' but trouble, are you?"

Grace nodded thoughtfully. "Yeah. I am."

The industrial zone in El Segundo was a bleak, grimy area just north of Long Beach. Scattered over a wide expanse of acreage were an oil refinery left over from a dystopian movie, numerous storage tanks, sludge pools, disused railcars, warehouses, and dirt parking lots. WSSI's training facility was a sprawling cement building with the forlorn look of a distribution center for discount carpets. No lights, no cars. Walczak's team hadn't arrived yet. Isaiah parked the Audi behind a berm. They got out and he went into the trunk.

"What are we doing?" Grace said.

"Isaiah's got a war chest in there," Dodson said. "He can't get busted because he buys everything on Amazon."

Over the years, Isaiah had been in situations where he needed something but didn't have it at hand. A tool, a surveillance device, a weapon. He started carrying them in the trunk of his car but they became such a jumble he couldn't find what he needed when he needed it. His solution: he removed the floor panel and spare tire for more room and organized his things in plastic boxes. They were labeled HAND TOOLS. DRILL/CIRC SAW. SOLDER/WELDER. PRY TOOLS. LOCK TOOLS. RESTRAINTS. WEAPONS.

"Why ain't we calling the police?" Dodson said.

"No," Grace said quickly. "We can't."

"Why? We tell 'em two people got kidnapped and they'll come out here and arrest everybody." He waited for Grace to answer. "What's the problem?"

"There's a murder warrant out for my mom."

"Well, why didn't you say so?" Dodson replied like it was as common as catching a cold. Isaiah was rummaging around in the trunk. He found a device that was so complicated it took a second for Dodson to realize what it was. "A slingshot?" he said. Its maker called it "the most powerful wrist catapult in the world." It was made from stainless steel and had a brace to keep your wrist straight. The Y was more like goalposts, two steel brackets holding high-tension springs that accelerated the speed of the four lengths of rubber tubing and rocketed a ball bearing fast enough to knock the head off a rabbit.

"Yeah, it's a slingshot," Isaiah said.

"What's wrong with you, Isaiah? You can't carry a pistol like everybody else?" Isaiah found the collapsible baton and put it in the back of his pants.

"What about me?" Grace said.

Isaiah rummaged in the trunk again. "Damn. I thought I had the pepperball gun."

"I used that the last time," Dodson said.

"This is all I have," Isaiah said sheepishly.

It was a modified caulking gun. In place of the tube of caulk, there was a spray can of butane. The plastic nozzle had been replaced with a short metal straw. A barbecue lighter was attached to the underside of the gun, its tubular nozzle shaped so its spark would light the butane as it came out of the straw. There were other homemade widgets and adaptors that gave the whole thing a built-in-the-garage-by-a-lonely-teenager look.

"What is it?" Grace said.

"It's a flamethrower. The one from Amazon was too big to fit in the trunk."

"You're kidding, right?"

He was embarrassed. "It was kind of an experiment. I, uh, made it myself."

"No shit?" Dodson said. "I thought it was for the military."

"It's got two triggers," Isaiah explained. "This one lights the bar-becue lighter. This second one releases the butane and creates the flame. It's got a range of about ten feet or so."

Grace said, "You're kidding, right?"

Isaiah kept rummaging and found a toy still in its bubble wrap. The label said THE SNOOPER. It was tubular, as big around as a penny whistle and about a foot long. It was made of pink plastic. The ends were curved and short, like a length of plumbing pipe with nothing attached.

"I feel ready," Grace said. "Don't you?"

"Them mothafuckas are strappin'," Dodson said, "and we gonna go in there with a slingshot and a caulking gun?" Isaiah was silent and frowning. "This is how he gets when he's making shit up on the fly," Dodson said.

"I know." Grace nodded.

Isaiah got some other things out of the trunk and put them in a shopping bag. "We need a distraction," he said. The three of them hurried over to the facility, Isaiah trailing, talking on his phone in urgent whispers. They arrived at the back door. Isaiah got the twenty-volt HSS drill with the cobalt bit out of the bag and gave it to Dodson. "You know what to do," he said, and Dodson went to work, drilling out the lock. The whine seemed loud enough to alert everybody in the city.

"Who were you talking to?" Grace said.

"When you finish, don't open the door," Isaiah said.

"Why not?" Dodson said.

"The alarm will go off. We have to wait for them to disarm it."

"Isaiah?" Grace said. A van was coming up the road. The head-lights would be on them in a minute. The drill's whine seemed to get louder, the beams edging toward them. Heart rates went up, everyone breathing faster. "Hurry, muthafucka," Dodson said to the drill. The lock finally came out and they hastily took a position behind a line of dumpsters with a view of the front entrance. Isaiah gave Grace a set of wire cutters.

"What are these for?"

"Cutting zip ties." The vehicles arrived. The crew dragged Sarah and her friend out of the van. They were tied up, bedraggled and terrified.

"*Mom,*" Grace said. She grabbed Isaiah's arm. "We have to do something."

"No. We have to wait." And then he told her why.

Walczak was where they'd left him, lying on his back in the chair, his torso tightly bound with duct tape, his legs above him in an L. He didn't panic. He didn't know specifically what he'd do, but he was confident he could figure something out. Hell, he'd taken classes on exactly this kind of situation. The first issue was mobility. If you could move, you could create an opportunity, find resources. He couldn't budge his arms or the upper half of his body, but his legs were free. He spread them wide and put his feet on the floor, the seat between his knees, his eyes on the ceiling. He pushed off, the back of the chair scraping and sliding over the hardwood floor. He'd moved maybe a yard and stopped. If he couldn't see where he was going there was no reason to expend the energy. He thought about what was around him. He could kick at the desk and hope the landline would fall to the floor. No, that wouldn't work. The desk was a solid piece of rosewood that weighed a ton and even if the handset fell there was no way to dial it. He visualized every item in the room, but there was nothing he could use to communicate with the outside world or cut the tape. Nevertheless, the tape was the only point of attack.

Or was it?

There was the chair itself. It was sturdy but spindly. An antique he'd bought at an auction. The top of the chair was rounded, two side posts and two fluted columns in the center where you rested your back. Without the use of his hands, there was only one force strong enough to break it. *Gravity.* Walczak planted his feet again and pushed himself across the study and down the hallway. It was hard work. He was sweating and breathing hard by the time he reached the edge of the staircase. This was going to hurt, he thought. He'd be sliding down the stairs on his back, headfirst, and his shoulders were wider than the chair. He couldn't see the stairs, but he didn't have to. There were twenty-one of them, a landing at the dogleg left, continuing on and ending in the foyer and the Italian marble floor, nothing to stop him but the wall underneath the Edwardian gilt mirror that took two workmen to hang.

"Here goes nothing," he said. He pushed off. It was worse than he'd thought. He was going *really* fast, like a goddamn snow sled, jolting over each step, his head and shoulders taking a beating as the chair banged into the solid oak banister again and again, skewing sideways as it hit the landing, smashing into the wall, flipping over, and tumbling the rest of the way down before he finally crashed onto the floor, stopping two inches from the wall.

"Ohhh shit," he moaned. The dog had chewed holes in him but this was pain on top of pain on top of pain. He could tell he was badly hurt, structurally hurt, so much blood he couldn't tell where it was coming from. He was still bound to the chair. His head and knees were on the floor now, his body in an inverted V, the chair legs pointed up at a forty-five-degree angle. The next part was a bitch too.

He spread his knees, raised his torso, and pulled his feet underneath him one at a time. And then, with a tremendous burst of energy, he stood up. Now he was bent over, wearing the chair on his back. He looked in the mirror. His head and face were bloodied, teeth were missing, he was bleeding from his scalp, bruises emerging on his face. One shoulder was lower than the other. Two of the chair's legs had been knocked off but that was no help. On the bright side, a side post was cracked but hadn't broken completely. Mission unaccomplished. He was still bound to the fucking chair. His hands were free, but they were down by his hips and useless. He couldn't even open a drawer. "FUUUUCCCKK!" he screamed. He caught his breath, steadied himself, then walked like a hunchback into the den. There was a landline on an end table. He sidled up alongside it, used his teeth, and pulled it by the cord until it dropped over the edge, the handset clattering to the floor. Then it occurred to him. He didn't know any of the crew's numbers by heart. They were in his phone, which Isaiah had taken with him. "FUUUUCCCKK!" he screamed again. He rested, trying to think through the pain and desperation. He couldn't stay like this. Patty and Noah would be home in the morning. There was only one alternative. Walczak closed his eyes and took a deep breath. Then he went back into the foyer and started climbing the stairs.

CHAPTER SIXTEEN
This Is for All of Us

Jimenez parked the van in front of the training facility, wondering why he'd let things get this far. He could have walked away long before this but it seemed natural, like no big deal. He was human shit and this is what human shit does. He knew why Hawkins was always pissed off and smoked most of the marijuana before he made the oil for his mother and he knew Richter was haunted by the old lady he'd nearly suffocated in his car and he knew why Owens drank and why she wanted him and he knew his wife had kicked him out because he'd beaten her one too many times and that his kids hated him and that he'd never get a good night's sleep again for as long as he lived. He knew he hated Walczak and as soon as this was over he'd kill that motherfucker if Hawkins didn't get him first. He also knew that he hated himself and if he ever got out of this mess he'd give his share of the money to his family and then he'd do what he'd wanted to do all along. Hang himself like the Iraqi man they'd strung up and buried outside the prison walls.

The crew brought Arthur and Sarah into the break room. There were tables and chairs, cupboards, vending machines, and a fridge. They sat the prisoners on the floor with their backs against the wall. Hawkins set the medical bags on the counter and opened them. A glow seemed to emanate like when Samuel L. Jackson peered into the briefcase in *Pulp Fiction.*

"Looka here, looka here," Hawkins said. He dumped the bundles of cash out into a satisfying pile. "Check it out, Owens. You could go to rehab in Malibu, play shuffleboard with the celebrities."

"Fuck you," she said, "and I want my share now."

"Later," Jimenez said. "We don't have time."

"And I said *now.*" She had her hand on her gun. She was dangerous. Hell hath no fury.

"The fuck you think you're doing?" Hawkins said, his hand on his own gun.

"Wait," Richter said. "Before we shoot each other like idiots, calm down, will you? Don't be stupid." Everyone relaxed but only a little. "Listen to me, okay? Let's say we get the pictures and all the copies. You guys get the million, right?"

"Oh, I get you," Owens said. "You want a cut, don't you?"

"No, I don't. It's small change."

"Maybe it is to you. But us peons think it's a lot of damn money."

"Hear me out, will you?" Richter said. "Suppose we *don't* give the pictures to Walczak and we keep them." The crew looked at each other.

"We'd have Walczak by the nut sack," Hawkins said with a wide grin.

"How? We're in the pictures too," Owens said.

"You ever hear of Photoshop?" Jimenez said. "We could hit Walczak up for a lot more than a million." They were all grinning now.

"Let's take that prick for everything he has," Richter said. Arthur groaned. His face was screwed up in pain, he was breathing in gasps, his head swiveling around like a baby's.

"What's wrong with him?" Hawkins said. "We hardly touched him."

"That Taser," Sarah said. "He's having a heart attack!"

"One bullshit thing after another," Jimenez said.

"Help him! Do you want him to die?"

Richter looked at Jimenez. "If he dies we have no way to corroborate what Sarah tells us."

"There's aspirin in my bag. Please!" Sarah pleaded.

"Get it for him," Jimenez said. Richter found the aspirin, Owens got him a coffee mug of water. Richter knelt down, put the aspirin in Arthur's mouth, and gave him a drink, most of the water dribbling down his chin. But Arthur's breathing got more ragged and strained, his face scrunched up in agony.

"If he stops breathing you'll have to do CPR!" Sarah shouted. "Cut him loose! What's wrong with you?" Jimenez reluctantly nodded again. Richter got out a folding knife and cut the zip tie off Arthur's wrists.

"I'm not doing mouth-to-mouth, asshole," Richter said, "so you better come through." Richter rose to his feet, turned away, and screamed, "OH FUCKING SHIT!" Arthur had a goddamn knife in his hand and was trying to get up. Jimenez ran over, kicked the knife away, and kicked Arthur until he rolled over.

"Stop it! Stop it!" Sarah screamed.

"Where the hell did that knife come from?" Jimenez said. He looked at Owens. "You were supposed to pat him down."

She shrugged. "I didn't think he'd do anything. He owns a bookstore for fuck's sake."

"You are the stupidest bitch who ever lived," Hawkins said.

Jimenez zip-tied Arthur's wrists behind his back and left him there next to Sarah. Richter had his pant leg pulled up. He had an open slash across his calf, his sock already soaked with blood. "Hey, I'm bleeding over here! Do you think you could give me a hand?"

"It ain't nothin' but a flesh wound," Owens said.

"Of course it's a flesh wound! I got slashed with a goddamn knife!"

"There's an infirmary," Jimenez said. "Down the hall, second left and it's on your right. Put a tourniquet on it. They've got all kinds of first aid stuff."

"Thanks a lot," Richter said as he hobbled out of the room. "Assholes."

Jimenez listened to the retreating footsteps. "We on the same wavelength?"

"Uh-huh," Hawkins said with a smile.

"What?" Owens said.

"Who needs him?"

When Walczak's crew had gone into the front of the building, Isaiah, Grace, and Dodson entered through the back. It was dark and smelled of disinfectant, cafeteria food, and cordite. Isaiah's injuries still hurt but he was loaded with Vicodin and the adrenaline smoothed over the pain.

They crept down a long hall. There were lots of offices and interconnected rooms and other hallways branching off. Signs with arrows directed you to the cafeteria, gym, lounge, library, gun range, admin, and so on. Isaiah made mental notes about the layout. An escape plan seemed like a good idea. He reasoned that the crew wouldn't take Sarah and her friend deep into the building. They'd go into the first available room that was relatively small. One, because they'd want their captives in a contained space, and two, they'd be eager to see the money. The odds, then, were that they were toward the front of the building.

They heard footsteps and someone muttering. Hurriedly, they darted into one of the dark rooms. Porkpie went by, limping badly. "Fucking assholes," he said.

A lucky break, Isaiah thought, and they needed one. That left three bad guys to deal with instead of four. The group continued on, making a couple of turns and reaching the main hallway. They kept moving until they saw an open door, light and voices coming from it.

"She's in there," Grace said.

* * *

Jimenez said, "Okay, it's showtime." He hauled Sarah up and sat her in a chair. "You tell us what we want to know or we'll go to work on you right now." He thought a moment. He didn't want to incapacitate her. "Wait, I have a better idea. We'll work on Arthur. Cut his ear off and you can watch."

"Yeah," Owens said excitedly, "like *Reservoir Dogs*."

"No! You wouldn't!"

Hawkins picked up Arthur's knife, knelt beside him, grabbed his ear, and twisted it. "They come off surprisingly easy. I'd say it'll take a minute tops, depending upon how much he moves around."

"Don't! Please don't!" Sarah said.

"Then you better start talkin'," Owens said. "He ain't foolin' around."

Hawkins ran the blade along the base of Arthur's ear. Arthur cried out, blood running down his neck.

"Stop! Stop!" Sarah screamed. "I'll tell you everything! I'll tell you everything!"

Grace heard the screaming. She started forward. "That's her, that's Mom." Isaiah held her back.

"We have to wait," Isaiah said.

"Where the fuck is he?" Dodson said.

"Now you're being smart, Sarah," Jimenez said. They cut her loose and he gave her a small notebook and a pen. "Let's start with where the copies are, and you should know, my bullshit detector is never wrong. Fuck around and we'll cut both his ears off and yours too."

A buzzer sounded. Someone was at the front door. Alarm flashed on everyone's faces. "Think it's Walczak?" Owens said.

"No, he's got a key card," Jimenez said. "Stay here. If they make a sound, beat the shit out of 'em."

Jimenez and Hawkins hurried down the hall, guns held at their sides. Behind the front desk in reception, there was a row of security monitors. Standing under the bug light at the front door was a cop in uniform. He looked legit, his squad car parked behind him.

"The fuck?" Hawkins said. "What's a cop doing out here?"

"I got this," Jimenez said. He stuck his gun into the back of his pants. He opened the door, Hawkins standing off to one side. "Hello, Officer. Anything wrong?" Jimenez said.

"Sorry to bother you, sir," the cop said in that flat, I-ain't-sorry-about-shit tone of voice. "Someone heard screaming coming from this location. Do you mind if I look around?"

"Someone heard screaming? From here? Not possible."

"But I'd still like to look around."

"Sorry. You need a warrant."

"No, sir, I don't. Exigent circumstances. Will you please move aside?"

"What exigent circumstances? That's bullshit."

"I told you, sir," the cop said, a warning in his voice. "Someone heard screaming at this location."

Jimenez looked past the officer into the darkness. "Someone like who?" he said, going falsetto. "There was no scream, the walls are made out of cinder blocks. This is bullshit. Who are you?"

"Officer Carter Samuels. Long Beach Police Department."

"Who's your commanding officer?"

"Doesn't matter," the cop said. "The fact is, I'm *your* commanding officer and I'm commanding you to step aside or go to jail."

When the buzzer sounded, the Latino guy and the black guy came out of the break room and headed toward reception. Isaiah and the others moved to the open door. Isaiah got out the Snooper. It was a child's periscope. He carefully extended one end so he could see into the break room. The tall woman was standing at a table, smiling as she divided the money into three neat piles, a gun resting next to them. Sarah and Arthur were on the floor.

"What's a third of a million?" she said. "Three hundred and thirty thousand and change? That's a helluva lot of money."

"So is a million," Arthur said in a croaky whisper.

"What?"

"Blackmailing your boss might work, but it might not. That's cash in hand." He paused, his face twisted in pain. "You saw how they cut the other guy out. Why wouldn't they do the same to you?" The woman looked at him.

"Shut up," she said, and went back to dividing the money.

The first person through the door was the likeliest to get shot and Dodson had a family. Isaiah gave him the collapsible baton and took the slingshot. "Come in behind me. Fast." Dodson made a face like this was the stupidest thing ever. Grace was eager to get into it, holding both triggers of the flamethrower. She looked silly, like a kid playing Star Wars.

Isaiah would only get one shot. He got a firm grip on the slingshot's handle, put a ball bearing in the leather pocket, and stretched the bands back as far as they would go. He took a breath and stepped quickly into the doorway. He locked eyes with the woman. She reached for her gun. Isaiah fired. The ball bearing hit her in the chest. She cried out, grabbed her breast but still managed to pick up the gun. Before she could raise it, Dodson slipped past Isaiah and cracked her over the head with the collapsible baton. "Down for the count," he said. "Shit, I shouldn't have hit her so hard."

Grace dropped the flamethrower on the floor and rushed over to Sarah. She got down on her knees and hugged her. "Mom," she said.

"Oh my sweet girl," Sarah said.

316

"Hurry," Isaiah said. Grace used the wire cutter to cut the zip ties. She and Sarah helped Arthur to his feet, his arms around their shoulders. They went into the hall and hurried back the way they came. They turned a corner just as Porkpie hobbled out of a doorway.

"Hey!" he said. He went for the gun in his shoulder holster, the group scattering in different directions. He fired. BLAM BLAM BLAM!

Jimenez was still arguing with the cop when they heard the gunshots. The cop went for his weapon, but Jimenez hit him with a roundhouse punch, all his weight behind it, knocking him back onto his squad car. He slumped to the ground, out cold. Jimenez and Hawkins ran back down the hall and into the break room. Sarah and Arthur were gone. Owens was lying on the floor, a huge lump on her head, blood running into her eyes. At least the money was still there.

"What a fucking idiot," Jimenez said.

The two men went back into the hall. Jimenez found the light switch and turned it on. It looked like a high school in a horror movie. A long empty corridor of speckled gray linoleum that looked vaguely green in the harsh fluorescents.

From somewhere they heard Richter shout, "They got loose. I'll cover the back door!" Without a word, Jimenez went left, Hawkins went right.

When Porkpie started shooting, Isaiah darted into a short hallway. He turned through a door into a rec room, then through a lounge and into a locker room. It was humid, smelling of wet towels and B.O. He hesitated. What was he trying to do here? Escape or take the guy out? Take him out and he was one less threat to Grace and the others. But he had to do it soon, before he ran into another member of the crew. He heard his pursuer coming. The damp air made him sweat. He looked for an ambush point that wasn't obvious. Nothing here. He cut down an aisle just as the lights came on. He had to get far enough ahead of the guy so he could set something up. He banged a locker closed and pushed over a bench to make the guy think he was taking a position and slow him down.

He went into the weight room. He couldn't run forever, and this was as good a place as any to try something. He got out the multitool Marcus had always carried with him, like a Swiss Army knife but more industrial. He quickly removed the light switch wall plate and snipped a few wires.

The room was L-shaped. There was nothing in the short end but chairs, a coffee table, and a sofa. He reached the corner and looked down the long end of the L. He could barely make things out in the dark. On the left was a loose herd of weight-training machines and benches for free weights. On the right, a long mirror for the weight lifters to preen themselves in and racks of dumbbells. Just past the mirror were rows of stationary bikes lined up like a cavalry charge. Beyond them, at the very end of the room, a red exit sign. In between, there were lots of hiding places, but his pursuer was a pro. He was a trained marksman with better-than-average reflexes and he'd know how to clear a room. Isaiah picked up a fifteen-pound dumbbell, went to the bikes, and hung his Harvard cap on a handlebar. He ran out the far exit, circled around through another room, and got back to the hallway. He wouldn't be able to see the pursuer and the slightest peek might give him away. He had to visualize the man's moves and figure out how much time they would take.

He heard his pursuer's boots treading lightly on the linoleum and then going silent. The man had entered the weight room. Isaiah waited for the pursuer's eyes to adjust. Five seconds. *Thousand one, thousand two, thousand three, thousand four, thousand five.* Another ten seconds for him to reach the corner of the L... *thousand eight, nine, ten.* Isaiah crept to the weight room entrance and took his first peek. The Latino man was just turning the corner into the long end of the L and out of view. Isaiah moved to the corner. He was behind his pursuer now but couldn't attack because he might be seen in the mirror. If he'd calculated correctly, the pursuer was creeping through the herd of machines. Fifteen seconds until he reached the bikes...*thousand ten, eleven, twelve.* Was he doing what he was supposed to do or had he stopped to watch for motion? Isaiah peeked but couldn't see him because of the dark...*thirteen, fourteen, fifteen.* The Latino man was seeing the Harvard cap now and realizing it was a decoy. He was crouching, knees bent, swiveling the gun, back and forth.

Go now, Isaiah!

Isaiah took off, running. The Latino man heard him and started to turn around, hard to do hunched over like that. Isaiah saw the man's snarling eyes and the gun rising as he raised the dumbbell over his head.

Grace and Sarah helped Arthur down a hallway. He was suffering from the beating and was bleeding profusely from his ear. His arms were draped around the women like iron yokes. "You should go on without me," he said. "I'll be okay. I'm a tough son of a bitch. I'll be fine."

"Sweetheart," Sarah said. "You have to shut up now."

They entered the mess hall. Rows of long tables and metal chairs. No place to hide here. Arthur was near collapse.

"We've got to make a stand," Grace said. The women helped him across the room, through the swinging door, and into the industrial kitchen. "It's here or nothing."

"Then it's nothing," Arthur said. "You'll get shot before you get within twenty feet of him. Stop being foolish! If you stay there'll be three dead people instead of one."

"I'm not leaving without you," Sarah said, adamant.

"And I'm not leaving without *you*," Grace said.

Arthur said to Sarah, "If you stay, you're condemning your daughter to death. Is that what you want?"

"I won't leave you, Arthur." She looked at her daughter, tears flowing down her cheeks. "But you have to go, my darling. For me."

This is too easy, Hawkins thought, following the blood trail like Hansel and Gretel followed those cookie crumbs or gumdrops or whatever the fuck they were. He entered the mess hall and turned on the lights. He never understood why the cops in the movies didn't do that when they were clearing a room. It looked cool with the gun-mounted flashlights shining around in the dark but it was still stupid.

There was no place to hide here so they had to be in the kitchen. A good place for an ambush if it wasn't for the Glock and the seventeen-round clip he was packing and his eleven years of soldiering. He had a knack for picking off snipers. Thought they were slick, aiming their guns between the curtains or popping out of a doorway or aiming down from a rooftop or hiding behind a burned-out car. The trick was anticipation. Knowing in advance where they'd come from and how. Sometimes he aimed at a spot before the motherfucker even showed himself, the asshole surprised as hell when the bullet exploded in his head before he could pull the trigger.

Hawkins kicked open the kitchen door just in case somebody was hiding behind it like a moron. He stepped inside and turned on the lights. A long stainless steel counter ran down the middle of the room, pots and pans hanging over it. There was no need to worry about Arthur, he was too banged up to do anything. The women would have to be shot in the foot or better yet punched in the face. He couldn't believe Grace let a goddamn pit bull maul Walczak. The bitch had a mean streak.

Hawkins jumped on top of the counter so he could see the whole space. *Weren't expecting that, were you, rookies?* At least they weren't crouched behind a box of broccoli or curled up on top of the fridge. On his left were the kitchen pass-through, the steam table, and an aisle where the food servers stood. Nowhere to take cover unless it was under the counter he was standing on. He hopped down on the right side. Now the counter was to his left, the stoves, fridge, and prep stations on his right. There was a big splotch of blood on the floor where they'd stood around making their battle plan, and there was the blood trail again leading directly to the walk-in cooler. The likeliest scenario? They'd set up some bullshit kind of trap. The blood was supposed to lure him into the cooler and somewhere along the way, Sarah would jump out of a microwave and hit him with a cast iron frying pan. The odds of that working were exactly zero. Or they'd try the same thing in the cooler. Throw turnips at him or drown him in chili sauce. He heaved a condescending sigh. *Okay, kiddies, here we go.*

He went down the aisle, ducking to look under the counter, then up again, opening oven doors with his foot, the gun following his eyes, aiming sharply at ambush points. He almost wanted to be attacked. He reached the end of the aisle. So they were hiding in the cooler. Given the amount of blood, they couldn't drag Arthur any farther. The door was closed but these things had inside latches. He opened the door, staying behind it as he did. He waited and then swung around fast, crouched and aiming into the darkness. He reached around with his free hand and turned on the light. He saw what he expected to see, rows of tall shelves and boxes piled on top of boxes, an aisle down the middle. He moved a worktable to hold the door open. Then he got a tray full of silverware and dumped it on the floor. If anybody tried to close the door behind him he'd hear them and they'd be dead.

He went inside, the gun going up, down, and side to side. No turnips or chili sauce. He kept going until there was only one more stand of shelves they could be hiding behind. He tossed a can of peas into the space, see if he could get a reaction. Then he heard Sarah say, "Please don't hurt us." And there they were, Sarah and Arthur huddled in a corner. "Please," she said again. "We'll do anything you say."

"You're goddamn right you will," Hawkins said. "Where's Grace?"

"She's gone. Escaped."

"Bullshit."

"I made her go. Why should she die too?"

"Good point, but I still don't believe you."

Hawkins made them get up, Sarah lifting Arthur by the arm. He groaned, still bleeding, hardly able to stay upright. Too bad, Hawkins thought. He was taking no chances, staying behind his prisoners as he marched them along to the break room. Owens was still lying on the floor facedown. "That is the most useless bitch ever," Hawkins said, and in that moment, somebody came up behind and hit him with something made of cast iron. He heard a *clonk!*, felt his skull splinter. He fell to his knees, heard another *clonk!* And there was darkness.

"You okay?" Grace said, putting down the heavy pan. She had left the kitchen through the back door, circled around, and gotten to the break room before they did.

"Yes, I'm fine," Sarah said, "but Arthur needs to go to the hospital." He was half conscious and covered with blood. Sarah looked around for something to staunch the flow and found a napkin container. She took a handful out and held the wad tightly to Arthur's ear. He groaned.

"We can't move him," Grace said. "Wait here. I have to find Isaiah and Dodson." She picked up the tall woman's gun.

"No, Grace, don't—" Sarah said, but her daughter was already gone.

* * *

Grace came out into the hallway holding the gun. It felt frightening and familiar at the same time. She wondered if she had the nerve to use it and decided she'd shoot whoever she had to. Anything for Isaiah and Dodson. She went the way she'd seen Isaiah go, into the short hallway. She went through a door and kept going until she reached a locker room, the lights still on. She entered the weight room. The wall plate was on the floor. Isaiah had been here. Was he *still* here? She hustled through the darkness, whispering, "Isaiah? Isaiah?" She saw a body on the floor. Abject horror gripped her chest, choking her heart and squeezing the blood out of her veins. She rushed over and knelt beside him. "No-no-no-no! Please no!" It was one of Walczak's crew. She nearly wept with relief. She texted Isaiah and Dodson. Where are you? Are you okay? No answer. What the hell were they doing? Were they captured? Hurt? Dead? She hurried toward the exit sign.

Owens woke up, groaning. The pain was mortar fire behind her swimming eyes, the bump on her head was the size of a plum. She was dizzy, confused. A concussion. She saw Sarah and Arthur huddled together on the floor, trying to make themselves small. Owens got up, shaky, blinking repeatedly. Her gun was gone. She saw Hawkins on the floor. His gun was gone too.

"They're going to cut you out," Arthur rasped. He looked barely alive. "That's what they said."

"What?"

"The man there on the floor and the other one, the Latino. They're going to cut you out just like they did the guy in the hat."

He was right, Owens thought. Why wouldn't they? They'd shoot her and bury her under an outhouse. She scooped the money into the medical bags, staggered down the hallway, her shoulder against the wall, the urge to sleep overwhelming. There was no plan except to get the fuck out of there. She couldn't see for the blood in her eyes. She wiped it off with her sleeve. She would go back home, she thought. See her parents and her brother, Wallace, and smell the cattle and feel the wind coming off the mountains. She reached reception and the front door and there was a goddamn cop lying on the ground. *Oh shit,* she thought. The police would get involved and if they found out she'd been in the building she was fucked. Her fingerprints, blood, and DNA were all over the place. Make a run for it? No. The FBI would be after her, her face on TV. She'd never get away, from them or from Walczak. What she was going to need was lawyers. Expensive lawyers. Walczak's lawyers. No other option except to go back and help the troops. She took the cop's gun, dropped the money bags in reception, and lurched into the hallway again. She could barely see and wanted to vomit but she kept going.

Dodson had turned off the phone. The vibration was too loud in the echoing halls. He crouched and peeked around a corner. He could see Porkpie at a T-shaped intersection. You had to go through him to get to the back door. He looked like shit, leaning back against the wall, in pain, a gun in his shoulder holster. His pant leg was cut off, his leg bound with a mess of bloody gauze and white tape. Dodson's plan was to rush him and hit him with the baton before he could get the gun out. Shouldn't be too hard. The guy was over-weight and could barely stay on his feet, and there was what, ten yards between them? Dodson was quick. In high school, he played point guard.

Porkpie got off the wall, hobbled into a room, and came back dragging two metal chairs. He sat down on one and put his injured leg on the other. Even better, Dodson thought. The guy got out his phone and sent a text. "Where the fuck are you assholes?" he said.

His hands were busy. Dodson took off, slower than he remembered, the baton ready to whop this bitch into dreamland. He couldn't believe how fast the man got out his gun and shot him. BLAM! The bullet caught him in the shoulder. He twisted around and crashed to the floor. The pain was a branding iron, searing his pain center so black he couldn't cry out. Now Porkpie was standing over him. It reminded Dodson of robbing Junior and Booze Lewis, being in the exact same position, seconds away from death.

"What happened, Slick?" Porkpie said. "Things didn't work out?" Dodson couldn't talk, growling through his clenched teeth. "Let me think now," Porkpie went on. "Given the situation and given that you're a witness and you've seen my face, I'd say you're expendable. What do you think?" His grim smile was fading into something that resembled despair. He looked like he was about to either apologize or walk away. He aimed at Dodson's head. "So long, homeboy." BLAM! And just like the robbery, Dodson thought he was dead. But it was Porkpie who cried out, staggered, and went sprawling. Grace appeared, a gun in her hand, a wisp of blue smoke curling out of the barrel.

"You okay?" she said.

"Do I *look* okay?" Dodson said. "Cherise is gonna kill me."

Porkpie was lying on the floor in an expanding tide of blood. Nothing to be done about that now. Grace took off her chambray shirt and folded it up. She pressed it hard against Dodson's shoulder. "Keep it there. Keep pressure on it." She texted Isaiah. Where are you? Are you OK? No answer. She gave Dodson Porkpie's gun. "I'm going to find Isaiah." She ran off.

"Where the fuck you going?" Dodson shouted after her. "I need a goddamn ambulance!"

Isaiah heard a gunshot and headed toward the sound. He saw a blood trail. Footprints went into the mess hall and came out again.

One set was very large. A lot of the blood was smeared around, prints on top of each other, obscuring the individual tread marks. Isaiah had a lot of skills, but he was no expert at reading footprints. He couldn't tell if everyone who had gone in had come out again. Was somebody still in there, wounded or dead? He went through the mess hall and into the kitchen. The blood trail led into the cooler. His phone buzzed. A text from Grace. Where are you? Are you OK? Gunshots exploded at very close range. BLAM BLAM BLAM. He dived to the floor, his hands over his head.

Grace heard the three gunshots and knew they were coming from the kitchen. She ran down the hall and stumbled to a stop. The tall woman had collapsed in a heap like she was dead. Her mouth was open, her eyes rolled back in her head. Grace raced past her and into the kitchen's rear entrance, where she'd come out before. She heard voices. She crept forward and peeked around the corner. Isaiah was in the narrow aisle. His back was to her, his hands were up. Over his shoulder, she caught a glimpse of Walczak. He was almost unrecognizable. His eyes were nearly swollen shut, two knots on his head like budding antlers. His nose was bulbous, purple and off-center, a mixture of what looked like blood and egg whites oozing from it. His upper lip was torn in half, his mouth more like a gash, the white teeth like maggots squirming around in a puddle of red muck.

"You fucked up...everything," Walczak said in gasps. "And now...I'm going to kill you." Isaiah didn't beg or ask for mercy. He just stood there. Walczak went on. "Aren't you gonna...say something before...you die?"

"What I said before," Isaiah said, his voice not even shaking. "Why don't you do mankind a favor and go somewhere and die?"

"I wish...we were back...at Abu Ghraib." Blood bubbled through Walczak's lips. "Oh my...God...I would...take my time with you."

Grace was in a panic. She couldn't get a shot. Her only option was to run up behind Isaiah and try to shoot past him, which was likely to get them both killed.

"I'm not...gonna kill you...right away," Walczak said. "Your...kneecaps first? What do you...think? Maybe one...in the gut? Oh, I know. In the...crotch. Yeah, that hurts...believe me. He tried to smile but it was too painful. "Naah, fuck it. I'm just gonna kill you."

Grace could see Walczak's shoulder, he was raising the gun. *Go now, Grace! Go now!* Suddenly, there was a *whoosh* and a *flash* and Walczak let loose a screech so loud and primordial it didn't seem possible a human being had made it. Grace shouldered Isaiah aside. Walczak was staggering around, flailing and banging into the counter and stoves. *He was on fire.* And there, behind him, stood Sarah with the flamethrower, blue flames still licking out of the barrel.

"This is for all of us," she said. "This is for everybody."

CHAPTER SEVENTEEN
Kind and Wonderful Isaiah

Chester's deadline had passed. He called and texted Dodson a dozen times but got no response. He was furious. That filthy toad of a lawyer wanted his retainer *right now* and the landlord had tacked a THREE-DAY NOTICE TO VACATE on the shop's front door. Chester yanked the Dane axe off the wall but decided not to destroy another custom-made display. Instead, he went outside into the alley and hacked viciously at a telephone pole until his neighbor, Mr. Gonzalez, came out and said, "The fuck you doing, ese? Why don't you go to the park and cut down a tree?"

Very well then, Chester thought. He would do as he'd promised and tell Junior about the robbery. His crew would have no compunction about killing Dodson and his cohorts. Chester was facing utter and complete destruction, but at least he'd have the satisfaction of destroying them too. He was thinking about how to do it. Email? Text? No. He'd be more personal, more direct. He'd knock on Junior's door and tell him face-to-face. Egg him on. Remind him of his injuries, urge him to show no mercy, to exact his revenge in blood and more blood. He was straightening his tie and putting on his coat when the front door was kicked opened and

Junior, who looked remarkably like a pug, stormed in, his angry crew of thugs right behind him.

"My goodness!" Chester exclaimed.

"Well, I hope you've contrived yourself to be deregulated," Junior said, "because your ass is on the docket."

"I beg your pardon?" Chester said. One of the crew, probably the overly muscled fellow, punched Chester in the face, the pain blowing up like a grenade. He felt cartilage crunching, his eyes detonating, blood spurting from his nose as he fell into a display and slid to the floor. He thought he'd gone blind but the toupee had slid over his face.

"See here now!" he shouted. Someone kicked him in the stomach and he couldn't breathe. "Wait—" he wheezed. But he was kicked again. And again. Junior stood over him.

"You thought you could recapitulate my premises and not forfeit the residue?" he said. "You must have misplaced your corpuscles if you thought that was substantiated."

Chester thought his hearing was impaired. "I beg your pardon?"

The thugs were ransacking the shop. Smashing, upturning, looting. "Wait, stop, please!" Chester said. "Why are you doing this?" The muscleman took over the conversation, perhaps to save time.

"This your card?" He held up Chester's business card.

"Why yes, yes it is."

Muscleman showed him a penknife. "You make this knife?"

"Yes, yes, that's a Babbitt, that's my emblem on the handle."

"What was they doin' in Junior's crib?"

"I have no idea. Many people have my card and . . ." Chester had only sold three of those penknives. One to Sylvia, one to a collector in Chicago, and one to . . . *that girl!* She'd asked for his card too.

Muscleman kicked him again. "I *said,* what was they doin' in Junior's crib?"

"There was a girl," Chester gasped. "She came in here one day and—"

"So some girl put this shit in Junior's crib? Now why the fuck would she do that?"

"You was the one in my constabulary," Junior said. "You absconded with my economic feasibility."

"I beg your pardon?"

"You broke into Junior's house and stole his money," Muscleman said.

"That's not true! I don't even know where Junior lives! We've never met. We've never even spoken, and how would I know anything about Junior's money or where he keeps it? How would I know Junior had money at all? I'm not part of your world. Look at me. Do I seem like the sort who would break into someone's house? My God, man, I wear a bow tie!"

That gave them pause. They looked questioningly at each other. One of the thugs entered from the back of the shop. He tossed something to Junior.

"Check this out," he said. It was Junior's platinum lighter, his initials engraved on it. "It was back there with the tools and shit."

"This is my asset," Junior said. "I reacquired this ornamentation from a store we robbed in Lynwood."

"What you got to say now?" Muscleman said.

"I've been set up!" Chester shouted. "It was Dodson and Deronda and—"

"Deronda?" Junior said. "You talkin' 'bout that girl who erupted my gonads?"

"I'm afraid I know nothing about your gonads, sir. Deronda was part of the conspiracy that robbed you. IQ was the mastermind!"

"Isaiah?" Muscleman said. "He's the one that found this shit in Junior's house."

"No no, wait, you're confusing the two robberies. I'm talking about the one that happened a long time ago, when Junior and Booze Lewis were shot."

"How you know about that?" Muscleman said.

"Okay, let me start at the beginning. My now-deceased wife, Sylvia, was a voodoo priestess, and one Christmas she took me to a party at her cousin's house—"

"Shut your orifice," Junior said. "Talkin' all that nomenclature." He went over and took the Dane axe off the wall.

"Damn, Junior," Muscleman said, "you not gonna cut his head off, are you?"

"No, not in the present tense." Junior took a practice swing with the axe. "All right, Chester. Select the digitation you find most inadvisable."

"I beg your pardon?"

Muscleman smiled. "Which finger do you want to lose?"

Laquez was at the bar waiting for Seb to get off the phone. Seb was sitting in his booth sipping tea like the punk-ass motherfucker he was. Laquez had started to sit down, but Seb gave him that look, like he was garbage, like he stank too much to be in the same room. Seb was still talking. He had that fucked-up smile on his face, the one where he was bullshitting and trying to convince somebody he wasn't. Seb was skimming, probably out of Manzo's account because that was who he was talking to. That was some dangerous shit right there. Manzo would kill you, wash his hands, and go home and play with his kids. Seb got off the phone, took his cane off the table, and got up.

"Seb?" Laquez said. Seb was pissed and went right past him. Laquez got off the stool and followed him. "Seb, we was supposed to have that talk?"

"Later. I'm busy."

"Come on, Seb, it's important. Leastways it is to me."

Seb stopped and took one of them big deep breaths, like he was doing you a big favor just breathing the same air. "Yes? Get on with it."

"It's about that five thousand dollars. The money you got from them people who came about the girl?"

"Yes, yes, what about it?"

"I'm the one who found her," Laquez said. "That money is mine. I mean, I'll give you like a finder's fee, but that's it."

"A finder's fee?" Seb nodded, like he was taking it seriously. "And how much were you considering?"

"Ten percent. All you did was make a phone call."

"That's very generous of you," Seb said, still with that sincere look.

"Well, can I get the money now? I got bills to pay just like you."

"Of course." Seb lashed out with the cane. Laquez staggered back, holding his face, blood running from a cut on his cheekbone. "Finder's fee?" Seb said. He was trembling and his eyes were red. "You're going to give *me* a finder's fee? You filthy rat. You're fortunate to be working for me at all."

"Damn, Seb," Laquez said, starting to cry. He touched the wound and looked at the blood on his hand. "Why you gotta be that way? I ain't never done nothing to you."

"You're an idiot, Laquez. You're useless and stupid and I wonder why I ever—" Laquez took the gun out of his belt and shot Seb twice. The first bullet went through his throat. The second broke the cane in half.

Carter Samuels didn't want to explain to his superiors why he'd been driving around the industrial zone in El Segundo in the middle of the night and how he could hear someone scream through cinder block walls so Isaiah took him to Elena's house. Carter had ugly bruises and his jaw was swollen. There was nothing Elena could do except give him ice and ibuprofen. Carter called his wife and told her he'd been in a fight. It was nothing serious, he told her, he'd be home as soon as the paperwork was done. You know the bureaucracy. If you're not filling out forms something is wrong.

Dodson went to the emergency room and explained to the police he'd been shot in a drive-by. One of the detectives knew Isaiah and when Dodson told him they were partners he said, "With *Isaiah?* Does he know about it?"

The hardest part of the whole experience was waiting for Cherise to arrive. What would he say? That he'd nearly been shot to death at TK's wrecking yard? That he'd been running around chasing bad guys with a goddamn slingshot? That payment for risking his life amounted to one half of a fucked-up painting? Every time he turned around, he was asking himself the same question. *Now what?* He'd been useful to Isaiah, he felt good about that. Bridgette, Carter, Grace, Sarah, Arthur. That was something to be proud of, and thus far in his life, that hadn't happened too often. But the shit that went down with Walczak had him worrying about his family and that was unacceptable. He could dissolve the partnership with Isaiah, but what came after that was no man's land. There was nothing in his old life he wanted to repeat and nothing in his new life but a pinch of hope and unlikely possibilities. He didn't know where he was going or what he would do. He just didn't know.

Cherise was horrified. "Oh my God." She rushed over to the gurney, kissed Dodson's hand, and held it to her tearful face. "Oh my baby. Oh my sweet baby."

"I'm all right. I'm okay." Dodson tried to prepare himself for what was coming next. The worst part of all. Worse than the wrecking yard, worse than getting shot.

"I thought so," Gloria said as she stepped into the room, her opinion of him an undeniable reality. "You were a useless bum before and now you're a useless bum with a bullet hole in you." She puffed herself up and folded her arms across her bosom. "Maybe now my headstrong daughter will listen to me for a change. I told her this would happen."

"Mama," Cherise said. "Could you do this another time?"

"I told her I told her I told her," Gloria said, relentless. "Do not marry that worthless hooligan. He will bring you nothing but misery and shame."

Dodson didn't reply. Maybe, he thought, she was right.

Nothing about what happened at the training facility showed up on the news. There was an article in *Businessweek* about Walczak temporarily stepping down as CEO of WSSI due to health issues. Another article appeared in the *Long Beach Press-Telegram* about a veteran who'd served in Iraq named Antonio Jimenez. He hanged himself on a playground chin-up bar.

Sarah anonymously released the Abu Ghraib pictures. The networks and cable stations ran them on a loop. *Some of the images may be disturbing and are not suitable for children.* The board of directors ousted Walczak and there was a clamor for his arrest.

After leaving the training facility, Arthur was taken to the emergency room. Sarah sat at his bedside and explained what had happened.

"After Grace left the room, I was so angry at myself. I hadn't done anything for my daughter in ten years, and now I'd let her go running off with a gun." At that point, she told Arthur, he was semiconscious. She had kissed him on the forehead, gotten up, and seen the flamethrower where Grace had dropped it on the floor. "I picked it up and pulled the trigger but nothing happened," Sarah said. Then she saw the second trigger and pulled them at the same time. "There was a whooshing sound and a flame came out but not very far." She left and wandered around aimlessly, feeling out of her depth and stupid. She found the tall woman on the floor and heard the three gunshots. "They were coming from the kitchen," she said.

She went through the mess hall and heard voices. "The door was open and there was Walczak, holding a gun on Isaiah." She cringed as if she was seeing it happen all over again. "That's when I shot him. That's when I shot him and watched him burn."

Arthur had to stay in the hospital three days. Grace and Sarah had long weepy conversations full of hugs and love. Deronda flew up to Reno and drove Grace's car back. When Arthur was released he insisted on leaving right away. They went to CarMax, bought a Ford Expedition, and left for New Mexico.

Isaiah and Grace sat in the backyard on lawn chairs, drinking beers and reading the paper, hardly speaking, sometimes holding hands. They took Ruffin to the beach and watched him bound around in the breakers. They played chess. Isaiah beat her three times in seventeen moves and she quit. She cooked him dinner, which was almost as bad as her coffee. They sat on the sofa and watched a nature program on his laptop, her head resting on his shoulder. But somehow Isaiah knew, even after they'd washed the dishes together and stopped to make out, their soapy hands all over each other, and even after they fell on the bed and made love three times and even after he awoke the next morning and smelled coffee and toasted bread—even then he knew she was leaving.

They stood in the driveway, not knowing what to say. He thought about asking her why she had to go, but if she'd wanted him to know she'd have told him. He didn't want to kiss her or hug her or even say anything. There were only the pale green eyes and the almost-pretty face gone slack, her small hands shredding a Kleenex. Finally, she stepped in close and put her forehead against his chest. He wondered if she could hear his heart, which he thought at any moment might stop beating.

"Take Ruffin," he said.

"What?"

"Take the dog. Take him with you."

"I can't. He's yours."

"I want you to take him," he insisted. "You *have* to."

"Why?"

"Because then I'll know you're safe." Her eyes were wet and so were his. She opened the car door.

"Come on, Ruff." Without a moment's hesitation the dog jumped in. She got in herself, then she backed out of the driveway and drove off, not looking at him as she went past, the dog with his head out of the window, tongue flapping, happy as could be.

Isaiah didn't move, hoping if he stayed there long enough he'd see her coming back. He went inside, sat in the easy chair, and thought of nothing until dark, the house so empty it might have been abandoned. He put some kibble into Ruffin's food bowl and left it there. He stayed in the house for the next several days, hardly eating or drinking but checking his emails and texts every fifteen minutes. Sarah had given him fifty thousand dollars and the same amount to Dodson, but he didn't care. He knew Grace had gone to New Mexico to be with her mother but ruled out going after her. That was understood, but why Grace had to end the relationship was a total mystery.

After a week, he knew he wouldn't hear from her and he tried to go about his business. He went to visit Dodson.

"I'm still upset with you, Isaiah," Cherise said. "You almost got my husband killed."

"I'm very upset with myself. I'm sorry, Cherise."

"Tell me it won't happen again."

"It won't happen again."

Gloria came in. "Is this him? Well, you don't look that smart to me."

"I'm not," Isaiah said.

"Well," she huffed. "Anybody who takes Juanell on for a partner must have something wrong with him."

Dodson was lying in bed, shoulder bound up, his arm in a sling. "Cherise is upset," Isaiah said.

"Yeah," Dodson said. "She was ready to kill both of us 'til I showed her Sarah's money. She wanted to give it back but I said we could make a big donation to the church and send Gloria on a cruise to the Bahamas or outer space." An awkward moment passed while the eight-hundred-pound gorilla came in and sat down. "The partnership," Dodson said. "It ain't working out, is it?"

"It is for me," Isaiah said sincerely. "I wouldn't have made it through if it wasn't for you."

"True enough. But I can't put Cherise through that again and you can do your own books." Dodson shook his head. "I can't bring in big cases any more than you can. I'm sorry I told you that."

"It's okay. I understand."

"But the main thing is, I gotta be my own boss and so do you."

"Yeah, I guess so," Isaiah said.

"I'll be around," Dodson said. "If you need me, pick up the phone."

He heard about Seb's death but felt nothing. Not victorious or relieved or glad. Nothing. And none of it mattered anyway. Marcus was still gone. Isaiah's hate had gained him exactly nothing. He divvied up his share of Sarah's money. He gave some to Harry Haldeman at the animal shelter. He gave some to TK and the senior center at McClarin Park and he bought Louella Barnes a new pair of glasses and he gave some to Beaumont for remodeling his store. He put a big chunk into Flaco's college fund and he bought the Carver Middle School Science Club new laptops. He bought himself a new pair of Nikes and another Harvard cap and he installed better speakers in the Audi. He went to a physical therapist and an acupuncturist to help heal his injuries. He worked his cases. Someone stole all the tools out of Néstor's plumbing truck.

Mrs. Wheeler's niece had run away from home. Chaco was into drugs and failing all his classes. Maynard White got scammed out of three thousand dollars by a man who claimed he was his grandson. Isaiah didn't find the man but he said he did and gave Maynard his money back.

He had terrible nightmares that left him gasping, his sheets tangled and drenched with sweat. He was screaming, his mouth full of dirt. His arms were cut off and flopping around on the ground. His eyes were missing. And despite all his professional caution and watchfulness, he didn't feel safe anymore. He couldn't imagine what full-on PTSD was like. Living hell must be an understatement. His loneliness was paralyzing. He hadn't felt this isolated since the days after Marcus had died. It was the same thing, really. Something inside you killed by a hit-and-run.

The house was regressing. The lawn hadn't been cut in weeks. He went into the garage to get the lawn mower and stopped in disbelief. The Mustang was there. He stared at it for a long time. Then he got in the car and thought about Grace and her dad, racing joyfully through the streets of San Francisco. There was no note. Only empty quiet. Only loss and grief and yearning. Isaiah put his hands over his face and cried until he couldn't cry anymore; for Grace, for himself, for a world so full of pain and sorrow and wickedness.

It was three months later when he got the letter, postmarked Santa Fe, New Mexico. He almost ripped it open but took it inside, afraid people might see his reactions. It was written in a firm, artful hand on nice stationery. In the top right corner, there was a tiny drawing of a beach, a smile of foam breakers around the bay.

Dear Isaiah,

I hope you are well. I'm with Mom and we're getting to know each other again. It is wonderful but strange to say the least,

338

saying things we've held in for ten years. She's incredibly strong and courageous. How she survived is a miracle. She was traumatized by what happened with Walczak. Arthur too. Not so much physically as emotionally. Arthur goes for long walks in the desert, smokes a lot of weed, and watches TV, which he never did before. Cameron quit the bookstore and went to live with his parents. All Mom can talk about was how she had no choice but to fire the flamethrower. "You were there, Grace, you saw what happened," she tells me over and over again. "I had to. I had to," and then she'll break down and weep. They haven't touched the money. I'm sorry to say your dog doesn't seem to miss you. Ruff loves romping around in the desert. He met a kangaroo rat the other day and promptly ran back into the house. He ignores Arthur's Lab, Gusto. I think it's beneath him.

I'm stalling, of course. I know you've figured it out by now. Mom didn't shoot Kyle Munson, I did. After the home invasion, he was the main suspect and I couldn't stand that he was alive and my dad was dead. I got one of my dad's guns and went over to Munson's. He was in his garage doing something with his car. It was a little after eleven. He knew me so he smiled and asked what I was doing out so late. I said you killed my dad and I shot him. I remember the sound was deafening and the gun nearly jumped out of my hand. After that, everything was a blur. Cops, sirens, people asking me where Mom was. She knew instantly that I had done it and fled to make herself seem guilty. There's more to the story, but that doesn't matter now, except to say, some illusions are better left alone.

I've carried around a burden of guilt since I was fifteen years old. Not only had I killed an innocent man, but I'd let my mother take the blame. I retreated into my art, afraid my shameful secrets would be exposed. And afraid of myself. I had killed. I was dangerous. It's not rational, I know. It seems like something you *could talk yourself out of, but it's like trying to talk yourself out of your nationality or that you're a woman. The violence defines you, changes who you are, and I am a killer. I've said that to myself a million times. That's why I've never let anyone get close, and that's why I had to leave.*

I'm seeing a therapist. She is wise and very smart. I've learned it doesn't matter which end of the violence you're on. Whether you've hurt someone or someone's hurt you, it's both of you who suffer. The therapist says I'm making progress, but I've still got a lot of work to do. It's hard to change who you are when you've been that way for so long. I don't have any plans really, except to paint and get better. I hope to come back someday. I realize you can't wait for me but know that the memories of us are safely tucked away, and you—kind and wonderful Isaiah—are always in my heart.

Your

Grace

Isaiah folded the letter and put it back in the envelope. He hadn't realized Grace had killed Kyle Munson until that night when they first made love. He was in the bedroom, packing things in a duffel bag. He could see the painting even though the lights were off. The black stump of the fatal gunshot, its malignant tendrils infecting the blue-sky life she would never have, the tormented swirls of grays and browns and the terrible fracture where she'd split in two, the artist on one side, the killer on the other. His interpretation might have been a flight of fancy, or maybe she intended something else or nothing at all, but that was how he would always see it. Whether she knew it or not, Grace had painted her sadness. He went out in the backyard, sat on the stoop, and read the letter again.

"I'll be waiting," he said. "I'll be waiting right here."

Acknowledgments

MY THANKS TO:

Abby Fairbrother for her enthusiastic and much needed assistance with my books, social media, scheduling, and pretty much everything else. Stasha Fassbender for her keen insights into many aspects of the story. Elyse Dinh-McCrillis for her kindness, advice, and unique knowledge of the book world. Hap Tivey—artist, life doctor, and Buddhist raconteur. The sales staff at Little, Brown: I am here because they are there. Production editor Ben Allen and copyeditor Barbara Perris, the most exacting, patient people in America. Craig Young for his musical expertise, pink socks, and all-around good-guyness. Esther Newberg and Zoe Sandler—my protectors, advocates, and educators. They are the absolute best at what they do. Reagan Arthur for her breathtaking faith in me. I am in awe of her except for the alarming lack of pork in her diet.

I am especially grateful to Pamela Brown, Sabrina Callahan, Nicky Guerreiro, and Alyssa Persons. It's almost impossible to put a new writer before the public in any meaningful way, and yet here I am, writing acknowledgments for my third book. They are consummate professionals and the best kind of people and I am better for having known them. And to my wife, Diane. Her love is everything.

About the Author

Joe Ide grew up in South Central Los Angeles. His favorite books were the Arthur Conan Doyle Sherlock Holmes stories. He held a variety of different jobs—including Hollywood screenwriter—before writing *IQ,* which went on to win the Anthony, Macavity, and Shamus awards for best debut novel. Ide lives in Santa Monica, California. Visit his website at joeide.com, or follow him on Twitter @joeidetweets.

MULHOLLAND BOOKS

You won't be able to put down these Mulholland books.

THE MAN WHO CAME UPTOWN *by George Pelecanos*

WRECKED *by Joe Ide*

THE SHADOWS WE HIDE *by Allen Eskens*

FROM RUSSIA WITH BLOOD *by Heidi Blake*

LAST NIGHT *by Karen Ellis*

GOLDEN STATE *by Ben H. Winters*

THE STRANGER INSIDE *by Laura Benedict*

TRIGGER *by David Swinson*

Visit mulhollandbooks.com for
your daily suspense fix.